Keep Me If You Can

If You Can Series: Book 3

Cheryl Terra

Author's Note

This is the third book of the If You Can series, however if you want to jump into Keep Me If You Can without reading the earlier books or just need a refresher on what happened, a summary of the series **containing spoilers** begins on the next page.

There is also a character summary **at the back of the book** featuring names and basic descriptions of important characters.

Please note that this books is written in Canadian English, which has rules and spellings from both UK and US English. It also contains phrases and words specifically from Québécois French. Translations of those can be found **at the end of the book**.

Content Warnings: Full content warnings can be **found on my website** (cherylterra.com/trigger-warnings), but please note that the If You Can series contains characters who engage in casual relationships with characters not involved in the main relationship dynamic. This will not include adultery of any kind between the MCs.

This book contains plots surrounding toxic parenting and family situations, slut shaming, references to non-consensual activity, risks of unplanned pregnancy, and multiple explicit scenes. There are also scenes featuring on-page emotional abuse, discussions of neurodiversity including harmful misconceptions (which are corrected on page), and discussions of the death of a friend (does not occur on page or within the timeline of the series).

The Road So Far

The If You Can series is intended to be read in order, however if you want to jump into Keep Me If You Can without reading the earlier books or just need a refresher on what happened, here is a summary of Nellie's story so far.

THIS SECTION CONTAINS MASSIVE SPOILERS FOR THE PREVIOUS BOOKS IN THE IF YOU CAN SERIES.

If you would rather read the full books, get your copies here: geni.us/iycseries

The Boy Next Door: The series prequel. Set the summer before Nellie starts university.

After realizing she can't afford to pay for university on her own, she asks her insanely wealthy but probably sociopathic father for help behind her mother's back, not understanding why her mom has told Nellie to cut ties with her dad. With the help of her best friend, Anne-Marie, Nellie decides she doesn't want to start university as a virgin, but also doesn't want to get into a relationship after her high school boyfriend spread horrible rumours about her that ruined her reputation.

After an unsuccessful summer of misadventures and bad dates, Nellie unexpectedly connects with JP, Anne-Marie's older brother, when she gets locked out of Anne-Marie's room in nothing but a towel. Telling him about her ex-boyfriend telling everyone she was a slut. JP tells Nellie it's okay to want sex but not a relationship and Nellie decides she wants to lose her virginity to him, though she doesn't tell him she's a virgin until after they've started hooking up. When they're done, Nellie asks him not to tell anyone and rushes away because she's afraid her religious, conservative father will find out.

Want the full story? Get your copy of The Boy Next Door here: **geni.us/bndct**

Kiss Me If You Can: Three years after The Boy Next Door, Nellie is a self-described "joyfully promiscuous" college student who doesn't do serious relationships, but does do anyone who seems like a good time... except JP, who she's successfully avoided seeing since that day in his bedroom when she lost her virginity, despite his attempts to get in touch with her.

After unexpectedly running into JP at a social event, Nellie's dad tries to get him to convince Nellie to go to law school again since he is now a successful junior associate with his dad's law firm. Much to Nellie's dismay, JP offers to tutor her for the LSAT if she doesn't get the internship. Well aware of her dad's toxic nature and tired of him trying to control her life, Nellie tells him she's so certain she'll get the internship that if she doesn't, she'll take him up on the offer so she can take the LSAT and consider going to law school.

Unfortunately, after offending a former flame who has connections to the internship, Nellie isn't accepted. She decides to hide this from her dad and gets a job at a restaurant to pay her bills, but her dad discovers her lie and tells her that until she takes the LSAT and attends the events he wants her at with a date who Nellie despises, he will withdraw all financial support. Upset, Nellie impulsively spends the weekend hooking up with Ben, her former psychology professor who she's been regularly flirting with all summer.

Not able to avoid JP any longer, Nellie finally tells him she's been avoiding him because he kept trying to get in touch with her and she didn't want a boyfriend. JP tells her just because he wanted to check on her after they hooked up didn't mean he wanted to be her boyfriend, he just wanted to make sure she was okay. He tells her he only offered to tutor her for the LSAT because he didn't think she'd need it and encourages her to stand up to her dad. They eventually agree to a friends-with-benefits situation since Nellie will be spending a lot of time in Montreal over the summer and hook up again. With casual hook ups arranged in both Ottawa and Montreal, Nellie is surprisingly looking forward to her summer even if she has to spend more time than she wants with her dad.

Want the full story? Get your copy of The Boy Next Door here: **geni.us/bndct**

Hold Me If You Can: Beginning approximately a month after the events of Kiss Me If You Can, Nellie and JP have met up several times as part of their friends-with-benefits arrangement, though Anne-Marie has nearly caught them a few times. Nellie is also still casually seeing Ben, both of them knowing their fling will come to an end when Ben moves to California at the end of the summer.

When Nellie is left scrambling after Bruno, her go-to date so she doesn't have to go with creepy Clinton Thibault, cancels on her last-minute for an event, she has the brilliant idea to dress her best friend, Sydney, in a tuxedo and fake mustache and take her as a date. Their charade delights some of the party goers, including the mysterious Claire and her fiancée Julie, but Nellie's dad is livid. As punishment, he tells Nellie she will be attending the final and biggest event of the season, the Diamond Gala, with Clinton. Desperate, Nellie says JP is taking her. Once her father approves, JP agrees to take Nellie on the *joking* condition that they have anal sex after the gala.

Nellie is obligated to attend the funeral of a prominent social figure. After inadvertently insulting the billionaire widow of the deceased--a woman Nellie's dad is trying to impress because he wants to take her on as one of his financial clients--and running into a former teacher who mentions she thought Nellie had ADHD, Nellie sneaks over to the Marchands to ask JP how he got out of attending the funeral with his family.

JP reveals the last funeral he attended was a for a close friend, Sam, who was killed unexpectedly when he got into a vehicle with a driver he didn't know was impaired after JP left a party they were at together without him. Nellie begins to realize there may be feelings developing between her and JP. After she returns to Ottawa, she decompresses and discusses the situation with Ben, admitting things aren't quite as casual with JP as they used to be.

At the Diamond Gala, Nellie and JP see the mysterious Claire and Julie one more time. After introducing JP, Claire and Julie discuss their non-monogamous relationship and how Claire has brought her other girlfriend along with Julie to "test the waters" with her mother and make sure their unconventional relationship will be accepted. Nellie commiserates with her about "the things we do for family." She reveals her dad is trying to impress this billionaire client and keeps getting upset with her because she keeps ruining it, not realizing that Claire is actually the daughter of the billionaire until Claire brings Nellie over to introduce her to her mother. Claire's mother is impressed by Nellie's quirkiness and agrees to meet with Nellie's dad about her financial needs.

After the event, Nellie and JP return to her house. JP confesses he was joking about wanting anal sex in exchange for being her date, but Nellie tells him the joke is on him because she'd wanted to try it anyway. After they hook up, there is a moment of emotional connection, but when JP tries to talk to Nellie about it the next day, she denies anything happened and reminds him she doesn't want a serious relationship. He agrees and she drives off, back to Ottawa and assuming she won't be returning to Montreal ever again.

In the epilogue, JP panics about realizing he's in love with Nellie and knowing that he can't do this "again."

Want the full story? Get your copy of Hold Me If You Can here: **geni.us/hmiyc**

Prologue

I Can Do Anything

WHEN JP MARCHAND HAD his first kiss, there was popcorn in his hair.

I shouldn't have known that. Just like I shouldn't have known the girl he kissed had a sunburn on her nose, even though it was winter. Or that they were missing the best scene of *Jurassic Park*, where they see the Brachiosaurus for the first time, but it kinda worked out because the song was playing in the background. Even though I was only eleven, I figured that had to make the whole thing pretty epic.

Everything was epic when the *Jurassic Park* theme song was playing.

Which I knew because I'd seen the stupid movie before, even though Mr. Marchand said Anne-Marie and I couldn't watch the movie with the older kids.

"It's not a movie for young ladies," he said.

Anne-Marie, who was not used to her dad telling her no for anything, looked both insulted and devastated. "But Daddy—"

"My dad lets me watch *Jurassic Park*," I said loudly.

Mr. Marchand gave me an unimpressed look. "Does your father allow you to talk back to him?"

He didn't, so I didn't say anything else. Mr. Marchand turned back to Anne-Marie, who had the corners of her mouth turned down into a sad pout, and shook his head again.

"It is your brother's birthday party, *ma chouette*," Mr. Marchand said. "We said Nellie could sleep over during JP's party so you did not bothering them—"

"We won't *bother* them!" I said. "They weren't even paying attention. They were throwing popcorn at that one guy because he wouldn't shut up!"

"And if you interrupt me again, you will be sent home," Mr. Marchand snapped. My face warmed with embarrassment and anger as he turned back to Anne-Marie. "*Ma puce*, all JP wanted to celebrate his birthday was an evening with his friends to watch movies. You and Nellie can watch *Jurassic Park* another time. Right now, your mother and I are asking you to please leave them alone."

He left us in the living room, the TV playing some boring kids' movie.

"This is so unfair." Anne-Marie flopped forlornly onto the couch. "I cannot believe my parents are so *mean*. Do they even love me anymore?"

"I'm sure they love you," I said.

She sniffled, though I didn't think there were any actual tears in her eyes. "You wouldn't understand, Nellie. Your parents would give you anything in the world."

More anger flared up, making my shoulders tense and my jaw tighten. That time, though, I suppressed it before snapping at Anne-Marie to stop being so unbearably dramatic. Which was a big deal, honestly, because lately it seemed like words burst out of me before I even thought them.

I did think them that time, though. I thought that Anne-Marie was being ridiculous. Her dad telling her no about one stupid thing didn't mean he didn't love her. It wasn't like he and her mom told her to pick a restaurant for dinner, but her dad wanted to go somewhere fancy and her mom wanted to go to Tee Dee Daisy's so they could play air hockey, and her dad said that was immature and her mom said he was immature.

It wasn't like she tried to tell them she didn't *want* to pick a restaurant the whole time they were arguing and that she just wanted things to go back to how they were because she was so sick of them yelling all the time.

It wasn't like the boiling anger built and built and built and finally burst out and she screamed that she was sick of them fighting and she hated them, she fucking *hated* both of them more than anything in the world and her mom pointed a finger at the stairs and told her to go to her goddamn room and she was *grounded* and there was no way in hell she was going over to the Marchands' for a sleepover with Anne-Marie while her stupid brother had a stupid birthday party.

It wasn't like any of that at all.

But after my mom had stormed out, my dad had come upstairs and told me I wasn't grounded and I could go to Anne-Marie's and that I never had to pick a restaurant again if I didn't want to. And Anne-Marie was my best friend, and now she was sad because she couldn't watch a movie.

And I might not have been able to stop my parents from fighting, but I *could* help Anne-Marie.

"I have an idea," I said.

Anne-Marie looked up, a heavy look in her warm brown eyes. "You do?"

We snuck into the basement, silent and unnoticed as we crept into the storage room. Once we were there, I pulled the door open and revealed the place that had made me the undefeated hide-and-seek champ at the Marchands' house since the very first time we'd played.

"This is *brilliant*!" Anne-Marie breathed as we crept into the hole that led to the crawl space beneath the stairs.

"I found it by mistake," I breathed. "I came in through the door in the entertainment room and then went back as far as I could and there was this gap here."

The crawl space was just large enough to let us sit with our legs crossed and peer through the angled slats of the door. And we *should* have had a perfect, clear view of the giant TV on the wall, but as usual, JP ruined everything.

"What are they doing?" Anne-Marie whispered.

I shook my head, not daring to speak. In the twenty or so minutes since we'd been kicked out of the basement, JP and his friends had moved the furniture around. The coffee table was pressed up against the door, blocking part of the TV from our view. Instead of sitting on the furniture, they were in a loose circle on the floor, alternating boy-girl all the way around. In the middle, a green Perrier bottle was lying on its side. I could see JP in profile, sitting to my right with his back resting against the couch. He was taller than me, but if he turned his head and looked over at the right angle, we would've made eye contact.

"It doesn't count," said a boy with flaming red hair, his arms folded across his chest and his frown so deep that his eyebrows were curled into each other.

The boy everyone was throwing popcorn at before Anne-Marie and I got kicked out snickered and nudged the girl sitting beside him. "Tell 'em it still counts, Courtney. That's what the rules say."

The girl gave him a twisted look. "They're twins, Logan. You sick freak."

"Okay, but Brooke doesn't get to spin again just because she doesn't wanna have her first kiss with her brother," Logan said.

"Then I guess we're not playing anymore," said the red-haired girl with glasses and a sunburn on her nose. Brooke, I guessed, and she mirrored her twin by folding her arms across her chest.

"I said before we started we'd only play if we didn't have to..." The red-haired boy trailed off, then gestured vaguely in the air.

"He did say that," JP said.

Logan rolled his eyes. "Well, she's gotta kiss someone, and she doesn't get to spin again. So are you volunteering to be stuck with Brooke for your first kiss?"

"Kissing?" Anne-Marie breathed beside me, and I could almost hear her eyes widen. Some of the other people in the circle giggled and Brooke recoiled, a hurt expression flashing across her face and her sunburned cheeks going an even brighter shade of red. JP glanced at her, then turned back to Logan.

"What do you mean, stuck with Brooke?" he asked. "I'd be *honoured* to kiss Brooke."

Logan snorted. "Go for it then, Birthday Boy."

So JP got to his knees, shuffled across the circle, and didn't even hesitate before leaning in to plant a kiss on Brooke's lips.

It was a brief kiss. The people around them let out soft *oooing* noises, but they'd barely started giggling when Brooke pulled back, her face and neck now red enough to match her nose. JP smiled, the corners of his eyes crinkling.

"Aw," Anne-Marie whispered. I guess I could understand why she thought it was cute, even though I sure wouldn't have wanted to be the one stuck kissing JP. Plus, it was kinda weird that JP hadn't kissed anyone before. Not that I had, but I knew a couple of people in my class had and JP was a whole teenager and stuff.

And then as the Brachiosaurus appeared on the screen, he kissed her again.

And, like.

Kissed her.

Like, really kissed her

And it made me feel sad.

Because it was so gross, obviously.

It was so gross that it made me sad because that was Brooke's first kiss and she'd always remember that JP Marchand had popcorn in his hair and that he'd lifted his hand to her cheek to touch it gently and that she'd put her hand on his thigh, probably to steady herself because she was so grossed out.

Because why *else* would seeing JP kiss a girl make me sad? I didn't like JP. Even if I did, he was sixteen. And blonde. And tall.

But my mom always called him a heartbreaker. Which had to be a bad thing, because who *wanted* to break hearts?

That was why I was sad, I thought. I felt bad that poor Brooke, with her pretty red hair and her sunburned nose and her cool gold-rimmed glasses, was going to have her heart broken by JP Marchand.

And then all thoughts were ripped from my head as JP put his *tongue* in her mouth.

His tongue, which was pink. And shiny with spit. And probably felt slimy and tasted like someone else's chewed gum.

The sight of it made me want to throw up everything in my stomach, including my stomach itself since my parents never did pick a restaurant and I'd only eaten a few crackers off the snack table before Anne-Marie and I got kicked out of the entertainment room. And I tried to stop it, but my whole body lurched and I *gagged*.

"Nellie!" Anne-Marie hissed from beside me, like that would stop anyone from hearing the retching sound I let out. It didn't, of course; Brooke had already yanked her face away from JP's, and the head of every teenager in that room swivelled towards the crawl space door.

Including JP, who was staring into the slats in the door as I stared out of them, his eyes as dark as blackberries and his face as red as Brooke's hair. Climbing to his feet, he took two steps across the room before shoving the coffee table out of the way and wrenching the crawl space door open.

"What. The. Fuck?" he growled.

It was a question, but apparently not one that JP wanted an answer to, because when I blurted out that I thought it was very nice of him to have his first kiss with Brooke so she didn't have to kiss her brother, his face went even redder and he turned around and stormed out of the entertainment room.

"How did you think you were going to get out of this without getting into trouble?" Mr. Marchand demanded after coming downstairs to escort me and Anne-Marie out of the crawl space while JP stood behind him, arms folded across his chest.

"We wouldn't have gotten in trouble if JP wasn't a bastard who told on us," I grumbled.

"You know, when I was your age, my parents would have put soap in my mouth for using that kind of language," Mr. Marchand said.

"Sounds fucking delicious," I said, and two minutes later I was trudging home through the rain because Mr. Marchand told me I wouldn't be welcome back at his house until I could behave myself.

It shouldn't have been raining. I don't know why it was. It was February, after all. Late February, since JP's school did spring break in February and it was the same week as his birthday so he'd done his party after.

But it was warmer than usual that winter. Even though it wasn't exactly *warm*.

I wasn't supposed to be home, so my parents hadn't bothered to keep their voices down. They were fighting loud enough that they didn't hear the door open, either, loud enough that the shouts echoed through the hallway.

"—undermine what I fucking *told* her—" my mom yelled.

"You think it was best for her to sit upstairs by herself?" my dad snapped. "You punished her for—"

"For fucking swearing! She can't use language like that—"

"Can you blame her when you can't get a sentence out without throwing at least one curse in it, Victoria?"

"Oh, sure, this is all *my* fault—"

"Yes, it is!" my dad roared. "I let her go to the Marchands so she could get a goddamn break from all of this! You punished her for not wanting to go to a childish restaurant with you, swore up a storm as you fought with me yet again, and left her here for me to deal with all night. So yes, Victoria, this is *your* fault."

Silence followed. Loud silence. Louder than the screaming, the fighting, the swearing.

"That's it," my mom said.

"What is?" my dad asked.

"I want a divorce."

No one spoke. The silence thundered in my ears like heartbeats.

"No," my dad said.

"Can you honestly say you're happy, Max?"

He said nothing.

"Can you honestly say this is working?"

Still, he stayed quiet.

"Can you honestly say you love me?"

"Yes," he said immediately.

"You don't."

"I do. Victoria, I do. I love you."

Her voice wavered. "Well, it's not enough to keep me anymore."

"It's enough—"

"It's never been enough. We tried, okay? We gave it twelve years. We're both miserable. We're so miserable that we're making Nellie miserable. You know she got another detention last week? Her teacher told me my daughter is misbehaving so much that she thinks Nellie might have a learning disability. She's going stupid with how much we're fucking her up, Max."

"Do not call my daughter *stupid*," he said.

"I'm leaving," my mom said. "And I'm taking her with me."

"*No.*" There was heat in my dad's voice that time. "No, you cannot—"

"It's over, Max."

"You cannot do this."

"I can do anything."

They were quiet for a bit before my mom spoke again.

"I'll stay in one of the guest rooms tonight," she said. "I'll talk to a lawyer tomorrow. Not Jean-Luc Marchand, obviously. I'm assuming you're using him."

"I have never given it any thought," my dad said, his voice quiet.

"You should've," my mom said. "And we'll have to think of how to tell Nellie. I won't say anything until we decide. I expect you to do the same."

"Vicki, please—"

But her light footsteps faded towards the back of the house. A moment later, my dad's heavier ones started towards the front and without thinking, I opened the front door and slipped out into the rain.

I went to the Marchands' because I didn't know where else to go. I knew Mr. Marchand wouldn't let me back in the house, but that was probably a good thing if my dad used him as a lawyer like my mom said he should. JP had told me once that you weren't allowed to lie to lawyers and I didn't want anyone to know what I'd heard, so I just sat on the front step with my backpack of sleepover stuff at my feet, shielded from the rain but letting it numb everything around me.

And I sat.

And sat.

After a while the front door opened and I nearly jumped out of my skin, only to realize JP's friends were leaving. I shrank against the wall as best I could, but as invisible as I felt, I wasn't. After a few of them walked by and some hushed whispers, the door opened again. I winced, preparing myself for Mr. Marchand to yell at me, but he wasn't the person who spoke.

"Nellie, what are you doing?" JP asked.

Great. Just *great*.

"Sitting," I said.

"I can see that." He sounded as annoyed as he was annoying. "But my dad told you to leave."

"I know."

"Then you know you can't be sitting here."

"I can do anything," I said.

"So you can go home."

My chin trembled. "I... can't."

"You can't walk across the lawn because of a bit of rain?"

"That's not why."

"So you can ruin my birthday party, but not walk back to your own house. Is there any particular reason you can't do that?"

And just like so many words that had fallen out lately, I barely thought before I responded. "My mom said she's leaving and she's taking me."

Then, like a big stupid baby, I started crying.

"Shit," JP said, then took a couple of steps outside and closed the door. A moment later, he settled on the stairs next to me. "Nellie, I'm sorry. I didn't know."

"It's okay," I sobbed.

"Can I... um. Do you, uh... do you want a hug?" he asked.

"Ew." I sniffled. "No. Gross."

Then I twisted, my head bowed so it bumped his arm, and a second later he hugged me, and kept hugging me even when the front door opened again and I heard a couple of JP's friends talking.

"Ohhh," said the annoying one, Logan. "JP, be careful. Brooke's gonna get all jealous of your new little girlfriend."

"Fuck off," JP said, looking over his shoulder. "Can you go get my dad, please?"

"Wait." I sat up, pushing him away. "No. He can't *know*."

"What? Why—"

"He's a *lawyer*, you bastard!"

That seemed like enough of an explanation to me, but JP blinked at me like he was confused. But for better or for worse, he accepted the explanation, because after Logan shouted across the house that JP was cuddling with the bratty kid from next door—which got not only Mr. Marchand's attention, but Anne-Marie's, too—JP said I'd been sitting out here for hours because my parents weren't home and I couldn't get inside.

And that I hadn't wanted to knock on the door because Mr. Marchand had kicked me out and I didn't want to upset him.

And that I'd said I was sorry for bothering them during his party, and that he knew Anne-Marie was in trouble too but could we all just forget about it so I could come inside because I was just a kid and I was *freezing* cold.

It was raining, after all.

And Mr. Marchand might've been super mean sometimes, but he wasn't evil, so he said of course I could come in and told me that if this happened again, he didn't mean I wasn't allowed to ask for help if there was an emergency or something.

And since Anne-Marie didn't know the truth either, when we got up to her bedroom and crawled into bed and turned out the lights, she teased me about sitting on the doorstep with her brother, and asked if he'd really been hugging me, and said that maybe I was secretly falling in love with him.

"Of course not!" I snapped, my face burning red in the darkness. "Ew, Annie."

"Is that why you were so sad when he kissed Brooke?"

"I literally do not care about that," I said.

"Sure you don't, *chérie*." She giggled again. "I think you have a crush on my big brother, Nellie."

And I insisted I did not, and I told her it was gross because he was a teenager and I was a kid, and that her brother was ugly and I'd *never* liked him, not even a bit.

But even though I secretly might've thought he was kinda okay sometimes, I knew there was no way I would ever fall in love with a bastard like JP Marchand.

Because I was never gonna let myself fall in love with *anyone*.

Chapter One
The Pussy Cat Caper

IT WASN'T MY FAULT I didn't finish my weekly Forensic Science and Law case study.

That was the fault of whoever thought *I* was the right person to lead an orientation group without considering the likelihood of me getting distracted by giving sex tips to a library table full of wannabe freshman sluts.

And that was sluts (*affectionate*), not sluts (*derogatory*), which was lesson one. Well, lesson one of the Nellie branch of the orientation, since lesson one of the actual orientation had been about balancing school life and social life. But that had quickly devolved into the whole "Okay, listen up, sluts, here's how to fuck around without finding out," because good *God*, they weren't teaching kids anything these days.

Not that they taught kids anything in my day either, considering I was barely four years older than most of these kids. I mean, I was an entirely self-taught slut. Which meant these students had a unique opportunity to speak with the campus expert about how to embrace their sexuality in a fun and safe way.

Or some bullshit like that.

Look, the point was, someone brought up sex—probably me—and they had questions, so instead of blandly reading out the orientation advice that none of them were going to follow anyway, I gave them my most useful tips.

"Take your socks off," I said.

"Because it's not sexy?" asked one girl.

"Because your feet probably smell," I said.

A girl with thick brown hair and freckled white skin named Katelyn frowned. "You think he'd notice that?"

I shrugged. "I dunno. That's not your problem. But if he gets you on your back and puts your legs up on his shoulders so he can start really pounding away, your feet end up pretty close to your own face and *then* it's your problem."

"What about hand jobs?" asked a blonde girl who'd definitely given more than one hand job before.

"What about them?" I asked.

"What's, like, your top tip for giving a hand job?"

"Put it in your mouth," I said. "Next question?"

"How do you make anal hurt less?" asked a person with shaggy black hair and dimples in their cheeks who'd introduced themself as Ridley.

"Take your time and use lots of lube," I said.

"Lube?" they repeated, blinking in confusion. "My boyfriend said we don't need that."

"Oh, honey." I shook my head. "Dump him."

"But—"

"Sort of related to that," piped up Sierra, a skinny girl with fair white skin who was wearing foundation meant for medium white skin. "He's not doing it on purpose—like I think maybe his aim is bad—but what if he keeps trying to put it in the wrong hole?"

"Which wrong hole?" I asked.

"The..." She glanced around the table. "The wrong one."

"Yes, but *which* hole is the wrong one?"

She scoffed. "The *ass*, obviously. What else would it be? It's not like there are guys out there trying to put it in your belly button."

Mentally, I flashed back to the dingy mattress I'd told my best friend, Anne-Marie, I'd lost my virginity on, and the nameless guy I'd told her I lost my virginity *to* so that I didn't have to tell her I'd fucked her brother earlier that day. Emotionally, I suppressed a shudder at the memory of him trying to stick his tip into my belly button. Physically, I just shook my head.

"You'd be surprised," I said. "And anyway, the asshole isn't the wrong hole if that's the hole you're aiming for. If it's *not* the hole you're aiming for and you think he's legitimately got depth perception issues, turn the lights on so he can see better."

"But what if it's, like... you know... um..." asked Zara, a pretty eighteen-year-old with brown eyes so dark they were almost black and light brown skin marked by the occasional acne scar. "Like... too *big*?"

"Too big for what?" I asked.

Her eyes darted to the side. "Like, to... you know. *Fit*."

One of the other girls at the table giggled, but I waved a hand to shut her up. "I mean, it's possible, but not all dicks are like the ones you see in porn, no matter what people claim their measurement is. Some men don't seem to realize that from an evolutionary perspective, it makes zero sense for the average dick size to be double what the average vagina can accommodate." I tapped my finger to my temple. "That's fuckin' science."

"Okay, but won't it, like... stretch?" asked Madison, who had large blue eyes that peered out from beneath the fringe of her warm brown hair, giving her an angelically innocent sort of look.

"Yeah," I said. "It's a vagina. It's supposed to stretch."

"But it never goes back to the same size," she said. "That's why women's hips get wider after sex."

"After *birth*, maybe," I said. "God, did you go to Catholic school or something?"

"Yes," she said.

"Right." I shook my head. "Look, if it feels like it's so big that it hurts, it's one of three things. One, you're not turned on enough and need more foreplay. Tell him to put his mouth to use. Two, you're turned on enough, but you need lube or something because sometimes things don't get wet enough on their own. If that happens, don't worry. It's normal. Or three, it's actually too big and you can find something else to do."

"What if he doesn't want to do something else?" asked Connor, who was the only guy at the table, but who had quietly assured everyone he was gay after Sierra had looked at him nervously.

"Tell him it's nice to want things, like how you want to keep his boy bits out of your hole of preference."

"How do you get a guy to go down on you?" Katelyn asked.

"Tell him to," I said.

"What if he says no?"

"Tell him his best friend and/or worst enemy offered to do it."

"I have a question, but it's not really sex related," said Sabrina, who had goldish-brown skin and brown ringlet curls with streaky blonde highlights in it. "More relationship related."

I shook my head. "I'm not the person to ask. I don't do relationships. See lesson one about being a slut."

"Oh." She swallowed hard and nodded, not quite meeting my eyes. "That's fair."

A prickling of guilt ran across my chest. "But what's it about? Maybe we can workshop this as a group."

"Yeah," Ridley said. "I've had a couple of partners before."

"Me too," Madison said. "Even if we didn't, um, do *it*."

Sabrina bit her lip, then nodded again.

"Okay, well… I wanted to know if anyone had advice on, like, getting something back from an ex?"

And then she started crying.

We'd talked about a couple of heavier things during my sex orientation, so it seemed like a weird question to trigger tears. But after a bit of prodding, Sabrina explained she'd followed her now-ex boyfriend to Ottawa, where he'd already been living for a year, after she graduated. She and her cat had moved in with him and his roommate a few weeks earlier.

"This is Salem," she said, sniffling as she pulled her phone out to show us a picture.

"Salem?" repeated Zara. "Like—"

"Sabrina the Teenage Witch," Sabrina said, smiling under her tears. "I know. I thought it was funny when I got him."

We passed her phone around the table as she explained she'd caught her ex not only sliding into the DMs of nearly every girl in her English class, but failing spectacularly at it.

"Russell says I'm being stupid for breaking up with him because he didn't cheat on me," she said. "But it's only because everyone kept turning him down. So I went to stay with the girl who told me what he was doing and now"—her face crumpled—"he won't give me Salem back."

"He stole your cat?" Madison said, her voice surprisingly feral.

"I've had him since he was a little kitten." Sabrina started to sob again and Zara passed me the phone while the group tried to comfort Sabrina.

I looked down at the screen. Salem was a black cat, of course, with startling green eyes. He looked like a little puffball, his coat shiny and well-groomed, and he probably shed like a mother-fucker. Sighing, I put her phone on the table and dug my phone out of my pocket.

"What are his socials?" I asked.

Sabrina looked up, her eyes still wet. "What?"

"And on a scale from one to five, one being Einstein and five being a lobotomized cane toad, how objectively stupid is he?" I continued.

"Probably an eight," muttered Connor, who had a protective arm around Sabrina's shoulders.

She let out a shaky giggle. "I mean, objectively, he's not *stupid*, but he's also an idiot. So like, a three?"

"I can work with a three." I unlocked my screen. "Give me his socials. We're getting your cat back."

Two hours later, I was sitting on the couch of a small apartment that smelled like cat pee because being slightly smarter than a lobotomized cane toad did not, in fact, mean that someone was smart enough to know how to clean a litter box.

"Oh, you have a kitty," I called as a beautiful black cat jumped onto the couch and sidled up to me. Glancing at the kitchen to make sure Russell was still getting me a can of his finest discount beer, I winced before shying away. "What's his name?"

"That little brat is Salem," called Russell.

I blinked hard as my eyes started watering. "He's adorable. How long have you had him?"

"A couple of years." Russell returned to the living room and handed me a beer. "If he's bothering you, you can shove him off the couch."

"Oh, I couldn't do that," I said, forcing myself to pat Salem's head. "Besides, aren't we, ah... heading to the bedroom right away?"

I parted my lips, hoping it wasn't obvious that I was breathing shallowly, and fluttered my eyelashes coyly at Russell. Luckily, Russell's three on the stupid scale had a "too horny to think" modifier on it, and he grinned before setting his barely sipped beer on the coffee table.

"If you want to get right down to business, don't let me stop you," he said, deepening his voice.

"I'm the one who slid into your DMs." I put my beer down and stood up. "If you don't like a girl who knows what she wants, I can go."

"No!" He almost sounded panicked, which was perfect. "No, of course. I'm totally into letting you take charge."

I lifted an eyebrow. "Is that so?"

He nodded eagerly.

"Because if it is, I have a kinky little idea that you might be into..."

It took a bit of making out and teasing him through his jeans to get there, but ten minutes later, I had Russell's wrists bound to his bedposts with neckties. By the time I finished blindfolding him with a third necktie, he was hard, his cock tenting the boxers I'd stripped him down to.

"What are you gonna do now?" he asked, his words breathless with excitement.

"Oh, I was thinking of playing with my pussy a little," I said, glancing around the room.

"But I can't even see you, baby."

"You know what they say about anticipation."

"What do they say?" he asked.

I tried not to roll my eyes, then stepped forward and patted his head. "I'll tell you when I get back from the bathroom, cutie."

He jumped at the contact, not realizing I was that close. "I see how it is. You're making me wait."

"Imagine that," I said. "Don't go anywhere, now."

"I couldn't if I tried," he said.

Which was bullshit. He wasn't tied *that* tightly to the bedframe. Russell might be a cat-stealing asshole, but I wasn't going to put him in danger. And as soon as I grabbed Salem off the couch and got downstairs to Madison's car, where Sabrina was sitting in the back seat with Ridley and Connor, I grabbed Sabrina's phone and sent the pre-typed text to Russell's roommate telling him to go untie Russell.

"...and he did," I finished. "And that's the whole tale of the Great Pussy Cat Caper of OttawaTech."

"Wow," said Glitch.

"Right?"

My TA shook their head in disbelief. "I mean, that story had everything."

"I know. Theft. Sex. A guy learning a valuable lesson about not letting strange women tie him up. Drugs."

They cocked an eyebrow. "Drugs?"

"Yeah. I took an unholy amount of Claritin after Madison dropped me off in the hopes I could breathe again. I'm super allergic to cats."

Glitch leaned forward, putting their elbows on their desk and resting their head in their hands. If I didn't know any better, I would've said they were exasperated. But not only were their shoulders shaking with laughter, I also *did* know better.

The best way I could describe Glitch was chaos, which they both knew and owned. Even that day during what were supposed to be their professional office hours, they gave off a sort of "stoner chic" air. They were wearing a tight T-shirt with the words "My Pronouns Are May/Hem" on the front tucked into a belted pair of cargo pants. Their waist-length brown hair was pinned back on the sides with one long braid trailing over their left shoulder and they had drawn dark brown freckles on their warm beige-white skin.

Glitch was the coolest TA I'd ever had, which wasn't saying much. But they were also one of the coolest people I'd ever met, and that was saying a *lot* since they were a law student. They were the TA for my Forensic Science and Law class, which was bad enough, but it was also taught by a stuck-up lawyer named Bruce Shelby. If it wasn't for Glitch, me failing the class would've been a near certainty considering there was a worrying amount of potential for that to happen anyway.

"Look, it's an epic story, Nellie," Glitch said. "And kudos to you for putting your actual health on the line for this girl you just met."

"Well, and to get payback on a dirty cheater," I said. "Don't forget the justice aspect of it. Which directly relates to this class, doesn't it?"

They tried not to laugh again. "The thing is, I don't see how you stealing a cat last night caused you to miss class and not be able to hand in your case study *today*."

"I took Claritin last night and it makes me drowsy," I said. "So I overslept."

"The class starts at eleven."

"It was a *lot* of Claritin."

Glitch failed at holding their laugh in. "Look, best I can do is give you the ten point deduction for submitting a late assignment if you give it to me now."

I shrugged and opened my backpack, pulling out the case study sheet. "Fair's fair, I guess."

Glitch took the paper from me and glanced down at it. "This isn't even complete."

"Well, yeah," I said. "I was volun-told to do the orientation sessions and then got busy stealing a cat last night."

They shook their head, even though they were smiling, and handed my case study back. "Nice try, but you know Shelby will eat you alive if you hand in an incomplete assignment. No dice, kiddo."

I sighed and took the paper from them. "It was worth a try, I guess."

"Totally, but the answer's no." They drummed their fingers on their desk, then looked at the door before turning to their laptop. "But look, I think your case study list had a typo on it or something, because it seems to me"—they typed quickly, then hit enter with a flourish—"that this case is *next* week's topic. So maybe if you go to the library now, I can pretend I didn't see anything and you can submit it for your next one."

"You rock," I said, putting my paper back in my bag.

"I know. Don't make me regret it." They waved a stern finger at me. "Seriously. Get your shit together."

I raised my eyebrows, but they'd barely moved before Glitch's face cracked and they started laughing.

"You can't even say that with a straight face," I said.

They snorted. "There's no hope for you if you think *anything* about me is capable of being straight."

"Your hair?" I suggested.

They rolled their eyes. "Go to the library and finish your case study, slacker."

"Alright, alright," I said. "I'm going."

"To the library?" they pressed.

"I'm going to the library," I said. "I'm on my way. Right now. Ready to spend my Friday night surrounded by books."

Chapter Two
Completely, Totally, Unequivocally Fine

"It is about damn time!" Anne-Marie exclaimed, bursting out of her seat when I walked up to our table in The Library ten minutes later.

She threw her arms around my neck before I even put my backpack down, half-strangling me and half-mashing her boobs in my face because she insisted on wearing four-inch heels despite being nearly five-eight. "Weeks I have not seen my best friend, and you decide it is okay to make me wait even *longer*?! Rude, *chérie*."

"I had to talk to my TA about getting an extension," I said. "Which they said no to, by the way, thanks for the sympathy."

"You are still late," Anne-Marie scolded. "*C'est tres impoli.*"

"Like, ten minutes late," I said.

"It's twenty-six minutes, actually," Remy said, not looking up from the book in front of him.

"You talked to Glitch for twenty-six minutes?" Sydney asked skeptically. "And they *still* said no to an extension?"

The answer to that was no, I hadn't been talking to Glitch for twenty-six minutes. I'd talked to them for close to fifteen minutes, then rushed to meet Anne-Marie, who'd decided a few days earlier to take an impromptu weekend trip to Ottawa with Remy to celebrate their anniversary. But I'd barely made it out of the building when my phone went off.

And of course, instead of being someone I wanted to talk to, it was my dad.

"I can't come to Montreal," I'd said after reluctantly accepting the call.

"Good afternoon to you too, *ma fille ange*," my dad had said, a subtle sarcasm floating through his otherwise performatively pleasant tone. "I hope you are doing well. How has school been going?"

I'd closed my eyes and took a steadying breath. "It's been busy. I have a lot of papers already, plus my internship applications, and my final thesis project."

"Are you not taking fewer classes this semester than usual?"

"Yes. I'm taking the recommended number of classes for a full-time course load instead of overloading my schedule like I did before." I'd dug my finger into the side of my thumb, using the sensation to ground myself enough to keep my voice even. "But the courses I have this year are a lot more involved."

"Hmm," he'd said. "And you are keeping up so far?"

"It'd be pretty bad if I was behind when it's only the second week of the semester," I'd said like I hadn't just left my TA's office where I'd been pleading for an extension for what wasn't even the first time.

"Good," he'd said. "It would not be too much for you to make a trip out here, then? Perhaps next weekend?"

And I'd said no, and he'd suggested the weekend after that, so I'd had to talk in circles with him for a few minutes before saying I'd see what I could do and hanging up. But the absolute last thing I wanted to do was tell Anne-Marie that. Partly because as much as I loved her, she was the world's biggest gossip, but mostly because I didn't want to bring the mood down.

"At least I suggested a cool bar for you to hang out at," I said to Anne-Marie.

"Certainly, but I know Remy and I would have much rather spent an extra twenty-six minutes visiting with you," Anne-Marie replied.

"It's okay," Remy said. "I'd rather be reading anyway."

I pressed my lips together, but it didn't stop my shoulders from shaking as I stifled a laugh. Anne-Marie and Remy had been together since we were about fifteen, but my parents had been divorced for four years by that point and I didn't live in Montreal. It wasn't until this past summer that I felt like he'd comfortable enough around me to relax, which was fair. We hadn't known each other all that well. Now that we did, I knew he didn't mean it personally; he'd rather read than socialize in general, not just with me.

But knowing that didn't stop it from being funny.

Anne-Marie sighed, though I could hear the affection in it, and stopped strangling me for a second to reach out and press a touch to Remy's shoulder.

"*Mon beau loup*," she said. "*S'il vous plaît?*"

He looked up, blinking, then stuck a napkin into the book and closed it.

"Hi, Nellie," he said.

"Hi, Remy," I replied, the words muffled by Anne-Marie's chest. "Whatcha reading?"

"A book about the history of the Canadian mint," he said. "We went on a tour earlier today so when I saw it on the shelf here, I thought it would be interesting to compare the information we got during the tour to what was written. So far, it seems like the tour was more thorough."

Anne-Marie let go of me. "Did it answer the question you had about the specimen coins?"

Remy shook his head. "I'll check online when we get back to the hotel later."

"I have to say, I was worried when you said you wanted to meet at a library," Anne-Marie said as I took the empty seat next to Remy while she sat across from him and beside Sydney. "I thought perhaps you'd left Montreal and stopped being fun. But this, *chérie*?" She gestured around her. "I love it. It makes you seem so... academic."

The Library was one of OttawaTech's best kept secrets. Seriously. I'd lived less than six blocks from the place for nearly four years and had only found out about it when Reid wanted to introduce us to his new girlfriend, Hope, but didn't want to take her to our usual near-campus haunt, Lou's Pub.

In what would be a shock to no one who had even an ounce of common sense, it was called The Library because of the books, which filled the entirety of the second floor of the two-storey bar. Shorter shelves sat under the windows, potted plants and other knick-knacks sitting on the tops, and the rest of the shelves went to the ceiling. Every single one was stuffed with used books that people could take or exchange with some of their own. It was like a life-size version of the Free Little Libraries that existed in some neighbourhoods.

Which I guess would be a regular library, sort of.

Whatever. The Library had a great ambiance. It was the kind of place that made me sad I didn't read more. I'd always wanted to be a reader, but my mind always wandered while I was reading. But for the kind of person who lived and breathed books, The Library was the perfect place.

They also made an *amazing* sangria.

"So what's new, Annie?" I asked, pouring myself some sangria from the pitcher Sydney had bought.

"Oh, not all that much," she said, which was clearly a bold-faced lie since there was always something new that Anne-Marie wanted to gossip about.

"How's your family doing?" Sydney asked.

I tried not to let my jaw twitch in annoyance. The conversation would've veered that way eventually, but I'd hoped it would be a while so I could pretend I needed to go to the bathroom or something.

But to my surprise, Anne-Marie didn't launch into hints that I should marry her brother.

"Honestly, that is half the reason we are here," she said, sighing as she lifted her drink and took a sip through the straw. "I needed a weekend away from home."

"Why?" I asked, frowning.

"Things have been odd." She stirred her drink with her straw. "My father and brother are not getting along. It is not like it is the first time they've gotten at each other's throats, but it does not happen very often. My dad is saying it is work-related, which means he cannot tell me because of attorney-client privilege, apparently. And Jean-Paul moved out."

"I didn't know JP's condo was finally ready," I said.

In an instant, Anne-Marie's head snapped towards me and a smile so predatory that I half-expected fangs to pop out of her mouth spread across her face.

"Is there a reason you should have known, *chérie*?" she asked.

Ah, shit. That was the trap.

"I thought you would've mentioned it," I said, running my fingernail along my thumb. "You tell me everything about everyone else."

"Well, yes." Anne-Marie tilted her head side to side. "But I thought perhaps my brother told you."

"*Why* would you think that?"

"You and Jean-Paul had such a lovely evening together at the Diamond Gala,. I assumed you were friends now," she said, her voice light with the airiness of delusion. "And since friends talk to each other regularly..."

"He took me to one event as a favour, Annie," I said. "That was it. We're not friends."

She glanced at her nails. "So you say."

"I haven't talked to JP since I left Montreal and you have literally no reason to think it was ever anything more than him helping me out of a tough spot."

"I am teasing, *chérie*," Anne-Marie said, waving a hand at me. "I know what you meant. But a girl can wish for her best friend to wake up and realize the man of her dreams has been in front of her face for nearly her entire life."

"He's not—"

"But yes, he moved out last weekend," she continued over my protests. "And something about it was not quite *right*. He got the call his condo was ready and he was gone within two days. I know he was looking forward to moving out, but Jean-Paul is a planner. He does not impulsively do things. So for him to *leave* like that…" She trailed off, fidgeting with her straw. "It felt wrong."

"Maybe you just miss him," Sydney suggested.

"It is not like he hasn't moved out before," Anne-Marie replied. "He lived in residence during university and such. But maybe." She shrugged. "My mother noticed it too, though."

"I mean, your dad and JP work together, don't they?" I said, knowing full well that they did and belatedly remembering that she'd also *just* said that. "Maybe they spend too much time around each other."

She tilted her head to the side in consideration. "That could be true. My dad hasn't said much since he left. Neither has Jean-Paul, and I have been texting him every single day so he doesn't miss any AMNN broadcasts."

"What's AMNN?" Sydney asked.

"The Anne-Marie News Network." She picked up her margarita and took a sip. "It is my brother's snarky term for me making sure he stays in the loop about all the latest information. Although, that reminds me!" She perked up, a smile spreading across her face. "Do you think I could be a news reporter? Like a television anchor or something?"

"I can think of no better job for you," I said.

Anne-Marie beamed. "Really? Because after I found out Jean-Paul called it that, I thought about it for a while and I think I would be *very* good at it."

"You would be good at it," Remy said, not looking up from his book.

"Remy thinks I should do it if I want to," Anne-Marie said. "And you know, I was talking to Michele, and her aunt's sister-in-law's niece is an entertainment correspondent on a morning show and she said she could get me in contact with her. I do not know if she will, though, since she would probably want a favour in return and the only thing I could think of was trying to get Jean-Paul to take her on a date again. Bu-*ut*"—she drew the word into two syllables and turned her head towards Sydney so she could look at me out of the corner of her eye—"I do not think my brother would agree to that, since I imagine he is very much enjoying the freedom that having his own home comes with as he can now get laid as much as he likes with complete privacy."

I sighed. "Anne—"

But she was talking again before I even got the second part of her name out. Across the table, I could see Sydney's shoulders shake as she laughed, and I threw a glare at her from beneath my eyelashes before picking up my sangria and taking a long sip.

I'd expected Anne-Marie to tease me about JP. After all, she didn't know we had hooked up. Not once, and not repeatedly. There had been a few harrowing moments where she nearly caught me fucking her brother, but none of those moments had actually tied me to JP.

She had no reason to suspect I'd been sitting on JP's face instead of jogging like I'd said the night she insisted I do the Illumi-Nite run.

There was no reason for her to think the panties she'd found in JP's room were mine, even though I'd been hiding naked on the floor beside his bed during that harrowing conversation.

And when he and I had disappeared during the Diamond Gala so he could use my pussy to jerk off into my panties, there was nothing that hinted that was what we were *actually* doing.

But then JP, asshole that he was, told her that he'd spent the night with someone after the Diamond Gala. And Anne-Marie, desperately pushy and delusional as she was, had clasped at that little joke like it was a frayed safety belt on a roller coaster.

Luckily, nothing was going to happen if that frayed safety belt snapped. The roller coaster was off, shut down, overgrown in an abandoned amusement park. Anne-Marie was never going to discover anything had happened between me and JP because it was over and we hadn't spoken in weeks.

Which was fine.

Completely, totally fine.

Because why would we? Both of us had known our arrangement was a temporary thing, just like my arrangement with Ben had been temporary. And it didn't bother me that I hadn't heard from Ben since he left for California. We'd been clear with our expectations and there was no reason for us to get in touch with each other, especially when we hadn't been texting each other or anything before he left for any reason but to arrange when we were next hanging out.

And sure, JP and I *had* sometimes texted each other about things that weren't related to hooking up. Sometimes we'd share gossip or jokes. And maybe sometimes we'd send each other pictures. But not, like, *nude* pictures.

Well, not completely nude.

Or, well, not full-body nude.

And maybe not *we*. Maybe it was more *I* sent him pictures, but only ever of certain nude parts. And he sent me pictures too, sometimes. Not his full dick or anything, but I had a couple of decent shots of his stupidly sculpted body in low-slung shorts with certain kinds of imprints showing through the fabric. He probably would've sent me pictures of his dick, too, but he'd made an off-hand comment once that he wouldn't do that without asking permission first and I'd never actually asked him for one and—

It didn't matter.

The point was, JP and I both knew it was temporary. I had no intention of going back to Montreal, even though my dad had asked no less than six times if I'd come to a dinner party or a gala or a benefit.

So there was no reason for me to message JP. And there was no reason for him to message me, either.

Though I guess if I *had* to pick a reason, I might've thought he'd text to check on me.

Not because I needed him to. I wanted him to even less than that, but JP had spent three years leaving Post-It notes on my car when I was in Montreal because he wanted to make sure I was okay after I popped my cherry on his dick. So it wouldn't have been unusual for someone to assume he might message to see how my ass was after he'd fucked it so hard we both nearly passed out.

He hadn't, though. And that was fine.

Completely, totally, unequivocally *fine*.

And the fact that I was curious about what was going on with him was totally normal. We had spent a good amount of time together over the summer, so it made sense for me to wonder what was going on with him. And to be, like, happy for him that he finally got into his own place after waiting for ages.

And since Anne-Marie had hinted that he might be having a rough time right now, it would also be totally normal for someone to text him and say congratulations.

Because it might cheer him up to hear that someone was happy for him. And once in a while, I tried to be a nice person who did nice things for people like cheer them up while they were having a rough time.

So it was entirely normal that when Remy got up to go to the bathroom while Anne-Marie was talking about... uh...

"—why she is suddenly so interested in trampoline workouts, but my mother says she is having fun with it." Anne-Marie took a loud slurp of her drink. "Between us, though, I think it has more to do with the instructor being young, Spanish, and known for wearing grey sweatpants to the gym."

...the gym or something, I guess.

Whatever. It was completely normal for me to pull my phone out of my backpack.

It was *totally* fine and normal and not at all weird that I scrolled down in my messages until I found his name.

It was completely, totally, unequivocally *fine* for me to send him a friendly message expressing my happiness for him.

Me

Congrats on finally moving out of your parents' metaphorical basement, loser

Totally normal.

Chapter Three
Hypothetically Hypothetical

Dɪᴅ I, ɪɴ ʜɪɴᴅsɪɢʜᴛ, have to text JP at that exact moment, considering his sister was sitting at the table with me? No.

Did I think of that before hitting send? Also no.

But did JP at least have more common sense than me and hold off on texting me back because he knew Anne-Marie was in Ottawa that weekend and made the connection that I texted him because she'd told me he moved out and therefore would likely be sitting right there?

Of *course* not. JP was a dumbass and I was at least three times smarter than he thought he was. If I hadn't thought of those things, there was no way he would, either.

Which meant I ended up trying to subtly text him back while simultaneously listening to Anne-Marie go through the past month's worth of gossip, since apparently the hour we chatted on the phone each week wasn't enough to make a dent in everything that had happened.

Bastard

I was wondering if I'd hear from you. AM's driving you up the wall already?

I tried not to glower at my phone, glancing up at Anne-Marie to make sure she was absorbed in her story about how her coworker at the place where she was a personal shopper had helped a politician's wife drop over ten grand on lingerie three days before it was revealed that she was having an affair with a politician from the opposing party, and sent a response.

Me

> I just wanted to say congrats, jerk pants. Didn't mean to bother you with my well wishes.

As soon as I sent it, I flipped my phone face down on the table next to my beer and looked up, nodding as if I'd been listening to Anne-Marie all along.

"—love how *subversive* it is," she said. "It is like the Martelle group is daring anyone to say something about Claire's... relationship? Relationships?" She frowned. "I do not know if it is plural."

"It should be," Sydney the linguistics nerd said. "It would be one relationship if they were all with everyone else involved, but from what Nellie said, Claire and her fiancée are one relationship, and then Claire's thing with her girlfriend is another relationship."

"And Claire's girlfriend's thing with her two boyfriends is a relationship," I said. "If I'm remembering it right from the Diamond Gala."

Next to my hand, my phone vibrated. My hand twitched because there was nothing I hated more than an unread notification, but I forced myself to ignore it.

"That is what I just said, *chérie*," Anne-Marie said, her eyes sparkling.

"Right," I said. "I was making sure I heard you right."

"Well, yes. In any case, I do not think Tessa—that is her girlfriend, we met at the *Saisons de Changement* celebration over the Labour Day weekend—will move here permanently. It seems more that they are making it clear that the Martelles will hear no criticism of Claire's lifestyle, and honestly, that is so good for them. I think—"

And then I lost my focus on her as my phone vibrated again. I tried to ignore it again, but when it vibrated a third time, I had no choice.

The first message was just a set of laughing emojis because JP was apparently incapable of sending a single emoji to get his point across, followed by two texts.

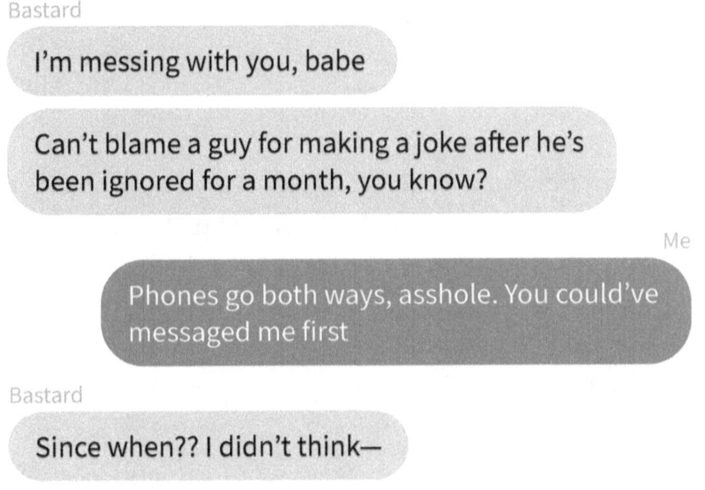

The chair next to me pulled out before I finished reading and I jumped, nearly dropping my phone. Fumbling it, I slammed the power button to turn the screen off.

"Are you okay?" Remy asked, giving me a strange look as he sat down.

"Fine," I said.

"Are you sure, *chérie*?" Anne-Marie said.

"Why wouldn't I be?" I asked.

"Well, your face is red."

"No, it's not," I said.

She looked at Sydney with a smirk on her face. "It is, yes?"

Sydney shrugged somewhat apologetically. "A little, I guess."

My phone buzzed in my hand, the screen flashing on. I pressed the power button quickly.

"If you are texting someone who makes you blush, *chérie*, I think you should be telling me about it," Anne-Marie said, her voice pitching up as her eyes sparkled.

"I'm *not*," I insisted, even though I could feel my cheeks burning hotter. "It's a classmate I'm doing a group project with."

"What group project?" Sydney asked, frowning.

"The one for my Forensic Science and Law class," I said.

Her frown deepened. "Really?"

"What do you mean, really?" I asked.

"You have a group project in that class?"

I tried to keep my voice even as I willed her to understand me telepathically. "Yeah. And you know him. He's a total bastard."

I watched three confused blinks flutter Sydney eyelids before realization flashed in her eyes.

"*Oh*," she said, drawing the word out. "Right. The bastard from your Law class."

Somehow, that convinced Anne-Marie to drop it, although Sydney gave me a meaningful look that plainly said she expected details later. Which was unnecessary because she was one of my two best friends and since I'd never had a secret friends with benefits arrangement with *her* brother, she was the first person I'd give details to about it.

Anne-Marie started talking about one of the benefits she'd been to and Remy opened his book. I waited, my palm sweating against my phone until he was absorbed in it again.

Then, heart racing in my throat, I looked at JP's messages.

Bastard

Since when? I didn't think this app let me do that

In all seriousness, I thought you were done with me.

Me

What's that supposed to mean?

Bastard

I didn't want to make it awkward if you were trying to ignore me.

And no hard feelings if that was the case, okay? I promise. I knew our arrangement, Nell.

My heart floated out of my throat and back into place, relief cushioning it as I let out the softest, least obvious breath I could. "Seriousness" and "JP" were two words I didn't want to think in the same sentence, but seeing him say, spelled out in writing, that he knew what this summer was held more comfort than I thought it would.

Me

I wasn't ignoring you. I haven't been back to Montreal.

I don't know if I'm ever going back, either.

I don't know if that answers whatever you mean by if I'm done with you.

"—hate that Nellie was right about it," Anne-Marie said.

My name caught my attention and I looked up from my phone. Next to me, Remy mirrored the action, putting his napkin back in his book.

"I don't know if she's completely right," he said.

"Why wouldn't I be?" I asked, wishing I'd heard a crumb of context so I knew what Anne-Marie meant.

"I don't know if what he's doing is gaslighting him," Remy said. "It's not so much that Niko is convincing Bruno about things that didn't happen, but—"

Anne-Marie cut him off with a heavy sigh. "Technicalities, Remy. You know what I mean. Niko is bad for him. He all but said to us that he got Bruno to cancel on Nellie as a loyalty test."

Oh.

Shit.

I didn't want to be right about Bruno ditching out on being my approved-of date for the social events I'd had to attend over the summer because Niko had manipulated him into it.

"Is he okay?" I asked. "Bruno, I mean?"

Anne-Marie looked at me apologetically. "Had I known Niko was like this, I would never have tried to get him and Bruno together. But it wasn't until after that he started acting like this. Not that I saw, anyway."

I looked from her to Remy. "Is anyone helping him?"

"No," Remy said.

I whipped my head back to Anne-Marie. "No one's doing anything? Why—"

"He does not want help, *chérie*," Anne-Marie said. "Trust me. I *have* tried. But he is embarrassed to admit he was wrong. And he's been convinced people are trying to break them up because they have something against Niko. By Niko, of course." She looked pointedly at Remy. "Which *is* gaslighting."

Remy nodded, then looked back at me. "We are making sure he knows we are there for him. So when he is ready for help, he can get it."

The four of us were quiet for a moment.

"But all is not bad!" Anne-Marie finally said, her voice brightening. "Actually, Bruno came to the *Saisons de Changement* event and Niko was not with him. It was a beautiful event and the company that organized it is doing the police benefit at the end of the month." She turned to Sydney. "If you are still seeing your cop friend, you should ask if he is going!"

"Oh," Sydney said. "Well, yeah. Sort of."

Anne-Marie raised her eyebrows. "What happened?"

"I haven't been back to Montreal and she usually gets a ride with me," I said.

"That's not all of it," Sydney said loyally. "Olivier was away for a couple of weeks because of the wedding he was in."

Anne-Marie raised her eyebrows. "He did not take you as a date?"

"Well, it's not like we're *super* serious," Sydney said. "And it was in Alberta, so I would've had to pay to—"

"Wait," I said, frowning. "The wedding for… what was his name? Colin?"

"Cody," Sydney said. "Yeah. Olivier was the best man."

I frowned. Sydney had met Olivier at Cody's bachelor party after one of the other groomsmen enlisted me so Cody could win a scavenger hunt. Well, he'd enlisted Anne-Marie, actually, but she'd left the bar wearing the panties he'd given her to give Cody, so I'd taken one for the team and surrendered my favourite panties to make up for it.

It worked out. I ended up having a threesome with a cowboy and a bad boy, and I was almost certain they'd ended up together.

But that had happened months ago.

"They planned the bachelor party, like, six months ahead of time?" I asked skeptically.

Sydney shook her head. "The wedding was supposed to be in April, I think, but the venue flooded the night before. The bride had her heart set on this place, so they postponed it instead of trying to find a new place that day. And, like, new decorations and stuff, since it was all there."

Anne-Marie clutched her chest. "*Crisse de tabarnak*, I would have died. Can you *imagine*—"

She launched into another string of words, which worked out well because my phone vibrated again.

Bastard

> I mean hypothetically, if we had the opportunity, are you into continuing what we were doing?

> Basically I wanna know what the chances are of, say, me getting a pic of your tits is

For fuck's sake. He couldn't be serious right now.

Me

> Are you asking me for nudes?

Bastard

> Hypothetically speaking, yes. If you're not done with me.

Me

> Hypothetically speaking, you're a perv.

Bastard

> Can you hypothetically blame me?

Me

Who else would I hypothetically blame?

Bastard

Look, babe. I'm not ashamed to admit that you're hot as fuck. And I went and got myself spoiled by getting that ass regularly over the summer

Which sucks. Now when I want to get laid, I have to work for it again. I figure I'm way more likely to get a pic by asking for one

Me

And you think you're going to convince me to send you a picture of my tits by calling me easy?

"But your father wasn't there, for better or for worse," Anne-Marie said. "Has your dad said if Kimberlee was feeling better, Nellie?"

"No," I said. "I haven't been talking to him much."

Anne-Marie frowned. "Excuse me?"

I looked up, confused. "What?"

"Who called you *easy*?" she asked, looking disgusted.

I stared at her, then looked down at my phone, where the message I *thought* I'd sent JP was actually what I thought I'd said to Anne-Marie.

Me

No, I haven't been talking to him much

Bastard

Uh... was that meant for me?

Shit.

Shit.

Across the table, Sydney had her napkin pressed to her mouth, trying not to laugh. What had I—

"Oh, it is the bastard from your class still, isn't it?" Anne-Marie said. "What's he trying to convince you to do?"

Oh, good. Apparently I hadn't said the tit-pic part out loud.

"Finish his section of the report," I said. "It's fine. He's just, uh… he's being stupid."

Anne-Marie scoffed. "More than stupid. How dare he say that about one of my best and dearest friends? Tell him to back off or I will come deal with him myself."

It was touching that she was willing to do that for me, but unnecessary given that my classmate was fictional. "I'll let him know. But, uh, what did you ask me?"

"If Kimberlee was feeling better," Anne-Marie said. "I have never known her to miss an event before, so her flu must have been outrageously bad. And since your dad missed it, too, I thought perhaps she was in the hospital or something."

"Oh," I said. "No. He didn't mention anything."

Anne-Marie frowned. "Really?"

I nodded. "Keep in mind my dad only calls to ask me to skip the classes he's paying for so I can go to Montreal and impress the Martelles again." I forced a laugh, hoping it made my bitterness less obvious. "He wants me to help him network or something. But I don't have time."

She nodded, sympathy in her dark brown eyes, but before she could say anything else, the server stopped by our table. I tried to ignore the guilty feeling of being distracted while I was supposed to be visiting with Anne-Marie as she ordered another drink and dipped my head to message JP again.

I tapped my foot nervously beneath the table. Anne-Marie had somehow started talking about the gym again, Remy flipped the page in his book, and Sydney was paying attention to the conversation like a good friend would.

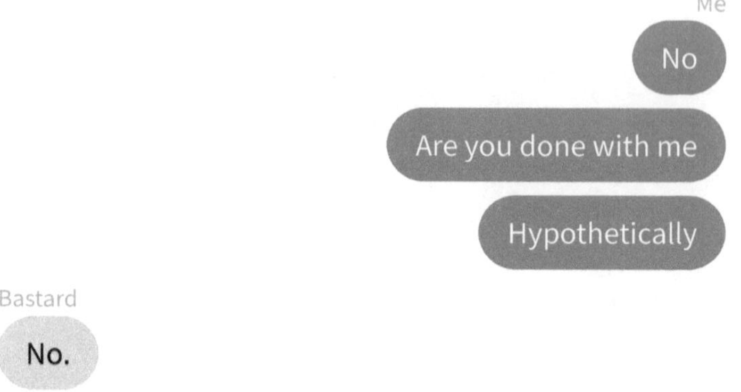

And maybe he should've been.

Maybe we both should've been.

Maybe I shouldn't have waited until Anne-Marie finished talking about her friend Lisette's totally not noticeable nose job but extremely noticeable lip fillers to excuse myself to the bathroom.

But, I figured as I lifted my shirt, aimed my camera at the girl reflected in the mirror, and made sure the phone blocked my face so the pink tinge still on my cheeks wasn't noticeable, none of it mattered anyway.

Because hypothetically, this was all hypothetical.

Chapter Four
She's Got A Great Rack

"Spiderwebs cling to your armour, leaving sticky trails of residue behind. The monstrous beast has been slain, and you collect the hoards of treasure left in its abhorrent lair," Calvin said from behind the cardboard screen blocking his sheets from the rest of us. "Among the piles of discarded skeletons, you find a pouch containing magic crystals, an ancient map on a delicate scroll, and for some reason, a freshly baked pie."

"I eat the pie," I said immediately.

"You can't eat the pie," said Hope, Reid's new girlfriend.

"I think what Himaya means is that you *shouldn't* eat the pie," Brandon said, giving Hope a pointed look.

"Borean," I said, calling him by his character name as I gave him an exasperated look. "It's *freshly baked.*"

He tilted his head and looked at Hope helplessly. "She makes a sound argument."

"So you eat the pie, Neelu?" Calvin asked.

"Sure do." I picked up one of the Filipino egg tarts Calvin had baked for us and popped it in my mouth.

"Alright," Calvin said. "Roll for constitution."

Hope let out a loud groan. "This is *exactly* what I was worried about."

I picked up my dice, shook it in my hand like that would make a difference, and dropped it on the table.

"Hell yeah!" Brandon said, peering at it before I could say anything.

"Nat twenty," Reid added. "Great roll, Nellie."

Sydney shot me a thumbs up.

Hope glared at me.

"Damn," Calvin said, sounding impressed. "Well, uh... I guess Neelu burps so loudly she regains three HP and the rumbling stops."

Sydney cackled so hard she snorted and the game came to a pause as everyone burst out laughing.

Well, everyone except Hope, of course.

"Great," she said. "You ate a disgusting pie. Now, is there anything else you can do to help us? Because I've yet to see why bringing her on our adventure is beneficial."

"Ah, hush up, Himaya," Brandon said. "Neelu may not be strong or all that smart—"

"Or particularly skilled," added Reid.

"And she's not especially agile," Sydney said.

"Plus, I barely know how to play the game," I said.

Hope looked at me, exasperated. "What, exactly, do you bring to the table, then?"

There was a pause. Brandon glanced at Sydney, who looked at Reid, who determinedly stared at the dice sitting on the table in front of him.

"I've got a great rack," I suggested.

"She's got a great rack," repeated Brandon, his round cheeks flushing slightly as Calvin and Sydney murmured in agreement, though Reid wisely kept his mouth shut and his eyes down.

"She's a *Satyr*!" Hope said.

"Are you saying Satyrs can't have great racks?" Sydney asked.

"Yeah, actually, I am," Hope said, glaring at her. "Because Satyrs are traditionally male and—"

"—and Calvin said I could be a female Satyr named Neelu with a great rack," I said. "And what he says goes. Isn't that, like, rule one? The Dungeon Master gets final say?"

"I'm so impressed you know that," Hope said dryly. "Is it because it's the same as the other kind of dungeons you have experience with or—"

"So while this is all happening," Calvin said, trying to change the subject before I could tell Hope I hadn't been to a sex dungeon yet but would gladly take her recommendations so I knew which ones to avoid. "Are you still walking forward?"

"Uh... yes," I said.

"No," Hope said immediately. "No, we're not."

"Yes, we are."

"We're *not*."

"Except that we *are*," I said. "In fact, we're walking forward so forwardly that I'm prancing on my little goat feet ahead of everyone, shaking my goat ass and—"

"You said you're in the front?" Calvin said.

"Yeah," I said.

"Great. Roll a Perception check."

And that was how I fell into a pit of lava and died, which despite her having nothing to do with it and not even saying anything to defend me at any point, Hope decided was Sydney's fault.

"I'm so *sick* of her!" Sydney vented as we walked home a little while later. "Reid had the fucking audacity to say I'm antagonizing her!"

"Have I called Reid a dick to his face recently?" I asked. "Maybe I need to make a point of it again."

"I don't know what his fucking problem is," she said. "I didn't even do anything. *You* were the one pissing Hope off."

I chuckled. "Yeah, that's true. I should be the one getting yelled at."

"You should," she said grumpily. "You know as well as I do that she's insecure about being with Reid because for some goddamn reason, even though we've been friends for years and I'm literally *seeing someone else*, he keeps picking girls who have a problem with him having a female roommate."

"Yeah, but it doesn't make it my fault that Reid yelled at you instead of me."

"No, but then you're flirting and—"

"I did *not* flirt with Reid," I interrupted.

"Yeah, but you were flirting with everyone else there," she said.

"And that matters why?" I said. "Please explain to me why me acting the same way I've always acted with Calvin and Brandon affects how Hope acts towards *you*."

Sydney's throat flexed as she swallowed, but she didn't say anything.

"I'm waiting," I said. "Because seriously, Syd. I was trying to help. I agreed to come to this *solely* because I wanted to be there since no one else seems to call her out for how she treats you."

She blinked rapidly a few times. I felt bad, despite not being in the wrong, because I knew a second later, her eyelashes would be wet.

"Don't you dare cry," I said. "You did your makeup way too nice today to ruin it with tears over *Hope*."

She let out a watery laugh. "I'm sorry."

"How can you be sorry for crying when you're not crying? Seems suspicious to me."

She laughed again, her strawberry blonde hair swaying as she shook her head, then took a deep breath and let it out.

"I'm sorry I'm taking this out on you," she said. "You're right. And smart."

"Don't forget my great rack."

"You're right and smart and have a rack that would make angels weep."

"Explains why you're crying."

Sydney let out an unattractive snort of laughter, but before either of us could say anything else, the Spongebob Square Pants theme song started blaring from my pocket, which sent both of us into another fit of giggles.

"You have *got* to change that," she said. "It's obnoxious."

"Counterpoint: it puts me in a good enough mood that I don't want to throw my phone into the canal instead of answering when I see who it is."

It probably sounded like a joke, but it wasn't. It was an exaggeration, maybe, but the flat tone I said it in made Sydney frown in concern. Not looking at her, I sighed, then tapped the screen and used the slight burst of happiness from the sound of my ring tone to sound as cheerful as I could.

"Hi, Dad," I said.

"*Ma fille ange*," my dad responded. "How is your second week of classes going?"

"Fine," I said. "How's... life?"

"Excellent," he said, sounding disconcertingly convincing. "I need you to share with me what your schedule looks like for the next few weekends."

"Booked solid," I said.

"All of them?" he asked.

"For the foreseeable future."

"*Ma fille ange*, I am not asking much," he'd said. "I am asking—"

"—that I make a two-hour drive, spend a couple of hours getting ready for some social gathering, attend the gathering so I can make Pia Martelle laugh like I'm some kind of court jester, spend the night in Montreal, then make the two-hour drive back to Ottawa after having brunch with you and Kimberlee because you never let me leave without having at least one extra outing," I blurted. "I don't have *time*."

There was a heavy beat of silence and I tensed, preparing myself for my dad to snap at me for talking back to him and possibly threaten to stop paying my rent again.

"So not next weekend, then," he said. "The one after, perhaps?"

I said no. He pushed back again and I pushed forward, and between all the pushing, by the time I hung up the phone, Sydney and I were nearly back at our apartment building.

"Like, is he purposely not getting it?" I grumbled as we turned down our street. "Or is he playing stupid because he thinks there's some competitive advantage to pretending he's surprised every time I tell him I don't have time to go to Montreal?"

"Maybe he's hoping you'll change your mind," Sydney said.

I scoffed. "Not a chance."

"Really? None at all?"

I turned to stare at her incredulously. "Uh... yeah. Zero chance. Why would you—"

She held up her hands defensively. "I just thought since you and JP are talking again—"

"I'm not changing my mind for JP Marchand, of all people," I said, rolling my eyes. "His dick isn't worth having to see my dad."

"Nell." She gave me a semi-patronizing look. "I know you'd rather tie up another sophomore douchebag and steal his cat than admit you like anything about JP, but you've straight-up said he's given you some of the best sex of your life."

That was true. JP was so infuriatingly good in bed that I couldn't even convince myself to pretend he wasn't, and that was saying something considering how delusional I could be. "So maybe you should realize it's less of a testament to the quality of his dick and more to how much I can't stand my dad."

"Even if I believed that, it's not like you'd have to. JP doesn't live next door anymore."

I glared at her. "So maybe then you should realize that I don't like him."

Sydney's lips pressed together, a laugh hidden behind them. "You text him an awful lot for someone you don't like."

"I do not!"

"If I opened your phone right now, you're saying his chat wouldn't be right under mine as most recent?"

"It's not," I said. "I texted Brandon when my lecture was done to say we were on our way over."

"Right. And you didn't take a sneaky picture of your dice sitting in your cleavage and send it to some mystery person while Hope and Brandon were arguing about which cell door they should open first?"

Right. I'd forgotten about that.

"Look, I'm just saying, maybe a trip to Montreal wouldn't be the worst thing," she said.

"And it has nothing to do with hitching a ride so you can see Olivier?" I asked.

Sydney twisted her mouth to the side and didn't say anything, which sent guilt pin-pricking along my chest and arms.

"You can borrow my car, Syd. Or get a train ticket. Or a bus ticket. Or take a freakin' Uber."

"You can't Uber to Montreal from here," she said, laughing.

"You totally can," I said. "I hooked up with a guy in my second year who somehow put in Montreal instead of Montreal Road when he got an Uber to bring his grandma back to her retirement home and didn't find out until she called a few hours later to ask how she was supposed to get back."

"He did not!"

"Totally did. With tip and surcharge and stuff, I think he said it was over a grand for both trips."

"He sent her *back* in an Uber, too?!"

"How else would she get back?"

She gave me an incredulous look. "What other options did you just suggest to me?"

"Oh yeah."

There was still a smile on my face when Sydney and I hugged goodbye and went to our respective apartments, but it faded once I walked in and remembered I'd left my internship applications spread over the coffee table to force myself to work on them once I got home. Dropping my backpack in the kitchen, I stripped out of my jeans and left them on the armchair in the living room before flopping to the floor, staring dully at the work in front of me.

There were two for me to apply for. The first was the FAI internship that I'd been rejected for the previous year because I'd pissed off Shitstain Humprey, who ended up being the nephew of Shithead Humprey, the head of the FAI Internship program.

The second was the CCFS Labs internship. If the FAI internship was competitive, CCFS Labs was like the Olympics. Applying was more like taking an exam than it was filling out an application. And considering they almost never accepted anyone with anything less than a Masters, I had a better chance of working as a go-go dancer on an Antarctic cruise ship than I did of getting accepted to CCFS Labs.

But I'd promised Ben I would at least apply for it when he wrote me my reference letter.

The problem was that it was eating even more of my precious time.

This was the most difficult semester of school I'd ever had, even though we were only three weeks in. Between my projects, applications, and general inability to properly manage my time, I hadn't even had time to go out and get laid like I usually did. I couldn't think of a point in my entire university experience that I'd gone a month without getting laid, except maybe last year when I'd had strep throat right before winter break.

But in fairness, I'd come back and immediately gone to a party, hooked up with a girl in the bathroom, and then went out to the garage to get myself another beer and ended up bent over the hood of a parked car hooking up with a guy I'd met earlier that night.

I had no stories like that from this semester. No, this semester, I had a week's worth of furtive tit pics taken in campus bathrooms and semi-staged photos of my ass in the full-length mirror in my bedroom and on one particularly horny night, a short clip of my fingers tracing my pussy lips. Or, more accurately, I had the results of those things: pictures in return, and on that same horny night, a video of a hand wrapped around a thick, throbbing cock, stroking it teasingly as pre-cum leaked from the tip.

The bastard hadn't even left the sound on, either.

But regardless of what Sydney thought, none of that meant I *liked* JP.

I liked that he was easy. I didn't mean it like he was easy to talk into having sex—which he was, but that wasn't the point—but things with him were easy. We'd hooked up before. I didn't have to figure out what he wanted, what he liked, what would make him buy in to what I wanted.

And I liked that he was fast. Not in the premature ejaculation kind of way, but in the way that I could get what I needed from him and move on. Like, I could get naked, throw my clothes in the washing machine, send JP a picture of my ass and ask for a picture of his dick and a couple of messages telling me what he wanted to do to me, and get off on my trusty vibrator before my load of laundry was even done.

Yeah, it wasn't quite the same as having a dick inside me or a pair of breasts to play with while I sat on someone's face, but it was also helping me do my laundry more regularly.

So really, it was a time management strategy.

Which was important. I had cases to study and applications to fill out, like the ones currently spread out on the coffee table demanding my attention.

So I picked up my headphones, put them on, and proceeded to put my face down on the coffee table and listen to the latest episode of the new podcast I'd gotten into.

Normally, I was a true crime girl. But when I'd found the *Why Am I Like This* podcast, I knew I not only had to listen to every single episode that existed, but also convince everyone in my life to listen to it, too.

Not because it was useful or anything.

Because it was fucking *hilarious*.

"My *mother* is a *saint*, Santiago, you fucknugget!" John shouted, even though he was laughing.

"I'm not saying she's not," Santi replied. "I'm saying I found a giant blue tentacle dildo, probably eight or ten inches around, in her bedside drawer."

"Bull. Fucking. Shit."

"Your mother likes tentacles, John," Santi said patiently. "Which explains why you look the way you do. That's a straight-up octopus beak you have instead of a nose."

And that was when Liam lost the game of Spit or Swallow they were playing, the sound of water spraying from his mouth echoing in my ears.

Spit or Swallow was exactly what it sounded like, so long as you didn't think it sounded like something sex-related. One of the guys would take a mouthful of water and the others did their best to make him laugh or react in some way, thereby spitting out the water. If they didn't, he'd swallow it.

Simple.

Hilarious.

And it had become a goal of mine to one day play it myself.

I was grinning into the hard surface of the coffee table when my phone vibrated with a notification. I considered not looking at it, but hadn't even started laughing at myself for thinking I could ignore a notification before another one came through. Annoyed, I lifted my head and glanced at the screen as a third notification came through.

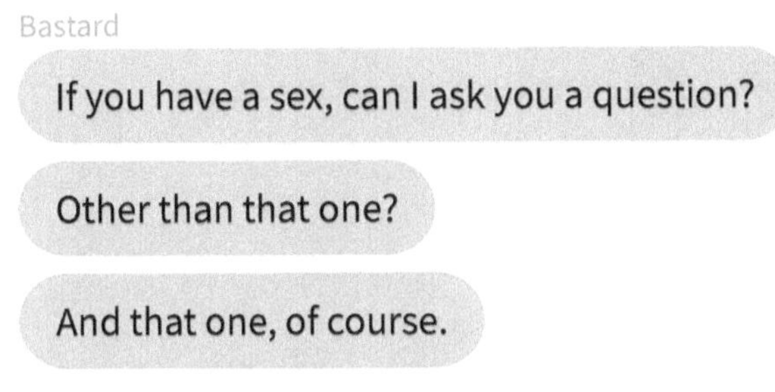

I glared at my phone.

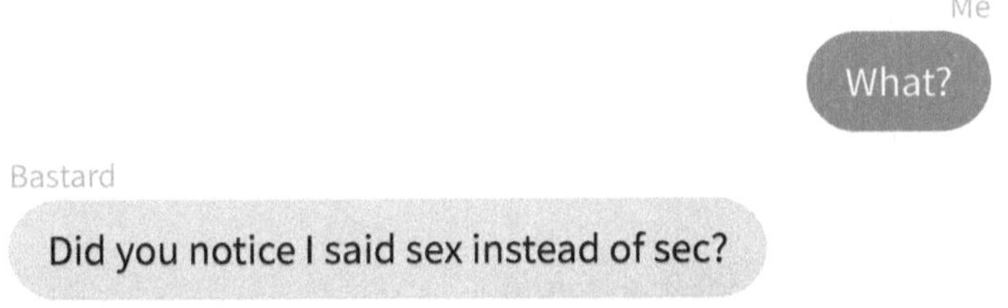

I read the message, glanced at the first one again, and went back to my podcast.

"—could have been so much worse," Liam was saying, his voice hoarse with laughter. "What if it was your *dad's*?"

"I hate you," John said. "I fucking hate you both. So much."

"Liar. You love us," Santi said. "Just like your mom loves tenta—"

And my phone vibrated again.

Bastard

Is that a yes?

I ignored it, not even bothering to open the message, which nearly killed me because I *hated* not looking at notifications.

"—convict me," John said. "No jury in the world."

"It would be completely justified," Liam said.

"Whose side are you even on?" Santi asked, cackling.

"The audience's," Liam said. "Because trust me, the longer this conversation goes on—"

"Oh, don't even," John said. "Do not *even*, bro."

"Oh, he's pulling out the 'bros,'" Santi said, snickering.

"Bro, shut up," John said. "Liam's just trying to keep us all talking so I don't tell everyone about what I found in *his* mom's drawer, which was—"

"You wouldn't *dare*!" Liam gasped.

"What was it?" Santi asked.

"I would absolutely dare," John said.

"Bro, *why*?!" Liam begged. "I'm not the one who found your mom's tentacle dildo!"

"And yet I'm the one who found—"

My phone vibrated again.

And then again.

And again.

Bastard

Babe

Babe did you notice

Babe did you see what I did there

Babeeee

I let out an aggravated groan and paused the podcast.

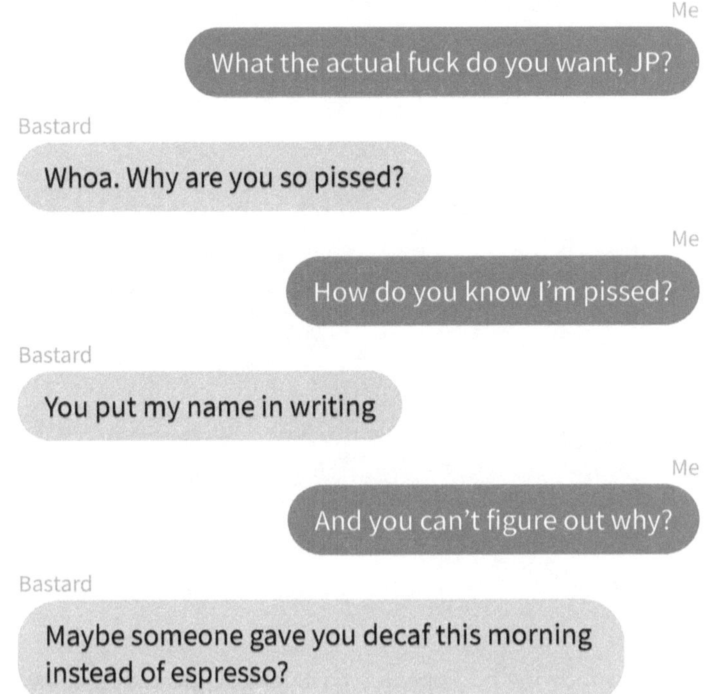

And I just...

I don't know why I unloaded the way I did.

It wasn't like JP was my go-to person to talk to when I needed to. That person was Syd. Or Anne-Marie, as long as what I needed to talk about wasn't JP. Or Ben, at least during the summer before he'd left. JP was the annoying bastard who blew up my phone with pointless texts and dicked me down when I was in Montreal.

That was *it*.

But for some reason, I started typing, and typing, and *typing*.

And for some reason, instead of deleting it all, I hit send.

Maybe someone had a crappy day. Maybe someone's dad called bugging her to go to Montreal even though she said no because he wants is her to help him impress his stupid rich clients. Maybe someone said no again and someone's friend is sad because it means her friend can't bum a ride from her so she can visit her slightly-more-serious-than-a-fuck-buddy, and it's bothering her because she doesn't like letting people down like that. Maybe now she's trying to fill out some fucking applications and can't focus on this boring crap because she realized she hasn't gotten laid in forever and now she's getting texts every five seconds from someone who STILL hasn't told her what he wants?

The marks showing he'd opened the message appeared right away, even though it took me a while to type it all. Not bothering to unpause the podcast, I closed my eyes and put my head back on the table until my phone vibrated again.

Well, I can't do much about your applications or make your dad less of a dick or help (I'm assuming) Sydney see her cop buddy

But funnily enough, I might have a solution for the other part

Me

Wow, you have a solution for telling me why you're messaging me? Shocking.

Bastard

Oops. Typo.

I meant the other partS.

And then he sent me a winking emoji.

Chapter Five
Good Golly

ONE TIME, I SKIPPED class because my blender broke.

I'd been on a smoothie kick. Not as part of a diet or anything, but because no one would question what I drank so long as I said it was full of protein and antioxidants.

And yeah, they might have been milk proteins and the antioxidants were from the blueberries in my blueberry cheesecake ice cream, but that was no one's business but my own.

But that morning, my blender stopped working. And instead of making something else for breakfast or stopping at a coffee shop or eating the ice cream without blending it into a milkshake first, I took the base of the blender apart and tried to fix it.

Three hours later, my blender was working again, but I'd missed all my morning classes and it was also past lunchtime, so I didn't feel like a smoothie anymore.

Another time, I skipped class to have a threesome.

Surprising, I know. I'd started chatting with two super-hot girls in my biology class, we realized we were all into women, and when the class finished, we went to one of the girls' dorm rooms and spent the rest of the day in an endless cycle of orgasms.

But of all the classes I'd skipped and all the reasons I'd justified it, I had never, not *once*, even considered the potential of skipping class to clean.

I figured I hated cleaning so much because my mom hated it, too. The little townhouse we'd lived in was never truly dirty, but it didn't have the stark spotlessness that my dad's house had before they got divorced. So when I needed to be punished, her go-to was chores, chores, and more chores, and always the ones that required me to go through everything and sort it, decide what to keep and what to throw out, and lose track of where everything was because while things were a mess, it was a carefully curated mess.

So I wasn't sure I wanted to know what it said that I skipped my Tuesday morning classes to clean my apartment.

I didn't want to think about why I finally put the pile of clothes that had been living beside my dresser into the closet.

Or why I took the textbooks from last semester and set them on the bookshelf in the spare room. Why I washed all of my dishes and put them all away instead of leaving them in the sink to dry. Why I put fresh sheets on my bed and opened the curtains to let in some light and lit a goddamn candle even though I wasn't supposed to have candles according to my lease.

And I *refused* to acknowledge that even though I did all that work, it didn't bother me that JP noticed exactly none of it when he showed up at my apartment Tuesday afternoon.

"Welcome to the Center for Chronic Testicular Inflammation, how can I help you?" I asked when my phone went off. The number for the front door wasn't saved in my contacts, but I'd had enough people over to know what it was when it popped up.

"Yeah, I have a dick appointment," JP said, his voice taking on the strange warble that happened every time someone buzzed to be let in from my building's foyer.

"What's the name?"

"Last name Heretofuckyou, first name Ima."

"Sorry, the only Ima I have scheduled today has the last name Fuckyougood and that *clearly* isn't you. Bye now."

And I hung up without buzzing him in.

A moment later, my phone rang again. Smirking, I answered it.

"Who is it?" I asked.

"It's me," he said.

"Me who? I wasn't expecting a 'me' today."

"Oh, don't you remember? We were messaging on the Monster Fucker Ottawa forums about the two-dick dragon dildo you wanted to sell because it was too small for you? Have you decided if you're willing to part with it yet? I've got cash."

"Absolutely fucking not," I said indignantly. "I'll tolerate a lot, but that ship sailed when you told me you were a giraffe furry. Good day, sir!"

The third time my phone rang, JP was laughing before I even said anything.

"Let me in, Nellie," he said.

"What's in it for me?" I asked.

"My dick, preferably," he said. "And the longer it takes for you to let me in, the more time I have to talk about how I'm going to tear your panties off the second I get up there loud enough for the people waiting for their Uber outside the foyer to listen, so—"

"Fine," I said, heaving a heavy sigh before pressing the button to unlock the door.

He was in the Ottawa area for a client meeting, he'd said when he texted me a few days earlier. And even though it wasn't a very long meeting, it was a two-hour drive in each direction, so he didn't have to get back to work afterwards. And since we hypothetically weren't done with each other, if we wanted to, we could meet up for an orgasm or three before he had to go back to Montreal.

And there was nothing hypothetical about how much I wanted that.

"Who is it?" I called again when he knocked on my door a few minutes later.

"Giovanni Cockeverlasting, the male escort you ordered?" he replied, so loud that the door barely even muffled his voice. "I told you I charge by the minute, sweetheart, so if you don't want that clock running down—"

I wrenched the door open. "You know I have *neighbours* who can hear—"

And I was pretty sure there was more to that sentence, but nothing else came out. JP was standing there and I...

I just...

Fuck.

It wasn't like he'd become a totally different person in the past month. He was still the same JP, with the same golden blonde hair and tanned white skin that made me think of beaches and oceans and surfboards. He was the same height and probably the same weight. The same crooked tooth flashed on the left side of his mouth, the same faded pink of his lips widening into a wolfish grin that made his startling blue eyes sparkle. And while I might not have seen him wear the same outfit before, it was his usual style: a white dress shirt with subtle dots on it and a complementary tie, though he had on fitted tan pants instead of ones matching the navy suit jacket he wore.

"Well," JP said, taking a step forward and pushing my door the rest of the way open. "I hope for their sake that your neighbours have good ear plugs, babe."

The door wasn't even closed when his arm snaked around my waist, pulling me in close and crushing his lips against mine. He used his body to guide me backwards, not breaking his kiss as he pushed us far enough into my apartment that he could swing the door shut behind him. As soon as it closed, he dropped the bag he was holding to the floor, then wrapped his other arm around me. I rested my hands on his biceps, trying not to melt, trying to not to let him distract me with the electricity of his kiss and the relief of his embrace and the enticing bulge of his cock pushing against my belly, already hard for me.

"Asshole," I breathed, to remind both myself and him that he was an asshole.

He smirked against my mouth. "I missed you too, babe."

"Don't ca—*ah*!" I let out a soft cry, more of surprise than pain, as he nipped at my lower lip.

"Don't call you that," he whispered. "I know."

"If you know, why are you still doing it?" I gasped between kisses.

His laugh brushed against my mouth. "Because I missed seeing that snooty little look I like so much."

I pulled back, staring up at him with a scoff on my breath. "*Snooty*?!"

His grin widened. "Yeah, just like that."

I tried not to laugh. "Fuck you."

"Oh God," he sighed, and his smile faded into something wistful as he tugged me in closer and slipped his hands down to cup my ass. "Yes, *please*. Please fuck me. It's been too long."

"What are you waiting for, then?" I asked.

He let go of my ass and lifted a hand to my chin, notching his fingers beneath it so he could connect his burning eyes with mine.

"You have to the count of five to show me where your bedroom is, otherwise I'm going to bend you over your kitchen table," he said. "One... two..."

"Three..." I said, grabbing his hand and directing it to the waistband of my jeans. "Four..."

His chuckle was dark as he batted my hand away so he could unbutton my pants. It came undone easily and a single tug was all it took to get the zipper down. He pushed my jeans and panties down at the same time, then shoved his hand between my legs and let out a pleased hum as he realized I was fucking *soaked* for him.

"Four and a half..." I murmured.

He took his hand back, grabbing me by the hips and forced me to turn around. Before he could push me down onto the kitchen table, I bent over it and craned my neck to look at him.

"Four and three-quarters," I said.

"You're a fucking brat," he said, laughing over the sound of his belt unbuckling and his pants unzipping.

"You're the one who threatened me with a good time and isn't following through," I said, swaying my hips from side to side. "Four and seven-eigh—"

"Five," JP grunted, grabbing my hips and pushing his cock in with one swift, deep thrust.

I cried out and he paused, maybe in case I needed to adjust or maybe because if he didn't, his cock would've decided to end things before they'd fully started. Whatever the reason, it was barely enough time for me to brace myself against the table before he started fucking me.

Hard.

Hard enough that I could barely hold myself up. Hard enough that I saw stars. Hard enough to make me think maybe it wasn't so bad, that maybe a month of not getting laid so I could feel *this* way in *this* moment was worth every sexually frustrated second.

Maybe.

Maybe... definitely.

I squeezed my eyes shut, stifling what could only be described as a sob of pleasure as JP's cock slammed into me. His hips slapped my ass, the sound filling my ears as a backdrop to the steady moans he fucked out of me. Everything about him felt like more than I expected. He felt bigger than I remembered, reaching deeper inside me than I recalled, his cock thick and throbbing and hot in a way I must have forgotten. His head dragged against my G-spot, making me shiver and shake, building up that warm, familiar intense sensation in my core way sooner than I thought it would.

Sooner for both of us, apparently.

"Oh, jeez," JP grunted, his body shuddering. "I... oh *gosh*."

"My goodness gracious," I said, my voice staggering because even though he was clearly fighting to hold back, he hadn't stopped thrusting. "Since when do you use such obscene language?"

He laughed at my teasing, his breath coming hard. "I can make it even dirtier for you, babe."

"What, are you gonna throw a 'jeepers' or a 'good golly' in there for me? Start calling it fornication instead of fucking?"

"You want to hear about how much I missed fornicating with you, baby?"

My head tilted back as I started to laugh. JP let go of my hip and brought his hand up to the back of my head, so smoothly that I barely noticed until his fingers were woven through my hair and my laughter cut off with a choke. He pulled my head back even more and plunged inside me again, my body slamming against the kitchen table as he hunched forward so his lips were next to my ear.

"Golly, babe, if I'd known just how darn-tootin' desperate your sweet little caboose was to be filled, I might've come to see you a whole heck of a lot sooner," he said in a confusingly hot growl.

"You're the worst," I said on a stilted breath. "My pussy's gonna go dry if you keep talking like that."

"That's a whole lot of malarkey," he said. "Considering I'm inside you right now and it's gotta be the hottest"—he stopped, a strangled noise betraying the joking air he was putting on—"and *wettest* little fanny I've ever copulated with—"

"You're such a bastard."

His cock twitched as he chuckled. "Really? I think I'm more of a scoundrel."

"On top of it all, you're a gigantic dork."

He let go of my other hip, wrapping his arm around my body, and with a not-unexpected-but-somehow-surprising amount of accuracy, pressed the pad of his middle finger to my clit. "Doesn't matter. You can sit here pretending all you want, but we both know nothing I say is gonna stop you from coming all over my cock, babe. Not when I can tell how badly you wanted me to stretch this pretty fucking hole of yours."

I nearly choked on my next inhale as he fingered my clit, his thrusts coming faster than they were before.

"And goodness gracious, I'm gonna make a mess of you," he murmured, and fire flared through me at the depth of his voice even as he said the *stupidest* shit. "Such a mess. And here I thought I'd be worried that I wouldn't last long enough." He pressed a kiss to the side of my neck. "But that doesn't matter because you're so close already. Aren't you?"

I couldn't speak. He slowed his fingers.

"I said, *aren't* you?" he repeated.

"Yes," I whimpered. "Yes, I am."

"Damn right you are." He started rubbing my clit faster again. "You're gonna come, and this hot little cunt is gonna choke my cock until I can't hold back. Are you gonna let me come inside you?"

"Uh-huh," I said.

His hand tightened in my hair. "You want it, babe?"

I nodded. Well, I tried to. I jerked my head forward as much as JP's hand would let me and I knew he felt it, because he chuckled.

"Say it. Say you want it."

"I want it." I squeezed my eyes closed as pleasure shot through me. "I want you to come in me."

"Of course you do," he said. "Because good fucking *golly*, you're still a perfect, needy little slut for me, aren't you?"

And I came. Because of course I did.

Because of *course* JP was the person who could use good-fucking-golly in his dirty talk and make me explode into a hundred thousand sparks. Of course I cried out, tears springing into my eyes as JP fucked me through my bliss, pounding me harder and harder and harder as he chased his own orgasm.

He groaned when he caught it and followed through with his words, filling my pussy with cum and my head with guilt as I reminded myself I shouldn't let him come inside me, that I was stupid, that just because I hadn't gotten laid for a month didn't mean he hadn't. And we weren't exclusive. We never had been. He could've been with someone else and not worn a condom.

But, a little voice whispered, JP wouldn't do that to me.

He stayed behind me, holding me close as he softened inside me. For a while, we were silent, both of us catching our breaths, neither of us quite sure what to say or do next. Finally, he sighed and pressed a kiss to my neck again.

"Jeepers, that was good," he said, and I'd never told someone to get their stupid dick out of me so fast in my life.

Even though I was laughing the whole time I was doing it.

Chapter Six
Big Talk, Small Talk

THE SIGHT OF JP Marchand standing in my kitchen, suit jacket and tie hanging on the back of a chair and his shirt sleeves rolled up to his elbows while he dished out pad thai and spring rolls from takeout boxes onto the plates he'd taken from my cupboards, was horrifying.

Absolutely fucking horrifying.

"Do you not like pad thai?" JP asked, misreading the look on my face as I stared at the situation before me.

"I do," I said, which was even more horrifying.

He raised his eyebrows. "Are you not hungry, or...?"

I was. I was crazy hungry, actually, and hadn't even realized it.

But why did he want to have lunch with me?

And why was the stereotypical sight of a guy in my kitchen, being all domestic and cute and shit, as hot as it was?

And why was it completely, totally, horrifically terrifying that I liked it?

"Oh," JP said when I didn't say anything. "You thought I was gonna come over, fuck you, and leave?"

"No," I said, which wasn't even a lie. I hadn't thought anything. Beyond cleaning my apartment and having sex with JP, I hadn't considered what to... you know.

Do with him once we were done.

His mouth twitched in amusement and he started splitting the pad thai between the two plates. "I figured we'd need something to eat before I'm ready to go again. Gotta make sure the trip was worth it, babe."

"You don't think three minutes in my pussy was worth it?"

He put the empty takeout box on the counter and the plates in places he'd set on the table, then looked up with a smirk on his lips. "I'd've done it for the chance at ten seconds inside you."

I willed the warm feeling in my chest to cool off before my neck and cheeks started turning pink. "You better last longer than ten seconds for the next round."

"No promises, but I'll try." He motioned at the table. "Eat. Otherwise you'll be trying not to choke on your noodles during round two since I'll be ready to go again in eight-to-ten minutes."

"Ten minutes?" I said skeptically, taking the seat he'd motioned at. "You think you're gonna be able to get it up again in ten minutes?"

He grinned as he sat in the other chair. "Is that a challenge?"

"No." I picked up the chopsticks he'd set next to my plate. "And why would I choke on the noodles? You wouldn't wait until I finish eating to fuck me?"

"You'd make me wait to get back inside you? After I spent two hours driving to get here?"

"You spent two hours driving to get to a client meeting. I just happened to be here."

"And yet I'd make the drive again to spend ten seconds in your pussy, as we've already established."

"I didn't realize you had so much trouble getting laid in Montreal."

He smirked. "Maybe I just got spoiled with you."

My face heated up and I ended the conversation by taking a bite of my food. I didn't know what to say to any of it. For as long as I'd known JP—literally most of my life, since we'd first met when I was four—we'd never done anything like this before.

We didn't hang out. Not without reason. The times we'd been around each other without the intent of hooking up always had a purpose. We saw each other at a charity run, or he came as my date to a gala, or we'd been literal kids who lived next door to each other and so were forced to tolerate each other's presence at birthday parties and other such events.

But this? Sitting at a table, just the two of us, eating together?

This was new.

And I didn't know how I felt about it. I wasn't sure I liked the intimacy of sitting at a table and having a meal with him. Because somehow, even though I'd had him in every fuckable hole in my body, *this* felt like something else.

Something bigger.

Something wrong.

But something that was only wrong because it felt terribly, horrifyingly, confusingly right.

And it feeling right made it feel even *more* wrong because we were quiet, both of us eating, neither of us sure of what to say to make this entire thing feel less... something.

It wasn't supposed to be something.

Which was how I ended up blurting a boring, generic, and entirely uninspired question.

"How's work going?" I asked before taking another bite of pad thai.

"Work?" JP repeated.

"That thing you do to make money?" I said through my noodles.

He chuckled. "Yeah. I just never saw you as a small talk kind of person."

Somehow, that seemed offensive, even though it wasn't. I swallowed my pad thai and picked up one of my spring rolls. "Fine. Why are things so tense with your dad right now?"

The flicker of surprise on his face was satisfying. "There's no line between small talk and big talk with you, hey?"

I shrugged. "You're the one who didn't seem to want small talk, so deeply probing personal questions it is."

"Good to know." He picked up some of his pad thai. "What makes you think things are tense with my dad?"

"Anne-Marie mentioned it when she was here."

He frowned thoughtfully at his plate. "It's that noticeable?"

"I guess. She said you moved out really fast. I said it was probably because you spend too much time around your dad, what with, like, working together and stuff."

He nodded slowly, still looking at his food. "I mean, yeah. It's helped being in my own place." Glancing up, he smiled, though his mouth was tight. "It's not a huge thing. My dad has certain expectations of me, which isn't anything new, and when I don't meet or abide by those expectations, he gets unhappy."

I nodded. "Relatable."

He half-laughed. "Things haven't gotten any better with your dad, either?"

It wasn't until later that I realized how smoothly he'd switched focus, how he'd given me an answer that was as specific as it was vague before guiding the conversation back to me. It should've concerned me how easily he managed it, but at that moment, I just rolled my eyes.

"Better, no," I said. "But they're not worse, so that's something, I guess."

"It is," he agreed. "Are you gonna be back in Montreal anytime soon?"

I tried not to glare at him and succeeded by glaring at my plate instead. "Not you, too."

"What?" he asked. "I'm just asking."

I sighed. "My dad's constantly calling to ask me to come to some event or another because he wants me to impress the Martelles for him again. He doesn't seem to get that I ran into Claire, like, three times and barely know her. And that I have classes. He thinks I can drop everything and show up when he wants me there because what he wants is more important than what I'm doing. Meanwhile, I'm... well."

"Well what?"

I picked at my noodles, not looking at him. "It's just been a rough semester."

"How so?"

"It's nothing to worry about."

"Are you telling me that or yourself that?"

When I looked up, JP was watching me. "What do you mean?"

He smiled as he collected more noodles in his chopsticks. "We're friends, Nell, but that doesn't mean I'm worrying about how rough your semester is. I don't know that much about it."

It was a good point. I nodded slowly. "Well, it doesn't matter either way. It's just a bad class schedule."

"What classes are you taking?"

"Forensic Pathology, which is boring because Dr. Spitzki is awful." I rolled my eyes. "And he hates me."

"Your prof?"

I nodded.

"Why does he hate you?"

"Probably because I don't put my phone on silent while I'm in his lectures and in his last class I took, I handed the final paper in printed on mustard yellow paper with purple writing."

"Why?"

"Because he docked me points on my midterm essay for using one-point-five line spacing instead of double spacing it." I picked up more pad thai. "So I made sure my final met all the standards he set out in the syllabus and then did whatever I wanted for the rest of them."

JP burst out laughing. "I bet he was pissed."

"Livid. I think he cried a little when he realized I was in his four hundred level course this year." I ate a bite of my food. "But that's not the worst class I'm taking."

"What's the worst?"

"Forensic Science and Law."

He raised his eyebrows. "Law?"

"Mm-hmm. I hate everything about it, including the fucking case studies that we have to do every *week*. I have one due tomorrow and there's no way I'm going to finish it, and my TA isn't going to give me an extension. More proof that not only could I never be a lawyer, but all lawyers are the literal worst."

"We do suck," JP said. "What's the trouble you're having with it?"

I lifted an eyebrow. "Why do you want to know?"

"Because, Smarty Pants, maybe I can help," he said, his mouth flicking into a grin. "Believe it or not, I've taken some law classes in my day."

"'In your day,'" I mocked. "Okay, Grandpa."

He snickered. "I was gonna tutor you for the LSAT. I bet you I can help with this."

"You said you didn't actually want to tutor me for the LSAT," I said.

"But I would've." He motioned at my plate. "Finish eating and show me your case studies."

I stared at him, not bothering to hide the disgust on my face. "You're not serious."

He looked amused. "Why wouldn't I be?"

"I thought I had ten minutes to eat before you fucked me again. Now you want to do *homework* with me? I brought you here to have sex, not to learn shit."

I thought he might laugh, but even though the corners of JP's eyes crinkled and his lips pressed together in a roguish smirk, the way his eyes trailed down from my face to my chest—and they would've probably gone lower, had I not been sitting, but the table was obviously in the way—sent a shiver rushing through me.

"I can do both," he said simply.

I rolled my eyes. "Sure you can."

And yeah, it was sarcasm.

But if it hadn't been sarcasm, it would've been right.

I don't know how he thought of it. I don't know *why* he thought of it. I don't know why I agreed to strip to my panties and sit between his legs, my back against his chest, his chin resting on my shoulder as he looked over it at the laptop in front of me.

I don't know why having one of his hands cupping my breast and the other between my legs, his fingers making slow circles over my clit, made something click in my mind as I read over the source material about a lab illegally retaining voluntarily submitted DNA samples. By all accounts, it shouldn't have; it should've been distracting me, making it harder to focus, frustrating me as he teased my nipple and sent aches of desire shooting into my core.

And that was weird. It was so fucking weird to be turned on while I was studying *that* kind of thing.

But somehow, it worked.

Somehow, I typed faster than I ever had before, my pussy getting wetter and wetter as I explained the precedence and relevance set by the case, as I summarized the key points, as I shared an opinion on the lasting effect of that particular case on the forensic science field.

"Done," I breathed when I finished writing. "Can we fuck now?"

"Mm-mm," JP said. "I'm gonna read it for you first."

The groan I let out was almost painful, my body desperate for release. "Please, JP. I want to come."

"You'll come when I say it's good enough." He kissed the side of my neck. "Turn your screen towards me a bit."

Hands shaking, I moved my laptop so he could read over my work. His fingers kept moving lazily in my panties, barely giving me enough friction to survive, even though I was so wet I could feel it coating his hand and my folds and soaking my panties. I tried not to think about how badly I wanted those fingers to slip inside me, how I craved the sensation of being filled, how I could feel JP's hard cock on my lower back. My eyes were closed and I opened them only when he found a mistake that needed correcting, my fingers trembling as I made the changes.

When he finally reached the end and decided my paper was good enough to call complete, he didn't say anything. He didn't tell me.

He just pushed two fingers inside of me, ground the base of his thumb against my clit, and laughed in my ear as I cried out.

"That's it," he murmured. "Now you can finish, Nellie. And when you're in your midterms or your finals, you're gonna remember how fucking hard you came all over my hand and sit there, wondering what kind of weird-ass person gets a wet pussy when they're thinking about what the Criminal Code says regarding the destruction of DNA analysis for ruled-out suspects."

"Shut up," I gasped. "I'm not gonna remember any—"

But then he curled his fingers and pressed them against my G-spot, and my vision went black, and I came so hard my head went light and I thought I was going to pass out before finally coming down.

Chapter Seven
No and No Again

"Who the fuck is K. DUNN?" I asked, staring at the name flashing on my phone screen.

"Probably a telemarketer or a wrong number," said no one since I was studying by myself in my apartment a few days after JP's visit.

But I did think it, and I thought about not answering it like I always did when I didn't know who was calling, and then I tapped on the screen.

"Hello?" I said.

"Hello," said a familiar but unrecognizable woman's voice. "Is this Nellie?"

"Yes," I said. "Who's this?"

"It's Kimberlee."

I blinked in surprise. Or annoyance. Or confusion. Or all three.

I'd never been close with any of my dad's girlfriends. I'd never wanted to be close with any of them. Before Kimberlee, some of them had tried, like they thought if they got on my good side, it would be less obvious they were just looking for a sugar daddy. But it had always been obvious that it was all a show, just like every other plastic thing in my dad's life.

Kimberlee, on the other hand, confused the hell out of me. She was nothing like my dad's ex-girlfriends. I couldn't figure out why she was with him; if I separated the fact that she was dating my dad from the rest of what I knew about her, I might think she was a decent person.

But she knew what kind of person my dad was.

She'd seen what kind of person he was.

She'd watched him empty my closet as punishment for doing the best I could in a bad situation. She'd listened to him berate me for daring to express my condolences to a widow at a funeral because he was trying to make a business connection. She'd stood by while he pressured me to change to a career I didn't want so I could make him look good. And yeah, she'd said a few things to him here and there, but it wasn't like it bothered her enough to leave.

Which was fine. It wasn't like I expected her to end a relationship she was clearly getting some kind of kickback from just because the guy she was with was awful to his daughter sometimes. I didn't need her to do that for my benefit.

But I didn't need to like her, either.

"Kimberlee," I repeated.

She chuckled. "I know it is a little out of nowhere and I apologize. But I wanted to speak with you about something and I wanted to make sure you understood it was coming from me."

"Okay," I said unsteadily, both suspecting and dreading where this was going. "What's that?"

"Well, I know you are very busy with classes this semester and have told Max you cannot attend any events, but I'd like to plan a dinner party—"

For fuck's sake.

"Can't make it," I interrupted. "I'm busy that day."

"I haven't set a date yet," she said, her voice gentle.

"Yeah, but I'm busy that day."

Kimberlee reacted with the same infuriating grace she always extended to me. "It will be a small dinner party, with only the important people in attendance. Close friends and some of my family and, I hope, you as well. Because you are one of our important people, Nellie."

I tried not to roll my eyes, then remembered Kimberlee couldn't see me and rolled them to my heart's content. "I don't have time to drive to Montreal, attend a party, and come home. I have a ton of work for school."

"I know," she said. "Which is why I was thinking of the Thanksgiving long weekend, so—"

"Kim, I've *told* my dad I'm going to Toronto for Thanksgiving and that I can't be there. So no. Definitely not. I am not coming to your dinner party."

"Okay," Kimberlee said, and I cringed with guilt at the soft disappointment in her voice. "I understand. Is there perhaps another time—"

"No."

"You would only need to be here for a bit," she said. "I would take care of everything and—"

"No." I picked at the skin around my thumb. "You've seen what my dad is like. You know how he acts around me."

"He will not be like that," she said. "I swear to you. I will not allow it."

"Well, you've got nerve, I'll give you that."

"Excuse me?"

"It takes a lot of audacity to think you could change anything about my dad," I said.

She sighed in frustration. "Nellie, can you please just consider—"

"No," I said.

"But—"

And I hated that it happened. I hated that I couldn't control it.

But I snapped.

"No," I said. "And no again. And no as many times as you need to hear it to get it to stick. Because honestly, Kim? I don't like him. And by association, I don't like *you*. I don't want to spend time with either of you. I want to finish my year of university and move on with my life. I get that you're with my dad because he's got a fat bank account and—"

"I am not," she snapped back, and I was almost stunned by the anger in her voice. "That has nothing to do with why I am with Max."

"Sure it doesn't," I said. "It's totally normal to date a sociopath in his fifties when you're in your thirties. Just another one of those phases, like being emo or pretending to like country music."

I heard the deep inhale she took to steady herself. "It is not my place to tell you what to do or ask you to understand what is going on, but I promise you, I am not with your father for his money."

"Whatever," I said. "It doesn't matter. I don't care what he promised you to get you to call and pretend like he's not behind all of this, but the answer is no."

"He did not—"

And I hung up, fuming.

Then, still fuming, I tapped on my messages.

Me

You'll never guess what—

And then I stopped.

And I stared.

And I deleted the four words I'd typed, mindful of avoiding the arrow that would've sent them away from my control, before closing my chat with JP.

I considered texting Sydney, but part of me knew I'd end up telling her my instinct had been to text JP over her or Anne-Marie or literally anyone else. That problem wouldn't exist with Anne-Marie, since the last thing I wanted was for her to find out that I was talking to her brother at all, but I realized as I looked at my chat with her that I hadn't actually heard from Anne-Marie for a few days. Guilt ate at my stomach and I opened the chat, firing off a quick message asking how she was because it felt weird to jump into my own problems when I hadn't even realized she wasn't texting me as much as usual.

Then I chewed my thumbnail for a moment before calling my mom.

I couldn't tell her any of this, of course. I hated lying to her, but I hated the idea of disappointing her even more. And picturing the look on her face if she ever found out I'd asked my dad to pay for my degree was enough to make my stomach fold in on itself again and again and again, until it was twisted into a little ball small enough to move up my throat so I could spew it on the ground in front of me. In her mind, I'd cut ties with him the moment I'd turned eighteen like she'd told me to.

Especially because the only reason any of this had worked in the first place was because of how fiercely independent both me and my mom were. It wasn't weird to her that an entire summer had gone by without me going back to Toronto. When she was around my age, she'd gone over a year without seeing her parents because she was travelling around the country doing her own thing.

It wasn't that she didn't care. She did, and I'd never question that. The way she showed she cared was by trusting that I knew what I was doing and letting me do it.

Even though I had no idea what I was doing and clearly shouldn't have been trusted.

So I couldn't tell her why I was upset. I didn't even tell her I was upset at all. I just knew hearing her voice would help, and like always, it did.

"John was *absolutely* in the wrong!" my mom said heatedly as I sprawled on my living room floor, laughing.

"Okay, but you can't tell me you don't think Santi deserved it after the tentacle dildo episode," I said.

"All his clothes, Daughter of Mine. He had nothing to wear but maid outfits and cat ears for the entire trip!"

"Mother of Mine, do you seriously think he didn't go out and buy different clothes after realizing John switched the luggage?"

My mom didn't go silent immediately. She made a noise that was kind of like a high-pitched "ah," like she was about to say something, then cut herself off when she realized she couldn't argue with me.

"Or he could have borrowed something from Liam," I continued. "Remember that episode where they were fighting about the sweaters because they both wanted the only large one and they ended up measuring *everything*?"

"I can't believe you got me into this damn podcast," she finally said. "Why are *you* like this?"

"Blame yourself," I said. "You raised me. And anyway, you haven't even listened to the next episode yet."

"Oh God. It gets worse?"

"Well, you know what they say," I said. "Don't give someone a raccoon tail butt plug and a maid outfit unless you're ready to see them wear it."

"No one says that, hon."

"Well, they should."

"You're joking. He didn't seriously use the butt plug."

"Well, either all of them lied or Santi's really good at PhotoShop, because John said there were pictures."

"Oh Lord thunderin' Jesus," she said. "You can't be serious. Santi would not use a butt plug."

"Are you saying you don't think Santi's the kind of guy whose wife owns a strap-on?"

"Nellie!" she exclaimed, scandalized even as I cackled. "How do you even know about that kind of thing?"

"I'm almost twenty-two, Mom."

"Oh, God," she said. "You don't own one, do you?"

"Mom!"

"I'm just curious," she said. "You don't have a boyfriend so it wouldn't make sense because who would you even use it on, but—"

"Uh, a girl?" I said pointedly.

"Right," she said quickly. "But you don't have one of those, either. So it's not like you need a strap-on if you're not... well." She giggled. "Getting together with someone to use it, you know?"

And all I could do was force a laugh.

My mom wasn't exactly conservative about anything—obviously, considering the topic at hand and the fact that she was even listening to the *Why Am I Like This* podcast in the first place—but there was a difference between joking about raccoon tail butt plugs and telling my mom that the only reason that my bedpost hadn't fallen from all the notches ruining its structural integrity was because I didn't have a bedframe with posts.

And sure, maybe it was pretty normal for people to keep details like that from their parents, but for me, it was just another reminder of all the things I'd been hiding from her.

"Daughter of Mine? Are you still there?"

I dug my finger into the side of my thumb. "Yeah, I am. Actually, speaking of changing the entire topic of conversation because this is getting awkward, Thanksgiving?"

But that made everything worse.

"Oh," she said. "Right."

"Don't sound so excited," I said. "I'll have to get a therapist or something."

My mom let out an awkward laugh. "Oh, hon. It's not that."

"What is it, then?"

"Don't be mad."

"Mad about *what*?"

She sighed. "Well… I just… I have an opportunity. Something I haven't gotten to do in a very long time. And it would have to be that weekend. But I thought, you know, do we need to do Thanksgiving things on *Thanksgiving?* Maybe instead, we could get together another weekend."

"What opportunity?" I asked.

"A vacation."

I frowned. "With who?"

"Just a friend," she said far too quickly to be anything but a lie. "We'd be going to Las Vegas. And hon, I haven't gotten to travel since before I escaped the devil"—she meant my dad, of course—"when we went to Disney World. Remember that?"

I did remember that. I'd been ten and we'd missed the character breakfast at the Crystal Palace because my dad had been tired after three days at Disney. He'd wanted to stay at the hotel and my mom wanted us to all go as a family, so none of us went anywhere.

"Yeah, no, I get it," I said. "I hope you have fun."

"Don't be mad," she said again. "And I promise, I will make it up to you, okay? I'll pay for you to change your flights and maybe you can play hooky from classes on Friday or Monday some weekend. And we'll still have a turkey dinner. I told Jack that was part of what I was worried about and he said he'd make one of his two-person dinners for us whatever weekend we choose."

I didn't bother telling her that I couldn't justify skipping classes to stay an extra day in Toronto or that I wouldn't let her pay for my flight change since my dad covered all my expenses. "Who's Jack?"

I had to hope I was a better liar than my mom since her voice was suspiciously flippant. "Oh, you know Jack. He owns the little cafe in the same parking lot as my store."

"What little cafe?"

"Jack's," she said.

"I know it's Jack's cafe, but—"

"No, it's *called* Jack's. It's in where the Vietnamese restaurant used to be before they bought the new location downtown."

I didn't bother pointing out that they'd sold the restaurant the previous year and I hadn't been to the liquor store she worked at for far longer than that, so there was no reason I'd have known about Jack or his cafe. "And he's your friend?"

I tried to keep my voice careful and neutral. My parents had been divorced for over ten years, but where I'd met a new girlfriend of my dad's almost every other month until he'd started dating Kimberlee, my mom had never so much as mentioned someone in that forced casual voice before.

But unfortunately, my mom saw right through my nonchalant tone.

"I know what you're implying and you're wrong," she said bluntly. "Jack is a friend and he's doing me a favour so you and I can stuff ourselves on the best damn turkey and mashed potatoes you've ever eaten."

The call with my mom didn't last too much longer after that. When we hung up, I stared at the books in front of me, not quite seeing them.

I had no excuse not to go to Montreal over Thanksgiving weekend.

It wasn't like my dad knew that. No one was going to call him up and tell him I wasn't going to Toronto for the weekend. I could stay home and do homework and hell, maybe I could go out and pick someone up at the bar or something.

Or I could call my dad and get him off my case about visiting him. I could go to his place for one stupid dinner party and that would hopefully shut him up until at least Christmas. And if I was going to be in Montreal anyway, I might as well see what JP's plans would be like that weekend and—

I hated that my phone was pressed to my ear before I even finished the thought.

"*Ma fille ange,*" my dad answered dryly. "Are you calling to explain to me what Kimberlee is so bothered about this evening?"

I instantly regretted calling him. "You don't have to pretend like you don't know, Dad."

"I do not know," he said. "I see that she is upset and has asked to be left alone for a bit, which is very unusual for her."

My stomach clenched with guilt. Maybe Kimberlee had deserved it a bit, but maybe I'd been a bit meaner than I should've been.

"And I know it has something to do with you," he continued. "But she will not tell me why. Which is rather disappointing, since all I want is a daughter who will be open with me about what she's done."

And yes, I should have taken a moment to calm down. In hindsight, that was obvious. Kimberlee's call had upset me, and my mom's call had frustrated me, and talking to my dad always made my stomach coil into ropes. I'd already snapped at Kimberlee more harshly than I should have. So I should have just hung up right there and walked away.

Instead, I opened my mouth.

"You'll have to settle for what you've already got, then," I said. "Because I'm not playing this game where I pretend like I don't know you told Kimberlee to call and guilt me into coming to your house for a dinner party that I've told you I can't go to. I was calling to talk to you about that and see if we can make something else work, but if you're going to act like I'm too stupid to figure out what you're doing, then I guess we're all too stupid to figure out another solution. So I guess I'm calling to remind you that no, I can't go to your dinner party."

My dad said nothing. He wasn't silent; I could hear him breathe, a steady in-and-out that betrayed nothing about his thoughts.

"What are you hiding, Eleanor?" he finally asked.

My lips parted. "Excuse me?"

"This is unlike you," he said, which was bullshit because this was *exactly* like me. "My daughter does not speak this way. My daughter knows the value of compromise. *My* daughter would not give a blanket rejection to everything unless there was something she was hiding. So what is it?"

"I'm not hiding anything," I said.

"I imagine it must be something I would be able to see," he said, ignoring me. "Since you have hidden plenty of other things from me before without insisting that you cannot even spare a moment to attend something that is obviously important to us. So what is it? Have you coloured your hair blue and pushed studs into your face and gotten tattoos everywhere? Because my daughter certainly cannot be stupid enough to have gotten herself pregnant, and those are the only excuses I can currently imagine."

My mouth fell all the way open.

"*Ma fille ange?*" he asked.

"I have to go," I said.

"Eleanor—"

But I ended the call.

Then I slammed my textbooks shut, stood, and went to the door to grab my purse.

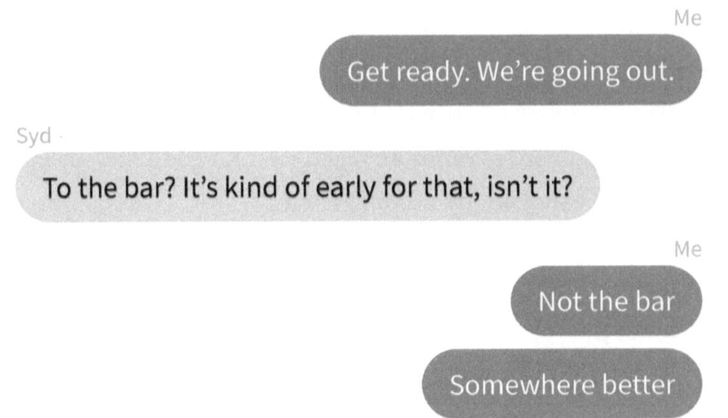

Chapter Eight
One Handed Texting

"CAN YOU GO OVER the plan for me? One more time?" Sydney asked.

"I'm getting a tattoo," I said.

"You're getting a tattoo," she repeated.

I flipped the page in the book of flash tattoos. "You seem to have a pretty good understanding of the plan."

"Right, of course," she said. "It's just that people usually know what they want to get before they waltz into a tattoo shop."

I flipped the page again. "I figured I'd see something I like."

"It's a tattoo! Not a t-shirt at the mall." She put her hand on the portfolio, stopping me from flipping the page again. "This is crazy. Even for you."

I scoffed. "Since when are you the mature voice of reason? What's next, telling me I need to eat more vegetables and go to therapy instead of working my issues out by sleeping around?"

"I mean, fuck vegetables, but the other part isn't that bad an idea now that you're not sleeping with a psychologist," she said.

"Seriously?!"

"Yes and no." She frowned, worry in her eyes. "You're my best friend. I want to make sure you're okay."

"I am," I said, smiling. "I promise. I just really want a tattoo."

"To piss off your dad."

"Not *just* to piss him off," I said. "I've wanted a tattoo for ages. I don't know why it's so unexpected. I mean, I have a belly button piercing. But your concerns are noted."

She sighed. "Alright. I'll drop it for now. Do any of these look like something you want drawn permanently on your body?"

"I kind of like this bearded merman playing the ukulele," I admitted, pointing at a drawing on the page.

"You've got to be fucking kidding me."

I was bracing myself against the desk as I laughed when someone came out of the back room. Through my laughter, I saw a woman with chin-length bleach blonde hair, upturned eyes, and tattoos covering nearly every visible inch of pale white skin that wasn't on her face or the palms of her hands. An amused expression pressed her lips in as she watched me—and to some extent, Sydney—giggle madly.

"Let me guess," she said after a few moments, her voice deeper and huskier than I expected. "You're here to get your ears pierced."

"Close," I said. "I was thinking nipples."

"Sure," she said. "Left, right, or both?"

"What do most people get?" I asked.

"Wait, are you seriously considering it?" Sydney asked.

I shrugged. "Maybe."

The woman chuckled. "Well, I say do both at once otherwise you're gonna chicken out. But some people get one done before the other since they can take a year or so to heal and you can't fuck with them while they're healing."

I stared at her in horror. "You can't fuck at *all*?"

"Fuck as in play with," she said. "You're more than welcome to drag your boyfriend in so I can lecture him about no touching and subtly imply that it's hard to suck on the nips when your jaw is wired shut, so he better not get his mouth anywhere near them lest I punch his little face."

"You don't have to worry about that," I said. "I don't have a boyfriend. Or a girlfriend."

Her eyebrow flicked up. "Well, you're pretty much set, then. Wanna get started?"

"Nah. I don't want to not play with my own nipples for a year. And there are a lot of things I'd rather have you do to my face than punch it."

"Like sit on it," muttered Sydney.

"What was that?" the woman asked.

"She said 'Like sit on it,'" I replied loudly.

Sydney's face turned red, which was fair because there was a chance the woman wouldn't find that as funny I did, but luckily she started laughing.

"Maybe later, sweetheart," she said. "For now, what can I help you with?"

"I'm Nellie," I said. "I'm here to get a tattoo."

"Sweet. I'm Tricia. I'm here to give you a tattoo." She leaned over and looked at the portfolio. "Is that the one you're thinking of?"

She was hot. *So* hot. Hot enough that having her lean in close like that and being able to smell what I was pretty sure was her shampoo made my stomach flutter. And she was about to *touch* me. Sure, it was to use needles to draw on my skin, but I couldn't stop picturing how pretty the colourful backs of her hands would look cupping my breasts, or wondering how far under the collar of her crewneck t-shirt her tattoos went. Or how inappropriate it would be for me to hit on her after she was done my tattoo.

Because I might have been insanely attracted to her, but I wasn't stupid enough to potentially upset someone when, again, they were using needles to draw on my skin.

After, though?

After, maybe I'd see how serious she was when she told me she might sit on my face later.

The point of this all was that Tricia was hot. Hot enough that I wanted to sleep with her. And she seemed like she'd potentially be into it. Especially after helping me decide on a tattoo—a super fucking cool but elegant dragon in flight with scales trailing behind it—and where to put it.

"It would look best on your ribs," she said, tracing a spot on her body just below her breast and to the side. "If you're okay with getting it somewhere a little less visible."

"It's only less visible if I keep my clothes on," I said. "So yeah. That sounds great."

"Awesome." She took the portfolio back and jerked her head towards the back room. "Let's go get set up. Your, uh, friend can come. If you want. But we'll be using one of the private rooms since you'll have to have your shirt and possibly your bra off while I'm working."

Sydney shook her head. "I came for moral support. I was going to do some shopping while she's in there."

Which was a complete lie, but Syd was an awesome wing-woman, and she texted me before I even had the stencil on to say she'd headed back to her place because she assumed I was gonna fuck my tattoo artist, but if that changed to let her know so she could see my new tattoo.

So I had the motive: Tricia was hot.

I had the means: Tricia potentially sitting on my face.

And good golly, did I have the opportunity: not only a private room in the back of the tattoo shop while I was topless, but the subtle mention that she was the only one working that day and the receptionist who'd checked me in was leaving in about twenty minutes.

"You sure you're ready?" she asked after confirming no less than three times that I was happy with the placement of the stencil.

"Hell yes," I said.

She nodded, then sat on the stool beside the tattoo chair I was sitting in and picked up the tattoo gun.

"It's gonna hurt," she warned.

"I'm looking forward to it."

Tricia snorted. "Just my luck. Last tattoo of the day and I get a masochist."

She leaned forward as I laughed, putting one gloved hand beneath my breast, and brought the tattoo gun towards me. Moments later, a sharp pain pricked at my skin. It wasn't strong enough to make me gasp or flinch, but I definitely took a shallower breath than normal. After a few seconds, she moved the tattoo gun away.

"Doing okay?" she asked.

I nodded.

She smirked. "Good. This is the easy part."

I tried not to laugh, knowing it would make my chest shake. Tricia went back to work, tracing over the stenciled lines.

It was hard to explain the sensation. It hurt, certainly, but at first, it seemed tolerable. It was only as she got further along that I really understood why people said tattoos were painful. The sensation built up, becoming more intense each time she passed the tattoo gun over my ribs.

"Do people usually talk while they're doing this?" I asked the next time she took the gun away.

"Sometimes," she said. "Some people find it distracts them. Some people go almost meditative. Does it hurt as much as you thought it would?"

"Maybe a bit more than I expected," I admitted.

"Well, you're doing great so far," she said.

I was oddly proud of that, but she'd brought the tattoo gun back to my ribs and started again, so I didn't say anything. It must have shown on my face, though, because when Tricia glanced up a few moments later, she let out another low chuckle.

"You got a bit of a praise kink there, Nellie?" she asked.

"What? No," I said. "I mean, I like a compliment as much as the next person, obviously."

"Mmm," she said.

"Come on. Who doesn't like compliments?" I rolled my eyes. "That doesn't mean I'm into being told I'm a good girl or something."

"Of course it doesn't," Tricia said lightly. "Don't worry, I won't argue when you're doing *such* a good job proving your point, sweetheart."

"I—oh, fuck off," I said, laughing.

She smiled. "Maybe when we're done."

And if you'd asked me right then, I would've said we were for sure going to. Fuck, I mean. We flirted a bit more, and laughed a bit more, and she had to have noticed the fact that my nipples were hard the entire time she was touching me.

But we didn't.

I didn't fuck her.

Not only that, I...

Fuck, I couldn't believe I was admitting it.

I *chose* not to fuck her.

And all because some asshole texted me halfway through the appointment.

Bastard

How'd you do on your case study?

"What's wrong?" Tricia asked.

"Huh?" I looked up.

"You're frowning," she said. "And you tensed up. It won't hurt as much if you relax."

"Just like anal," I said.

She pulled the tattoo gun away so she could laugh without messing anything up. "Can't say I've ever experienced it. But is everything okay?"

"Oh, yeah," I said. "Just a text from someone I didn't expect to hear from."

"Mmm," she said knowingly. "An ex?"

I snorted. "God no. I burn those bridges until they explode so I look cooler while I'm walking away."

She chuckled again, then went back to doing my tattoo while I clumsily texted JP back.

Or is it "doing who?"

He sent a set of laughing emojis.

Bastard

Sure you are, babe. Since when have you wanted a tattoo?

I didn't want to admit why I'd impulsively ended up sitting topless in a tattoo parlour. And I could've just not responded and come up with something later. But I was impatient, and I wanted to know why JP was texting me.

Also, I loved proving JP wrong.

"Do you mind if I take a picture?" I asked Tricia.

"Of what?" she replied.

"Me being tattooed."

She glanced up. "To send to your not-an-ex that's texting you?"

"He would've had to be something in the first place to be an ex. But we might mess around now and then."

She smirked. "Alright. Go ahead."

So I held up my camera and pointed it down my body, making sure both of my tits were showing in the photo, and sent it. The checkmarks showing he saw it appeared immediately, but it took almost a minute before he messaged me back.

Bastard

See, exactly what I said. You sure are getting a tattoo

Me

jelus?

Bastard

I wouldn't say jealous, but I do wish I was as close to your tits right now as she is

"Here," Tricia said, and I nearly jumped as I realized she'd stopped tattooing me and stood up. "I'll lean you back a bit and you can prop your elbow up on this stand so it's easier to type."

"Thanks," I said as she helped me adjust.

"No problem, sweetheart. I want you to be comfortable."

The low huskiness of her voice was definitely doing it for me, but I didn't say anything else. And I didn't text JP back until Tricia sat down and started working again.

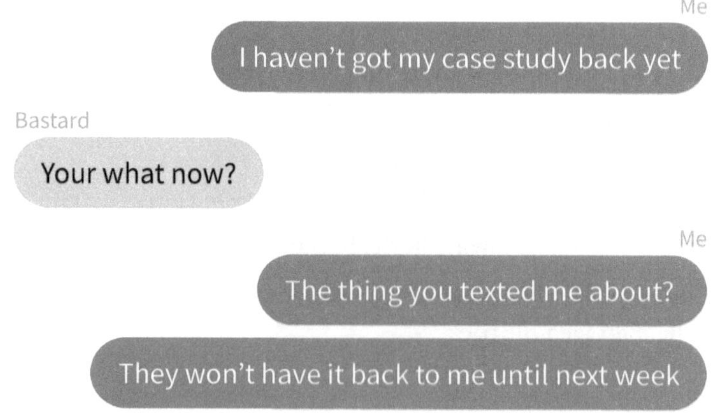

Bastard

You can't blame me for getting distracted

Seriously, look at your tits right now

Me

I can see them. So can she. So unless there's anything else you want, I'm gonna go since I'm trying to seal the deal here

Bastard

Go for it, babe

I frowned again, but Tricia didn't comment on it that time. Something about JP's message felt strange, like he was...

I don't know.

He shouldn't have *been* anything. We both knew that. So I didn't know why he thought he needed to give me the go-ahead.

Me

I don't need your permission to get laid

"Are you still doing alright?" Tricia asked.

"Yeah," I said, probably too quickly. "I'm fine."

She studied me for a second, something flashing through her mind that I couldn't have guessed at, then nodded. "If you say so."

I did, but before I could tell her that I did, my phone went off again.

Bastard

Of course you don't. But I figured it'd be extra hot for you to know I'm picturing it and jacking off while you're with her

Oh God.

Oh *God*.

I mean, it was. It absolutely was. Somehow, even though it felt like wasps were attacking my ribcage and stinging it repeatedly, the thought of JP touching himself while thinking of me was...

I shouldn't have liked that so much.

Me

Narcissist much?

Bastard

For what?

Me

Thinking it's hot for ME to think about YOU when I'm with someone else. And please. You would think two women going at it was hot regardless of if I was involved or not

Bastard

Technically true, I guess. Pretty much anyone going at it would be hot to think about

I swallowed hard. I did trust JP. Especially when he was telling me to trust him, for some reason. JP didn't take things like trust lightly.

So he was into this.

He probably was joking. It's not like it was late at night and he was texting me while he was in bed or something.

But my pussy didn't want to believe that.

Especially because my pussy seemed to insist on conjuring up an image in my head. An image of JP in his bedroom—which I knew wasn't the right background because he didn't live at home anymore, but I didn't know what his new bedroom looked like—with his fist around his cock, stroking lazily as he texted me.

Of him sitting on his bed, leaning against the headboard, his legs spread and his shirt lifted so when he came, he wouldn't mess up the fabric.

Of his eyes closed, his head tilted back, his lips parted, his breath shallow as redness crept up his neck and cheeks.

Of a mop of hair belonging to some anonymous girl in his lap. Blonde and pin straight one moment, brown in pigtails the next, natural curls after that, and then red and wavy and mussed up like he'd been using it to guide her up and down on his cock.

Of what she was tasting.

Feeling.

Hearing.

In the new image, his fist was no longer wrapped around his shaft, but twisted in her hair. His pants weren't just pulled down, they were off, and he was shirtless, and he was fucking up into her mouth while pressing the back of her head down the way he did when he emptied a load down my throat. I didn't know if he did that to other people, but it didn't matter; it was my image, and my daydream, and my pussy getting wet while I thought about JP fucking another girl and understood exactly what he meant about the little something extra.

"Nellie?"

I almost jumped as Tricia said my name. She had sat back on the stool, another amused look on her face.

"It's done," she said. "Go take a look."

My legs were unsteady as I got out of the chair. That had to be from the adrenaline of the tattoo and not what I'd been picturing, obviously. And I forgot all about JP for a few minutes as I looked in the mirror and nearly screamed in delight at the dark dragon outlined on my ribs, the skin surrounding the ink swollen and tinged red. Tricia took a few photos for me, then cleaned it off and put a clear bandage thing on it with strict instructions on how to change it, how long to keep it there, and what I could and couldn't do during the weeks it would be healing.

"That should be it," she said when she finished, then glanced down. "Unless there's anything else?"

And there was.

But there wasn't.

"I think that's all," I said, not quite looking at her, but able to see enough of her in the corner of my eye to catch the smile hiding a look of disappointment.

"For sure," she said. "If anything comes up, you can call the studio here. Or come in and see me. Anytime, sweetheart."

And I agreed I would, even though I was pretty sure we both knew I wouldn't.

And I paid for my tattoo and left a way bigger tip than I originally planned on because it turned out they did take credit cards instead of just cash like I'd thought and I decided the only thing better than getting a tattoo that pissed off my dad was making him pay for it.

And then, adrenaline surging through me and barely feeling the ache in my ribs because the ache in my pussy was more demanding, I walked out of the tattoo parlour and pulled out my phone.

Bastard

> Are you soliciting a dick pic from me?

Me

> I'd prefer a cumshot video with the sound on but I'll settle for that, yeah

Bastard

> You gonna listen to it while you're getting tattooed?

I didn't reply. Not with words. I just sent him one of the photos Tricia had taken before I put my bra back on.

Bastard

> Damn, that's hot. And the dragon looks amazing, too. Suits you, babe

> If you're done, aren't you going home with your new friend?

Me

> Didn't work out

> So show me

I had a photo by the time I got back to my apartment. And I forced myself to take the time to send one in return before pressing my vibrator to my desperately throbbing clit.

After, when I was lying on my bed with my phone sitting next to me, I vowed to never tell *anyone* I'd rejected a sure thing with a hot tattoo artist and chosen to go home and masturbate to a picture of JP's dick instead.

And when my phone went off again before I'd even caught my breath, they wouldn't have been able to torture it out of me that I shoved my vibrator out of the way, dug my much more powerful rabbit out of the night stand, and came harder than I'd ever been able to make myself come before while watching—and listening—to the cumshot video he sent me.

Chapter Nine
That Fucking Fucker

"Look, kiddo, the answer is no."

"Come *on*, Glitch. Help a girl out."

"Okay," they said. "I will."

I perked up, surprised. "Really?"

"Of course not."

I groaned. "Was that necessary?"

"Necessary? No." They smirked. "It was funny, though."

"It hurt my feelings," I said.

"Poor baby," they replied.

"I think there's a rule that if your TA hurts your feelings, they have to give you an extension," I said.

"I think there's also a rule that if a student fails to hand in an assignment in a timely manner with no justified explanation, they get a zero," Glitch replied.

"That sounds like a stupid rule," I grumbled. "There's seriously nothing you can do? I need, like, an hour. An *hour*, Glitch. It's not my fault I'm terrible at these."

"Except you're not, though." They tapped the case study they'd handed back during class that day, which I'd set on their desk after I walked in. "This was not only the best you've done all semester, but I think it was the highest grade in the entire class. What was different about it?"

"I wrote it while my fuck buddy was fingering me," I said. "But he lives in Montreal so he can't come and do that every single week."

Glitch rolled their eyes. "You know, if you spent more time working on your assignments instead of coming up with crazy shit like that, you wouldn't need extensions all the time."

I didn't bother insisting I was telling the truth. Glitch wouldn't have believed me anyway, and more importantly, I was a little unsettled that I'd gotten such a good grade on the case study JP had "helped" me with. Unsettled and upset, because it meant his stupid idea had worked.

Which would mean if I wanted more help, I'd have to tell him he was right. And admit that I'd tried to replicate the results myself, but I got way too distracted with my vibrator to keep working on my paper.

And that...

That wouldn't be a good idea.

Not when I was already questioning what the hell was going on with JP.

We'd been texting every day.

Every single day.

Multiple times a day, even. Sometimes it was so we could do this weird sort of long-distance-mutual-masturbation thing because both of us were apparently too busy to go out and get laid in real life. And for some reason, sending pictures and texts and knowing that two hundred or so kilometers away, one of us was getting off to the idea of the other person getting off was better than erotica or porn or my own imagination.

But that was only sometimes.

Bastard

What was that podcast you were telling me about?

Me

Why am I like this

Bastard

You'd probably be better off asking Professor Sexy instead of me, but if I had to guess, I'd say the daddy issues

I'd sent him middle finger and eye roll emojis.

Me

The name of the podcast is Why Am I Like This, asshat

And for the record, I HAVE asked Ben why I'm like this

Bastard

Did he say it was daddy issues?

Me

He said it was because I have to put up with stupid questions from the bastard who grew up next door to me

Bastard

I knew it was all Marc-Andre's fault

Me

> Yes, of course. Your younger brother that I think has said less than ten words to me since he learned to talk is definitely the problem

Bastard

I'll let him know he needs to apologize for making you a sassy little sex addict

How is Professor Sexy doing, by the way?

And that had turned into me telling him about how I hadn't heard from Ben since he'd left, which was fine and truly didn't bother me because it was expected, except that it meant I was stuck filling out the CCFS Labs internship application on my own. And that had turned into explaining why I had to apply for it, and why I didn't think I'd get it, and the real story behind why I hadn't gotten the FAI internship the previous summer.

Bastard

Seriously? He told his uncle to reject your application because you didn't want to be his girlfriend?

And his uncle listened?

Me

Yep

Bastard

And you're applying for it again? Why would you even want to work there?

Me

I don't. But there are only so many places to do internships like this. It's the only one in Ottawa

So I couldn't tell JP his idea worked and see if he would come back to Ottawa to help me with my next case study. Because when he said he would've driven two hours for the chance to spend ten seconds with me, I'd rolled my eyes and assumed he was exaggerating.

But now I wasn't so sure.

"Look, Nellie," Glitch said after scoffing at the notion that I'd written my highest-graded case study of the year while being edged towards an insane orgasm by my best friend's older brother. "I like you, okay?"

I raised my eyebrows. "Like, you like-me like me?"

Glitch blinked, looking startled. "What? No. I mean—"

"Because if you do, that's cool," I said. "But I refuse to sleep my way into good grades, so we'd have to be full-on celibate until at least Christmas, and that doesn't work for me. You know I'm a total hoe."

They burst out laughing. "As a *person*, I like you. You're fun. You're smart as hell. Honestly, if you ever decided forensics wasn't for you, you'd make a great—"

"I swear to God if you say I'd be a good lawyer, I can't be held responsible for my actions," I interrupted.

They hesitated, lips still parted, before speaking again.

"A great, uh, consultant of some kind," they said, then wove their fingers together and put their elbows on the table. "I *want* to help you. But I can't give extensions for any reason other than the approved ones on the syllabus. So if you end up in the hospital or have a death in the family or get a university-approved education plan for additional accommodations or something, come talk to me. Otherwise, the answer is going to be no."

"What's an university-approved education plan?" I asked.

"Well, if you're Autistic or dyslexic or something, you can get an education plan to allow you to use a computer for everything, for example," they said. "I had one in my undergrad for extra time on tests because I have ADHD."

"Oh," I said.

"So if you have ADHD, you should talk to student services," they said.

"I don't, though."

They raised their eyebrows. "Really?"

I mirrored their expression. "No, I'm lying about it even though it would get me what I want in this situation, which is an extension on my case study."

They tilted their head in concession. "Fair, I guess. You just seem like the type."

"I do not," I said. "I have no problem paying attention to things."

"That's not... well. Never mind." They shook their head. "Unless you're on your deathbed, your direct family is on their deathbed, or you've got a case of the neurospicies, you're not getting an extension."

"Jeez, if you don't want to see me in your office so often, you could just say so," I said.

"Oh, you're more than welcome to keep trying. I just don't want you to hold onto hope that you'll eventually wear me down." They unfolded their fingers and pushed the chair back, standing up and collecting the stack of case studies from the students in the class who weren't there pleading for an extra hour to finish. "Now get out. I need to go smoke before my meeting with Shelby."

I lifted an eyebrow. "Since when do you smoke?"

They rolled their eyes. "You'd need a joint too, if you had to meet with him three times a week."

"Oh," I said. "You mean weed."

"Of course." They smirked. "You wanna come? The strain I've got right now is way better than what they've got in the dispensaries."

I pretended to be scandalized. "Are you offering to sell me drugs?"

"Are you offering to buy them?"

I started to laugh, but Glitch looked serious. "Wait, do you actually...?"

Instant regret flashed across their face. "It's nothing major. I just have access to some good stuff here and there, and law school isn't cheap, so I do what I can to make a few dollars on the side."

"Oh."

Their jaw twitched, eyes darting to the side before looking back at me. "Are you cool about that?"

"Yeah," I said. "It's fine. I won't say anything."

They studied me for a moment, then sighed and sat back down. "Fine."

"Fine what?"

"If you can promise me you'll *absolutely* get it done, you can give the case study to me in an hour. I'll tell Shelby I lost track of time before our meeting."

I stared at them, my mouth half-open. They stared back at me, trying to cover the worry in their eyes with a hard look.

"I won't have it done in an hour," I said.

Glitch's jaw twitched. "Nellie, I seriously can't—"

"So you better get those to Shelby before you lose track of time." I took my case study from their desk and stood.

"But—"

"If I'm not going to sleep with someone for a good grade, I'm not going to blackmail them for an extension," I said. "At least if I'm sleeping my way into passing there's a chance of orgasm. There's nothing fun for me in blackmail."

They stared at me for a moment, then nodded.

"I appreciate it," they said.

I smiled cheerfully. "No problem. See you next class."

And then I left.

I mean, obviously I'd *thought* about taking that hour to finish my case study. But I'd thought about it in the same way I thought about thousands of options I'd never take. Like sure, I'd considered impulsively throwing a raw egg on the floor while cooking or driving my car into the river instead of going to Montreal to visit my dad, but not in a way where I'd ever *do* it.

Glitch wasn't hurting anyone. Weed wasn't even illegal. And post-secondary school wasn't cheap, let alone law school.

Considering I'd basically sold my soul for four years to get my tuition paid for, I didn't exactly feel qualified to judge them for doing what they had to do.

"I mean, I think you could judge them a little," Sydney said skeptically as we settled in to study at her place a few hours later. "There's a pretty big difference between getting your dad to pay your tuition and being a literal drug dealer."

"They're not really a drug dealer," I said, pulling things out of my bag to find the highlighter I knew I'd thrown in there earlier. "It's just weed. I can buy that from a store."

"Yeah, I guess."

"Like, I'm not sure what they were so worried about. It's not like they offered me meth."

"If you say so," she said, distracted.

I frowned as my arm reached the bottom of my bag with no highlighter in sight. "What's wrong?"

"Nothing's wrong," she said in a way that made it very clear something was wrong.

"Syd, clearly something's going on." I peered into the bag one last time, then gave up my search and started loading everything back in. "You've never had an issue with weed before. You've smoked more of it in your life than I have."

"That's not it at all." She sighed and leaned back on the couch. "I try so hard to like Reid's girlfriends. But they always seem to have a problem with me. Hope's been the worst of them, but Reid won't stand up for me even though it's so obvious she dislikes me and it's probably because the only thing all these situations have in common is me." A wry smile twisted her mouth. "I'm the common denominator. So I'm the problem."

Reid had said some borderline awful stuff to Sydney in the past, but never in a way that made me think he was *trying* to hurt Sydney. That, though? I stared at her, my mouth half-open.

"He said that?" I asked.

"No, no," she said. "Of course not."

"Who said that, then?"

"Maybe I thought of it myself."

"I don't believe that for one second. My best friend is a badass. It's not *her* fault Reid has crappy taste in women." In the process of shaking my head, I noticed my highlighter sitting on the coffee table and grabbed it, then fidgeted with it as I looked up at Sydney. "So who said that? Was it Hope?"

She didn't say anything.

"I see." I put my highlighter back down. "Unrelated question. If I got arrested for running someone over with my car, do you think Glitch would give me an extension on my case studies?"

Sydney started laughing, even as she blinked rapidly like she was trying not to tear up. "I don't think that's on their approved list of reasons to give extensions."

"Great. I guess I'm dropping out."

"It's not worth it."

"Did you talk to Reid?"

She sighed and shook her head. "I'm just so tired of it. Of all the drama. I'm keeping my head down and avoiding them both whenever I can. No one tells you how exhausting it is to be disliked, but causing shit with her would be worse."

I disagreed, but of course, I was going to respect what my best friend wanted. So when Hope and Reid walked in after I'd cheered Sydney up enough to work on a paper for her English class while I pretended to do my next case study but actually read transcripts of interviews with a serial killer currently on death row, I decided to get back at her in my own subtle way.

"Oh," Hope said as the apartment door closed. "Sydney. We didn't know you were here."

"Why wouldn't I be?" Sydney asked flatly.

"I thought you said you were hanging out with Nellie," Reid said, followed by the two thumps of him removing his shoes and kicking them to the side. A moment later, he popped into the living room and caught sight of me. "Which you are. Hey, Nellie."

"Hi," I said. "You don't mind, do you? Your apartment is cleaner than mine right now."

Which was true, even though I'd done all that cleaning before JP showed up.

Reid gave me a strange look. "Of course I don't mind. Why would I?"

"Because maybe we had plans to sit in the living room and watch a movie?" Hope said, her voice dry.

"Oh no," Reid said, playful sarcasm in his voice. "We'll have to watch it on the smaller TV in my room. And I have no seating, so we'll have to sit on the bed. Together. With the door closed."

"Maybe we should go to your place," Sydney said to me. "I'll clean your kitchen for you."

"I'm kidding," Reid said, plopping on the couch next to her. "We'll wait until you're asleep later. Right, baby?"

"Apparently," Hope said, crossing the room to the other chair.

"Did Syd tell you I got a tattoo, Reid?" I asked.

"Oh yeah!" He shifted forward excitedly. "Let's see it."

I could've shown him a picture or carefully lifted my shirt to let him look at the dragon on my ribs. But Hope was there, she'd been an asshole to my best friend, and I hadn't bothered putting a bra on before coming over.

So I stood up, turned to Reid, and lifted my shirt *just* high enough that my underboob was showing.

It wasn't much, as far as revenge went, but it was enough that Sydney pressed her lips together to hold in a laugh. Hope looked like she was about to burst into an explosion of green powder, but Reid just looked at the dragon and nodded in approval.

"It looks great," he said. "And it's healing nicely. You did the Saniderm thing on it, right? The clear bandage?"

"Yeah," I said. "She said it might be itchy but I've barely noticed anything, honestly."

"Maybe I'll check her out for my next one," he said. "The artist I was going to moved to San Francisco and I've been wanting to get another tattoo done for a while."

"I definitely recommend Tricia," I said. "And not just because she's hot, either."

"Yeah, she seems good," Reid said. "The linework on this is—"

"Maybe we could continue this conversation after Nellie puts her shirt back down," Hope said.

"Why?" I asked. "It's just my ribs."

"We can see—" She cut herself off, then motioned towards me.

"You can see what?" I asked. "Me? That's because I'm standing right here and I'm not a ghost."

Her lips curled up into an unamused smile. "Well, I was *trying* to be polite so I didn't embarrass you, but your boob is hanging out."

Reid blinked and sat back. "Sorry, Nellie. I didn't even notice."

"I find that hard to believe," Sydney said. "She has very noticeable breasts."

"Prominent, some may even say," I said, lowering my shirt. "I can put them on the table if you need a reminder of how great my rack is."

"I don't need a reminder," he said, snickering.

"You don't?" Hope said, her voice deceivingly light.

Reid grimaced. "I didn't mean it like that."

"How did you mean it, then?" Hope asked.

Reid started to answer, but as he did, my phone started vibrating on the coffee table with Anne-Marie's name flashing on the screen. Which wasn't super common, since she usually texted me before calling, but it wasn't entirely out of the ordinary. Leaving them to their awkward situation, I answered my phone.

"Hey, Annie," I said.

And then I winced and yanked the phone away from my ear as a piercing shriek of garbled words poured out of it.

"—swear I could *never* have expected this to happen, not for this, but I do not think there is a way for him to get out of it!" Anne-Marie let out a gleeful, wordless squeal. "If his father has any sense, he will already know there is no buying his way out of this, not when it was so public and involved the SVP. Oh, and my mother spoke with Emile LeBlanc, who, I do not know if you know him but *he* said—"

"Anne-Marie!" I finally said. "What are you talking about?"

"*Chérie*!" She squealed again. "How have you not heard the news?"

"I think you have to say the news for me to hear it."

"Yes, but it's all *over* the news. The actual, on television news. Here, at least. I suppose maybe in Ottawa—well." She took a deep breath. "Clinton Thibault was arrested. He is in *jail*."

My first reaction was the same kind of gleeful excitement Anne-Marie had.

My second was relief so strong I almost cried. It wasn't like I planned to go to any of my dad's events ever again, but now there was no *way* my dad would ever want to be associated with the Thibaults like that. There was no chance that I'd ever have to be Clinton's date for anything. My dad couldn't ever hold that over my head again.

My third reaction was less of an emotion and more of a sudden dread in my stomach, something that dropped so low that it pulled the moisture from my mouth and replaced it with a sick, horrified feeling.

Clinton was not a man who respected the word "no."

"What'd he get arrested for?" I asked. "Did he... you know. Do something to someone?"

"No, no," Anne-Marie said. "I mean, yes, he severely injured someone and hurt a few others, but not like the way you are thinking. Which, honestly, of *all* the things to take down Clinton Thibault, I would have never expected it to be crashing his Maserati into the middle of the police benefit."

"He did what now?" I said.

She launched into another stream of words, as twisted and convoluted as ribbons in a windstorm, and even though Sydney had leaped off the couch and leaned in to listen, neither of us could make out a thing she was saying.

"Annie, you have to slow down," I said. "You said he crashed a Maserati. Where did the Uber come from?"

She let out an aggravated noise. "I do not have *time* to slow down! I have so many calls to make. I will—actually, if you go to—search his name with the word 'crash,' I guarantee a video will come up right near the top. His parents are attempting to get it removed from the media but it's viral. There is no chance they will get it off everything. But I will call back later after I talk to Remy again, because *he* said he does not think Clinton will get jail time but I think—oh, never mind. I will call later!"

And then she hung up.

"What the hell?" Reid asked, staring at me and Sydney.

"It's this guy from Montreal," I said, turning and plunking myself in front of my laptop so I could search for the video Anne-Marie was talking about.

"The one Nellie's dad tried to make her go to those events with," Sydney said.

"Ah," Reid said. "The handsy one."

"That's a word for it." I typed quickly and like Anne-Marie said, a video showed up near the top, even though it had only been posted a few hours earlier. Sydney sank to the floor beside me, kneeling so she could slide in closer to the screen. Reid lifted his legs off the floor so he could shift behind us and even Hope got caught up in the curiosity of it all.

Or at least, she pretended to so she could take Syd's spot on the couch.

In hindsight, Anne-Marie had done a reasonable job of simplifying the story. It boiled down to Clinton being rejected by a girl at a club. Clinton, being Clinton, refused to take no for an answer after he bought her a drink, and the girl, being a girl, was nervous around him, so she and her friends tried to slip out of the bar unnoticed and go home.

Except Clinton noticed.

The women had just gotten into their Uber when Clinton stormed out of the bar—allegedly drunk, according to the news, but only because they couldn't outright say he was without proof even though it was obvious—and like the psychopathic narcissist he was, got into his car and went after them.

The cops were called, of course, but the car chase ended before they got there, since technically, they were all there before Clinton was. One of the women in the Uber knew about the police benefit because her brother-in-law was an officer and directed them there, thinking someone would be able to arrest Clinton.

But she was wrong.

"Despite being surrounded by a selection of Montreal's finest, it was not a SVP officer who captured the suspect," the news anchor said. "After crashing his vehicle into the lobby of the hotel where the benefit took place, sending four people to hospital including a bellhop who was set to retire next week and an officer who is still listed as being in serious but stable condition, the suspect exited the vehicle and ran. In the chaos, it was actually the wife of an officer who brought down the suspect."

The camera switched to an interview with, according to the bar of text at the bottom, two of the women who had been in the Uber.

"It was amazing," said one woman in muted French so the voiceover in English was clear. "Like something from a movie. We saw him running towards us and the driver turned the vehicle back on, but before we even moved, a woman in heels and a ball gown flew into the man and tackled him to the ground."

"There were rhinestones everywhere," said the other woman. "But she is our hero. She came to the car and she was bleeding, you know, from her knees and elbows. Scrapes from the road. But she checked on us first."

"That's actually so sweet," Sydney said.

I nodded. "I hope she was okay."

"She must have been," she said. "I mean, it'd be a very different story, right? If she was hurt or something? I wonder if—"

But the camera switched again and she didn't finish her thought.

"If what?" Hope asked.

"Syd—" Reid started.

"No," Sydney said, her voice high-pitched.

"You didn't know," I said, reaching for her.

"Know *what*?" Hope demanded.

But Sydney had gone silent, her eyes wide and unblinking and her expression frozen as she stared at the couple on my laptop screen, a chubby woman with rosy white skin and red hair standing next to a man with curly brown hair and who was shorter in person than one would expect.

"—spoke with Officer Olivier Courbet," the news anchor said.

"Of course I am horrified," Olivier said to someone off-camera. "She was put in a position that she was not prepared for when there were so many others who should have been there instead of her. But that horror is nothing at all compared to how proud I am of my wife."

"That fucker," Reid said, his voice heated and rumbling and growly. "That fucking *fucker*."

"Oh my God," Hope said. "That's your guy, Sydney. You're the other woman!"

And Sydney just stared at the screen.

Chapter Ten
Vengeance But In A Fun Way

"You're not going to tell him you know?"

Sydney stared into her beer. "I haven't decided yet."

"Syd—"

"I know." She sighed and picked up her beer. "I need to tell Clara."

She said Olivier's wife's name like they knew each other. They didn't, but given the deep dive Sydney had done on social media, I understood why the past four days made it feel like she'd known her for four years.

The day after we found out, Sydney had skipped class. I'd gone over once mine were done expecting to find her moping in bed or maybe on the couch, trashy TV on with candy wrappers and melted ice cream surrounding her. Not that I wanted my best friend to be suffering, but secretly, I was almost disappointed to find her dressed and showered and sitting at her kitchen table in front of her laptop instead of surrounded by chocolate I could steal.

"Are you studying?" I'd asked as I kicked my shoes off.

"In a way," she'd replied.

And that was when I'd walked behind her and saw all the tabs she'd opened as she tracked down Clara Bouchon-Leville.

Those tabs had stayed open most of the week, if not on her laptop, then at least in her mind. She'd only skipped one day of classes, but it was the weekend before I convinced her to go out for a couple of beers with me at Lou's. But even as we ordered a plate of mozza sticks and chicken wings and the two-for-one happy hour special on draft beer, it was clear she was still thinking about Olivier's wife.

"Technically, you don't *need* to tell her," I said as carefully as I could. "But—"

"But I should, and everyone will judge me if I don't, and even though I want to walk away and forget this whole thing, I'm supposed to be a girl's girl." She took another long sip of beer. "That's what I'd say, if this was happening to someone else. But once it's happening to *you*…"

"It's not that easy," I said.

"I thought if I didn't tell Olivier I knew, it would give me time to figure out… you know." She waved a vague hand. "How. But he's starting to wonder why I haven't called him back."

I twisted my mouth to the side, thinking. "Well, I think the problem is we have *too* many options."

Sydney raised her eyebrows. "We do? And what do you mean, we?"

"We do," I said. "And I mean 'we' as in '*we*,' as in I'm your best friend and like hell am I letting you figure this out by yourself. Especially when it can be so much fun."

Sydney looked at me incredulously. "Fun. You think this is going to be fun?"

"I think getting vengeance on that doorknob is going to be fun in that it'll be satisfying," I said. "Like not 'Oh yay a day at the circus' fun but like… you know. 'My name is Inigo Montoya' fun."

That drew a light chuckle out of her. "I don't think Inigo Montoya would necessarily call that *fun*."

"Whatever." I straightened up a bit and pulled in closer to the table. "Okay. We could get them to go out to another benefit or event or something and then they'd need to hire a babysitter. So we get them to hire you, not knowing it's you—"

"This sounds like the start of a bad porno," Sydney said. "But also—"

"Okay, fine," I said. "They hire *me* as the babysitter, and Olivier's just sweating, right? And he's so concerned that I'm going to do something that he doesn't realize until it's too late that *you're* at the event too, and *bam*!" I slapped my hand on the table. "You pull out the receipts and show Clara and she kicks his ass to the curb."

She jumped when I slapped the table, but started laughing in earnest.

"Why do you need to be there as the babysitter?" she asked. "And also, why do they need a babysitter? I'm pretty sure they don't have kids."

"I'm hearing a lot of problems and not a lot of solutions, Syd," I said. "But fine, we can scrap the babysitter. What if we just show up at the event—"

"What event?" she asked, cackling.

"The one we're planning as a charade to catch Olivier. Keep up." I snapped my fingers. "So we plan the event, we show up and cause a huge scene—"

"But wouldn't the event have to be in Montreal?" she asked. "Your dad wouldn't be super thrilled if you caused a scene."

That was a good point. "Fine. What if we get someone to seduce Clara so *she* can get revenge?"

"I think it would be more likely for you to seduce Olivier. Clara's socials have a lot of Jesus-y things on them."

"Not a chance. First of all, I have standards."

"You do not," she shot back.

She was starting to sound like the Sydney I knew and I grinned. "I have *some* standards. Olivier is a limp, unwashed salad of soggy lettuce, stale croutons, and male disappointment. And second of all, Olivier knows who I am. He's a dumbass, but he's not stupid."

She pursed her lips. "Good point. Maybe Anne-Marie could seduce him."

"Ooh!" I said, perking up. "Anne-Marie and Remy could play their little jealousy game."

"I don't think we want to put Remy in that position, though," Sydney said carefully.

"Shit. Good point." I tapped my fingers on the table. "So are we back to trying to seduce Clara? Jesus-y stuff on her socials doesn't mean she isn't open to doing things other than praying while she's on her knees."

"Who would even seduce her?"

"JP."

The answer left my lips faster than it should have, and with far more confidence than was warranted. Especially since the whole thing was meant to be an over-the-top joke to cheer Sydney up.

"JP," Sydney repeated. "You think he'd do that?"

"JP loves justice," I said. "This would be right up his alley."

"Clara doesn't seem like his type," she said.

"I mean, she's curvy and hot, so I'm pretty sure she is," I said. "But I can promise him anal again. I could probably get him to do anything from suck on my toes to clean my bathroom with that."

Her laughter was interrupted by gags. "That's disgusting."

"The toe-sucking or the bathroom cleaning?" I asked. "Because my bathroom's not that bad, but also, no kink-shaming."

"You don't have a foot fetish," she said. "I would know about it by now."

I shrugged. "True. But either way, if you want me to take one for the team, I'll tell JP he can put it in my butt if he seduces Clara."

"JP could put it in your butt by asking nicely," she said.

"Not true," I argued. "I'd still consider it if he asked meanly."

By the time we paid our bills, Sydney was more herself than she had been. At the very least, she felt a lot less guilty, which was the whole point, really. It wasn't her fault Olivier was a cheater. And she *definitely* hadn't known he was married. And he was the one stupid enough to continue the charade for months instead of being a cheating prick for one night and then never calling Sydney again.

That being said, I was still livid on her behalf. So livid that I was still thinking about a couple of days later instead of paying attention to Dr. Spitzki's pathology lecture and decided it might be worth finding out if one of our unlikely plans might be possible.

Me

> Would you seduce a guy's wife to get revenge on said guy for cheating on said wife?

Like always, JP replied almost immediately.

Bastard

> Hypothetically? Or are you asking for another favour?

Well, it wasn't an instant no. So that was good.

Me

> Maybe both

Bastard

> I'm gonna need more context

I glanced up. Dr. Spitzki was pacing the front of the lecture hall and showing off his incredible talent for making something as interesting and morbid as wound ballistics sound less entertaining than reading the windshield wiper blade catalog at Canadian Tire. Not that it mattered; he liked to wander around without his glasses on and wouldn't have seen me looking at my phone anyway.

So I started texting JP back. But I was barely into the story when the Captain's voice blared out of my phone, asking if the kids were ready, and the Spongebob Squarepants theme started playing.

"Bastard," I muttered, which was both an exclamation of frustration and the name that was flashing on my screen.

"Ms. Belanger," Dr. Spitzki said. "How many times do I—"

"I know," I said, grabbing my laptop and shoving it into my bag as I stood up. "I'm going."

"Could you silence the damn thing while you go?" he asked sarcastically.

"Sure." I tapped the screen. "Hello, Nellie speaking. How can I help you?"

"That is *not* what I—"

But I'd already pushed the classroom door open and ducked into the hallway.

"You sound hot when you talk all formal like that," JP said. "How's it going, babe?"

"It was better before you got me kicked out of class," I said. "Thanks for that, asshole."

He started laughing. "It's not my fault you weren't paying attention in class."

"It is your fault that you're an impatient dickhead who couldn't wait for me to text him back."

"Well, I figured after three minutes of watching the typing dots that this was pretty complex for a hypothetical and that it would be easier to call and get the details."

He was right, of course, but I wasn't going to tell him that. "Whatever. So you know my friend, Sydney?"

"Yeah, the one fucking the—oh fuck, no," he said. "Nope. I would not do that."

"You don't even know—"

"She's sleeping with a cop, right? The cop she met back in the spring at that bachelor party where you had a threesome with those two other guys?"

I plunked myself on a bench down the hall from Dr. Spitzki's class and rubbed my fingernail along my thumb, frustrated JP had put the dots together so quickly. "How did you even remember that?"

"I remember a lot of the hot-as-fuck stories you tell me," he said. "So it's the same guy?"

"Well... yeah."

"So no. Hard pass. No way."

"Not even if I promised you anal again?"

"Babe, you could promise me anal, a threesome, a foursome, an-as-many-as-you-can-find-some, and daily blowjobs for the rest of my *life* and I still wouldn't fuck a cop's wife."

"Even if he's the kind of cop who cheats on her for months?"

"So, a typical cop?" he asked dryly, but I heard the smile in his voice as I snickered. "Yes, even then. Jeez, Nellie. That's, like, one of the top lawyer life rules. Don't fuck with cops."

My quiet giggle trailed off and I sighed miserably. "But he hurt my friend. How am I supposed to get back at him if it's against the rules?"

"Last I checked, despite all the times you've stated that it's your dream career and a lifelong desire you're simply desperate to fulfill, you're not a lawyer," he said. "It's a rule for *me*. I'm not saying don't get back at him. I'm saying *I'm* not seducing his wife."

"Well, how am I supposed to get back at him, then?" I asked. "It's not like I can seduce his wife. I'm fairly certain she's straight."

"Which leads to the question of how seducing his wife gets back at him," he said. "Wouldn't it make more sense to tell her and ask if she wants revenge?"

I picked at my thumbnail, twisting my mouth to the side.

"Look, I'm assuming you know how to find this woman," JP said when I didn't say anything. "Why don't you tell her what he did and call it a day?"

"If it were you, would you be satisfied with that?"

He hummed in concession. "Fair point. But I know you, Nell. This shady, underhanded shit isn't you."

"You don't know me that well."

"Babe," he said.

"Don't call me babe," we both said at the same time, and I groaned.

"See?" he said, laughing.

"Fuck you."

"Mmm, I'd love to," he said. "Which brings me to the reason I called, actually."

"To get the rest of the story about why I want you to seduce a cop's wife?"

"Nah, but I figured two birds, one stone. I was going to call you later anyway."

It was my turn to put the dots together. I stared down at my hands and hoped the way my heartbeat had just skipped wouldn't show through my voice. "Are you coming to Ottawa for another client meeting?"

"Good guess," he said. "But, ah, not specifically."

"Oh. Apparently that dot-to-dot was harder than I thought," I said.

"The what?" he asked.

"Nothing. What's going on, then?"

"Well, uh..." JP cleared his throat. "Look, I need a favour."

"*Do* you?" I asked, not bothering to hide my delight. "My, how the turntables."

He chuckled, but it was far more forced than usual. My glee at having one over JP dropped into guilt at the tension suddenly filling his voice.

"The turntables have turned, for sure," he said. "Especially because I know this is a big ask. Probably too big."

I ran my fingernail along my thumb. "You want me to come to Montreal for something."

"Another good guess," he said. "But no."

I frowned. "You need me to ask my dad for something?"

"Also no. Maybe this will be easier than I thought."

I sighed in annoyance. "Are you gonna tell me what it is instead of being all cryptic or can I hang up and go to the library to finish my case study of the week?"

"It's this thing for a, uh, client," he said. "A prospective client, I mean. I have a huge opportunity to meet with them—a life-changing opportunity, it's that big of a thing—but this client is focused on, uh... appearances. And has assumed I'm in a relationship."

My stomach sank. "Is that so?"

He let out a sigh of his own. "You've connected the dots already, haven't you?"

"I am pretty good at dot-to-dots," I said. "This one's either you a picture of a lion in a party hat or you wanting me to be your fake girlfriend."

He let out a half-laugh that was semi-serious, a sound I wasn't used to hearing from JP. "Well, yeah. Except it's worse than that."

"Worse than a lion in a party hat?"

"Very much so. Because the client wants to meet during this personal development conference. In Mont Tremblant. So it's kind of an overnight thing and he's made it clear he expects me to bring a... my... girlfriend. The girlfriend he thinks I have."

I didn't say anything.

"You'd get a free trip to Mont Tremblant out of it," he said, like he already knew exactly how tempting that wasn't.

"And you figured I owe you one from the summer," I said.

"I know that's what it looks like," he said. "It's not the case, but it's a fair thing to assume."

I brought my thumbnail to my mouth and chewed on it. "Okay. So if it's not that, then why does it have to be me?"

"Because you get it," he said simply.

A warm sensation spread over my skin and into my chest. Which sucked, because it was kind of making me want to agree to it. "You know it sounds exactly like the kind of thing my dad would ask me to do."

"Yeah. Which is why it's killing me to ask. I hate how he treats you." More warmth. Ugh. "What if I say no?"

"Then you say no."

I picked at my nails again. "You'll be upset about it, though. And what about your client?"

"I'll figure it out," he said. "And no. I won't. It's entirely up to you. I figured it couldn't hurt to ask, you know? The only thing I'll be upset about is not getting to fuck you in Mont Tremblant."

"I mean, it would just be a hotel room," I said.

He scoffed, some of the playfulness returning to his voice. "You think I wouldn't find somewhere more creative than a hotel room to fuck you? There's a ton of stuff to do in Mont Tremblant. We could fuck on a boat tour, during a hike, on the zipline—"

"How would we fuck on a zipline?" I asked.

"Carefully," he said. "And we've never fucked in a hotel room anyway. We could hit two of them."

I frowned. "It would be two nights?"

"No," he said. "Your room and my room."

"We'd have separate rooms?" I asked skeptically.

"Well, of course," he said. "I don't want to risk you not having your own bed, so I'd book you a separate room."

"You're joking."

"Or am I tempting fate? How are we supposed to do the whole 'It's the last available room and there's only one bed' thing if we don't book two rooms in the first place?"

I rolled my eyes. "That's for romance books. You better not fall in love with me during this trip."

"Trust me, that won't be happening during this trip," he said with unwavering and relieving certainty. "But does that mean you're agreeing to it?"

"I guess I could spend a weekend getting fucked in Mont Tremblant," I said. "When is it?"

"Well, uh... that's the thing," he said haltingly. "It's kind of... not... on a weekend. It's this Friday."

Oh.

Shit.

"Don't worry about it," he said after a moment. "I knew it would be asking a lot. I can figure something else out."

Yes, I wanted to say. You should figure something else out. Because if I wasn't going to skip class to spend an extra day in Toronto seeing my mom, there was no way I was going to do it for JP Marchand.

Although, my mom was asking for me to skip class because she wanted to take a vacation, and JP was asking because he'd do the same for me.

I knew without a doubt he'd do the same for me.

"I can make it work," I said.

"What?"

"I said I can make it work, old man," I repeated. "Check your hearing."

"Nell, if—"

"Shut up before I change my mind."

And for once, JP kept his mouth shut.

Chapter Eleven
Afternoon Me Is A Different Person And I Hate Her

"I HATE YOU," I grumbled into the phone.

"I know," JP said. "But you did agree to this."

"That was a different me. Afternoon me. And seven a.m. me hates her, too."

"It's six-forty-two, actually."

I groaned. "You're *early*?!"

"If you'd been out of bed at six-thirty like you said you would, it wouldn't be an issue." I didn't respond with words, just muttered vocalizations mocking what he'd said. JP snickered. "Well, rounding up, can seven a.m. Nellie let me in? I have something that might get her out of bed."

I opened my eyes blearily. "You brought me something?"

"Mm-hmm. And you're gonna like it."

"Is it your dick?"

"Are you saying you like my dick?"

"I'm too tired to pretend I don't."

"Well, it *is* something thick and creamy that you'll want to put in your mouth, but—"

"I don't take cream in my coffee," I said.

"It's not coffee."

"You didn't even bring me coffee?"

"No, I—"

But I tapped the screen to end the call and shoved my face into my pillow, closing my eyes for the thirty seconds it took JP to stop laughing enough to dial my number on the intercom again.

"No coffee, no Nellie," I said when I answered, my voice muffled by the pillow.

"I don't know how you take it," he said, still chuckling.

"Yes, you do," I said. "Frequently and often from behind. Sometimes with a finger in my ass."

He laughed hard enough that I heard it bounce in the echo-y foyer and pressed my face into the pillow harder, trying to hide my smile. From who, I didn't know. Myself, I guess.

"What I brought is better than coffee," he said. "And I *fully* planned to stop for coffee on the way, to the point that I can tell you where the nearest Starbucks, Tim's, McDonalds, and two different local coffee shops are. I figured the promise of coffee later was better than getting your coffee order wrong."

It was a good point. I didn't tell him that, but JP probably figured it out since I sighed and hit the button to let him upstairs. By the time he knocked, I'd crawled out of bed and brushed my teeth, but my hair was still unbrushed, my eyes were protesting the fact that I dared to open them before eight-thirty, and all I had on was the ratty bathrobe I kept in case of fire.

You know. So I could still keep sleeping naked like I preferred, but wouldn't freeze to death if I had to run outside in the middle of the night.

"Don't you ever have to get up early for class?" he asked when I opened the door. "Or do they not start at eight at OttawaTech?"

"I went to one eight a.m. class my first year, dropped out, and signed up to take it in the spring semester instead." I looked at the reusable shopping bag in his hand. "What'd you bring me?"

"No hello, no kiss, nothing?" he teased as he kicked off his shoes. "I guess I should've expected nothing less from seven a.m. Nellie."

"It's why you love me," I said.

He flicked an eyebrow up. "You think so?"

"Well, there's gotta be something wrong with you. You keep coming back even though you know I think you're stupid and smelly."

"And hideous," he said. "Don't forget that I'm the ugliest person you've ever seen in your life."

"I don't get nearly enough credit for not puking every time I see you. Now show me what's in the bag."

His mouth twisted, but he turned and set the bag on my kitchen counter. Without a word, he pulled out a white bakery box.

My mouth dropped open. "You went to Trou de Beigne?"

"I figured I should do something more than dick you down at a fancy hotel to thank you for helping me out," he said. "And this was cheaper than getting wine or something."

"Oh, how you flatter me," I said, watching as he flipped the lid open and revealed a dozen perfect ring-shaped delicacies, then frowned. "Wait, they're open this early?"

"This early? No," he said. "And they weren't open when I left Montreal two hours ago, either. I got these yesterday."

"You brought me old donuts?"

"You know damn well they'll be just as good now as they were last night," he said, holding the box out to me. "Now go on, take one. They're your favourite. I got an extra Nutella Banana."

I did take one, not because he told me to but because he was right. They *were* my favourite donuts, and the Nutella Banana ones were the donut world's equivalent of an orgasm. I took an immediate bite and tried not to moan.

The fact that he was right was unsettling. He didn't know my coffee order, yet somehow knew these were my favourite donuts? I couldn't think of how, or when, or *why* he knew that.

And it wasn't that I was complaining he didn't know my coffee order. That made sense. For all the times we'd fucked, JP and I had never woken up next to each other, and it wasn't like there were any other times we would've had coffee together.

We weren't dating. We weren't even—well. It was getting harder to deny that we weren't friends, but we weren't *friends*-friends. We were buddies. Fuck buddies.

Who didn't sleep with other people. But only because both of us were too busy with our respective lives to find other people to sleep with and it was easier to mutually masturbate long distance. We were long distance fuck buddies.

Who sometimes texted about other stuff and helped each other out when they needed father-approved dates for galas or fake girlfriends for client meetings. But he'd only agreed to be my date because I promised him anal and I only agreed to be his fake girlfriend because...

Well, I could probably talk him into anal again.

But none of that meant anything. JP knew as well as I did there wasn't anything more than that between us.

Things started because they were convenient. They continued because they were easy. And they'd end, like all things like this do, when we were tired of each other.

That was just how it was going to be.

"Even if you were packed like I'm assuming you aren't, we don't have time before we need to leave," JP said, breaking me out of my thoughts.

I blinked a few times, my eyes focusing on the shit-eating smirk on his face. "What?"

"If you stare any harder, your eyes might actually pop out," he said. "But I really do need to be there by nine-thirty so I have time to get ready before my meeting. I don't think I can fuck the remaining three brain cells out of your head before we have to be on the road, no matter how bad you want me right now."

I snorted and ate another bite. "Don't flatter yourself. I was just appreciating how delicious this donut is and your face happened to be in the way of my wistful gaze into the distance."

His smirk widened into a grin. "Good to know your 'This is damn delicious' face is the same as your 'Damn, I'd sure love JP's delicious cock right now.'"

"I don't believe for one second that I, or anyone else, has ever called your cock *delicious*," I said.

"In words, no," he said. "But the way you suck it makes it pretty clear you can't get enough."

"It does not," I grumbled, taking another bite of my donut.

"Sure it doesn't, babe."

I swallowed, but before I could tell him not to call me that for the eighty bazillionth time, JP took a step forward and notched his fingers under my chin, tilted my head up, and kissed me.

And I hated that I'd expected it.

I hated that I'd swallowed my bite of donut a little faster than I should've because I was waiting for it.

I *hated* that there was always a quip ready on his tongue for everything I said, and yet my response wasn't to tell him to fuck off but to crave that tongue against mine. I hated the way he challenged me and I hated—absolutely fucking *despised*—when he got the best of me.

Like when he pulled back and before my mind even caught up with his whirlwind, he grabbed my wrist and lifted it to his lips, then took a large bite of the half-eaten donut I forgot I was holding.

"You fucking bastard," I gasped.

He let go of my wrist so he could cover his mouth as he laughed through his bite of *my* donut. "If you didn't want me to help you eat it, you should've eaten it faster. You can eat the rest of them in the car. Now come on, how much packing do we need to do?"

"I am packed, asshole," I muttered, popping the rest of the donut into my mouth because there was *maybe* an eighth of it left. "I just need to get dressed and grab my bag from my room. And put a couple more things in it."

"See? This is why I had to leave at five."

"You're this fucking perky and you've been up since *five*?" I said, groaning. "You're a monster."

"I left at five," he said. "I've been up since four-thirty."

I gagged as I walked into my bedroom to change and he laughed.

"Trust me, if I didn't have to work late, I would've picked you up last night," he said. "Instead, I decided four hours of driving before my meeting was a good idea."

"I said I'd meet you there," I said, grabbing the outfit I'd set out the night before and shrugging my bathrobe off so I could pull on a thong and leggings.

"Except then I'd have questions about why my 'girlfriend' was driving there separately," he said. "So instead, I get to do this all over again tomorrow when I drop you off."

I wasn't entirely sure about that. I had a feeling JP would end up "unexpectedly" staying the night in Ottawa. "Seems like a lot of driving for one stupid meeting. It couldn't have been an email?"

He chuckled as I grabbed the tank top I'd set out, only then realizing I hadn't set out a bra. "Not really. I need this client to see how dedicated I am."

I opened my underwear drawer, but it was empty. And there were no bras sitting in my usual pile of clothes on the floor. "It's that important?"

"It's a big deal, yeah," he said. "Probably the biggest thing I've ever tried to do, actually."

I frowned, putting my hands on my hips and turning in place, trying to figure out how every bra I owned had vanished. "And your dad sent you on your own?"

"Well, no." There was a hesitant pause. "He's not fully aware of this."

"Oh," I said knowingly. "Trying to lock it in before you tell him so he's more impressed?"

"Sort of. And he'd be annoyed I brought you."

The laundry. That was where all my bras were. On the other side of my apartment. I started towards the door, then stopped and frowned.

"Annoyed you faked having a girlfriend? Or annoyed that you brought me specifically?"

There was a hesitant pause. "Uh... mostly the first one."

I picked at my thumbnail. "But some of the second one. Because your dad doesn't like me."

"I don't think he knows what to make of you a lot of the time. He's got specific expectations for how people should act and you deviate from that."

"So, in simple terms, he doesn't like me."

"He doesn't know you well."

"It's fine," I said. "I can be your shameful secret girlfriend."

"Trust me, if you were my actual girlfriend, it wouldn't matter. You're not someone to be ashamed of."

Maybe he hadn't meant them to, but those words hung between us, filtering through the air in my apartment. I pressed my fingernail into my thumb, not quite sure what the feeling in my stomach was, not quite sure if I liked the fact that JP didn't see me as someone he'd be ashamed of.

Or the fact that he seemed to have considered it before.

"Are you sewing the clothes yourself in there?" JP asked suddenly. "Or are you dressed yet?"

"Yeah," I lied, springing into motion and frantically pushing clothes to the side hoping a bra would appear.

"Awesome." His voice got closer. "Let me grab your bag."

Fuck.

Well, I guess it was a no-bra day.

I grabbed the tank top and yanked it on just before JP entered my room. While he grabbed my bag, I ran a brush through my hair. I followed him to the kitchen, then remembered I needed a coat or a sweater or something and darted back to my room to get my volleyball hoodie.

Then I was physically halfway through the door when I remembered I didn't grab my backpack, which I needed so I could study while JP was in his meeting because I had a Forensic Science and Law midterm the following week. And after I'd grabbed it and tried to leave again, I had the key in the lock before I remembered I hadn't put on deodorant.

"Fuck off," I muttered as JP laughed. "I haven't had coffee yet."

"Are you sure you have *everything* now?" he asked as we walked to the elevator.

"I have everything," I insisted. "And if I realize I don't after the coffee kicks in, I'll buy it there. It's not like we're going to get halfway to Mont Tremblant and I'm gonna make you turn around."

Which I regretted saying when the coffee kicked in halfway to Mont Tremblant and I realized I'd left the donuts from Trou de Beigne sitting on the counter, so JP had to convince me they'd still taste good when we got back the next day.

Chapter Twelve
If The Gondola's A-Rockin'...

I PLANNED TO SPEND the time JP was in his client meeting studying.

Of course, studying was always more effective when one was relaxed. So taking advantage of the weekend special for a deluxe pedicure at the hotel spa was in my best interests.

And obviously since I'd be reading and highlighting and making notes while I studied, I didn't want to be distracted by how bad my nails looked. So it only made sense to get a manicure done at the same time.

And since all I'd eaten that day was seven-eights of a Nutella banana donut and an extra-large coffee and a few of the finger sandwiches and cut up fruit they had in the spa lounge for people to help themselves to while they sipped sparkling cucumber water next to a bubbling fountain, I *had* to go out and get lunch after I was done.

I mean, I couldn't study on an empty stomach.

And since we'd gotten to Mont Tremblant at the ungodly hour of sometime before ten a.m., it would still be hours before our room was ready for check in. So it didn't make sense to go back to the hotel right away when I could take a nice early afternoon digestive walk through the shopping village.

Of course, just when I finished wandering past the shops and was almost out of excuses to not go back to the business center at the hotel and crack open my Forensic Science and Law textbook, I heard JP call my name.

Or, well... not exactly my name.

"Babe!"

I swivelled my head towards JP's voice. It only took a moment to catch sight of him slipping through a crowd of people before jogging towards me like an absolute dork in his dark blue polo beneath a suit jacket and slacks.

"Don't call me—" I started once he was close enough to hear me.

But then he kissed me.

And he...

I mean, he *kissed* me.

The only way to describe it was deep. Suspiciously deep. But it wasn't the kind of sloppy, spit-swapping PDA of people purposely showing off how publicly horny they were for each other, either.

It was deep in the way that it felt earnest.

In the way that the world muted itself when his lips met mine.

In the way that it felt unburdened and unashamed and celebratory, like the kind hockey players give their wives after they win the Stanley Cup, where you know it's gross and sweaty and yet completely perfect because nothing else matters right then.

It was the kind of deep, intense kiss that felt far too familiar, especially as JP's hand moved up to push my hair back before caressing my cheek.

The kind of deep that could drown me in an instant.

The breath I pulled in when JP moved away felt cold, like the air was frozen even though it was an arguably nice October day. I looked up at him, my lips still parted and my eyes wider than usual. JP's eyes, on the other hand, were sparkling as they crinkled in the corner.

"Pretend you like me for a sec," he murmured. "Just until they're around the corner."

Oh.

Oh.

Of course. His client... clients? Potential... or maybe he kissed me like that because he'd gotten them to... whatever. Fuck. I couldn't think. But they were there. He'd told me he was going for lunch with them after his meeting and they must have just finished, so of course they'd all left together and he...

He was trying to convince them we were together. That's why I was there. I was JP's fake girlfriend and I was helping him get these clients to impress his dad. And to do that I had to pretend I liked him enough that I'd date him willingly.

So I kissed him again.

Not quite as deep, and not quite as intense, and only slightly as sudden. It didn't stun JP the way he'd stunned me, but I heard a hitch of surprise as our lips met again. Which was stupid of him because how *else* did he expect someone to respond to being kissed like that? It would've looked ridiculous if I'd pulled back and pretended like that hadn't affected me at all. In my head I knew it was fake, but it wasn't like my pussy had a brain of its own.

If it did, I would've never ended up in this situation in the first place.

But all my pussy knew was that JP's lips were soft and warm and enticing and his body was close to mine. All it knew was kisses from him almost always led to more. It didn't know people were around or that it wasn't real or that we couldn't do anything about this because our room wasn't ready yet.

So of course, after we got into the Panoramic Gondola JP suggested taking up the mountain since it was a not-too-chilly October day and the leaves were practically glowing gold and red and orange beneath the warm sun, I turned to him and asked for dick.

"Here?" he asked, laughing in surprise as he shrugged his suit jacket off.

"Where else?" I asked. "You knew our room wasn't ready."

"You think we have enough time before we get to the top?" he asked, the corner of his mouth twitching. "And you're not worried about someone seeing us?"

I rolled my eyes. "This wouldn't even be the most public place we've fucked before. But fine."

"Fine?" he repeated.

"Fine. I won't play with your dick. How did your meeting go?"

He opened his mouth, then nodded reluctantly, like he'd just realized what he'd stopped me from doing. "It went great."

"When are you telling your dad you got hired?"

He stared at me. "What?"

"Oh my God, JP," I said, half-groaning. "Did you hit your head or something? The client. When are you telling your dad that you got this new big client for him?"

Something like relief flashed on his face, which seemed odd, but he laughed and shook his head. "Sorry. I'm still trying to figure out how I got talked out of fucking in a gondola."

"You talked yourself out of it."

"Apparently. I'm also trying to figure out why you think they hired the firm."

I started to answer but realized before I even got a word out that telling him he kissed me like he was celebrating sounded stupid. "You seemed to be excited about something."

"Of course I was. I've been looking forward to this gondola ride all week." He snickered as I rolled my eyes at him. "How'd your studying go?"

"It didn't. I went to the spa."

"The spa?"

"Yeah. They had a special on pedicures and I splurged and got a mani done, too." I waggled my fingers at him. "What do you think?"

He looked down at my nails, studying them for a moment before shrugging. "Meh."

"*Meh*?!"

"I mean, they look alright, I guess," he said.

I let out an offended scoff. "Asshole."

"I did bring some lube," he said.

"Perfect. It'll hurt less when I bend you over later," I said.

He lifted an eyebrow. "You're gonna bend *me* over?"

"Why would I let you bend me over when you can't even compliment my nails?"

He shook his head, still chuckling. "It's a joke, babe. I was gonna say I won't be able to tell how nice your nails look until I see your fingers wrapped around my dick later."

"You could've seen how they look a lot sooner than that," I said. "But someone said he didn't want me to play with his dick."

"Someone said *nothing* of the sort," he said. "Someone knows you well enough to know you'd get me right to the edge and then stop so I'd have to walk around the top of the mountain with a hard-on tucked into my waistband."

"You think I'd do that on purpose?" I asked, feigning hurt.

"Yes," he said. "Not that it matters much now."

I glanced at his lap and tried not to laugh, mainly because guys didn't like it when you looked at their dicks and laughed even if it was only because they'd gotten conveniently hard at the most inconvenient time. But it didn't seem to bother JP, who chuckled even as he reached down and unabashedly adjusted his bulge as I watched.

"Although," he continued. "Maybe if you held it for a sec."

"Held it?" I repeated.

"To show off your nails." He glanced at his lap, then back up at me. "Just for a bit."

I twisted my mouth to the side like I was actually deciding whether or not I wanted to do it, then slipped from my side of the gondola to his. His eyes followed my hands as I reached down, unbuckling his belt. As I undid the button, his cock twitched beneath the fabric, and as much as I wanted to put my hand over it so I could stroke him through his boxers and feel him throb, I didn't. I just worked the zipper down, feeling him twitch again, and then once more when I carefully reached into his boxers and pulled his cock out.

"Fuck," he murmured, then let out a soft hum of approval as I slowly and deliberately let each of my fingers fall into place.

"What do you think?" I asked when my hand was wrapped around him.

"Fucking gorgeous," he breathed.

I glanced up. JP was looking at me, breathing slowly and steadily through parted lips, and I gave him an unimpressed look. "You didn't even look, JP."

"Yeah, I did," he said, still staring at me.

I tightened my grip, squeezing him more firmly. "You're the one who said he couldn't tell how pretty my nails were until he saw them displayed against your cock. The least you could do is pretend to look at them."

His eyes lingered a second longer, then trailed down to his lap. The muscles in his throat flexed as he swallowed, though he didn't say anything until I let go of his cock and extended one finger, lightly and carefully dragging one nail up the underside of his cock.

"What happened to just holding it?" he murmured.

"Do you want me to stop?"

"Of course not. But I dunno if we're gonna have enough time."

"What if I promised I'd try my hardest to make you come?" I whispered, then wrapped my fist around him again. "Would you trust me?"

His breath hitched as I stroked him firmly. "I trust you, yeah."

And then we staggered to a halt.

For a moment, we were silent. JP's cock throbbed in my hand as we both looked out the windows, the gondola swaying gently above the trees. The cable car in front of us was slightly higher, but even if whoever was in there looked down, they wouldn't have been able to see the lower part of ours. And across from us, the cars heading back down the mountain were positioned before and after us instead of right in line.

It was like the gods or goddesses of fucking in gondolas had heard us.

"How long do you think we'll be stopped?" I asked.

"I don't know," he said. "A couple of minutes, maybe?"

"Long enough for me to get my pants back on before we get to the top if I took them off to fuck you?" I asked.

The corners of his eyes crinkled. "You're the one who has to decide if it's worth risking someone catching you with your pants down, babe."

"And you're the one who has to decide if it's worth risking walking around the top of a mountain with blue balls if you don't finish in time."

He glanced out the window again before lifting his hand to my head and pulling my face to his.

"Worth it," he said, then kissed me.

Neither of us were stupid. I mean, we were stupid—fucking idiots, literally and figuratively—but we were smart enough to choreograph the second-most efficient way to fuck in a gondola. The most efficient way would've been if I had on a skirt, but I hadn't woken up that morning and planned my outfit around gondola fucking.

So instead, we used our not-insignificant amount of practice from fucking in the backseat of JP's car to get in position.

JP's lips hadn't even left mine before I kicked my left shoe off, and it was only seconds after he stopped kissing me that I yanked my leggings down. While he opened his pants just enough to pull his cock out through the flap in his boxers, I slipped my left leg out of my pants and made sure the fabric wasn't twisted or inside out so I could shove my leg back in if I had to dress quickly.

Then JP grabbed his cock and I swung my leg over his lap to straddle him. He guided himself to my soaking entrance and nudged my thong to the side, I lowered my body, and our lips met again to muffle each other's sighs of relief as I sank onto him.

And that was where we ran into what was probably both the biggest difference between fucking in a gondola and fucking in a car, and also the source of our downfall.

Not *literally*, of course. But I didn't know how much a-rockin' a cable car could handle before it went a-knockin'... to the ground or something.

And yeah, in hindsight, it was almost certainly more than two stupid people having a quickie while it was stalled. But JP and I weren't gondola experts, nor were either of us functioning at full brain capacity. His dick was so hot, and so thick, and it was throbbing inside me so hard, and I couldn't focus on anything except how full I felt, and how wet I was, and how badly I needed to fucking *come*.

Well, that and the thought that if I bounced on his dick the way I wanted to, we might fall.

"Just grind, babe," JP whispered instead of laughing at me like I thought he would when I admitted what I was thinking. He had one of my ass cheeks in each hand and squeezed, his fingertips digging in as he started to guide my body back and forth. "All you gotta do is grind on it."

"That's good and all," I said, trying not to whimper. "But seeing as I've made you come more times than I can count, I'm pretty sure that won't get you there."

"Maybe," he murmured. "Maybe not. Maybe you're gonna have to get on your knees and finish the job. But right *now*, you're gonna give me what I want. And what I want is the girl with the hottest, wettest, neediest little hole I've ever fucked to use my cock to get off."

"I—*fuck*." Any train of thought I had disappeared as JP gently spread my ass wider so he could press his finger against my asshole. As soon as he worked the tip of his finger inside me, he let go of my other ass cheek and tugged my tank top down, stretching it until he could lower his head and take one of my nipples into his mouth.

Because of course I still wasn't wearing a bra. And of course JP figured that out. And of course the second he sank his teeth into my nipple my whole body shuddered and I couldn't stop my hips from pulsing forward once, and then again, and then giving in and letting my body move into him like he'd told me, swaying back and forth so eagerly and so smoothly that it was less like I was moving and more like the world was moving around me and—

"Oh shit," I said.

JP lifted his head. "What?"

"We started moving."

He looked out the window and swore. "Started a *while* ago."

"What?"

He shoved the hand that wasn't currently fingering my ass between us.

"Come," he demanded.

"JP, I—"

"*Come*." He pressed his thumb to my clit and rubbed, pushing his other finger deeper into my ass. "Or do you want to get to the top and have all the people waiting to go back down watch you fuck yourself on my cock because you couldn't seal the deal in time? Because I'm not letting you off my lap until you come for me, babe."

"And if they catch us?" I gasped, even as my pussy suddenly developed a brain cell and screamed that we were so close and not to *dare* stop. "You're the one with a client to impress."

"If they catch us, then lucky—"

He thrust up, his cock hitting the perfect spot inside of me.

"—fucking—"

Again, he pushed up, and the flickering sparks began to catch.

"—me," he finished, and did it again. "Lucky me, getting to show off this pretty girl so desperate for my cock that she couldn't stop herself from riding me all the way to the top of the world."

And like, that last bit was corny as shit, but I came.

I came so fucking hard.

JP groaned as I did, his arm tightening around me and his thumb still working my clit as my hips bucked. I clung to him, lost in the sensation of falling, which is normally not a good feeling to have when you're in a small, enclosed room dangling from a cable.

But when JP was the cause of that sensation, it was perfect.

Fucking perfect.

The second my orgasm faded enough to let my mind take over again, I squirmed out of JP's grip. While I pushed my foot back into my leggings and slammed my shoe on my foot, he grabbed his dick and started stroking because every second before we reached the top of the mountain mattered. As soon as I was dressed, I made to get on my knees in front of him, but JP shook his head.

"Hand," he said.

I didn't have time to question him. My best guess was that he thought the extra few seconds it would take for me to get off my knees and look presentable when we reached the top wouldn't make up for how much better my mouth would feel on his cock. But it didn't matter. JP told me what he wanted, so I moved in beside him and replaced his large hand with my smaller one, letting the juices I'd left on his cock help my palm glide along his shaft. He groaned again, eyes closing as he put his arm around my shoulder.

"Harder," he murmured. "It feels so good, babe."

"Like this?" I asked.

He inhaled sharply and nodded, his eyes fluttering open, a cloud of need giving them a heavy, hazy look. I held that gaze for a moment before leaning in and kissing him. Humming pleased approval, he kissed me back eagerly, his breath puffing against my skin as he reached over and grabbed my breast through my shirt to play with my hardened nipple while I jacked him off.

And he was close.

He was so close.

Which is why I was almost devastated on his behalf when he let go of my breast and put his hand over mine, stilling my movements.

"But—" I started.

"We're almost there," he said, soft reluctance in his voice.

Which we were. We were close enough to the top that I didn't even have time to protest again. JP put his cock away and I patted my hair down and made sure my tits weren't popping out of my tank top. When the doors opened to let us off the gondola, both of us looked presentable, though I was pretty sure my face was still a little flushed and JP strategically carried his suit jacket folded over his forearm, somehow still managing to look casual and unsuspecting even though he was holding it in front of him.

"Told you so," he murmured as we strolled away from the crowd near the gondola.

"Excuse me?" I said, raising my eyebrow as I matched his soft tone.

"I told you I'd end up walking around the top of a mountain with a hard-on instead of getting to come."

"Need I remind you who insisted I grind on your cock instead of fucking you properly?" I said. "Besides, you said the risk was worth it."

He glanced at me, much in the same way he'd looked at my nails when I first showed them to him, and tilted his head to the side. "Meh."

And of course I knew he was joking.

Of course JP didn't think I was "meh." We're talking about a guy who, despite being as much of a slut as I was, had busted early on more than one occasion and said it was because I fucked him so good. A guy who'd put his tongue in my ass. A guy who'd bluntly stated, more than once, that he was attracted to me. I knew damn well he was doing it to get a rise out of me. That he liked my so-called "snooty" look I gave him when he got on my nerves. That he wanted me to look at him, insulted, so he could laugh and revel in the fact that he'd gotten on my nerves.

So of course, I mustered up the sweetest smile that I could and looked up at him.

"Well," I said. "If I'm so 'meh,' I guess you don't need me to take care of that on the way back down."

"Oh, you won't be," he said. "I'm holding off until I get you into the hotel room so I can take my time getting exactly what I need out of you."

But it wasn't long before he regretted that decision.

"I really am so incredibly sorry," the hotel clerk—Émeric, who hailed from Strasbourg, France according to the badge on his chest—said in apologetic French as we tried to check in a couple of hours later. "It seems there was a, ah… an influencer who requested a room last minute as they are doing an episode about our hotel, but the night shift did not realize it was already booked."

"Let me guess," I said. "You have no more rooms with two beds and the only thing left is like, the honeymoon suite."

Émeric frowned. "Ah, no. Your husband—"

"Oh, we're not together," I said without thinking.

"In marriage," JP added quickly. "As my girlfriend never fails to remind me. Right, *ma nounoune*?"

Oh. Right.

"Yeah," I said, probably unconvincingly. "Get on that, *mon... chenille*."

JP winked at Émeric. "She calls me that because she's hoping I'll have a glow-up one of these days and become *son papillion*."

"More like a moth," I muttered.

"Right," Émeric said, looking at me like I was crazy. "Well, ah, your boyfriend did book a room with only one bed, but there are no rooms."

We stared at him for a beat.

"No rooms," JP repeated.

"*Oui*," Émeric said.

"At all?" I asked.

"No rooms at all," he repeated. "Not here, and not at any of our sister hotels, and according to my supervisor, not at any of the other hotels either." He shrugged unhelpfully, though he looked like he really did feel bad. "Of course, you will receive a full refund, plus my supervisor has offered to give you enough loyalty points for a week of free stays in the future. And we can provide you with a food voucher for this evening, if that will help."

"Not really," JP said. "We're going to the dinner reception for the business retreat you're hosting here right now."

"I see." Émeric grimaced, typing quickly on his computer. "Ah, well, I can refund the cost of your girlfriend's spa visit from earlier, if you would like?"

"Actually," I said. "Do you have free passes for the gondola?"

I'm sure Émeric thought I was crazy. But he didn't get to see the look on JP's face when we got back on the gondola.

He didn't get to watch the easygoing mask JP almost always wore fall away to desperation.

He didn't get to hear the slight crack in JP's voice as he set his suit jacket to the side, his cock tenting his pants, and whispered "Please."

Just that.

Just "*Please.*"

And Émeric didn't get the semi-smug sensation of indulgent satisfaction that I did after making JP flood my mouth and throat with rope after rope of cum before we were even halfway back up the mountain.

Chapter Thirteen
Spit or Swallow

"—SO MANY OF THEM don't understand how impressive it is that this model outperformed the traditional benchmarks *and* helped the client achieve a sixteen percent higher return on their portfolio."

"Sixteen whole percents," I said flatly. "Wow."

"Exactly. And it's a rapidly evolving sector. So those benchmarks are now part of a proprietary—"

The man talking at me gave off the air of someone who bought condoms that were too big because he refused to accept anything about him was average. Yet the way he talked made him so sound generic and boring that I was afraid to blink, lest I fall asleep while he blabbed in my general direction. Instead, I focused my dry eyes on the glass of what apparently passed for wine at this event, trying to decide if it tasted the way it did because it was poisoned, or if it was just that bad of a wine.

JP had been vague on the details of whatever retreat or conference or convention this was, probably because it was for businessmen or finance guys or investors or other generic names for careers that were based on manipulating money. Bringing it in, spending it to make it, liquidating and illiquidating it in an attempt to avoid paying their share of the tax bill. Plus, of course, advising and protecting people in those careers so they didn't end wherever it is rich people go when they commit crimes instead of prison like everyone else.

Not that I thought JP was specifically that type of lawyer. All I really knew about JP's job was that he read a lot of contracts and didn't like it all that much.

But JP hadn't bothered pointing out who the fuck I was supposed to be impressing, even though he'd already introduced me to plenty of people. And that meant that when he excused himself to the bathroom, all I could do was sit there and imagine ramming whatever a benchmark was up Mr. Sixteen Percent's ass as he attempted to shoot his shot.

Though, to JP's credit, there was a good chance I wouldn't have remembered who I was supposed to be impressing, even if he had pointed him out. If someone told me I had to pick one of the business bros here from the sea of them, they'd all fucking drown.

"—multi-billion-dollar merger—and yeah, I said *billion* with a B," Mr. Sixteen Percent was saying. "So the analysis of the financial synergies and risks meant we could successful enhance the portfolio to—"

"Ah, *ma chérie!*" a loud voice interrupted, and suddenly there was a hand on my shoulder. "*Est-ce que tu apprécies la fête?*"

The man attached to the hand appeared to be in his late fifties. He was heavy-set and had short, cropped hair that was significantly thinner on the crown of his head, though it was still dark brown. He was otherwise clean-shaven and he wore an unassuming brown suit that, on closer inspection, was of surprisingly high quality. Cufflinks decorated the sleeves of the white shirt he wore underneath and there was a redness to the olive-toned skin on his nose. In one hand, he held a half-empty glass of what I assumed was the same terrible wine I was drinking.

"I'm enjoying it so far," I replied.

The man smiled cheerfully, switching to flawless but accented English as he removed his hand from my shoulder and leaned on the cocktail table we stood at. "Excellent. You know, I say the most important thing at these events is that everyone enjoy themselves. Isn't that right, Rob?"

"It is," Mr. Sixteen Percent said quickly. "Of course."

"You must pardon me for interrupting," the man said. "I did need to speak with this lovely young woman for a few minutes."

Mr. Sixteen Percent nodded. "Pleasure to meet you... uh... I didn't get your name, darling."

"No, you didn't," I said.

He waited just long enough for it to be uncomfortable, then chuckled awkwardly and excused himself. The older man smiled again.

"*Je suis désolé*," he said. "But you did not seem to enjoy that conversation. And I am good with faces, you know, but I am sure I haven't seen you here before."

I wasn't quite sure if I could trust this man or if he and Mr. Sixteen Percent had some kind of wingman arrangement where they swooped in to "save" someone from an awkward conversation with the other, but I figured JP had to be coming back soon either way. "It's my first time."

"Newcomers are always welcome," he said kindly. "Have you been called to the bar yet?"

"No," I said. "The line's been too long so I've been drinking the wine on the tables."

The man stared at me, then let out a bright laugh. "Clever. And tell me, what do you think of it?"

"It's shit," I said.

"Is it?" His eyebrows knitted together. "May I—"

"My boyfriend's coming back with something for me in a minute," I said before he could offer to buy me a drink.

"That is a relief to hear," he said. "But as I was saying, may I have a sip of your glass to see what you mean?"

Great, I thought. He was going to lift my wine glass up and go through the whole wine-tasting show, sniffing it and swirling it and taking a sip before declaring that I simply did not know good wine, and then I was going to have to tell him my dad had subjected me to more than one lesson with connoisseurs he hired so I wouldn't embarrass him at events like these and could unequivocally state that this wine was from the bottom of the bargain bin at a liquor store, and that the bin was probably next to a south-facing window that received direct sunlight for most of the day because it clearly hadn't been stored in a proper wine cellar.

But I still hadn't figured out if the wine was poisoned, so at least there was that.

"Go for it," I said, holding out my glass.

Sure enough, the man took my glass and eyed it carefully, first from the top down and then by lifting it to let it catch the light. He swirled it, then eyed it from the side again, then took a gentle whiff before bringing the glass to his lips and sipping it.

Then his face contorted almost painfully and he spat the wine directly back into my glass.

"*Crisse d'ostie de tabarnak*," he swore, sticking his tongue out like that would get the taste out of his mouth. "My God, that is horrendous. How—why—" He let out an annoyed noise, then turned and lifted a hand in the air. "Sophie!"

A woman wearing a slinky black dress and a headset with a clipboard clutched in her hands rushed up to him. "*Oui, Monsieur La Cloche?*"

"*D'où vient ce vin?*" the man demanded. "*C'est pas le vin que j'ai demandé pour les tables.*"

"Ah..." Sophie's lips tightened into a worried pucker. "*Ce vin est sur les tables des dirigeants. Monsieur Richard a insisté pour que nous changions le vin sur les tables d'hôtes.*"

"Of course." The man scoffed loudly. "A cheapskate to everyone but himself. Sophie, have bottles of the original wine sent to every single table. Please give my wife the bill. And for Monsieur Richard, since he is not covering that bill, you may serve him the swill he purchased for the rest of the evening." He handed her the glass. "Have someone bring this young lady a new glass immediately. Her beverages are to be on my tab for the rest of the night."

And sure, he could've been trying to impress some random blonde he'd never met. I might not look as polished as I usually did at these types of events since JP told me it was the closing reception of a personal development conference for legal and business professionals. So I'd picked a simple black dress that my dad had surprisingly approved of for a casual luncheon, despite the inclusion of two stripes of mesh around my ribcage and the V-cut neckline.

That approval had occurred when I was wearing a bra, though, and this dress was low cut enough to make it *very* clear that I'd forgotten to pack one.

But not only had the man mentioned his wife, when Sophie nodded before scurrying away and he turned back to me, there was clear and genuine annoyance on his face.

"My apologies," he said. "There are many things I am easygoing about, but good wine is not one of them. You know, I am horrified that my colleague thought it acceptable to replace the table wine like that."

"It's fine," I said, my tone guarded only because I wasn't sure what to make of him. "It wasn't bad enough to stop me from drinking it."

"The wine they are bringing you is much better," he promised. "My father would rise from his grave and cut out my tongue for saying it, but while the French make an excellent wine, you know, nothing they have ever created compares to the grapes from Piedmont."

"Oh!" I said, both surprised and not that I knew what he meant. "Is it a Barolo or a Barbaresco?"

The man's eyes went wide with excitement and he pressed a hand to his chest. "My dear. You know, there is nothing more trustworthy in this world than a young woman who knows her wine. You must tell me what firm you're with so I can poach you immediately."

"What?" I said.

"I joke, of course," he said, chuckling. "Unless you are actually looking to move. I have just hired one new associate but I can certainly make room in our offices for another, the other partners' opinions on the matter be damned."

"I have no idea what you're talking about," I said.

The man frowned. "You are not one of the lawyers here for the personal development seminars?"

"I'm not a lawyer," I said. "I'm here with my boyfriend."

"That is positively devastating," he said.

"That I have a boyfriend?" I asked.

He chuckled. "For the younger men of the world, certainly, but I meant that I cannot hire you. Who is this lucky boyfriend of yours?"

"That would be me."

I was too cynical not to wonder if JP had been standing by, waiting for the perfect moment to stride up to the cocktail table and slip his arm around my waist. I think anyone would've thought the same thing, and I had half a mind to be pissed off that he'd sacrificed checking on me and making sure I was okay for movie-level timing. Like yeah, I was fine, but from the outside, JP wouldn't have known that.

But when the other man laughed warmly and stepped out from the table with his hand extended, if that was the case, he would've actually known I was fine.

"Jean-Paul!" the man said. "I should have known you would be the one with this delightful young lady."

For half a heartbeat, my stomach dropped with the worry that this was JP's prospective client and I'd potentially messed things up for him. But JP's client wouldn't be another lawyer, so my stomach returned to its usual place as JP shook the man's hand with nonchalant confidence.

"The prettiest girl in the room? Of course." JP looked at me, his eyes crinkled with a smile. "He hasn't been giving you a hard time, has he, babe?"

"The opposite," I said. "He saved me from a terrible glass of wine."

"No one should be subjected to that garbage," the man said. "My apologies again. Your new glass will be here shortly."

JP chuckled. "Nell, this is Louie LaCloche. He founded one of the top law firms in Quebec. Louie, this is my girlfriend, Nellie Belanger."

"Ms. Belanger, it is a pleasure," Louie said, extending his hand to shake mine. "So you say you are not a lawyer. What is it you do for a living, my dear?"

"I'm still a student," I said. "But I'm taking Forensic Science."

"That must be fascinating," Louie said. "Is that the program at Carleton?"

"Ottawa Tech," I said.

"Ah, of course." Louie tapped the side of his nose. "Well, forgive my bias, as of course my profession makes me think anyone suited to it should be an attorney. But you know, the commonality between law and forensic science is the pursuit of justice, and that is entirely noble regardless of the path one takes."

"You don't think I should give up on the science aspect and become a lawyer because I might be good at it?" I asked.

"The day I deem myself more qualified to decide if someone is better suited for something than they themselves are is the day I should retire," Louie said. "Passion plays a much larger part in our careers than any of us expect, as Jean-Paul knows."

I almost told him I loved him.

The words wanted to burst from my mouth. Luckily, I held in both that and the semi-concerning request for him to please be my new dad but not as a sex thing, as a legitimate parental figure. "Wow."

Louie tilted his head to the side. "Wow?"

"You're the least lawyerly lawyer I've ever met."

He let out another one of his bright laughs. "You know, I'll take that as a compliment."

"Coming from her, it's the highest possible," JP said, grinning. "Louie could write a manifesto about how law professionals need to focus more on genuine connections. Both as a service type of thing and as a reminder of why people choose law careers. It's a little out there compared to other firms, but it makes a difference."

He said it in a matter-of-fact way, but there was something beneath that paired with the way he was determinedly not looking at Louie that was almost sad. Almost envious, like that was the kind of lawyer he wanted to be. I rubbed my finger over the edge of my thumbnail, a quiet sense of sympathy making my chest ache. JP's dad didn't see things the same way that Louie LaCloche seemed to. And deep down, I knew JP wasn't thrilled about where his career had taken him.

But there wasn't a hell of a lot I could do or say about that. I'd only really said anything to him once, at the Diamond Gala, when he admitted he felt like he wasn't making a difference. And yeah, maybe the response of "Go make a difference, then" wasn't the most helpful thing I could've said, but I hadn't meant it to hurt the way it clearly had when he responded with a lash of sarcasm.

So I didn't say anything. I just smiled and stupidly put my hand over top of JP's where it was resting on the cocktail table. A moment later, he flipped his hand over, interlocking our fingers and pressing his palm to mine in a way that felt just a little too good.

"Focusing on genuine connection seems very worthwhile for lawyers," I said. "Is that what this conference is for, then?"

Louie's cheeks rounded as his smile widened. "That it is. And you know, I think they do a damn good job of it. Though I may be biased as I'm involved in organizing it and teach several of the sessions. But I have already begun thinking of some new things to try out for next year, you know. There is one I'm particularly excited about, but it was too late to implement by the time I'd fully developed it." He shook his head sadly. "Perhaps if I find some volunteers, we could do an impromptu demonstration for everyone tonight! It is an *exceptionally* entertaining exercise."

I had a hard time believing any exercise at a personal development seminar could be described as entertaining, but JP was still holding my hand, so I guess anything was possible. "What kind of exercise is it?"

The moment he told me, I looked at JP, who let a slow, reluctantly affectionate smile spread on his lips. "Alright. Let's go for it, babe."

"Don't call me babe," I said without thinking.

"Sure thing, babe," he said.

I shot half a glare at JP, but Louie clapped his hands together in glee. "You know, the two of you *are* the perfect couple for this."

And despite my instinctive objection to anyone thinking JP and I were a perfect couple, ten minutes later, we were sitting across from each other on the stage, each of us holding a bottle of water.

"—but Nellie and JP have been kind enough to assist me with giving you a preview of an exercise we will do at our next conference," Louie said into the microphone to the crowd of half-drunk and intrigued-looking business bros and their wives or girlfriends. "This is an exercise I developed after discovering it on a podcast my sixteen-year-old was listening to—and yes, she got sent to her room when I began listening and realized how vulgar it was—called *Why Am I Like This*."

There was a hum of recognition and a few laughs from the other attendees.

"For those who do not know, the original game is called Spit or Swallow"—there was another round of laughter, louder this time—"and the point of the game is to say something to make the other person spit out their water, or swallow it so they can take their turn. And you know, you're probably thinking 'Louie, how does this relate to creating a genuine connection with my colleagues and clients?' Which is fair. Usually, you will not want to spit water on your clients."

It was a few more minutes of laughter interspersed with an explanation, but once Louie finished describing the somewhat questionable reasons he had for using this as an exercise—pinpointing information about someone you're speaking to, creating connections over laughter, determining the line between humour and hurt, and a few other things that I'm sure he hoped covered the fact that he obviously just found the idea of a bunch of business types trying not spit water at each other hilarious—he turned to me and JP.

"Now, you know, of course we want this to be all for fun," he said. "So you do not want to be *too* mean with your remarks."

"We'll be okay," I said. "My mother always said never to let a man who can't grow a beard get to me, so he has nothing to worry about."

"She's right," JP said. "I've always told Nellie I'm jealous of her mustache."

"Well, I suppose that shows we have started the game!" Louie said over the laughter from the crowd. "The first person to spit out their water loses, and the other person will win a bottle of the lovely Barbaresco we had on the table this evening. You may begin, Nellie!"

And like, I'd already decided I was going all in on things. I didn't need a game to insult JP; I'd do it whenever I had the opportunity.

But now that there was a prize on the table, I'd do *whatever* I could to beat him.

I waited until JP had taken his first mouthful of water, then looked at him with the closest thing I could manage to a swoony expression.

"JP, I know you don't know this," I started in a solemn voice just breathy enough to sound romantic. "But I can't look at you without feeling like I'm looking at the sun."

JP blinked, his eyes darting to the side in unsettled confusion. I couldn't blame him. I was pretty sure I'd never looked at him with that kind of earnest expression or spoken to him with that amount of dreaminess in my tone. Frankly, that should have been the tip-off for him, but it wasn't my fault he was too slow to realize I was faking it.

"You hurt my eyes and make me want to cry," I finished.

The roar of laughter was much, much louder than I'd expected. JP hadn't seemed to expect it either because he got really, really close to spitting, but by twisting his mouth and stifling a cough, he kept it in.

"Babe, I want you to know I'll never forget the day we met," he said when it was his turn, matching my solemn sincerity. "But I swear I'll keep trying."

I almost let some of the water dribble out of my mouth as the audience laughed again, but kept it in. After all, I had a *lot* of practice not laughing at anything JP said.

And that was the problem.

Louie had no reason to know it, but JP and I were far too experienced at insulting each other for this game. I think he expected us to trade a few lines back and forth before one of us cracked, but even as the people in the room laughed and our jabs got a little more risqué than was probably appropriate for a work event, both of us kept a straight face.

"You seem like the kind of person who still has their Little League trophies displayed in their bedroom," I said at one point.

"They're part of the decor," JP said when he swallowed his mouthful of water.

"You don't even live with your parents anymore."

"I don't care what anyone says," JP said after I'd taken my next sip. "You can barely even tell you have daddy issues."

I swallowed my water. "It's because the mommy issues cancel them out."

JP lifted his water bottle to his lips. "That's not how that works."

I waited half a moment for him to take a sip before responding. "Some people stop speaking when they don't know what they're talking about, but you'd never let a little thing like that stop you."

"It doesn't matter to me what my friends say," JP said when that didn't get him. "You are almost as pretty as all their girlfriends."

Even Louie let out a low *ooo* that underscored the chuckles in the audience. "Jean-Paul, the point of the game is not to get her to break up with you!"

That part nearly got me to laugh, but I swallowed my water as JP took a swig from his bottle. "Oh, I won't. He's by far got the biggest—"

And I don't know *who* was looking out for me right then—maybe the god or goddess of gondola-fucking called in a favour from the god or goddess of trying to impress your fake boyfriend's potential client, who was obviously working overtime because oh my God, why had we agreed to play this in the first place?—but I cut myself off before I said something *hugely* inappropriate at a work event.

And also inaccurate. While I was bisexual and therefore happy with any and all genitals as long as they were attached to a decent human being, JP was proof that dick size didn't matter. Not because he was small—he was maybe a hair above average—but because not once had the size of his cock affected how good sex with him was.

But I'd also never fucked any of JP's friends, so I couldn't say for certain if he was the biggest.

"Uh," I said. "I mean, he... is... the best kisser. Of all his friends."

It fooled no one; everyone knew what I'd been about to say and they *lost* it. Even Louie had to put the microphone down because he was laughing so hard. JP's face was turning red and his shoulders were shaking as he stifled his laughter, and for a few seconds I was certain he was about to spit his water out.

But he didn't. He held it in, and then he swallowed, and took a steadying breath as Louie wiped a finger under his eye.

"My God," he chuckled. "If that did not get him, I don't know what will. We may be here all night, folks!"

But we weren't.

Because JP, bastard that he was, figured out how to get the best of me.

"Nellie," he said after I'd taken a mouthful of water before everyone had even caught their breaths. His voice was deep and solemn and his bright blue eyes were laser-focused on mine. "I love you."

And water went *everywhere*.

Chapter Fourteen
Sniff, Sip, Shoot

"The bartender said this is the one they're putting on the tables," JP said, putting a glass of wine in front of me.

I swirled the glass twice and lifted it to my nose before taking a small sip.

And oh, *God*. I almost wanted to cry.

Not because it was tear-inducingly good. And surprisingly, not because I had the realization that I'd somehow become enough of a wine snob to recognize how fucking good it was. Like, I wasn't even twenty-two. I was supposed to be sticking straws into a four-liter box of wine and drinking it like a juice box, not appreciating the burst of tannins and hint of citrus.

No, I wanted to cry because I knew what I was about to do.

"He said it's a Barbaresco with rich notes of red fruits and a complex layering of aromas," JP continued. "And a lingering finish with—"

He cut himself off as I knocked back the rest of the wine in a single gulp and set the glass on the cocktail table we were standing at.

"I may be a bit rusty, but I don't think I've ever been to a wine tasting where they suggested *shooting* a glass of wine," he said after a moment.

"Obviously you're going to the wrong wine tastings," I said. "It's all the rage these days. Sniff, sip, shoot. Really brings out the... you know." I gestured vaguely. "Oakiness."

The corners of his eyes crinkled with laughter. "Pretty sure it's unoaked."

"Pretty sure you're full of shit. Barbaresco wines are required to be oaked by the DOCG. For nine months minimum."

"That's oddly specific."

"The Italian wine connoisseur my dad hired to make me sound smart about this shit made a comment about nine months being the magic number to develop human brains and excellent wine. I'm never going to forget that."

JP tilted his head in concession. "You got me. Want me to ask for another? It's still on Louie's tab."

I did want him to get me another one. I wanted another, and another, and enough to make me throw up on the side of the road on the way back to Ottawa in the hopes that the echo of JP's voice saying the L word would spew out with it.

Because yes, he had been joking.

Yes, it had made me—and everyone else in the room—laugh.

Yes, I was slightly annoyed that he won the bottle of wine even though he said I could keep it because he didn't drink wine that often.

But somewhere deep down, part of me had latched onto the words, even though we both knew they weren't real.

And I couldn't say why.

But instead of telling JP that yes, he should go get me another, and by another I meant he should grab the bottle and a straw if they had any tall enough, I shook my head.

"I need to be sober enough to make your sorry ass look good for once in your life," I said.

He frowned. "What?"

I shot him an unimpressed look. "The client."

"The client?" he repeated.

"Yes, the client," I said. "The client you want to impress? That client? You know, the whole reason I'm here?"

An amused dimple appeared on his cheek. "And here I thought you were here for my boyish charm and massive co—"

"Trust me, if your dick was as massive as your ego, I wouldn't have any complaints," I interrupted.

Instead of letting my jab bruise said ego, JP grinned and put an arm around my shoulder, pulling me and using the guise of pressing a kiss to the side of my head to whisper in my ear.

"Pretty sure you don't have any complaints about my dick," he murmured. "Considering you just told an entire room full of people about it."

"I implied to a room full of people that you had the biggest dick of all your friends, and considering I don't know any of your friends, that's saying literally nothing."

"Yeah, but you've done such a good job convincing everyone we're a couple that they'll naturally assume you know all my friends, so…" He chuckled as I elbowed him away from me. "And anyway, I thought you forgot about the client thing."

"Why would I forget the literal reason for me being here?"

"I mean, you did get up on a stage to play a game where we were assholes to each other and then implied I have a huge dick."

Oh.

Right.

My face burned and I glared. Not at him, because it felt like the ropes of guilt and embarrassment knotting together in my stomach had wrapped around my neck so I couldn't turn my eyes towards him, but I glared all the same.

I was such an idiot sometimes.

I hadn't even thought of that. Now it was way, way, *way* too late. This whole thing had started because JP's client was apparently somewhat traditional and focused on appearances. Which meant that client was probably similar to the type of person my dad was, and that type of person would *not* find what we did funny in any way.

I was supposed to make JP look good. And instead, I'd told everyone he had a big dick and Little League trophies decorating his bedroom.

Maybe that was why he hadn't bothered saying anything. I'd probably already cost him the client.

I fucked it up.

And God, it felt bad enough when I fucked things up for my dad. I didn't even like him. To fuck things up for JP, who I... you know. Tolerated. More than tolerated, even.

Fuck.

Fuck.

"Stop," JP said.

"Stop what?" I asked.

"Blaming yourself."

I frowned, then glanced at him. He was studying me, the smirking asshole gone and replaced by someone with a soft smile on his lips. "What do you mean?"

"Come on, Nell." He tilted his head, playfully patronizing. "Even if there was something for you to feel bad about, I got right up there with you. I had a ton of opportunities to say we shouldn't do that. I said stuff that was just as—no." He shook a finger at me. "I said stuff that was worse than you did, considering I won. You don't think I either figured it was worth it or that maybe the client left already?"

I dug my fingernail into the side of my thumb. "How did you—"

"It doesn't take a genius to see where your mind went."

"Clearly, since you figured it out."

"There she is." He grinned. "Sometimes I'm not as stupid as you look."

"That's a stretch. You're pretty—hey!" He cackled as I figured out what he said and smacked his arm lightly. "You're a bastard."

"So I've heard."

I shook my head. "I can't believe you made me skip a day of classes, dragged me out here, and then didn't even introduce me to your client."

"Oh, I did."

I looked up at him. "What?"

The corner of JP's mouth twitched. "I introduced you earlier."

All I could do was stare at him for a moment. "I must look pretty damn stupid, because you're an idiot."

He burst out laughing. "The personal development exercise is over, babe."

"You introduced me to your client and didn't even warn me who they were?!" I tried to keep my voice down, but the urge to blow up was making my hands shake. "What if I'd said something wrong?"

"So?" he asked.

"So?!" I nearly threw my hands up in the air. "You brought me here to make you look good, JP. How am I supposed to do that when I don't even know who I'm supposed to impress?"

"Do you think people aren't impressed by you unless you fake it?" he asked.

I opened my mouth to respond. Normally, even if I didn't think I had a response figured out, something came out.

But not this time.

I didn't go to shit like this for me. I was there to be the perfect daughter. The perfect girlfriend. The perfect person to make someone else look good. I was supposed to laugh at people's jokes and talk about appropriate things and sip my wine politely.

I wasn't supposed to sniff, sip, shoot.

But I had. And JP had just played along.

"Babe," he said, his voice soft. "It doesn't matter who you were here to meet. I brought you because I needed a fake *girlfriend*. Not a *fake* girlfriend."

"But—"

"But nothing. I wouldn't have asked you to do this if I wanted some Stepford-esque robot giving canned responses." His eyes flicked down for a moment. "You're more impressive as yourself."

My throat felt dry and I silently wished I hadn't shot all my wine. "Okay."

"You don't believe me," he said.

"What if I let you down?" I asked.

"Then I'd get down there with you." He shrugged. "You can't let someone down if you're on the same level."

And he...

He couldn't say that.

He couldn't *say* that.

That wasn't what this was. It wasn't who I should be to him. I shouldn't have been the person standing there, locked under his gaze, my heart thumping in the base of my throat and sending something coursing through me.

Something warm, so warm it made my palms sweat.

Something heavy, so heavy it weighted my feet to the floor.

Something terrifying.

"Nell—" JP started.

"Don't," I whispered.

He blinked. "What?"

"Don't... you... do that." I blinked too, like my eyelids were knives that could shear through the look he'd been giving me. "Don't do that."

"Do what?"

My chin trembled.

I wasn't ready.

"This," I said.

I wasn't sure that either of us knew what "this" was. But JP looked at me for a moment longer, then nodded. Lifting his hand to my cheek, he dipped his head and pressed his lips to mine. His kiss was so warm, so scorching hot, that whatever warm thing had been coursing through me was overtaken, overshadowed, overflowing into that place deep in my core until I was leaning into that kiss like I was addicted to fire.

"We should probably leave," JP said, pulling back and clearing his throat. "I've still got a long drive home."

"Aren't you staying with me?" I asked.

He flicked an eyebrow up. "Am I invited?"

And I...

I probably shouldn't have shot that wine.

"Yes."

Chapter Fifteen
Labelless

If we had a room at the hotel, things might have gone differently.

If we had a room, we might have talked. Maybe with words and maybe with actions. I might have let JP kiss me and hold me and break me down bit by bit until all those things I'd never admit to spilled out of the cracks. I might have said things I did and didn't mean, things I wanted that were at odds with what I needed, things that would've hurt me to reveal and hurt him to have taken away.

Because if we had a room, if we'd given in to *this* and *that* because JP Marchand had the audacity to say something that made me feel like I was less of a fuck-up, I might have believed him.

And in the morning, I would have had to pick up all the pieces, shoving them back through the cracks as best I could and praying he'd forget they'd ever been revealed at all.

If we had a room at that godforsaken hotel in Mont Tremblant, it wouldn't have been just fucking, and it would have ruined everything.

But we didn't. We had JP's car, and two hours of driving down a dark highway, and two people who had no idea how to address what was going on. So we defaulted to our fall back.

Which was also fucking.

Because of course it was. Things with JP suddenly felt too intense? Better fuck it out. And when we *couldn't* fuck it out because despite all my adventurousness, distracting a driver with road head on the surprisingly quiet highway as we drove back to Ottawa was *not* my idea of a good time?

Well, then we just spent the entire drive doing our *other* fall back.

Which was one-upping each other.

About fucking.

"So I'm telling them about this girl, right?" JP said as we motored down the highway. "And yes, in hindsight, I sounded like a complete douchebag, but in fairness, it's because I used to be a douchebag."

"You still are a douchebag," I said.

"Yeah, but I used to be one, too," he said. I rolled my eyes, which he obviously couldn't see since I was staring out the windshield, but he laughed like he knew I'd done it anyway. "Anyway, I fully admit the shit I was saying was *not* cool. I know that now."

"Like what?"

"You know. Commenting on her body. Telling them where I'd like to see her mouth. That kind of awful locker room talk that I should've known better than to be part of." He drummed his fingers against the steering wheel. "I don't know why I thought it was a good idea to tell you this story. It makes me sound awful."

"Don't worry," I said. "I already thought you were awful."

"Yeah, but actually awful." He sighed. "I know better, okay? I would never say anything like that now."

"I know you wouldn't," I said, which was true. Of course I didn't like that JP had been that kind of guy once upon a time, but also, people do stupid things. At least he'd learned. Some of them never did. "But also, I'm really curious about how this led to the laziest sex of your life."

He laughed. "Okay, well, I'm sitting there being a douchebag and talking about how I'm gonna get her number later, and one of the senior associates is laughing at me and says unless I'm exaggerating, there's no way this woman is gonna go for a lowly intern like me when we're at this swanky club. And with perfect timing, the girl I saw walks out of the bathroom on the other side of the room. So I point her out to everyone at the table and go, 'Trust me, man, by the end of the night I'll—.'" He stopped and cleared his throat. "Uh..."

"Just tell me," I said.

"It was pretty vulgar," he said. "Let's just say it had something to do with where on her face my balls would be. And the senior associate turns to me and goes, 'That's my daughter.'"

"*No!*" I gasped.

JP nodded. "And I think he's joking at first, right, except all the other guys at the table look like they're about to witness a firsthand castration. But there's no way out of this. Like, I just told him I was going to fuck his daughter's mouth so hard her chin would leave a bruise on the nutsack her dad was probably thinking of cutting off. There's no coming back from that."

"Oh, God," I said. "So what did you do?"

"I looked back at her, then at him, and I go, 'Well, I should've known that. Look at you, sir. Of course you'd make beautiful babies.'"

I snorted back a laugh. "And you thought that would work?"

"It shouldn't have. But he just stared at me and then goes, 'Shut the fuck up, Marchand,' and slams back the rest of his beer."

"That's it?"

"Well, he also stormed across the club and told his daughter to stay away from me." He grinned. "But he was apparently as much of a prick at home as he was at work and she didn't like being told what to do. And let me tell you, there's something to be said for the starfish."

I frowned. "The starfish?"

"You know." He extended one arm slightly to the side. "Flat on your back. Do whatever you want to me. All I had to do was lie there and keep my dick hard while she did her thing. Which was *not* difficult, considering how hot she was. I mean, her tits were just—"

"You're a pig," I said, but I was laughing.

"She wouldn't mind me saying it," he said. "We kept in touch after I left Quebec City. She's got an OnlyFans now."

"Really?" I asked.

He nodded. "And it's her dad's fault."

"Daddy issues usually are."

He chuckled. "Look, the guy was obviously loaded. But his oldest son fucked around in university and flunked out two years after she'd started business school. So he told both of them he wasn't giving them a free ride anymore and refused to pay the rest of her tuition."

"Seriously?! But she—"

"—didn't do anything wrong, yeah." He shook his head. "Bet he regrets both that and the fact that he made her go to business school now. She started up an OnlyFans to pay her bills and by the time he found out and cut her off, she was doing well enough that she could've just dropped out of school. She didn't, though. Graduated valedictorian, actually."

"Good for her," I said. "For both of those things."

He nodded. "She's so good at what she does that she started running some courses for people wanting to get into the industry. When she retires from making content, she wants to start an accounting firm for people in the sex work industry." He tapped his hands on the steering wheel again. "She's a great person. If she ends up doing it, I said I'd help her out with the paperwork and contracts and stuff."

"You think your dad would be okay with that?" I asked, surprised.

"Of course not. But I'd do it for her pro bono."

"Pro bono or pro—"

"Don't say it," he said, but he was laughing. "Okay. Your turn. What was the best sex of your life? Other than with me, of course. So I guess, like, the eightieth best sex of your life."

"We haven't had sex eighty times."

"I'm sure a few of those sessions were worth two or three spots on the list," he said.

I couldn't argue that. JP *did* have a number of the "best sex of my life" spots. Not all of them, though.

"Erin," I said without needing to think about it. "She was a rugby player."

"I am already liking where this is going," he said.

I rolled my eyes. "We were fuck buddies for a couple of months. She was kind of like... quietly dominant? If that makes sense? Like, she liked to be in charge, but she wasn't into bondage or ordering me around or anything. She was very gentle about it."

He tilted his head. "I wouldn't have guessed you were into that."

"I'm not *not* into it," I said. "It's not my usual thing, but most of the time our hook-ups were pretty good. Not, like, mind-blowing. Until this one night."

Even in profile and with only the streetlights brightening his face, I saw JP's smirk widen. "What happened this one night?"

"I was being a brat."

"Now *that* I would've guessed," he said. "You are a brat."

"Shut up." He was right, but that wasn't the point. "Like I said, we were fuck buddies, but we weren't together. So we were at this frat party and I was flirting with some people. And Erin came up to me at one point and asked if I was coming home with her. And I don't know what I was thinking but I asked her if she was going to make me."

"And she made you?"

"She dragged me to the backseat of her car, pinned me down by my throat, and growled 'The safe word is red'—which, incidentally, was the colour of my ass the next morning—'otherwise, keep your mouth shut.' And then she just—" I stopped, sighing. "Not exaggerating, I'm pretty sure I came at least ten times. She was *torturing* them out of me by the end of it."

"Holy shit."

"I know." I smirked, remembering the taste of cranberries on Erin's lips and the feel of her muscular shoulders beneath my thighs, lifting my lower body off the seat of her car as she ate me out. "My abs hurt for like a week afterwards from all the orgasms. But she graduated last year. I wonder what she's up to these days."

"Fuck." JP shifted in his seat. "Why is it so fucking hot?"

"I find it fairly temperate," I said. "But you can open the window if you want."

"I meant the thought of you getting fucked."

"Probably because I'm hot."

"That's some of it. But there's something about thinking of someone you've fucked being fucked by someone else that's just... you know. Or am I weird?"

"You are weird," I said, though I was picking at my thumbnail when I said it because I'd been picturing the girl he'd just told me about using his body while he lay there enjoying it. And that wasn't even the first time; there was also the fantasy I'd conjured up about an anonymous girl sucking his dick that I'd been so into, I'd given up hooking with my tattoo artist. "But... yeah. It is hot. So maybe I'm weird, too."

JP nodded but didn't say anything. I glanced down and tried not to smirk when I saw the bulge on his lap.

"Do we need to pull over for a quickie?" I asked.

"As much as I'd love to, it's probably not a great idea," he said reluctantly.

"What the fuck, JP?" I asked, trying to sound mock-offended even though I was actually a little offended. "That's the second time today you've turned me down."

"I am *not* turning you down," he said. "I *am* very aware that I've been up since four-thirty and if I fuck you the way I want to right now, I'll be tired enough that I shouldn't be driving."

That was unfortunately, reasonable. "I'd offer to drive—"

"Absolutely fucking not," he snapped, and so did the sweet longing of the atmosphere in the car. "I wouldn't let you drive my car in the first place, but *especially* not after you've been drinking. Jeez, Nellie. You know better."

I waited until a beat after he was done before finishing my sentence in a flat tone. "—but you probably wouldn't let me drive your car even if I hadn't been drinking."

JP's jaw twitched. "Right."

"Apology accepted," I said dryly.

"I'm sorry."

I folded my arms and turned, looking out the passenger window at the streetlight-illuminated highway. "I'm not as stupid as you look either, you know. I wouldn't do that."

"I know." He sighed. "I shouldn't have snapped. But you heard about the whole thing with Clinton getting arrested, right?"

"That's how we found out Sydney was getting cheated on."

He frowned. "Huh?"

"The woman who tackled Clinton was Olivier's wife. The cop she was hooking up with."

"Small world, I guess." He drummed the steering wheel again. "Clinton could've killed someone. He almost did. So I've been thinking about Sam a lot lately."

Oh.

Of course.

I couldn't say I'd forgotten about Sam, JP's friend who had been killed in an accident after getting into a car with a friend he hadn't known was high. But I hadn't known him. I'd never met him. And JP and I had only ever talked about Sam one time, right after sex that had been a little more emotional than it should have been and right before Anne-Marie had nearly caught us together.

So it wasn't reasonable to assume I'd make that connection, not that JP seemed to think I should have. But it made sense that he was thinking about Sam. They'd been close friends and JP had been half-destroyed by the accident.

And even though I knew JP had other friends and people to talk to, something told me I was one of the few who really *knew* how hard he'd taken it.

"That's understandable," I said.

"It doesn't excuse me snapping," he said. "I am actually sorry, Nell."

"Apology actually accepted," I said. "I get it."

Part of me thought he was going to chuckle dryly and tell me that no, I *didn't* get it, because I'd never lost a friend to a car accident by an intoxicated driver, but JP wasn't that kind of asshole. He just nodded, his cheek twitching, then cleared his throat.

"To make this slightly less depressing, I will say the way we fucked the night I told you about all that was the second-best sex of my life."

"Really?" I said.

He nodded. "The way you grabbed my chin and said... uh..."

I'd said he was mine.

He'd wanted me to say I was his. To pretend that was what we were, just for a moment. And I'd hesitated. He'd cringed, the guilt pouring off him in waves as he tried to backpedal, agreeing with my unsaid thoughts that I couldn't *say* that to him.

And then I'd put my fingers beneath his chin.

I'd forced him to look at me.

I'd stared into those deep blue eyes, no careful mask left to hide the vulnerability and shame of what he'd just said.

And I'd told JP that he was *mine*.

There had been a heartbeat or two or three, the world stopping as he stared at me, and then he'd lost it, coming inside me and clinging to me like he was in free fall.

JP laughed softly. "I don't know how I went from not being able to finish to nearly passing out because I came so hard, and I still can't explain what was so hot about it, but fuck."

"Well, I'm a good actor," I said, trying to keep my voice light as I subtly reminded him I hadn't meant it.

That it hadn't been *real.*

Thankfully, JP either got the hint or hadn't needed the reminder in the first place. "You are a hell of an actor. You completely nailed the role of bedside rug after Anne-Marie burst in. Complete dedication, right down to wearing your panties on your head."

"Thanks. It was all improv," I said, and he laughed. "So if that was the second-best sex of your life, what was the first?"

"Guess," he said.

"Does it involve me?"

"I wouldn't be making you guess if it didn't, babe."

I didn't bother telling him not to call me that. "Wow. I have your top two?"

"Top three, actually," he said.

I looked at him incredulously. "You need to get laid more."

"Or you need to stop being so good in bed."

"Well, that's not happening," I muttered, and he laughed. "What's number three, then?"

"Popping your cherry," he said without hesitation.

"Oh, fuck you," I grumbled.

"Yes, I did," he said proudly. "For your very first time."

"Shut up," I said. "You and Anne-Marie and literally everyone said the first time sucks. How was my first time your third best?"

"Are you saying your first time sucked?" he asked.

I rubbed my finger against my thumbnail. "I… no."

"Good, because I'd hate to call you a liar again," he said. "But I don't know what made it so good. Logically, it shouldn't have been. You shouldn't have been good at anything. Maybe it was because of how sweet and needy you were. Or maybe because I got to fuck you bare. Or maybe it was that you finally admitted you were a virgin and yet still swallowed my cock to the root when I came."

I hoped the warmth of the streetlights was still dim enough that JP wouldn't be able to tell my face was burning. "It's not like you were my first blowjob."

"I refuse to believe your high school boyfriend fucked your throat like I did."

His tone was arrogant. Aggravatingly arrogant. Especially because he wasn't wrong. But I wasn't going to tell JP that.

"So if that's number three, then number one is after the Diamond Gala," I said.

"How'd you guess?" he asked.

"Pretty sure you said something about it," I said, not looking at him.

"Really?" he said. "I told you that? That doesn't sound like me."

"He says in the middle of a conversation where he's telling me I'm responsible for his top three best sexual encounters."

He snorted on a laugh. "Fair. Well, yeah. You're right."

"I know."

He smiled. "So what's yours?"

"My what?"

"Best sex of your life."

"I told you. Erin—"

"Babe." He glanced at me so I could see the patronizing look on his face. "That sounded super fucking hot, but I *know* I'm in your top spot."

I gritted my teeth together. "You think so?"

"You wouldn't keep fucking me if I wasn't."

Fuck. He wasn't wrong. "Yeah, well... I don't want to tell you."

"Why not?" he asked.

"You're going to make fun of me."

"I won't," he said.

"You will. You make fun of me for everything."

He shook his head solemnly. "Not this. I promise."

I fidgeted with my thumbnail again, looking out the window at the road zipping past us for a moment.

"It's the same as yours," I finally said.

It surprised him more than I thought it would. "Really? You liked anal that much?"

"I'm not saying I'd want it all the time, but... yeah."

"Wow," he said, then chuckled.

Instant heat bloomed on my face and my throat went dry. "I knew you'd laugh at me."

"I'm not, babe. I'm—"

"—making fun of me," I said.

"—so fucking hard right now it hurts," he finished.

Obviously I couldn't confirm or deny if it hurt or not, but a glance at his lap showed that he was definitely telling the truth about how hard he was. "Oh."

"Like, yeah, I knew you liked it because you came so hard you started speaking in tongues—" I interrupted him with a scoff of annoyance and he laughed again. "But I still wasn't sure if it was *that* good."

"Why not?"

He shrugged. "I mean, it's your ass. How good could it feel to take it that way?"

"Why don't you take it in the ass and find out?"

"It wouldn't be a good comparison," he said. "You don't have a prostate."

I blinked. I'd thought he'd laugh and immediately shoot it down, but that sounded like...

"Have you done it before?"

"Never had the chance." I stared at him until he flicked his gaze towards me for a moment. "What?"

"You would, though?" I asked.

"Take it in the ass?"

"No, go berry picking in a strawberry patch," I said. "Yes, take it in the ass. You know, the thing we're talking about?"

He chuckled. "I mean, yeah. Absolutely."

"Like, from being pegged?" I asked. "Or..."

"Are you asking me if I'd fuck a guy?"

There was no point in denying it. "Yes."

"Yeah."

I glanced at him. "You would?"

"I have."

"You've fucked a guy before?"

He glanced back at me. "I didn't expect you to have a problem with that."

Part of me wanted to be livid at his assumption that I had a *problem* with it, but I buried the flare of anger. I'd come out to enough people and gotten enough unexpected reactions to know that sometimes people weren't who you thought they were, especially about sexuality.

"I don't," I said. "I was clarifying what you were saying to make sure I understood because I didn't know you were bisexual."

He was staring straight out the windshield, but a passing streetlight revealed the small smile on his face. "Is that what I am?"

Shit. That *had* been an assumption on my part. "I... no. I was saying... I mean, you can call it whatever you want. I meant—"

"It's okay, babe. I'm not saying I'm not. I just mean I don't... know. What I want to call it."

"You don't have to label it at all, either." I tapped my fingernail and thumbnail together. "I guess I was just curious."

"About what?"

"What else you're attracted to."

"Isn't that the question," he murmured, then chuckled. "I think that's the problem with labels. Like, I... If a person consents and is into it, I probably wanna fuck them. But sometimes naming something feels like too much."

"Yeah," I said.

His head tilted towards me. "Yeah?"

"Labels can complicate things."

My voice came out in a soft tone that I hadn't intended. JP quietly considered what I'd said. Probably because we both knew I was talking about more than whatever his sexuality was.

"So you're not judging me for not knowing?" he asked.

"Oh, of course," I said. "How dare you take time to figure out a complex thing like your sexuality and not be able to give me a detailed breakdown of what your specific pre-approved labels are?"

He started laughing. "Okay. Well, anyway, yeah. I have hooked up with a guy before. Neither of us were quite ready for anything past some making out and blowjobs and it took me a while to accept that I was... whatever I am. So he was the only one. But I wouldn't say no to trying more one day."

I nodded, chewing on my lip as a comfortable silence filled the car. A few streetlights went by, lightening and darkening the interior of the car, before either of us spoke again.

"So... would you let someone peg you?" I asked.

"Are you offering?"

"Offering, no. I don't like wearing strap-ons."

He shrugged. "Fair."

I couldn't tell if he sounded disappointed, not that he'd actually answered the question. But I'd never had much of an interest in pegging. It wasn't a deal breaker, but if JP *did* want to explore something like that, I was more likely to suggest a butt plug or a dildo or something. I couldn't picture getting behind him and grabbing his hips as I tried to fuck him, thrusting in a way that didn't feel natural to me and hoping that it felt good for him.

Getting him on his back, on the other hand? Pushing his legs apart so I could watch his face twist while I slid a dildo in his ass? Leaning down to suck his leaking cock as he squirmed beneath me?

I might be able to picture that.

"What are you thinking about?" JP asked.

"What are *you* thinking about?" I replied.

"On the count of three, both of us say what we're thinking," he said. "Okay?"

I held in a smile. "Sure."

"One, two, three."

"I think you should fuck me in the ass when we get home," I said.

"I should fuck your ass when we get back to your place," he said at the same time.

"Deal," we both said.

Chapter Sixteen
This Is...

I was not a morning person.

JP was, but that Friday had been a long, long, *long* day. He'd woken up at four-thirty, driven for four hours, spent a day in meetings, got fucked in a gondola—twice, technically—and had water spit all over him during the reception for the world's weirdest personal development seminar.

Then he'd had a surprisingly deep conversation over the additional two hours of driving he had to do before getting back to Ottawa.

So no one would have blamed him if he'd fallen asleep while I was in the shower, but when I walked into my bedroom, he'd stirred from the short nap he'd allowed himself to take.

And then he'd joined me for my second shower, which I'd needed to take after he turned both of us into shuddering, sweaty messes while fucking me in the ass.

So it made sense that despite being the kind of monster who woke up early enough to do things like go to the gym before work instead of barely making it to an eleven a.m. class on time, JP would sleep in the morning after we got back from Mont Tremblant.

It made complete sense, and yet, the bastard woke me up before ten. On a *Saturday*.

"You awake yet?" he mumbled.

"Why are you touching me?" I mumbled back.

A mindless hand traced the curve of my waist above the covers. "You're soft."

"You're stupid."

"So you are awake?"

"No thanks to you."

His smirk was such a trademark expression that I could almost hear him doing it. "Great. Any chance I can have some of those blankets back? You've been hogging them all night."

I blinked, slow awareness washing over me as I realized I was curled into a ball, blankets tucked under my chin. My back was to JP and my face was half-buried in the fluffy pillows on my bed.

It wasn't where I'd fallen asleep, which meant I'd stirred at some point during the night. The last thing I remembered was a kiss on my forehead and strong arms around me, a steady heartbeat drumming in my ear as my eyes slid closed without even consulting me.

But I *hadn't* meant to fall asleep on JP's chest. I hadn't meant to be in his arms at all. The plan had always been for us to share a bed that night, so it wasn't like it was unexpected that he was there, but I'd thought if he tried to cuddle with me, I'd shove him away and tell him I didn't like to be touched while I slept.

Which wasn't even a lie. Most of the time.

I'd liked it when Ben cuddled me. And Ben had explained it was a scientific thing because post-sex cuddling added endorphins or something. It hadn't mattered because Ben and I were very clear about what we were to each other. He was my former psychology professor; I was a student. We had a summer fling that ended when he moved to California for a year of sabbatical. It didn't matter if he cuddled me to sleep once or twice because on the few harrowing occasions that one of us thought the other might be feeling things we didn't want to be felt, we'd both very clearly indicated that we didn't want anything more.

But JP...

JP was fucking with my head.

One moment, he was kissing me like my mouth was his favourite flavour.

Like the world was churning around us and I was the only thing holding him steady.

Like his body had suddenly decided it was allergic to air that hadn't been processed through my lungs first.

It was ridiculous and unsettling and so, so hard to fight because those kisses made me think *his* mouth was my favourite flavour. That the world was spinning and *he* was holding me steady.

But the next moment, he'd smirk that stupid smirk of his and push all my buttons before fucking me until the only thing I could remember was that this was what I wanted. I wanted to feel good. Nothing more, nothing less.

That was what I was supposed to want, anyway.

All I was supposed to want was his body. His pleasure. His fingers and tongue and cock. I was supposed to want him to eat me out from behind before he fucked me, making me see stars and sob as I came with his cock buried in my ass. I was supposed to want him to finish inside me, then fall asleep on the other side of the bed so he could wake up the next morning and fuck me one last time before going back to Montreal.

I wasn't supposed to be a little sad that I'd woken up wrapped in blankets instead of his arms.

I wasn't supposed to loosen my grip on my blankets, hoping he'd curl his body around mine before tucking the covers around both of us.

And I wasn't supposed to feel a spark of warmth as he pulled the blankets away and did exactly what I wasn't supposed to want.

"About time, babe," he murmured as his chest met my back. "I thought I was going to freeze to death."

"Let me remind you whose bed it is," I said.

"Yours," he said. "Luckily for me, you're *so* good at sharing."

"I share with people who deser—*ahh*!"

He burst out laughing as I squealed and jolted up, my eyes flying open at the sudden chill from icy fingers resting on my ribcage, directly on top of my dragon tattoo.

"What the *fuck*?!" I screeched over his laughter. "Why are your hands so fucking cold?"

His breath was warm against my neck as he grabbed me even as I tried to wriggle away from him. "You're the one who stole the blankets, babe. I told you I was freezing my ass off over here."

I'd thrown snowballs warmer than his hands, yet he ran both of them along my perfectly-warm skin, making me squirm as I struggled away from him.

But not, like, actually struggled.

More like writhed back and forth, making my ass brush against his cock, so when I finally got the upper hand and rolled over to face him, it pressed firmly into my belly while I reached around to grab his ass.

"Your ass doesn't feel that frozen to me," I said.

"But my plan to make you find out worked," he said, then leaned in and kissed me.

"Ugh," I said against his lips, wrinkling my nose. "Your morning breath is awful."

Both of us laughed.

Neither of us stopped kissing.

He untangled one of his hands from around me and cupped it over my breast, the cold of his fingers making my nipple pebble beneath them. Though, I guess the fact that he was pinching it between his thumb and forefinger might have been part of it. I let out one soft moan as he brushed his thumb over the hardened nub and another as he brought his other hand down to my thigh, urging it up so he could wrap it around his hip and let his stiff cock rest against my pussy.

"Fuck the blankets," he said. "I should've asked you to rub your pussy on me to warm up."

"I don't think it would help heat up your ass," I said. "It's much more efficient in warming up smaller areas."

"Damn," he said. "I was gonna suggest sticking my cock in there to warm it up, but it's probably too big."

I let out an unattractive snort. For as much as I made fun of JP, I hadn't intended to imply he had a small dick. That was a result of sleepiness and lack of focus, since said dick was sliding along my dripping slit. But he didn't take offense; he just ran with the joke, confident enough in himself that he didn't need my validation for something as trivial as his dick size.

And God, I liked that.

I liked it as much as I hated that it was yet another item on the ever-growing list of things I didn't hate about JP.

Because as that list got longer, the list of reasons that I *didn't* want anything more than this with JP got shorter.

And shorter.

And shorter.

His hands weren't cold for very much longer. As he left lazy kisses on my lips, he traced my body, warming his fingers up even as he left chilled paths along my skin. I stopped trying to get away from him, instead returning those lazy kisses as he replaced my squirms with slow thrusts forward, grinding himself against my pussy.

There was no decision for his cock to slip inside me. There was no ceremony or warning or effort. It just pushed into my dripping hole like it knew it was meant to be there. I sighed against JP's lips as he entered me, my eyes opening only so I could let them flutter shut again. He murmured words that weren't quite words as he slipped his hand around my body, grabbing my ass so when he rolled slightly away, he stayed inside me. With my leg slung over him, I wasn't exactly on top, but the angle changed enough that JP could thrust a little deeper as he started a slow rhythm that filled me with simmering bliss.

It was quiet. Gentle. Unrushed and unhurried in a way we didn't often have. There were no furtive glances to make sure cars weren't pulling into the same parking lot. No worry that Anne-Marie would burst in. No ticking clock telling us when we had to be done by. There was only him, and me, and the blankets around us.

And, apparently, my phone.

"Fuck," I muttered as it vibrated on the nightstand.

"You can answer it if you want," JP said. "It might be important."

"Or it might be a telemarketer." It took more effort than I wanted to give, but I focused my attention on the man in front of me. "Anyone who knows me knows I'm probably asleep right now."

He didn't say anything else, instead bringing his hand to my side again and holding himself inside me as he nudged me onto my back. It shouldn't have felt so effortless, getting into that position while still attached to him, but apparently JP didn't let a little thing like anatomical limitations get in the way of what he wanted.

He pushed in deeper, his hips flush against my thighs. A shiver ran through me as he dipped to press his lips to my neck, a tingle of electric desire spreading from his kiss and across my skin. Moaning softly, I started to move my arms around his body so I could pull him in closer.

And then my phone started vibrating again.

"You sure you don't want to—" he said.

"*No*," I said, even though my hands were itching to reach over and find out who it was.

Despite my protest, he lifted his head and glanced at the nightstand. "It's a random number."

"Great. Extra not important." I dug my heels into the mattress for leverage so I could push my hips up insistently. "Make me come."

That snapped his attention back to me, deep blue eyes boring down into mine.

"Please," I added softly.

"Fuck," he groaned, then buried his face in my neck. "*Fuck*."

The next time he brought his mouth to mine, I felt it.

Not his lips. I mean, obviously I felt those. But I *felt* it, thrilling and terrifying and foreign, my heart skipping one beat and then another. JP must have felt it too, because his mouth didn't leave mine. He kissed me harder, drove his cock in deeper, held me tighter until I knew both of us were close, so fucking *close*, and I couldn't stop myself from moaning against his lips.

"Nell," he breathed. "Nell, babe, this... this is..."

"This is what?" I whispered.

Because he trailed off, but I needed the next word. I *needed* it. I needed to know what he thought this was.

Fake.

Too much.

A problem.

Not what I wanted.

So good.

He pulled away so his eyes could bore into mine, bright and blue and more serious than I'd ever seen them.

Not what he wanted.

Not enough.

Real.

"Babe—"

And then a door opened.

Not my bedroom door, thank fuck, but both of our heads snapped towards the sound of my apartment door opening.

In hindsight, my reaction was not the most intelligent thing I'd ever done. An intelligent reaction would have been to do something like listen for another few moments to figure out what was going on. Or look at my phone to see if someone had texted me, like Sydney, who I knew had the spare key. Or lock the bedroom door and call the police. Or scream that I had a gun, even though the entirety of my experience with guns was of the water variety.

Instead, I shoved JP off of me, leapt out of bed, and snatched my ratty old bathrobe from the hook near the door.

"Wait—" JP protested, but I'd already put my bathrobe on and wrenched the bedroom door open. I pinched the front of the robe together as I stormed into the hallway, pulling the door closed behind me.

Then three things happened in rapid succession.

First, my bedroom door slammed with a thundering bang.

Second, someone shrieked.

Third, I burst into my kitchen just in time to see Sydney whirl around. The moment she saw me, her eyes went wide and her face went deathly pale.

"Oh, no," she whispered.

"What the hell, Syd?" I asked. "I was in the middle of fucking—"

And thank God—thank *God*—I didn't finish that sentence.

"*Ostie de* fucking *crisse, qu'est-que* fucking *tabarnak*," Anne-Marie cursed, a hand pressed to her chest as she turned to face me.

Anne...Marie. My best friend.

Anne-Marie, who had *no* reason to be here.

Anne-Marie, whose brother had just pulled his dick out of me seconds earlier.

Chapter Seventeen
...Mean

"WHAT ARE YOU DOING home?" Sydney asked, trying not to sound
panicked. "I thought you were... away."

"What are you doing in my apartment?" I replied, my voice muffled
by Anne-Marie's shoulder, since she'd lurched forward and thrown her
arms around me even though I was pinching my robe closed in the front.

"It is my fault, *chérie*," Anne-Marie said as she let go of me. "I came to
town on a whim. I needed to see my best friends and I know I should have
called but I was not thinking entirely. I did not even think you would not
be home until I tried buzzing your apartment a few times before calling
dear Sydney."

"She said she needed the bathroom," Sydney said, her chin trembling.
"Reid and Hope are hogging the shower, so I thought she could use
yours."

"Oh," I said.

"I was going to call." She glanced towards the hallway. "I... I'm so
sorry."

Anne-Marie let go of me, her eyebrows pinched together. "It is that
big a deal that we came to your apartment, *chérie*?"

"No, I... I was, uh..."

She gasped, bringing a hand up to her mouth as her eyes widened again.

"Ohmigod," she said. "Who?"

"What?"

"You said you were in the middle of fucking." She giggled. "*Who* is he? Or she? Or... they?"

"No... no one," I said. "I was in the middle of fucking... sleeping."

"Fucking sleeping with who?" she asked lightly.

"Why—" I started, then realized this might be the best possible option and heaved a semi-fake sigh. "Fine. I was sleeping with someone."

She squealed and did a little dance where she stood, which felt highly unnecessary.

"So can you maybe just, uh, go... for a bit?" I said.

"Oh, absolutely not." Anne-Marie's smile grew into a sly grin. "We'll wait while you finish up."

"I'd rather not," Sydney said.

Anne-Marie waved her off. "You do not need to be embarrassed, *chérie*. We will make some coffee while you do what you need to do, and then you can come out here and introduce us to them so we can ensure they are good enough for our best friend."

"Yeah, that's not happening," I said. "We haven't, uh... we're not really..."

"Together? Pah." Anne-Marie waved her hand again. "I still want to see what fine person you are hooking up with. Sydney and I do not mind waiting."

I glanced at Sydney, my heart pounding in the base of my throat.

"I do, actually," Sydney said. "If Nellie doesn't want to introduce us, she doesn't have to."

Anne-Marie huffed and turned to put her purse on my kitchen counter. "Fine. You can go."

"Annie—" I started.

"Oh!" she said brightly. "But you should steal one of Nellie's donuts before you leave. Where did you get Trou de Beigne? I thought you said they did not sell these in Ottawa."

I watched as she opened the white bakery box, my stomach churning. "I, uh... got them from a friend."

Anne-Marie picked up a coconut lime donut. "Your friend in your bedroom? They are from Montreal?"

Shit.

Shit.

"No," I said.

Anne-Marie studied me for a moment, one eyebrow higher than the other. She looked back at the bakery box, then slowly turned her head to survey the rest of my kitchen.

Which would've been fine.

Except the way my apartment was laid out, the kitchen, entryway, and living room were all in one open area.

And JP had left his suitcase near the door.

"Hmm," she said. "This looks familiar."

"It's not," I said. "It can't be. It's mine and I just got it, so you've never seen it before."

"Is that so?" Her lips began to turn up, creases appearing in the corners of her sparkling eyes. "So if I opened it, it would not be filled with men's clothing?"

"Nope," I said, half-ready to jump forward and tackle her if she tried.

But she didn't. Instead, she motioned at a pair of shoes sitting next to my door.

"These are much too large to be yours," she said. "So they must be your friend's?"

"Yeah," I said.

"Mmm," she said. "Because they also look very familiar, *chérie.*"

"I thought you had to pee," Sydney said loudly. "Shouldn't you go to the bathroom?"

Anne-Marie ignored her. "I could swear my brothers both have shoes like these ones."

Fuck.

"They're shoes," I said. "Lots of people have similar shoes."

"Yes, but these are unique." She folded her arms across her chest. "My mother purchased two pairs like these for Jean-Paul and Marc-Andre last year for Christmas. They are custom-made by LB Bespoke. One of the preferred vendors for my company. You know, where I am a personal stylist?"

Fuck.

"They're probably knock-offs," I said.

Anne-Marie's smirk grew. "I see. So the donuts from Trou de Beigne are from your friend, but that friend is not from Montreal, where Trou de Beigne is located and where my brother Jean-Paul happens to live. And the shoes are knock-offs that just so happen to look like the custom pair my mother had made for my brother Jean-Paul. And the luggage here is yours, even though it looks *much* like my brother Jean-Paul's luggage, right down to the monogrammed luggage tag with the initials JPM on it."

Fuck. Fuck. Fucking *fuck* fuck fuck.

"This has nothing to do with JP," I said. "The donuts are from a few days ago and the shoes are clearly cheap knock offs and the tag is, uh, upside down. It says 'wdr.' Which is the brand. Wandering... Done... Right."

"I have never heard of this brand," Anne-Marie said. "Is it new?"

"You're trying to find patterns where there aren't any. That's called apophenia, actually"—inspiration struck and perked up—"and I learned it from Ben. This guy I was sleeping with who was a psychology professor."

"Mmm," she said, unconvinced.

"*My* psychology professor," I continued. "Which is why I didn't tell you. And that's way more interesting than whatever you think is going on here."

"Sure, *chérie*." She bit her lip, excited energy trembling off of her. "And this Ben, is he in your bedroom right now?"

"Well, no, but—"

"And so if I were to go over to your bedroom right now, I would see...?"

"Nothing."

"Well then"—without warning, she pushed past me and raced down the hallway—"there's no reason for me to not look, is there?"

"Fuck," Sydney said.

"Anne-Marie, *don't*," I said, starting after her. "Please."

But before I'd even caught up to her, Anne-Marie had her hand on my doorknob and threw the door open.

And there, in the room, was nothing.

The room was empty.

JP was gone.

Where, I couldn't say. Maybe the closet. Maybe dangling naked out the window, passersby on the street catching the rare phenomenon of a full moon in the middle of a sunny morning. Maybe underneath the bed, even though my bed frame was from IKEA and had convenient under bed storage drawers where I kept my spare linens and also a few stuffed animals I was too embarrassed to leave out.

Or maybe I was delusional.

Once I'd accepted that I was, indeed, delusional, it became clear that JP hadn't even bothered *trying* to squeeze himself in the three inches of space between my headboard and the wall and was sitting exactly where I'd left him.

"Hey, sis," I heard JP say as I reached the bedroom far, far, *far* too late to stop Anne-Marie from opening the door.

"I *knew* it!" she shrieked, jumping up and clapping her hands together. "Oh, Nellie Belanger, you sly girl. I *knew* you'd eventually—"

"Nellie, I'm so sorry," Sydney said from behind me. "I had no idea. I thought you were staying in—"

I looked into my bedroom. JP was sitting on the edge of my bed, the sheets around his waist. His hair was tousled almost artfully and there was a bemused expression on his face as Anne-Marie blabbered on.

"How long has it actually been?" Anne-Marie was rambling. "Since the Diamond Gala? Or was something going on before that? I suspected but you are so *stubborn* sometimes and—"

"—please don't hate me," Sydney said.

JP caught my eye and pressed his lips together, but he wasn't quite able to stop his shoulders from shaking with laughter.

At least one of us found it funny, I guess.

"—cannot wait to tell everyone! My mother is going to be thrilled that someone finally managed to get you to—except *you*," Anne-Marie said, her pitch lowering into a half-growl. "How could you ruin this for me, Jean-Paul? *Tu es un gros plein de merde.*"

Anne-Marie had insulted JP many times. Many, many times. They were siblings, after all. But I couldn't say I'd ever heard her say something in such a cutting, hateful tone.

"What?" JP said, taken aback.

She waved a hand. "I will not let it stop me being happy for you. But so you are aware, I am absolutely disgusted by you right now. You *and* Dad."

I had no idea what she was talking about, but clearly, that meant something to JP. Patches of pink appeared on his cheeks.

"It's not what you think," he said.

"Oh, of course not," Anne-Marie said sarcastically. "This has nothing to do with you telling Dad you want to move out of corporate law. There must be some other explanation for why you're defending Clinton Thibault on his horrible charges."

The idea of time standing still was strange to me. I could understand the concept of shock. I could understand how moments, big moments, could affect people. The concept of time pausing at those moments didn't make sense to me. A second is a second, no matter what is happening in that second, and a minute is a minute.

However, the moment those words left Anne-Marie's mouth, time slowed the same way things feel slower underwater. Her statement hung between us like water-logged fabric, too heavy to float but too light to fall straight to the bottom. Anne-Marie's lips were still moving, but the sounds didn't make it to my ears until what she'd said finally sank in.

JP was Clinton's lawyer.

Clinton, the man who'd started a drunken car chase because some girl decided she wasn't interested in him.

Clinton, who women warned each other about. Who no one wanted to be caught alone with. And whose parents paid off the ones who did get caught with him.

JP was defending him.

"And what would that explanation be, dear brother?" Anne-Marie was saying.

JP said nothing.

"He could have *killed* someone, Jean-Paul!" Anne-Marie said.

"I am *very* aware of that," JP said.

"Are you? Because if you were—"

"And you are very aware of the fact that I can't say—"

"You are still my brother and I still love you, but I have never been so ashamed," she said. "That is literally why I came here. Dad told me and I couldn't—I needed my friends. Remy is away this weekend and I needed a hug, so I drove myself here. And you know I hate driving, so you must know how upsetting this is if I drove all this way just for a hug. So if you want Nellie to stay with you, you had better—"

"I'm not with him."

JP and Anne-Marie both stopped talking and looked at me.

I think.

I wasn't looking at either of them.

"*Chérie*—" Anne-Marie started.

"Get out," I said.

"What?" she said.

"You heard her," JP said.

"Both of you. All of you." I stepped back in the hallway and pointed at the door, still not looking at either of them *or* at Sydney. "Get out."

"But—"

"Out."

"*Chérie*—"

"Out!" My voice cracked. "Get the fuck out of my apartment."

Anne-Marie turned, holding her hands up. "First let's talk about—"

"About what?" I snapped. "About you barging into my apartment and going into my room even though I *told* you not to? About you screeching about what you think is happening? You're calling him a pile of shit like you aren't pushy and overbearing and obnoxious. I said *no*, Anne-Marie. This wasn't fucking okay."

"Nellie," she said, her voice regretful. "I was just—"

"Mean," I interrupted. "You were just fucking *mean*. You think this is some big joke like it doesn't matter that it bothers me. You didn't respect me saying no. Just like the fucker you're pissed your brother is defending."

Hurt flashed across her face, which was fair, because what I'd said was also pretty mean. I would've lost my mind if someone compared me to Clinton. He was obviously far worse than Anne-Marie was, and I should've probably had some level of grace for my best friend.

But right then, she didn't feel like my best friend, and I couldn't quite bring myself to care.

"We're not together. We'll never *be* together. We're not even friends, Anne-Marie. I've told you a hundred million times I don't like your brother and *that* hasn't changed."

That was also mean. Mean enough that Sydney glanced at me in surprise.

"Nellie," she said softly.

"It's okay," JP said, his voice dry. "She's right. I'm pretty awful."

"Especially now," I said. "So get out."

From the corner of my eye, I saw JP shrug and start to get out of bed.

"Ohmigod, you're naked," Anne-Marie muttered, her face going red as she turned away.

"No, really?" JP replied. "I don't know how *you* usually do it, but most people take off their clothes. So unless you want the whole view, maybe you should listen to Nellie."

I was too angry to be grateful for him taking my side, so instead, I turned on my heel and walked three steps to the bathroom, slamming the door behind me without another word. My hands were shaking as I flipped the toilet lid down and sat on it, waiting for the three of them to...

To just *go*.

Anne-Marie finally listened to me. I assumed Sydney did, too, since it was after the muffled sound of my apartment door closing that I heard JP moving around my bedroom. I picked at my thumbnail until the skin was raw and painful and JP was knocking on the bathroom door.

"I told you to leave," I said.

"I know," he said. "But—"

"No buts. Get out."

"No."

I looked at the closed door, incredulous. "Excuse me?"

"I said no. Because—"

"Because what? You're the kind of guy who corners people now? Has defending an asshole like Clinton rubbed off on you already?"

"You'd think, since even though I'm not into this whole miscommunication thing where I have a perfectly good explanation that you refuse to listen to, no one is letting me finish a fucking sentence," he said. "But mainly because my stuff is in there."

I glanced at the counter, where a small toiletry bag was sitting next to the hand towel. "Your toothbrush is that important to you?"

"I, at the very minimum, need my contacts so I can drive without crashing."

Fuck. I'd forgotten he wore contacts. Gritting my teeth together, I stood and grabbed the bag, then cracked open the bathroom door enough to hand it to him.

"And I'm no longer working at my dad's firm," he said, taking his bag out of my hand. "Anyway. Bye, Nell."

My mouth dropped open and I opened the door the rest of the way. JP's back was to me, since he'd already started down the hallway. "You what?"

"I'm quitting," he said without looking at me, turning the corner as I followed him. "I had a job interview yesterday."

"In Mont Tremblant?"

JP walked into the kitchen, stopping at the sink and opening his toiletry bag, taking a contact case out. "I didn't technically sign anything, but they said they'd send the offer on Monday."

"I..."

He started washing his hands. "You what?"

I was lost for words. "Congratulations."

His mouth twitched as he turned the tap off and opened the small case with his contacts in it. "Thanks."

I looked down at my feet. Mainly because he started fishing his contacts out and I didn't want to watch him touch his eye, but also so he couldn't see my face burning. "I should have let you explain."

"Yeah, you should've."

"Why didn't you tell me before? Or say something when Anne-Marie...?"

I trailed off. He paused so he could pop his contacts in before taking a breath and letting it out. "I couldn't. It hasn't been announced that Clinton's defense is Dad's firm. And considering Anne-Marie blurted that little fact out like it was common knowledge, I now can't risk her knowing until I've officially accepted the other offer."

"Because your dad might find out?"

"And because I wouldn't want a new employer to find out I'm leaving because of a case." He washed his hands again, then put his contact case back in the toiletry bag. "That could fuck me over. Which is also why I needed you this weekend. I told the people I was interviewing with that 'my girlfriend' and I were looking to move, which backfired a bit when they invited me and said girlfriend to the retreat this weekend while I did the final interview."

I didn't say anything as he walked over to his suitcase and put his toiletry bag in it, even though I still had questions. Like how he'd expected me to cover for him if that little bit of information had come up during the retreat.

And where he was moving to, since it would still have to be in Quebec because I knew from my Forensic Science and Law class that moving from province to province as a lawyer took more than a job interview.

And if this was it as far as things went with us. Because I hadn't totally meant it when I said I didn't like him, but that Anne-Marie's reaction was exactly the reason why we shouldn't have been doing this in the first place.

I mean, one of the first things she'd said was that she couldn't wait to tell everyone.

Which meant there was a chance my dad would find out about this.

And that...

He couldn't.

"I'll make sure she doesn't tell anyone," JP said, like he could read my mind.

"Thank you," I said.

He reached down to grab his shoes, which were very clearly not knock-offs in any way, and I...

I didn't want him to.

"You don't have to leave," I said.

He hesitated just enough that the pause was noticeable. "I appreciate that. But I should still go."

My chest ached and a taste that felt as real as it was imagined filled my mouth. I knew what that hallucinated taste was, and I knew what I needed to say to get rid of it.

"I'm sorry," I said, glancing down because even though I knew I needed to say it, I couldn't bring myself to look at him.

"Don't be." He finished putting his shoes on, then straightened up. "Honestly, I would've thought the same thing. But if it'll make you feel better, apology accepted."

It did. I hated that it did, but it very, very much did.

"Okay," I said. "So we're still—"

And then I stopped, heat flushing my face as my own words echoed back at me.

That I didn't like him.

That there would never be anything between us.

That we weren't even friends.

"We're still what?" JP asked.

I swallowed hard. "We're... good?"

There was another moment of hesitation, though I wasn't sure which of us was hesitating. But a heartbeat passed, then another, and then JP's mouth twitched into a lopsided smile.

"Yeah, babe," he said. "We're good."

Before I could say anything, he brought a hand to my cheek, dipped his head, and kissed me.

"Don't call you babe," he murmured against my lips. "I know."

Then he pulled back, grabbed his suitcase, and left.

And not that I was an expert on kisses or anything, but something about that one felt like goodbye.

Chapter Eighteen
Goblin Mode

"Is it something about my face?"

Sydney and I looked up in unison as Reid slid into the booth next to Syd and set his elbows on the table, collapsing forward into his hands with an existential crisis in his eyes.

"What?" I asked.

"That's attracting these kinds of people to me," he said, forlorn. "Like, is there something about me that screams 'I'm peggable'?"

Sydney sprayed a mouthful of beer across the table. Thank God it was happy hour, since most of it ended up in my half-full pint and when she started hacking a moment later, she knocked the rest of her half-full pint over.

"Or 'I want to be dressed up in fishnets and told I'm a bad boy while you spank me'?" Reid continued as if there wasn't cheap beer pooling around his elbows.

"Let me see." I mirrored the way his elbows were on the table, though I clasped my hands together before putting my extended forefingers to my chin. Reid stared back at me, distress pinching his eyebrows together as I studied him intently.

"Well," I said as soon as Sydney stopped choking and started to mop up her spilled beer. "I'm not one-hundred-percent sure what it is, but there is something about you that's very submissive and breedable."

Reid responded exactly the way I thought he would, which was to glare at me instead of laughing. I responded to that exactly the way he probably thought I would, which was to burst out laughing.

"Thanks," he said, his annoyance clear. "That's just what I wanted to hear. That I look 'submissive and breedable.'"

"Do you have some kind of problem with people who like that kind of thing?" Sydney asked, shoving her napkin at him.

"Of course not," Reid said, taking it so he could clean up the beer around him. "But I'm not into it."

"Well, have you ever tried it?" I asked. "Maybe you'd actually like being pegged."

"Why do I even bother talking to you?" he muttered.

"Because of my great rack and hilarious antics," I said, reaching for my beer before remembering Sydney had spit in it. Which wouldn't be a problem, since spit was just spit, but she was drinking an ultra-hoppy IPA and I doubted that would taste very good mixed with my light summer lager. "So? How do you know you're not into it if you've never tried it?"

"I don't need to try it to know I'm not interested," he said, his cheeks red as he helped himself to my napkin so he could finish drying the table. "You can't tell me you'd need to try taking a dick in your ass to figure out if you'd like it."

I curled my lips down thoughtfully. "You make a good point."

"Thank y—"

"I knew I wanted to take a dick in my ass even before I tried it," I finished.

Sydney started cackling, her giggles broken by the occasional cough that made it clear she was still working some of her beer out of her throat, while Reid shook his head and sighed.

"Why does that not surprise me?" he asked.

"I don't know," I said. "Why are you being so judgmental about it?"

"I'm not," he said. "But I guess you knowing you wanted to try it is very similar to me knowing I *don't* want to try it."

"I think the real question is why are you asking?" Sydney croaked.

"Yeah," I said. "Was someone... *Hope*...ing for it?"

He gave me another dirty look and didn't say anything, which meant I was right. Surprisingly, to be honest. Hope hadn't been his girlfriend for a super long time, but it had been long enough that this sort of thing should have come up a lot sooner. But Reid didn't have time to answer before the server came over to take our order for another round of beer.

"How'd it come up this time?" Sydney asked after the server walked away.

"The fact that you have to say *this* time," Reid muttered, shaking his head. "Hope sent me a picture of her wearing a strap-on."

"She bought it without even checking if you were into it first?" I asked.

"She already owned it. But don't worry. She said she cleaned it real good after the last guy."

I tried not to laugh. I did. But all I managed to do was twist my face awkwardly and Reid sighed.

"Just laugh," he said, so I did.

It felt good. The laughter, I mean. It wasn't the first time that day I'd laughed, but the world hadn't seemed as funny as it usually did after Anne-Marie discovered me and JP together two days earlier.

I'd spent Saturday in goblin mode, which was the mode where I sat around in my pyjamas, getting frustrated when I couldn't find a new true crime documentary to hold my attention, then putting on old seasons of *The Simpsons* that I'd seen a thousand times before. For dinner, I'd had a handful of crackers, two packets of fruit snacks, and after realizing I didn't have any clean knives, a couple of bites of cheese directly from the block because fuck it, I lived alone.

Sunday had also started as a goblin mode day, even though I really had to study for my Forensic Science and Law midterm. I needed decent grades on both that and my midterm essay due the following week to make up for the case studies I'd missed handing in. But around three, a soft knock at my door had me scrambling to put my chewed-on cheese block back in the fridge before answering.

"We're going to happy hour," Sydney had said when I answered the door.

"I don't—"

"Please." She'd folded her arms across her chest, her eyebrows furrowing together in worry. "Let me buy you a beer to apologize."

I'd sighed. "Syd, I told you it was fine. You didn't know. And you tried to get Anne-Marie to go when you realized what happened."

"I know, but—"

"I'm not mad. Not at you, anyway."

She'd nodded, her lips pressed into a tense line. "Have you talked to Anne-Marie since yesterday?"

I hadn't, which Sydney already knew because Anne-Marie had been texting her about how I hadn't answered any of Anne-Marie's text messages.

She was sorry. I knew she was sorry. And I probably should have accepted it. Yes, she was pushy and obnoxious and completely inconsiderate sometimes, but she *was* a good person under all that. She was my best friend. She'd gone out of her way to help me countless times and was always the first person to defend me when I needed someone on my side.

And yeah, maybe some of it was embarrassment. The guilt of breaking whatever implied girl code there was that you weren't supposed to fuck your friend's siblings, even if they were kinda hot and pretty good in bed.

But the memory of the way my stomach had plummeted, the fact that she hadn't even considered *not* bursting into my bedroom, that she saw how upset I was and still felt entitled to that information about my life... it kept playing over and over in my head.

If she couldn't see how big a deal it was to me at that moment, what was going to stop her from deciding it wasn't a big deal at all? And if she decided it wasn't a big deal, what was going to stop her from telling people about it?

What was going to stop that information from getting back to my dad?

So I'd told Syd that no, I hadn't replied to Anne-Marie, and I wasn't planning to. And when Anne-Marie had texted again after Syd and I had gotten to Lou's Pub and ordered our beers, I asked Syd if she'd tell Anne-Marie to back off.

But Syd said this *was* Anne-Marie backing off, since even though the whole thing started because Anne-Marie was being disgustingly pushy, Syd had to convince her not to camp outside my apartment door waiting to talk to me.

"—I said I wasn't interested in being pegged by her," Reid was saying to Sydney after our beers were dropped off. "And she goes, 'Oh, so if it *wasn't* me, it'd be okay?' And I said—"

"You've got to be *fucking* kidding me," I blurted.

"Uh... yeah, pretty much," Reid said. "But I think she'd already decided we were breaking up, so—"

"Not that." I lifted my phone up and showed the screen to Sydney. "Did she go back to Montreal?"

Sydney frowned. "What?"

"Anne-Marie."

"I think so. Why—"

"That's the front door number," I said heatedly. "So if she's still here and trying to make me talk to her—"

"It might not be her," Reid said. "Are you expecting a package or anything?"

"On a Sunday?" I said.

"Why not?" Sydney said. "They deliver every day now."

"Okay, but no." I stared at the flashing screen on my phone. "I didn't order anything."

"You won't know if you don't answer," Reid said. "Maybe someone dialled the wrong number or something."

"Yeah, but if it isn't—"

"Answer it for her," Sydney said, nudging Reid. "If it's Anne-Marie, you can hang up."

It was as good an idea as any, so I passed my phone to Reid.

"Hello?" he said cautiously after tapping the screen.

Then he frowned.

"Uh... Reid," he said. "Who's thi—" He stopped, then grimaced. "Oh. Yeah, one sec. She's... no, no she's not home. I'm... No, you're mistaken. I'm not—"

"What the fuck?" I asked.

"—definitely not. *Definitely* not. One sec, here she is." He shoved the phone towards me. "It's not Anne-Marie."

"Who..." I lifted the phone to my ear. "Hello?"

"*Bonjour, ma fille ange,*" replied a flat voice.

I stared at Reid, barely able to blink.

"Dad?" I finally said.

Sydney's mouth dropped open.

"Why is a young man answering the buzzer for your apartment?" he asked.

"It's connected to my phone," I said. "He's not—"

"Let me in," my dad said. "*Now*, Eleanor."

"Okay, but I'm literally not home," I said. "I'm at the pub down the street."

"On a date?"

"With Sydney," I said. "And her roommate, Reid."

I don't know if he believed me, but I didn't have enough space in my brain to try to convince him. My *dad* was at my apartment and I…

I'd been living in the building for nearly four years and my dad had never visited me there.

There was only one reason I could see him changing that fact literally overnight.

And as terrified as I'd been that Anne-Marie would tell people about me and JP, it wasn't until that moment that I realized I hadn't thought she actually would. That deep down, I'd trusted she would see how important it was to keep quiet.

And fuck, did it hurt to think that she hadn't.

Part of me wanted to run. A big part. But ten minutes later, I was staring at my dad standing awkwardly in my kitchen, my palms sweating.

"I know it's a mess," I said before he could comment on the dishes in the sink or the clothes on the floor in the living room or the trash that definitely needed to be taken out. "I've been busy with school."

"I see," my dad said, his voice unreadable.

"If I'd known you were coming, I would've cleaned up a bit." I couldn't seem to control the speed of my voice, which was stuck on rapid. "I know I should keep it clean in general but it's midterm week and it hasn't been a priority."

"Mmm," my dad said. "Perhaps I should get a cleaner in for you, then."

Fuck.

I tried to figure out how he was going to twist that into telling me he knew I'd been hooking up with the boy next door and that he was disowning me. Maybe something about helping me clean up my act? Clean up my messes? Or that no professional cleaner would be able to hide the dirty things I'd been doing?

Or maybe he was going to be more subtle in his accusations. He could casually say that getting a cleaner would leave me more time for other things, like hooking up with JP.

Usually I'd say he was offering it as an attempt at bribery. Or blackmail. But neither of those things made sense if he was here because Anne-Marie had told him I was sleeping with her brother. My dad wouldn't bother trying to bribe me to not sleep around. He'd just cut me off. So—

"Nellie?" my dad said when I didn't say anything.

"I don't need a cleaner," I said.

"I can have Pierre look into someone for you," he said. "So you have a bit more time to focus on your schoolwork."

I stayed silent, waiting for him to drop the rest of the proverbial shoe. But he didn't.

He nodded brusquely, glancing around. My apartment wasn't especially big, but it wasn't small, either. It was technically a two bedroom, though I only had a desk and some bookshelves in the smaller one. My kitchen was a good size and the living room had space for a comfortable couch, an armchair, and a square storage ottoman, with room left over to let me sprawl on the floor when I used the coffee table as a study space.

But with my dad standing there, it felt cramped. It wasn't that he was an exceptionally large man; he wasn't much taller than me, and I teetered on the line of short as far as women went.

He just made everything else feel small.

"Did you, um, want something to drink?" I asked when the silence had stretched on and my dad still hadn't said anything. "I have some Coke. Or water."

"No," he said.

I swallowed nervously. "Okay. Did you just stop by for a visit or—"

"No."

That wasn't surprising.

"I am here to ask a favour."

That also wasn't surprising. I mean, it was, in that I thought he was there to tell me I was a disgusting disappointment for getting caught having sex with JP Marchand, but the idea of my dad needing a favour wasn't all that new. In fact, I could almost guess what it was: he was having a party, or there was a gala event, or he needed me to convince Claire Martelle to make her mother give him more money.

But the way he shifted in place, then cleared his throat and laced his hands together in front of him like he was suddenly uncertain...

That was unusual.

"What favour?" I asked when he didn't say anything else.

My dad squared his shoulders. "I have proposed to Kimberlee."

"Proposed what?" I asked.

He flicked an annoyed glance towards me. "Marriage, Nellie."

That didn't answer the question of what he needed from me. It just led to more questions. But as much as I wanted to blurt out some of those questions—mainly "What the fuck?!" and "Are you crazy?" and "Is *she* crazy?"—I held all but one back.

"And she said yes?" I asked.

His mouth tightened into a line. "She did."

"Oh," I said. "Congratulations."

He nodded brusquely. "Thank you."

"And this has to do with the favour you need?" I asked.

"Correct." He took a shallow breath. "We would like to have an engagement party."

I fucking *knew* it. "Dad—"

"I understand you are busy," he said. "We have not picked a date. Our proposition would be the Friday after Thanksgiving, but Kimberlee wanted to know when would work best for you. The party itself will be a small, intimate dinner, so there will be no need for you to have hair or makeup done prior to the event. That way, you could come to Montreal after your classes are done and be home late that night or early Saturday morning, if you would like to stay overnight and travel the next day. I can arrange for a town car to pick you up and bring you home if you would like. Then you do not have to drive and could instead study or relax while en route."

I didn't know what to say.

All of it was reasonable. Thoughtful. Considerate of the excuses I'd given him time and time again.

And completely unsettling, since "reasonable," "thoughtful," and "considerate" were not words I'd ever once thought about my father.

"Why?" I asked.

"Why?" he repeated, raising his eyebrows.

"Why is it so important for me to be there?"

It was a risky question. I half-expected it to backfire, to burn away the uncharacteristic nervousness in the undertones of my dad's voice as he snapped that it was important because he *said so*, like I owed him anything he asked for because I was, above any other meaningful part of my identity, his daughter, and that he had no obligation to explain his reasoning to me.

But it didn't.

"We would like to share this announcement with our close friends and family," my dad said. "Kimberlee's parents and her brother and sister-in-law, as well as their children, will all hopefully be there. She has a relatively large family." He paused, not quite looking at me. "You are my family, Nellie."

He didn't stay much longer. Just long enough to ask some tense questions about my classes and pay little attention to the answers I gave him, then tell me he'd have Pierre get in touch to arrange a ride for me to Montreal.

"I don't need a ride," I said. "I'll drive myself."

"I do not want to impede on your study schedule," he said.

"It won't. I'd just rather have my car with me so if there's anything else I want to do while I'm there…"

I trailed off, a pang of something regretful in my chest.

Because there was usually only one other thing I wanted to do in Montreal, and I wasn't sure where things stood with him.

Chapter Nineteen
After School Special

"No," Glitch said the moment I walked into their office the next day.

"Glitch—"

"There wasn't even anything due today, Nellie," they said, not even bothering to look up from their laptop.

"I know, but—"

"And there is no case study this week," they continued. "Your midterm paper is due. And if you think there's *any* reason I can give you an extension on that, my professional recommendation is that you seek medical help for your delusions."

"Glitch, I fucked up."

I didn't mean for my voice to crack. I didn't mean to sound like I was about to cry. I didn't mean to make Glitch finally look up from their laptop, only to see me sitting in the chair I always sat in when I asked them for an extension fighting back tears.

But I did.

And it was fucking humiliating.

"What?" they said.

"I fucked up." I pulled the syllabus out of my bag. "I mixed up the dates."

They sighed. "Nellie—"

"I thought the midterm was this Wednesday and the paper was next week." It was a fight to keep my voice steady. "All my other midterms are this week. It wasn't until Shelby was talking about the midterm today that I realized it's the *paper* due this week. And not even next class. He said it has to be submitted online by midnight tomorrow."

"I don't know what you expect me to do. I've told you I can't give you extensions unless it's one of Shelby's approved reasons."

"Yeah, but—" I cut myself off, not quite willing to resort to any more begging than I'd already done.

Glitch studied me for another moment, then sighed and spun their chair to the left so they could grab a printed stack of papers stapled together. They twisted back to face me, elbows and forearms resting on their desk as they flipped to the second page.

"Has one of your parents died in the last month?" they asked.

"What? No."

"A sibling?"

"I'm an only child."

They flicked up an eyebrow. "Is that a recent development?"

Between the morbidity and the stress, it was almost funny, but I couldn't force a laugh. "No. I've always been an only child."

"Too bad." They glanced at the sheet again. "Did you ever talk to student services?"

"About what?"

"Getting a personalized education plan."

"Oh, do they give education plans to people who miss massive details like the actual due date for their midterm projects and start working on their case studies way too late because they procrastinate boring things?"

"Yes," Glitch said. "When those people have ADHD."

"Great. So that doesn't help me at all." I groaned, burying my face in my hands. "Why am I like this?"

"Well, I'm a law student, not a doctor, so I can't help you there," they said, their voice flat. "But you have about thirty hours before it's due. You can get something done in that amount of time."

I laughed. It sounded like a real laugh, even though there was a lump in my throat. "There's no chance of that. My brain goes numb reading about this shit after, like, twenty minutes."

"What about that friend of yours?"

"What friend?" I mumbled into my hands.

"The one who 'helped' you with that one case study you rocked. Or was that bullshit like I said it was?"

It took a beat for me to realize they were talking about JP, and another beat after that before I could speak over the clenching guilt in my stomach that came from thinking about JP.

Maybe if things were different, he would've helped. But now... there was no way. Even if I could bring myself to ask him, I doubted he'd want to see me.

"It was bullshit," I lied. "What about if my apartment flooded and ruined my laptop?"

"*Did* your apartment flood?" they asked.

"Not yet."

"It's not spelled out on my list, but purposely flooding your own apartment to get an extension probably won't work," they said.

"So you're saying there's a chance it's possible?"

"Theoretically anything's possible, but considering there's a line here about extension approval being at Shelby's discretion, I'm going to say those chances are close to zero."

A prickling sensation started in my eyes. Even though I still had my face in my hands, I squeezed them shut before they could start stinging.

"But if the alternative is definitely not getting my paper done in time, not-quite-zero is still better than nothing."

They were silent for a moment, then drummed their hands on the desk. "How about something that has a slightly-better-than-not-quite-zero chance of helping you get your paper done in time?"

I frowned into my hands, then looked up at them. "What do you mean?"

Glitch studied me for a moment, then glanced at the closed office door behind me.

"Look," they said, lowering their voice. "You're not getting an extension. It's just not happening. But I have a way you can get it done in time."

"I'm not cheating, either," I said. "I need to pass this class, but it won't do any good if I get kicked out of university for plagiarizing."

They shook their head. "You'd be doing the work yourself."

"I just told you—"

"I can get you some study buddies."

I stared at Glitch like they were crazy, because they were. "Study buddies. How the hell is finding someone to study with going to help me finish a paper in time?"

"Not study buddies. 'Study buddies.' Like... dexies?"

"The fuck is a dexy?"

Their mouth twisted to the side, holding back a smile. "You're kind of a goody-two-shoes, aren't you?"

"I have literally never been described that way."

"Yeah, but—never mind." They glanced at the door again, then reached under their desk and pulled out a backpack. I watched, still confused, until they unzipped the inside pocket and pulled out a small plastic bag full of pills.

Oh my God.

It was happening.

The thing they'd been warning me about since sixth grade, when teachers and parents and the cool kids on TV all tried to convince us that strangers would try to give us drugs.

Considering the situation, I probably shouldn't have found it as borderline exciting as I did. Based on how many times I was told to say no to drugs, I'd assumed it would be a much more regular occurrence. And it wasn't like I'd never been offered drugs before. But it was the first time I wasn't at a nightclub or party or something.

"Study buddies," Glitch said.

"What are they?" I asked.

"They would give you energy," they said.

"So would cocaine," I said. "And I don't think that would help me finish my paper."

They laughed. "Fair point, but it's not *that* kind of energy. It's more to help you get stuff done. Stay awake so you can finish your paper. That kind of thing."

"And you think this would be more effective than flooding my apartment?"

They shrugged. "Less destructive, at least."

"Unless I develop a crippling addiction."

"True, but I'm pretty sure you'll be fine."

"I thought you said you weren't a doctor."

"Also true, but even though I'd definitely be able to use a lot more than forty bucks, I'm not willing to sell you more than two of these." They flattened the baggie on the desk. "Considering you didn't know what a study buddy was in the first place, I feel like you don't know many people who could sell you more."

I lifted my eyebrows. "They're twenty bucks each?"

"Yeah, but I accept tips, so you can round it up to fifty if you want."

I laughed.

I had to.

Because I couldn't actually be considering this. Like, yeah, I was desperate. I was panicking. I'd been panicking even before my Forensic Science and Law class because I had studied nowhere near as much as I'd wanted to. I'd convinced myself to do literally anything else on Friday while I was in Mont Tremblant. I'd spent Saturday and part of Sunday moping. And I'd spent almost all of Sunday night making up fake scenarios in my head about what would happen when I went to my dad's engagement party.

I couldn't help it. *Something* was off. For my dad to come to Ottawa, completely out of his way, to ask me to attend... the cynic in me said it was manipulation. That he'd known I would have a harder time saying no if I had to say it to his face.

But if that was the case, why hadn't he asked for more?

Why had he done so much to make the party as unobtrusive as possible?

And why hadn't he said anything about Reid?

That was the weirdest part of all of it. Sydney told me Reid had said he was pretty sure his balls had retracted so far into his body that he could feel them sitting under his lungs because my dad's voice alone had been sharp enough to cut them off. Which was entirely expected for my dad. So expected, in fact, that I'd had a nightmare about it the previous night.

It had felt real. Too real, even after I'd woken up and reminded myself that I'd never had sex with Reid, Anne-Marie was not actually a robot my dad had developed to spy on me, and she didn't have the ability to transform Reid into a wheel-shaped device that could teleport me from my apartment to a cavernous version of my dad's foyer, which had turned into some kind of courtroom where he was the judge.

In hindsight, maybe I shouldn't have eaten the rest of that block of cheese before going to bed.

But the weirdness aside, the rest of the dream had been me reliving Saturday morning when Anne-Marie had caught us over and over. It was convincing enough that I swore I could smell JP's cologne, a spicy, woodsy scent with a hint of floral that was still distinctly masculine. When I woke up, my lips felt swollen, like he'd just been kissing them.

Because even though my mind had conjured up someone who looked like Reid, everything from my heart to my pussy knew the person I'd been dreaming about was JP.

That didn't matter, though. What mattered was that even my subconscious knew something was weird about my dad not saying anything about Reid answering my phone, and that fact had thrown me off enough that I hadn't gotten around to studying the night before.

Which didn't even matter because I'd been focusing on the wrong project, and now my TA was offering to sell me two pills so I had a chance to get my paper done in time.

"So?" Glitch said, raising their eyebrows at me. "Are you in? Forty bucks for two, fifty if you're leaving a tip to make up for the pain in my ass you've been all semester. I accept cash or e-transfer."

I started to say no.

Because of course I did. I was *trained* for this. I'd been to enough "Say No To Drugs" presentations and seen enough after-school-specials to know what I should do. I was supposed to put my hands on my hips and loudly tell Glitch that only real big *losers* bought drugs. Preferably while they wore stereotypical baggy jeans and a belt with spikes on it or something to show their villainous nature while I sported a modest outfit featuring frilly socks and an out-of-style side ponytail.

I was supposed to declare that I wasn't the kind of impulsive person who bought drugs from someone.

That my mom and dad worked hard to make sure they raised me with strong morals—or my mom had, at least.

That I was *not* going to take drugs just because someone said they'd help me get my paper done in time, and that I *didn't* need drugs to have fun.

But the thing was, I didn't live in an after school special.

Strong morals or not, I *was* impulsive.

And I very well might need drugs to finish my paper on time.

"I'll take them," I said, and held out my hand.

Chapter Twenty
Seagulls Don't Have Tits

ONCE IN A WHILE, I wondered if I was secretly part wizard.

Coincidence was one thing, but there had been enough instances of me thinking something random only to have that thing happen shortly after for me to wonder.

I didn't mean things that had obvious consequences. If I thought to myself "I'm going to fail this paper because I mixed up the due date with the midterm date" and proceeded to fail the paper, it wasn't exactly unexpected.

But if I thought "Boy, I sure miss Ben right now, but I wish I could randomly run into him somewhere because I don't want to text him out of nowhere and dump all my problems on him" and then got kicked out of Dr. Spitzki's class because my phone rang unexpectedly, it would be *super* fucking weird if the person on the other end of the phone was Ben.

Unfortunately, it wasn't.

"Hey, Daughter of Mine!" my mom said after I answered.

"Hey Mom," I said, walking past Dr. Spitzki, who was still pointing at the classroom door in a silent order to get out. "One sec."

"No, no," Dr. Spitzki said, his voice full of bright sarcasm. "Actually, Nellie, maybe this is one call worth answering. Let me see your phone."

I looked at him incredulously. "You want to talk to my mom?"

"Normally I would refuse to speak to a student's parents since all of you are adults by the time you get into my classroom," Dr. Spitzki said. "But given how childish you act, maybe a dose of parental disappointment is what's needed for you to smarten up."

A few of my classmates let out awkward chuckles, though it seemed to be more out of discomfort than anything. Far more of them had looks of shock on their face, and at least one person in the second row let out a whispered "What the fuck?"

Which was fair. It was pretty harsh, though even I wouldn't argue that I didn't deserve it, given how much of a shit I'd been in Dr. Spitzki's classes over the past four years. But it also didn't bother me at all.

If anything, I felt sorry for Dr. Spitzki.

Because my mom heard him, too.

"Give the phone to that dick-cheese-licking-walnut-fucker, Nellie," she said.

I had no idea what a dick-cheese-licking-walnut-fucker was, but I wasn't about to correct her. "Okay, Dr. Spitzki. If you say so."

"Excellent," Dr. Spitzki said as he took my phone. "Hello, Mrs. Belanger."

Oof. Fumbled before he even had a fighting chance.

I couldn't hear everything my mom said, but given that he started the conversation by reminding her she'd once been married to my dad, "walnut fucker" was probably among the nicer things. The smug look on Dr. Spitzki's face was gone by the time he got another word in.

"I simply wanted to give you my opinion on the matter," he said. After a pause, his face twisted in confusion. "Seagulls don't have those, Mrs. B—right. Of course... No, they... Vicki, seagulls don't have tits. They're not *mammals*!"

The entire class burst out laughing, including me. I was willing to bet my mom had told him she didn't give a seagull's left tit about his opinion, but Dr. Spitzki seemed to be too hung up on the fact that my mom thought birds had tits to realize she was telling him she didn't give a fuck.

When he handed the phone back to me a few minutes later, it had been replaced by what I assumed would be the same expression as someone who just licked dick cheese out of a walnut he'd fucked.

"I see where you get it," he said.

"I tried to warn you," I said.

"Just leave, Nellie."

I shrugged and turned, even as the other students started laughing again.

"—piece of shit they hire to teach at that school," my mom was saying as I lifted the phone to my ear. "Of course seagulls have tits!"

"They definitely don't," I said. "Birds can't breastfeed."

"Explain chicken breasts then, smartass," she said.

"Sure. It's the chest part of the chicken. But they don't have mammary glands and 'tit' generally implies a nipple of some kind, so—"

"So you're smart enough to know how bird tits work, but not to turn your phone off during class?" my mom asked.

I twisted my mouth, trying not to laugh as I found a bench to sit on around the corner from Dr. Spitzki's classroom and office. "I thought you were on my side."

"I'm on your side when it comes to not embarrassing you in front of a room full of people," she snapped. "Unfortunately, that gull nipple you have for a professor is completely correct about it being rude to interrupt class like that."

"I know. I just forgot. But since I got kicked out anyway, was there anything in particular you were calling about?"

"Of course there is," she said. "I wanted to say Happy Thanksgiving before I go on vacation."

I bit back a smile. "When are you leaving for Vegas?"

"In about twenty minutes," she said.

"To go to the airport?"

"No, to get on the plane," she said. "We're waiting right now."

After making sure she wasn't getting arrested by air marshals for causing a scene in the middle of an airport or something, I circled back to the topic of her trip again, trying as subtly as I could to figure out who the other person in her *we* situation was.

"What are you going to do besides win the jackpot while you're there?" I asked.

"Oh, wander the Strip," she said. "Hit up the outlet malls. Maybe see a show or two."

"What kind of show?" I asked.

"I haven't decided yet, hon. There are so many to pick from."

"You should go see the Magic Mike one," I said.

"Nellie!" she said, cackling. "I can't do that."

"Oh. You like Chippendale's better?"

"I'm not going to see a male stripper show," she said.

"Why not?" I asked, sounding as innocent as I could. "That's the perfect thing to do with your friend on a girl's trip."

She didn't fall for it. "My *friend* and I are not interested in that kind of thing."

"No? What's she into instead? I'll look up some ideas for you while you're on your flight."

"Very kind of you, Daughter of Mine, but you should be focused on not getting kicked out of class instead of looking up shows in Vegas."

"Well, I already got kicked out, so I'm free for a while," I said. "It's really no problem."

"Right," she said. "Except it is."

I frowned. "What?"

She sighed. "Hon... listen. Please be more responsible."

My lips parted as I blinked down at my hands. "What?"

"Your professor might be more useless than a mesh raincoat, but as much as I hate to admit it, you're in the wrong here." She sighed, the sound uncomfortable. "If you've aggravated him to the point he's answering your phone in class, it's obvious this is an ongoing issue. You're paying to be there, Nellie. Wasting your tuition by getting kicked out of class isn't smart. You're better than how you're acting right now, hon."

I glanced at my feet, trying to suppress the familiar sensation of guilt that always appeared when my mom mentioned tuition or bills or anything to do with the money she didn't know I was taking from my dad, so there was room for the mostly unfamiliar feeling of disappointing my mom. Because while she hadn't outright said the whole "I'm not mad, just disappointed" line, I heard the intent of it in her words.

And is there anything worse than that?

Other than an entire list of things that are far, far worse than disappointing your mom. But it still sucked.

"Okay," I said. "Well, in that case, I have to go."

"Nellie—"

"I have to get to my next class." I was actually going to the library to study because I was done for the day, but that was a lot less time-sensitive than I needed my excuse to be. I scratched at my thumb with my forefinger. "Have a safe flight and a good time with your *friend*."

"Honey—"

"And Happy Thanksgiving," I said.

She sighed again. "I love you, hon. Have a good weekend."

After hanging up, I opened my messages app.

Then I hesitated, turned the screen off, and twisted my phone in my hands.

I wanted to tell someone about this. To rant. To have a sympathetic ear commiserate with me about the fact that my mom wouldn't even tell me who she'd ditched me for.

But Sydney was in class and more importantly, I'd been leaning on her for everything lately, even though she had her own stuff going on.

She still hadn't told Olivier she'd found out about his wife, let alone told his wife about it. She kept saying she wasn't ready, that she didn't know how she wanted to do it, that she was scared. And all of those things were very fair.

But it had gotten to a point that Olivier knew something was wrong. The day before, he'd finally told her he noticed she wasn't calling or texting him first. That she hadn't put any thought into coming to visit him, and had turned down his offer to come see her.

I didn't want to add more to her plate.

Then there was Anne-Marie. Or, rather, there *wasn't* Anne-Marie. She'd finally stopped texting me, which was exactly what I'd wanted, so I didn't know why it bothered me so much.

Maybe because I was starting to feel guilty about it.

Regardless, she wasn't an option. And JP wasn't an option, either. I'd never responded to the single text he'd sent asking how I was, despite the fact that the unread notification was killing me.

And for the second time that day, I thought about how much I missed Ben.

I missed talking to him. Sex with Ben had been great, of course, but I missed him far more on a platonic level. He had the right balance of understanding and gentle guidance that made me feel supported, but not judged. I didn't have to worry about what came out of my mouth around Ben. Even if I was wrong, he listened to my justifications for why I felt a certain way.

I needed that. With everything going on right then, I needed it more than I even wanted to admit.

But Ben wasn't here, and I wasn't a magical wizard who could conjure up his presence with a simple thought, and I had studying to do.

So I walked down the hallway that led to the library, which passed by another hallway that had a bunch of professors' offices in it, which was empty except for a single figure unlocking a door about halfway down the hall.

A single but very, *very* familiar figure.

I was seeing things, I told myself. It was probably another professor who had an office in the same spot. Or whoever was using that office for the year that Ben was on sabbatical. It *couldn't* be—

My feet started moving before I'd even tried to convince myself it wasn't him. I hadn't even finished the thought when I reached the office I'd seen the person go into, the door still sitting open and the nameplate that had always been there still displayed on the wall beside it. His back was to the door, a familiar messenger bag sitting on the chair on one side of the desk as he rifled through a file folder.

"I'm surprised you let them put 'Dr. Ben Cameron' on the door. I thought you hated being called 'Doctor,'" I said.

Ben jolted so violently that he knocked a cup of writing utensils off his desk. Pens and pencils clattered to the ground and scattered, a few of them going flying as he whirled around.

"Holy freakin' Christ," he gasped. "Nellie?"

Fuck, he looked good.

Ben's medium-gold skin had darkened from the California sun, though the biggest change on his face was the layer of scruff on his cheeks and chin. I'd seen him with a couple of days' growth on his face before, but this was more than that. His thick hair was pushed back off his forehead, showing off the surprise in his hazel eyes. And his smile...

Well, that wasn't there.

Once he'd finished gaping at me, his mouth closed into a worried line, not quite a grimace but most definitely not the pleasant expression someone would hope to see on the face of a person they'd missed.

In short, it didn't seem like Ben was particularly thrilled to see me.

Chapter Twenty-One
What If

"Hi, Professor Cameron," I said, pretending the fact that he was staring at me like I was his worst nightmare personified didn't hurt nearly as much as it did.

"Nellie," he said again. "What... why are you... uh..."

"I go to school here," I said. "And I just wanted to say hello. I hope your sabbatical is going well."

"It is," he said, still gaping a bit. "Yes. It's... it's going very well."

"Cool," I said. "Well, have a good day."

And I left.

Well, I turned and took three steps before Ben called after me.

"Nellie, wait. Don't go."

I told myself not to listen. He didn't want to see me. And that was well within his rights, as was him being nervous about my presence in his office. There were no hard feelings about that. It was to be expected.

So I kept walking.

For two more steps, at least, before a little tug in my chest made me stop and go back to the doorway of Ben's office.

"What, as the kids say, is up?" I said, trying to sound casual.

He lowered his voice a bit. "Is anyone, ah, in the hallway?"

I shook my head.

His mouth twitched. It wasn't quite a smile, not when there was that much concern in his eyes, but it had the hint of one. "You can come in if you'd like to talk, you know."

"It's okay," I said. "You're busy. I can leave you to whatever it is you're doing and—"

"I'm never too busy for you, Ms. Belanger."

The sudden warmth in his voice was jarring given his initial reaction. Or, well... what I *thought* his initial reaction was. I stared, not quite sure what to think or how to respond. Seconds earlier, he'd looked at me like I was the Ghost of Hookups Past come to drag him to a disciplinary tribunal. Like despite the fact that we'd parted on the best possible terms for a professor and his former student who'd spent the summer fucking each other's brains out, he would've rather seen an apparition clad in chains and moneyboxes and ragged nineteenth century clothing—because the ghost of Jacob Marley was visibly spookier than the Ghost of Christmas Past, obviously—standing there instead of me.

How in the hell was I supposed to believe someone who had just looked at me like that wanted to see me at all? Especially since he hadn't messaged or emailed me or anything since he'd left for California?

Before I could respond, Ben did that thing where he knew exactly what I was thinking and shifted, glancing past me before lowering his voice again.

"Let me explain?" he asked just loud enough that I could hear him. "If you have a moment, that is."

I didn't consider it.

Not for a second.

I just walked into his office.

You couldn't consider something you'd already decided to do, after all.

"Should I close the door?" I asked.

"No," he said, then frowned. "Wait. Yes."

"What was the thought process behind that?" I asked as I closed the door.

His mouth twitched in amusement. "A closed door between us and any potential witnesses invites far, *far* too much temptation."

"Fair. I do tend to misbehave more when doors are closed," I said. "So why'd you make me close it?"

"I figured the chance of someone overhearing our conversation is higher than us giving into those temptations," he said. "Especially given the fact that my reaction clearly upset you, I feel like the chance of misbehaviour plummeted."

I didn't meet his eyes as I wandered further into the office. "I definitely got the sense that you're currently anti-misbehaviour."

He sighed, bending down to pick up the empty cup. "That wasn't my intent at all. I'm sorry."

"It's fine."

"It's not." He started collecting some of the pens off the floor. "I needed some things from my office. I was worried about running into you, so I waited until I knew you'd be in class. Which meant I was extra startled when you appeared."

I dug my thumbnail into my finger harder. "So you didn't want to see me."

"Understandable conclusion, but incorrect." He straightened up and set the pen cup on the desk. "I am absolutely *thrilled* to see you, Nellie."

"You just said you waited—"

"Because I didn't know what the reaction would be if I ran into you," he said.

"You don't trust me to be good, Professor?" I asked.

"I should hope not," he said. "But I meant for me, mainly."

Frowning, I finally glanced up at him. "How so?"

"The first thing I thought when I saw you standing there—after 'Oh God, I hope I'm not going to have a heart attack from jumping like that,' that is—was that I wanted to kiss you," he said, half-laughing. "I tried to avoid running into you unexpectedly because I didn't trust myself to act like I don't know what it's like to be inside you. If I'd be able to look at you and maintain some kind of casual conversation without everyone being able to tell I was picturing you naked."

Damn.

I fought to keep my breath from hitching, instead tapping my hands against the desk. "You could've texted me. My number hasn't changed."

"And there lies the other aspect of things that I never thought to address before I left," he said, chuckling. "I didn't want to put you in an uncomfortable position. As many times as I've wanted to send a message to see how you're doing, I told myself I couldn't. I needed to leave it up to you to reach out. So I wasn't entirely certain... and then suddenly, you were standing there and before I could even process that you were clearly comfortable enough to come and say hello, you'd started walking away."

"Oh." Warmth stemmed up my neck and to my cheeks, but not the good kind. "I wish you would've told me. I thought you didn't want to hear from me, so I... I didn't want to bother you."

"Oh, Nellie." He shook his head. "I handled this badly. I'm sorry."

The sincerity of his apology sent an unfamiliar ache through my chest. "It's okay."

"It's not. I wish I'd thought this through a bit more. But I was preoccupied with Isabelle's recovery and—"

"Wait," I said. "Isabelle? Your ex-wife?"

"She had a medical emergency last week and had to have surgery. But her wife uses a wheelchair and Isabelle needs at least a week of assistance getting around and, ah... you know." His cheeks reddened. "Using the washroom and showering and such. Neither of them have anyone else they're close enough to ask for that kind of thing. Stanford has a fairly generous personal leave policy, so I offered to come back to help for the week." He held up the folder I'd seen him looking through when I first walked up to his office. "I also had some study results here that would be useful for the project I'm currently working on, so I drove to Ottawa to pick those up before I fly back."

"That was nice of you," I said. "I hope she's okay."

"She's more concerned with being cleared to run the marathon she's been training for in the spring," he said, chuckling. "It'll take a couple of months, but she'll be fine."

"Okay. Well, I guess it makes sense you didn't tell me, then," I said, heaving a fake sigh. "You're forgiven. And I'm sorry I ruined your plans to avoid me."

He grinned. "What are you doing out of class, anyway? I was sure you had a pathology class this afternoon. Dr. Spitzki only teaches it once a year and it's always been at the same time."

"I got kicked out again."

He flicked an eyebrow up. "Again?"

"Yeah. He doesn't seem to like my ringtone, even though I got rid of the Titanic one and now it's just Spongebob Squarepants."

He chuckled. "You're not going to fall behind though, are you?"

"Not in that class," I said without thinking.

Ben tilted his head to the side. "What class are you falling behind in?"

"We don't have to talk about that," I said.

"Don't we?" he asked.

"Nope. Let's talk about you. Do you have a girlfriend in California?"

"I do not," he said, frowning. "How's your semester going, Nellie?"

"It's fine. Have you been surfing yet?"

"No, but I've spent a good amount of time jogging on the beach." He folded his arms across his chest. "What's giving you trouble?"

"Nothing. How did—"

"Nellie," he said. "I can tell when you're lying."

"There's nothing to lie about," I said. "My classes this semester are a little harder than I expected. Probably because I've got other stuff going on and just need to pay more attention to things." I shrugged. "I mixed up some due dates for Forensic Science and Law. It's a stupid class anyway. And I got the paper done in time, no thanks to wasting fifty bucks on Glitch. And now I'm ready for the midterm next week so it's totally fine."

Ben nodded slowly. "What's Glitch?"

Fuck.

Fuck my stupid mouth.

And not in the fun way.

"The TA for that class," I said.

"What, ah... what was the fifty bucks for?"

I swallowed hard. "I couldn't get an extension so they gave me some... advice."

"What kind of advice?"

Fuck. I could feel my face turning red.

"Stupid advice," I said. "That I shouldn't have followed and that didn't help anyway, so it's not a big deal."

"Mmm," Ben said. "See, it sounds like it might be a bit of a big deal."

"Maybe it's just an embarrassing deal you're going to judge me for," I mumbled.

"Nellie, don't tell me you cheated."

"I didn't cheat."

"I know it can be tempting, but it's incredibly easy to find plagiarism and it would end your career before it even begins. You've worked so hard—"

"I didn't *cheat*," I repeated heatedly. "I thought you could tell when I was lying."

His eyebrows pinched together. "Yes, but—"

"So you should be able to tell when I'm telling the truth." I picked at the side of my thumbnail. "I didn't cheat. I wrote the paper myself."

"And Glitch helped you?"

I couldn't bring myself to look him in the eye. "Glitch, um... suggested... some help. From study buddies."

"What kind of study buddy charges fifty dollars to—oh." He nodded slowly. "The pill kind."

My shoulders tensed. "Don't lecture me."

"I'm not going to—"

"I was panicking and it was a stupid decision. I know." I crossed my arms. "You don't need to tell me that. And I already got the karma from it because the stupid pills didn't work anyway."

"What do you mean by that?" he asked.

"What do you mean, what do I mean?" I glared at the floor in front of me. "They didn't work."

"What did you think they were supposed to do?" he pressed.

"Glitch said they'd give me, like, energy," I said. "But they didn't."

He was quiet for a moment. "Did you feel calm?"

"What?"

"After taking them? Or focused?"

"Focused on what? I don't understand—"

"Humour me for a moment, Nellie," he said. "After you took the pill, you wrote your paper. Do you remember feeling focused on your paper or more productive than usual?"

I sighed, but did as he asked and thought back to a few days earlier. I'd taken the first pill as soon as I got home, then sat down in front of my laptop and started working. A while later, I'd looked at the clock and realized a few hours had passed, but I didn't have any more energy than I had before. So I'd taken the other one and kept working for the rest of the night.

"I guess so," I said. "I pulled an all-nighter and missed two classes the next day, but I finished the paper."

Ben nodded before drawing in a deep breath and let it out.

"I need to do something inappropriate," he said, turning around and reaching across his desk.

Oh thank God. "Does it involve taking my pants off or do we just need to do yours?"

He half-laughed. "It involves me suggesting something I probably shouldn't be suggesting considering the amount of times we've had our pants off together."

He turned back to me and started scribbling something on the scrap of paper he'd grabbed. After he handed it to me, I frowned down at the name and phone number he'd scrawled. "What's this?"

"You should probably get assessed for ADHD," Ben said.

And I fucking lost it.

"Are you serious?" I snapped, crumpling the paper in my hand. "This is getting really old. Why does everyone keep *saying* that?!"

"Who else has said that?" he asked.

"Glitch," I said. "They've asked, like, three times. And I had this teacher once, but she... I was going through some stuff. And now you, because apparently there just *has* to be something wrong with me, and—"

"There is nothing wrong with you, Nellie." Ben's voice was gentle, especially considering the iciness in my own tone. He reached out, taking the crumpled paper back and working it open so he could smooth it out. "But there are some things you've said that are fairly common in other people with ADHD. And with the study buddies not working as you'd hoped—"

"They were just shitty pills," I said.

"Maybe," he said. "Or they were one of the usual stimulants that people refer to as study buddies or dexies or whatever name students are using to describe what we prescribe as Adderall or Dexedrine or Vyvanse. For people without ADHD, it increases energy, but for people with ADHD, it can be calming and help with focus. It's why they're prescribed."

I stared at him wordlessly. He folded the paper in half, then held it out to me again.

"This is a colleague who does assessments," he said. "Call or don't call. It's up to you. I simply want you to have the resource if you need it."

I took the paper slowly. "But you think I have it."

"I think finding out if things could be better would be worth talking to someone far more experienced with that sort of thing than I am," he said. "I'm a forensic psychologist. He's a psychiatrist. He went to school with Isabelle and specializes in late diagnoses. It's a particular passion of his. If you say I'm the one who gave you the number, he may be able to get you in more quickly."

"If I do that, he might question why you gave it to me," I said.

"And?" Ben asked, unconcerned.

"You're not worried I'd tell him…" I trailed off, gesturing between us.

"If you do, so be it," he said. "I am still never going to ask you to keep that a secret to protect me, Nellie. But if you're concerned that you can't be fully open with him, I will say that as a psychiatrist, he doesn't take many—if *any*—patients for talk therapy. The shortage of doctors, especially mental health professionals, and *especially* ones who deal with adult assessments is—well." He shook his head. "I know he has a list of recommended psychologists. He asked me once if I would be willing to be on it, but I don't do that kind of therapy either. Regardless, if you feel the need—"

"I won't." I slipped the piece of paper into my pocket. "If I even call."

Ben nodded in understanding, but didn't say anything. A few moments of contemplative silence passed.

"Any other new and exciting things to tell me?" he asked.

"I got a tattoo."

"What?!"

I had to brace myself against the side of his desk as I laughed at his reaction. Ben looked so completely startled that I couldn't stop, although it might have had something to do with the relief of a change in subject.

"Why is that so surprising?" I asked. "Lots of people have tattoos."

"I just never pictured you with one," he said. "What did you get?"

I bit back a smirk. "Do you want to see it?"

The air between us tightened until heated tension filled the office.

"Is it in an appropriate location for me to see?" Ben asked.

"Of course, Professor Cameron. I wouldn't have to undress."

"Are you saying that because you could technically keep your clothes on to show me?"

"Yes."

He made a soft noise. "Where is it?"

"On my ribs."

"But you'd lift your shirt far higher than necessary, wouldn't you?"

"You know me."

He swore softly. "There's a line, Nellie. We've crossed that line, repeatedly, and admittedly enjoyably, but we're in my office right now. This line is so far beyond that line that you can't even see the original line anymore, that's how beyond that line we are."

"I see your point," I replied, glancing down at his lap. "May I counter with the fact that your cock is hard?"

He flushed red. "For the record, this is entirely wrong. Morally reprehensible. Completely unethical."

"So should I step back over the line?"

Ben opened his mouth, then hesitated.

"I'll go, Ben," I said. "You could come over later, if you wanted. If getting a blowjob while I kneel under your desk is too far over the line."

His throat flexed, then he let out a sigh that was dejected and secretly pleased all at once.

"Show me your tattoo, Ms. Belanger," he murmured, his voice husky and low.

A little while later, I let him smooth my hair down and adjust my t-shirt so it wasn't askew. He wiped a drop of cum I'd missed off my chin, then promised that he would always be happy to hear from me and I could message him whenever I wanted.

Then I cheerfully continued on my way to the library like I'd intended to before I got sidetracked sucking Ben's cock before letting him slip his hand into my jeans and finger me until I had to bite down on the sleeve of my hoodie to muffle the sound of my orgasm.

And I was going to study.

I really was.

But after I had my headphones on and my laptop open in front of me, I dug in my pocket to grab my lip balm and felt the little piece of paper Ben had given me.

He was wrong.

He had to be.

But even if he wasn't, what did it matter?

If I had ADHD—and that was very much an *if*—what was knowing about it going to do? I was almost done school. I could take care of myself. My life was good, aside from the stuff that sucked, but most of those things were out of my control. Knowing I had ADHD wouldn't fix my dad's materialism. It wouldn't change my mom's flightiness. It wouldn't make JP less of a bastard or make Anne-Marie forget that she'd caught me fucking her brother.

Adding some extra letters to my medical chart wouldn't fix anything. All it would do was answer the question of why I was the way I was, and what good was that? I was *fine* as I was. My life was fine as it was.

But.

But.

I couldn't tell whose voice it was whispering in my head. It wasn't Ben's. It wasn't my fifth-grade teacher who couldn't stand me because I was a shithead in her class. It wasn't my mom or dad's.

I didn't know whose it was.

Maybe it was mine.

But what if it could *be better?* it whispered.

I stared at my computer screen for a long, long time.

Then I clicked the browser and brought up the search engine.

how do you know if you have adhd

Chapter Twenty-Two
Donut Fuck With Me

"You know, just when I think I can't be any more impressed by your ass, it goes and shows how talented it is by learning how to make phone calls on its own," JP said.

"I didn't butt dial you," I replied in a hushed voice.

There was a breathlessness to his voice and in the background, I could hear clanging sounds over pounding music.

"Damn," he said. "It almost sounds like it's speaking to me."

"I *am* speaking to you."

"If only it was a little louder. I can barely hear it."

I gritted my teeth. "I can't talk louder right now. Maybe you could go somewhere quieter."

"Why would I pause my workout because an admittedly fantastic ass is on the other line?"

"JP, stop. I called you on purpose."

"Really?" he said. "Well, you have to understand my confusion, since it's been, oh... two weeks now?"

My stomach ached and I curled over the arm I had crossed across my lower body. "I know."

"Seriously, I can barely hear you. Can I call you when I'm done working out or—"

"No," I said. "I need your help."

"Is it the kind of help that involves your ass in some way? Because I could be persuaded."

I hated him.

I hated that he could somehow call me out the way he was while still being playful. That he was clearly bothered that I'd ghosted him—which was fair—but that his words, while tinted with sarcasm, didn't cut the way I probably deserved.

If he could've just been the asshole I knew he was capable of being instead of the person threatening to make me smile even as he teased me, this would be a lot fucking easier.

"I need you to be serious right now," I said.

"Uh... okay," he said. "What's wrong?"

I glanced up. My ensuite bathroom at my dad's house was reasonably large, but even though I was sitting on the edge of the tub at the far end of the room, the door seemed like it was right in front of me. And yes, it was closed. Yes, it was locked. Yes, I'd shoved a towel against the crack at the bottom and turned the tap and fan on *and* could hear the music playing in my bedroom loud enough to cover the way I was whispering.

But it felt like the person on the other side was waiting with an ear pressed right up against the door.

"I wouldn't be asking if I had literally any other option," I said as loud as I could manage. "Seriously. Your... Anne-Marie is here and I can't leave and I just, I can't... I need—" I closed my eyes, grimacing. "I need you to do something for me."

"What is it?" he asked.

I jabbed my fingernail into my thumb so hard I thought it might start bleeding. "And don't laugh at me."

"I mean, is it funny?" he asked.

"JP!"

"Okay!" he said, not bothering to mask his chuckle. "Even if it's funny, I won't laugh loud enough for you to hear it."

I scrunched my eyes closed.

"Nell?" he said after a moment. "Are you still there?"

"Never mind," I whispered. "I'll deal with it myself."

"Wait," he said. "Are you crying?"

I buried my face in my free hand, my cheeks burning with embarrassment.

Because yes, I was crying.

That wasn't the part I was embarrassed about. People cried. Whatever. And I wasn't all that embarrassed that JP knew I was crying. He'd seen me cry before, though mainly when we were kids.

But as an adult, he'd had his tongue in my ass on more than one occasion, so him knowing I was crying didn't really get to me.

I was embarrassed because it all started over a donut.

"I am sorry, but we are sold out," the cashier had said in French. "It is the most popular flavour. You need to come earlier in the day."

"I couldn't get here earlier in the day," I'd replied, staring at the display case.

"That is not my problem," the cashier said.

Which was true, but for one, they didn't have to say it. And for two, it didn't change the fact that all I wanted to get through the rest of this godforsaken day was a goddamn creamsicle donut from Trou de Beigne and they didn't *have* it.

I'd planned to leave Ottawa to drive to Montreal for my dad's dinner party before rush hour started, but then Glitch had handed back our midterm papers in Forensic Science and Law.

"Sorry," they murmured as they slipped me not the printed-out copy of my paper like everyone else was getting because the professor liked to leave notes scrawled in red pen when he was marking, but a single sheet of paper requesting I meet with Bruce Shelby immediately after class.

I'd stared down at it, confused, then glanced up at them. "What does this mean?"

But they just grimaced and moved to the next student, leaving me sweating until Shelby dismissed the class.

"You asked to talk to me?" I'd said, showing him the paper.

"Who are you?" he'd asked.

"Nellie Belanger."

"Belanger. Right." Shelby took the paper. "You have your laptop with you?"

"Uh... yeah," I'd said.

He'd pulled a folder out of his briefcase and flipped it open. On top was my paper, a red grade scrawled in the corner of the cover sheet.

A good grade.

A *suspiciously* good grade.

"This was well written," he said casually.

I knew too many lawyers too well to believe he'd made me sit through an entire lecture sweating through my hoodie just to tell me I'd done a good job. "Thank you. What was the problem, then?"

He slid the paper to the side, revealing a print-out of my grades from the rest of the semester, which aside from the case study JP had helped me with, were all significantly lower than the one on my paper. "I'm sure you understand how it appears to go from the grades you've been averaging to a grade like this. But I've been doing this long enough to know that before getting the university involved, there are easier ways to ensure the work is legitimate."

"Okay," I'd said. Despite knowing I'd done nothing wrong—aside from buying drugs, but that wasn't the kind of thing that would make my work illegitimate—my heart rate spiked. "What am I supposed to do?"

He'd nodded towards my backpack. "If you consent to let my TA check the program you wrote the paper in on your laptop, we can have this settled in the next few minutes."

And like, of course I did. I knew I didn't have to *let* either of them go through my personal stuff, but I also had nothing to hide and he wasn't wrong. Getting the university involved and proving I hadn't cheated could take months.

But Glitch was busy dealing with other things, and Shelby said I couldn't leave until they'd looked because then I might fake the information or delete the file or something, so I'd had to stand there until they were done.

Thankfully, once Glitch pulled up the file, it was clear from the version history that I'd typed and retyped and edited the whole thing myself. Shelby did raise his eyebrows at the fact that I'd done the paper in one day, but said it was enough proof for him that I hadn't cheated.

"Good job," Glitch had whispered after Shelby gave me permission to pack my laptop up and walked away. "Your study buddy helped a lot, then?"

I shot a glare at them. "I don't want to get into it."

They'd pressed their lips together, amused. "It helped more than you thought it would? Because if that's the case, you should know—"

"Shut up." I'd zipped my bag closed. "I know what it was, I know what that means, and I don't want to hear it."

They'd raised their hands in surrender. "Either way, congrats on your mark."

I'd rushed back to my apartment, but I still ended up leaving almost an hour later than I'd planned. Traffic out of Ottawa had been bad, and it got worse the closer I got to Montreal. And since the only things stopping Montreal drivers from being mistaken for Formula One drivers were the existence of a designated racetrack, an ability to follow the actual rules, and talent, I was a bit on edge.

And since my dad had planned dinner later than usual so I could be there, I decided to treat myself to a snack and detoured to Trou de Beigne.

But the donut I wanted wasn't there. And between that and the stress of someone nearly rear-ending me for the grave sin of not wanting to plow my car into a group of daycare kids being led to the park on the other side of a crosswalk, it was the last thing I'd needed.

"Miss, if you're not getting anything, I need to help the next person," the cashier had said.

"I'm still getting something," I muttered, trying to ignore the way my eyes were stinging. "I'll take, um... one of everything."

The Bourbon Fruit Loop donut I ended up munching on as I drove the rest of the way to my dad's *did* cheer me up quite a bit. But the universe was conspiring against me because it turned out I'd been delayed the exact amount of time it took to make sure I was walking up to my dad's front door just as it opened so Della Kinsley and Jean-Luc Marchand—JP and Anne-Marie's parents—could walk out.

"Nellie!" Della had said, her voice bright. "How good to see you. Kimberlee said she was starting to get worried that you hadn't arrived for tonight."

"I got stuck in traffic," I'd replied.

Della glanced at the white donut box in my hands, but graciously ignored it. "Well, I am so glad we got to say hello since we cannot attend the party tonight. Kimberlee had invited us to her soiree, but we had a last-minute obligation come up."

Mr. Marchand had scoffed vocally. "That's a polite way to say our son hasn't managed to remove his head from his ass."

I looked at him, shocked. Della grabbed her husband's arm like she'd gone to slap it but realized it would look bad, so dug her fingers into his sleeve.

"Darling," she'd said, letting out an uncomfortable chuckle. "That was incredibly inappropriate."

"I'm not wrong," Mr. Marchand had grumbled.

She forced another loud, awkward laugh. "Well, we must be going, Nellie. JP had to bow out of a work-related event so we are going in his place, but Anne-Marie will be here in our place. I'll let her know you've arrived so she can come over and spend time with you before the party!"

I'd tried to say that wasn't necessary, mainly because I couldn't tell Anne-Marie's mom that I didn't want to see her and was already trying to figure out how I was going to avoid her during the party, but Della had yanked her husband off the front step and started marching across the yard to their house.

So of course, before I'd even finished saying hi to my dad and Kimberlee, I had a new text from Anne-Marie.

Annie

> I know you are still mad, chérie. But may I please, please, PLEASE come over? You can pretend I am not even there if you don't want to talk to me.

I'd frowned at my phone as I closed my bedroom door. That didn't sound like Anne-Marie at all. And I just...

She was still my friend.

I hoped.

Me

> If we don't have to talk about what happened, then sure

She sent about eighteen hearts and kiss emojis and said she'd be right there, and I'd barely finished reading the message when the doorbell rang.

"Thank you so, so much, *chérie*," Anne-Marie had gushed as she entered my room after my dad's assistant let her in. "If Remy was not away again this weekend, I would not be home, I swear. I cannot tell you how awkward it has been lately."

"What's going on?" I'd asked.

She'd opened her mouth, started to say something, and then stopped. "I... ah... I actually cannot tell you."

I'd stared at her, confused, until her face started turning red and she shifted uncomfortably.

"Because you would not like to talk about what happened?" she added quietly.

Oh.

Oh, shit.

"Do your parents know?" I asked.

Anne-Marie shook her head quickly. "Not that part of it. But the... the reason I..." She'd stopped, distress on her face as she tried to think of a way of saying what she needed to say without saying the things I'd said she couldn't say.

And of course I gave in.

"Just say it," I'd said. "I don't want to hear anything about, like... me... and him. But what else is going on?"

She'd bit her lip.

Then her eyes started to water.

"Nellie, it was *horrible*," she'd whispered. "I have never seen my father so angry. But Jean-Paul... he *quit*."

"Oh," I'd said, not surprised, then reminded myself I wasn't supposed to know. "Oh! Shit. He's not working with your dad?"

She'd nodded, grabbing a tissue off my vanity and dabbing at her eyes. "Remember I came to Ottawa because I found out my dad's firm was defending Clinton? And I said Jean-Paul was on the defense team? It turns out my brother was so disgusted with my dad for the whole thing that he found another job." She sniffled, her blonde hair swishing as she shook her head. "I said those horrible things to him when I caught him with you and it turned out he was planning to leave the entire time."

"Wow," I said.

"When he told my dad he got a new job, the fight they had... I don't know if you know, but my parents, um..." She shifted uncomfortably. "My mother got pregnant before they were married and my father's family was very unhappy. My grandfather cut them off, actually, at one point. Not forever, obviously, since"—she gestured vaguely around my room, which I took to mean she was referring to them being well-off now—"but my dad finished law school and started his firm and all of that on his own."

"That's impressive," I said.

She let out a watery laugh. "Yes, well, my dad told Jean-Paul there is no way he could ever build something like this and that he's going to come crawling back one day after he loses all his savings or knocks up some poor girl or something. And my brother told my dad that he was perfectly capable of building something even better, since unlike my dad, he's good at managing money and smart enough to use a condom."

Which was funny. And badass. And I was secretly so, so proud of JP for standing up to his dad like that, even though I would never say that to his face even if I *was* planning on ever talking to him again.

And I probably should have been listening as Anne-Marie talked, since that's what a good friend would do, and she needed a good friend just then. The Marchands may not have been a perfect family, but where I'd spent most of my childhood hearing my parents hurl horrible words at each other, Anne-Marie hadn't.

And I hadn't been there for her to lean on during any of it because of what I'd done with her brother.

But the guilt wasn't enough to overshadow the insistent little warning bell that was ringing in the back of my mind.

It was quiet, at first, barely louder than my thought that JP didn't *always* use a condom.

And then a bit louder as I told myself it was fine, since I was on birth control.

And louder still when I realized I couldn't remember if I'd taken my pill that day.

And then louder as I tried to remember if I'd taken it the day before, and the day before that.

It rang quieter as I checked my phone and breathed a silent sigh of relief, realizing I couldn't remember taking my pill because I was supposed to be on my period.

And then it fucking *screamed* at me.

"Annie, hold that thought," I'd said, because Anne-Marie was still talking. "I have to use the bathroom."

I'd closed the door, locked it, and double-checked the lock before grabbing my toiletry bag and digging out the ratty old pad I always hid my birth control in so my dad wouldn't find it.

And then I'd sat on the edge of the tub and called JP, fighting back tears.

"Babe?" JP said, the worry in his voice bringing me back to the present. "Are you actually crying?"

"Do *not* call me babe," I snapped, a hot tear spilling down my cheek. "I'm not your babe. I never have been. We are—were—friends. Just because we sometimes fuck doesn't mean that you can call me babe. Just because I haven't texted you in two weeks doesn't mean you can call me babe. *Don't* call me babe."

I wasn't sure if it was because of or despite the heat in my voice, but JP chuckled. "Alright, jeez. Just take a breath and tell me what's going on. Otherwise I'm gonna start thinking you're pregnant or something."

Because of course.

Of fucking course he had to say it.

When I didn't respond, JP chuckled again, the sound nervous. "Nellie?" he asked. "What do you need me to do?"

"I need you to bring me a pregnancy test," I whispered.

Chapter Twenty-Three
I Ruined Everything

The only thing that stopped me from assuming JP had hung up was that I could still hear the faint sounds of the gym in the background.

Past that, there was only silence. He'd gone so quiet that I didn't know if he was even breathing.

"You're joking," he finally said.

I closed my eyes, my stomach churning.

"Babe," he said, his voice hoarse. "Are you joking?"

"It might be nothing," I said. "It's *probably* nothing. I'm late. Like, two days late. Which I know isn't a lot. But I missed a couple of pills this month and I'm freaking out and I can't leave. Anne-Marie is here and my dad's having this party tonight and I—" My voice caught and I shoved a hand beneath my nose as it started to water. "I'm scared."

I wasn't exactly *prepared* for any specific reaction from JP, but there were a few options I might have thought were likely. I might have expected him to get angry, or to panic, or to ask incredulous questions like "How the fuck did you miss a *couple* of pills?" and "How do you know it's mine?" and "So you're getting an abortion, right?"

But even though in hindsight it was by far the most likely reaction, I was still shocked when he took a breath, let it out slowly, and spoke in a calm voice.

"How long before people show up for the dinner party?" he asked.

"An hour, maybe," I said.

"Alright. Here's what's going to happen." The background sounds faded until all I could hear was JP's voice. "I'm going to go to the *dep* and pick up a test. And some Advil. I'll put it in a bag under your car and let you know once it's there. You tell Anne-Marie you've got a headache and forgot your Advil in the car and run out to get it. Then go to the bathroom, take the test, and call me while you're waiting. We'll find out together."

"I..." I said, then trailed off.

"What?" he asked.

"That's... smart."

A hint of laughter tinted his voice. Not much, but it was there. "It's amazing what you can think of when you're not freaking out."

"I think I have a right to be freaking out," I said.

"Sure, but it won't do any good," he said. "Shit happens. The first thing we have to do is figure out what we're working with and go from there."

My eyes watered again. "Since when are you so logical?"

"It's a pretty good trait for a lawyer, babe."

I didn't think he intended to let the pet name slip out after my rant about it, but I didn't mind all that much. "Don't call me babe."

"One of these days you'll stop saying that," he said.

"One of these days you'll stop doing it."

"I wouldn't do that to you. I know how much you love it."

I glared down at the bathroom floor. He wasn't wrong, but like hell was I going to admit that.

"Nell?" he said. "It's gonna be okay."

"Easy for you to say."

"It's not, actually," he said. "It'd be a hell of a lot easier if we were—"

"Don't," I whispered. "Don't do this to me right now."

"—friends," he finished after a pause. "If we were still friends, babe."

My heart dropped. "Are we not?"

"I wasn't sure," he said. "I haven't heard from you and then you just said we *were* friends, not that we *are* friends. So I guess it depends on what you want."

I bit my lip, but it wasn't enough to stop my chin from trembling. "I want to be friends."

"Friends it is, then," he said. "Now go get ready for your party so I can get the test."

After hanging up, I took a few minutes to let my heart rate drop as much as it could and dabbed a cool cloth on my eyes, willing the redness to go down. Once I was done, I took a deep breath and opened the door.

"Are you feeling alright, *chérie*?" Anne-Marie asked, glancing at me in the reflection on the mirror as she blended out her blush.

"Yeah," I said. "Just a, uh... unsettled stomach."

She nodded knowingly. "It happens. Do you need some stomach medication? I have some Imodium in my purse, which I am sure is too much information, but I keep forgetting to take my Lactaid pills before eating, so—"

"I'm okay," I said quickly. "Really. What were you saying before I left?"

"Oh," she said. "Just that my mother refused to let my dad cut off Jean-Paul completely and reminded him he has no say over the trust funds my grandparents gave each of us. Not that I think Jean-Paul would need to rely on his because he *is* quite responsible with his money, but I am glad he has it as a backup. Just so not *everything* is going wrong all at once."

"What else is going wrong?" I asked before I could stop myself.

She glanced at me, her eyebrows raised.

Right.

Me.

I was going wrong.

"*Chérie*," Anne-Marie said, her voice guarded. "May I say one thing about what happened—"

"You *promised*, Anne-Marie," I said.

"It's only that I want to apologize."

"What?" I asked.

She sighed, looking down at her hands. "In my mind, it wasn't such a big deal. It was just silly and playful, the way people are about things like this. But Jean-Paul explained... a lot. About why you didn't want anyone to know. I am sorry I didn't respect that. But more, I am sorry I wasn't a friend you could trust to share that information with." She looked up, her eyes glimmering. "I wanted so badly to talk to you about everything going on. And Remy, he kept telling me to call and explain, but I kept telling myself I did not deserve your help when I was never that person for you."

And just...

Fuck.

Fuck.

My stomach churned again, guilt and sadness and remorse blending together.

"Thanks," I said. "I, um... am also sorry. That I... I, um, slept with your brother."

She waved a hand. "*Chérie*, if I stopped being friends with everyone who slept with my brother, I would have perhaps three friends and at least two of them would be lying to me. As much as I would love for you and Jean-Paul to—"

"Annie," I said, my voice low.

She lifted her hands. "I will not lie to you and pretend my opinion has changed on that, but all I mean is that he has a tendency to get around. It is no big thing. And I understand why you did not tell me, so there is nothing for you to be sorry for. But if you would be willing to forgive me..."

"I do," I said. "Of course."

Aesthetically, Anne-Marie was incredibly beautiful. Even if she didn't curate her appearance with the latest fashion and high-end makeup and regular salon treatments, she would still be one of those girls that people looked at in awe because she was so *pretty*.

The way she smiled right then, though, was probably one of the most beautiful smiles I'd ever seen on her face. It was bright and relieved and genuine.

And it killed me because I didn't feel like I deserved it.

Anne-Marie threw her arms around me and I hugged her back, agreeing the same way we did when we were kids that we would simply never fight again, even though we both knew we'd probably fight again at some point. We went back to getting ready and Anne-Marie must have felt like she'd gotten enough of her family drama off her chest, because she switched to talking about how Bruno had finally admitted to Remy that he was unhappy with Niko and needed to break up with him.

Which was good, because obviously I wanted to be happy that my friend was getting out of a toxic relationship.

But it was bad, too, because the topic was distracting enough that I almost forgot I was freaking out about my period being late.

And that *could* have been a good thing, but it meant that I wasn't fully paying attention to my phone while I rinsed my makeup brushes in the bathroom.

"—and of course Remy said he'd be happy to be there while Bruno talked to him," Anne-Marie said as I walked out of the bathroom with the clean brushes. "And—oh! You got another message, *chérie*."

She reached for my phone, which I'd stupidly left sitting on the vanity. And I panicked.

"Stop!" I half-shouted.

And unlike the last time I'd shouted at Anne-Marie to stop, this time, she froze, her eyes going wide.

"What—" she started, but I lunged across the room, the makeup brushes scattering along the top of my vanity as I threw them down and snatched my phone up. The message popped up on the lock screen beneath one that had been sent a few minutes earlier.

Bastard

> Left it there in a white plastic bag

> You there?

Thank God he was smart enough to keep it vague.

"What is wrong?" Anne-Marie asked, concern in her voice.

"Nothing," I said. "I... I thought it was going to be something else."

She lifted her eyebrows and I knew *exactly* what she was thinking, but before she even had the chance to forget that she said we weren't going to talk about it, I started towards my bedroom door.

"I have a stomachache," I said. "I left my Advil in the car. Be right back."

"I don't think Advil will help with that, *chérie*," Anne-Marie said, but I ignored her as I ran out of my room, still clutching my phone in my hand.

My heart wasn't pounding so much as it was fluttering, like it was anxious vibrations scattering through my veins instead of distinct beats. Slipping my shoes on, I dashed outside, glancing around to make sure no one was watching as I strode up to my car. I unlocked it, yanking the back door open so I could at least pretend I was looking in the place it would make the most sense for me to find Advil, and leaned down to see where he'd put the bag.

Except there was no bag.

I blinked, staring at the stretch of stone beneath my car, empty except for a few pieces of gravel and a crunchy looking leaf.

Maybe I was looking at the wrong spot, I thought. Straightening up as gracefully as I could, I walked to the other side of the car and repeated the action.

No bag.

I went to the hood. No bag. To the trunk. No bag. To the Porsche parked on the driveway that JP knew damn well wasn't mine.

No bag.

He must have been watching for my text because he replied seconds after I sent it.

Fuck.

There wasn't much I could do but take a last look before going back into the house. I opened the door, bumping it with my hip as I typed another message to JP.

"Looking for this?"

I dropped my phone.

It clattered against the tile in the foyer, the sound not quite sharp enough to echo in the cavernous room, and came to a stop screen down about a meter away from my dad's feet.

My dad, who was holding a white.

Plastic.

Bag.

I opened my mouth. Nothing came out.

"I imagine you must be," my dad said. "Seeing it was your car I found it under."

"How—" I breathed.

"I believe you have heard of windows," my dad said dryly. "I happen to have several them in my house. A few of which look out the front, where I was very curious about why Jean-Paul Marchand was poking around my daughter's vehicle." He let one of the bag handles drop open so he could reach in. "Now I am even more curious why the boy next door was leaving *this* underneath my daughter's car."

And he held up the pink-and-white box containing a two-pack of pregnancy tests.

"Me too," I said. "I wonder what—"

"What is this for?" my dad asked, his voice like ice.

"Maybe you should ask J—"

"What is it *for*?" he repeated.

"I don't—"

"So help me God, Eleanor, I—"

"It's mine."

For a moment, I wondered how the hell I'd learned to say things without speaking, because while the pregnancy tests were most definitely mine, that voice wasn't. But as my dad turned to look at the staircase, I followed his gaze and saw Anne-Marie standing near the top.

"Is it?" my dad asked.

"Yes," Anne-Marie said. "I needed those."

"Bullshit," my dad said.

I looked at him, stunned. "Dad—"

"It is not *bullshit*, Mr. Belanger," Anne-Marie said stiffly. "I did not want my parents to know, so—"

"So you asked your brother instead of your partner?" my dad said. "You asked him to leave it outside under someone else's car instead of simply bringing it to you directly? You asked him to bring it *here* instead of your own house, even though your parents are not home?"

Anne-Marie hesitated. "Well... yes."

He stared at her, then turned back to me without another word. "Are these yours, Eleanor?"

I glanced at Anne-Marie. "She just said—"

"Tell me the truth or I will call Jean-Luc and ask him to come speak with his daughter," he said. "Given everything *else* going on right now, I imagine that would not be especially welcome, would it?"

"Dad, that's not—"

He shook the box in my direction. "Tell me my daughter is not this stupid."

"I—"

"Are you?"

"I'm not—"

"Were you stupid enough to get yourself pregnant, Eleanor?"

And maybe someone else would have been able to hold it together.

Maybe someone else would've kept denying it and denying it and denying it until a man who was not known for giving in finally gave in.

Maybe someone else would have cried, hoping tears would be enough of a distraction to turn the conversation around, or at least enough to suppress the sparks of rage from being interrupted every *fucking* time she tried to say something.

But I didn't hold it together.

I knew he wouldn't give in.

And even though the path to freedom existed right behind me, since the door was right there and I had my car keys in my hand and my shoes were still on my fucking feet, I couldn't see it.

So, like always, I ruined everything.

"I don't *know*!" I snapped. "That's what pregnancy tests are *for*!"

Predictably, my dad lost it.

Unpredictably, he'd never lost it quite like that.

From the corner of my eye, I saw Anne-Marie pull her phone from her pocket as my dad hurled words at me. Because of course there had to be a witness to the worst moment of my life. And of course it had to be her, who would probably memorize everything just so she could repeat it to everyone. Which was quite a feat, considering he let out a string of French profanity featuring a mix of things I could barely translate paired with insults I'd never considered my father even knew.

Not because I couldn't picture my dad swearing at someone. I knew he did. I'd heard him swear at my mom when they were still together. But the things he spat at me just then were words I pictured him thinking were too vulgar, too low-brow, too common for someone like him to use.

But apparently for me, he had no problem summoning up a variety of creative ways to call me a promiscuous embarrassment of a whore.

"Dad, stop," I asked when there was enough of a break in his words for me to cut in. "I'm not—"

"Stop?" His laugh sounded like knives stabbing through muscle and hitting bone. "Stop. As if you have ever once considered *stopping* your behaviour. You are belligerently hostile. You take and take and take, and in return mock me openly, insult me at every turn, and now do the one thing I was certain you were not stupid enough to let happen after seeing the disaster that is having an accidental child."

"Thanks," I said. "I appreciate knowing how much I ruined your life."

"I did not say that," he said. "Your mother is the one who chose that path and while I sincerely hoped you would not follow in her footsteps, here you are putting things in motion before you've even finished the degree you were so insistent on taking."

"I don't know if I am," I said. "It's just a *test*."

"I thought you were better than this," he said. "But I suppose you do have your mother's hair, her attitude, and apparently, her stupidity, because you are just as impulsive and stubborn and *moronic* as she is."

"Jeez, that's a horrible thing to say to your own child."

Maybe if I hadn't already felt like I was free-falling off a cliff, I would have jumped at the voice behind me, but all I could think was that the entire neighbourhood must already know because I didn't close the door properly. Though, it was entirely possible that he'd opened the door himself and I was so wrapped up in the viciousness of my dad's words that I hadn't noticed.

Regardless, I wasn't even shocked by JP suddenly appearing on the other side of the foyer. I wasn't shocked that he spoke, or by the realization that I'd shrank back from my dad so much, I was nearly pressed against the wall.

All I felt was relief.

"Jean-Paul," my dad said, his voice still cutting and sharp. "What happened to not sneaking in the back door to see my daughter?"

Instead of crumbling under my father's gaze like so many others had, JP let one of his easy, casual smiles spread on his lips. He put one hand in the pocket of his basketball shorts—because apparently he hadn't even changed before leaving the gym, which I had no idea how to interpret—and glanced around the room as though it wasn't filled with a cloud of boiling tension.

"I never snuck in, Mr. Belanger," he said. "I only came in the back door when it was specifically requested."

How he could make me want to laugh in a moment like that, I'd never know, but I had to clamp my jaw closed to hold it in.

"Do you truly think that blithe attitude is appropriate?" my dad asked. "Though, I guess I should not be surprised. Perhaps your shared lack of sense is part of the attraction."

"Dad, please," I said. "Stop."

"Why should I do that, Eleanor?"

"Because—"

I hesitated. There were a thousand words, a thousand reasons why, but they were all swirling around in my mind like leaves caught in twisted wind, just high enough that I couldn't snatch them out of the air.

"—you're embarrassing me," I finished, because it was the only thing I could find.

My dad scoffed. "I am doing no such thing. You alone are responsible for any embarrassment you feel. You made your bed—or his, I presume—and you can handle the consequences."

"Stop talking to her like that," JP said. "She's your *daughter*."

"*My* daughter would not be embarrassed by this kind of thing," my dad said. "Because *my* daughter would know better than to get herself into these situations, seeing as I did not raise *my* daughter to be a slut."

There was more he wanted to add. His mouth was still open to send slicing words at both me and JP.

But a roar from above silenced my dad in a way I'd never seen before.

"How *dare* you?!"

We all looked up, including Anne-Marie, who nearly stumbled off the steps as she turned. Standing at the top of the stairs was Kimberlee, her hair pulled back in a low bun. She looked to be about half-ready for the party, clad in a pair of leggings and a cute pink top with a bow on the front that didn't seem to be her style at all.

And she looked *furious*.

"How dare you, Max?" she said again. "Do not tell me you truly said what I think I just heard."

My dad's face twisted. "You do not get to—"

"I absolutely do!" She stormed past Anne-Marie, lifting a finger and pointing it at him as she stomped down the rest of the stairs and walked right up to him. "I *do* get to tell you that you should not—not *ever*—speak to Nellie like that. To anyone like that! How could you even *think* such a thing?"

Rather than look like a chastised schoolchild, which is what I would have looked like if Kimberlee had scolded me like that, my dad's nostrils flared into a sneer. "You do not understand."

"You're right," she said, her voice strong. "I do not understand how this monster lived in you the whole time."

That was what made my dad react. It was a blink and barely a shift of a facial expression, but coming from my dad, that was like a physical recoil.

"You promised me," she continued. "When you threw her clothing out and I told you how you treated her was the worst behaviour I'd ever seen. You promised me, Max. You *promised* you would change and never do anything like that again. I did not think I had to specify that you would do nothing *worse*, either."

My father said nothing.

"You have a smart, accomplished, strong, and talented daughter, no thanks to your own contribution," she said. "And who puts up with horrible things from you to receive the bare minimum. The things she should get by default. The things *you* signed up for when you decided to be a parent."

He'd never decided that. I was a mistake.

"We will discuss this later," my dad said. "Right now—"

"You may not have later," Kimberlee said. "Seeing as I am currently wondering if my decision to allow you to be a parent again is the greatest mistake of my life."

Silence.

Silence broken only by the sound of my heartbeat in my ears, faster than usual but somehow steady, despite the turmoil around me.

"What?" I said.

I couldn't see Kimberlee's face, but my dad was staring directly into it, a silent battle raging between them.

"Yes," he finally said. "That is why this dinner was planned. To announce that Kimberlee is pregnant."

Kimberlee was pregnant.

With my *dad's* baby.

She had to be fucking insane.

"How... how did..." I stammered.

"You certainly seem to understand the 'how' of it," my dad said. "Considering you're about to potentially experience it all on your own."

"She's not alone," JP said. "And potentially is the key word there, Mr. Belanger. Seeing as this whole thing started because I stopped by to bring Nellie a test so she could know for sure."

"How responsible of you," my dad said, sarcasm dripping from his voice. "At least one of the two of you has some semblance of a brain in their head. Perhaps there's hope for the little bastard, assuming it's yours and she hasn't been out there spreading her legs for everyone else."

Again, silence.

JP wasn't smiling anymore. No one was. Anne-Marie's mouth was open, Kimberlee was staring at my dad, and I couldn't even breathe, let alone say something. JP looked at me, his gaze finally meeting mine and holding it. His eyes were stormy and clouded and heated, betraying nothing more than his anger.

What if he agreed?

I'd hooked up with Ben just a week earlier, though JP didn't know about that and Ben had come in my mouth, so if I was pregnant, it was pretty damn unlikely to be his.

But all JP would know was that we'd never been exclusive. And he wouldn't choose this. Who would? Who would *choose* to stick around for the barrage of vitriol from my dad all over the *potential* of being pregnant?

For a long, terrifying, silent moment, I was nearly convinced JP was going to shrug, then turn on his heel and walk right back out the front door.

Then, not breaking eye contact, he jerked his head towards the stairs.

"Go get your stuff, Nell," he said. "You can come stay with me."

"She absolutely will *not*," my dad said.

"You absolutely do not get to make that decision," JP shot back.

"You do not come into my house and tell my daughter to—"

"If your daughter isn't a slut, then I guess I'm not your daughter," I said.

My dad looked at me, his mouth half-open.

"Space seems to be a good idea," Kimberlee said, stepping back from my dad. "I think I'll do the same."

Some people explode when they're angry. My dad wasn't like that. He blew up sometimes, certainly, but when he was angry—really, truly, furiously angry—he imploded. The room went quiet as every bit of tension and energy seemed to draw itself to him, and his face transformed to stone as he looked at Kimberlee.

"Fine," he said. "Leave."

And he turned on his heel and walked away, footsteps echoing down the hall as he went to what I assumed would be his study.

For a long, quiet moment, all of us stared at the spot he left, like it was a black hole that couldn't help but absorb our gaze.

"Babe," JP finally said. "Go get your stuff."

"Babe?" repeated Anne-Marie, her amused tone completely out-of-place in the tense room.

Part of me prickled, ready to snap at JP that he didn't get to tell me what to do.

That I didn't need him to protect me.

And for the love of God, to stop fucking calling me babe.

But I knew that anger wasn't directed at JP.

And I knew I needed to go.

"I'll just be a sec," I whispered, then avoided looking anyone in the eye as I started up the stairs.

Chapter Twenty-Four
You Say Daddy Issues Like It's My Fault

I drove to JP's apartment alone.

He offered to drive me. He insisted, actually, and I insisted right back that I take my car. I told him it was because I wouldn't put it past my dad to have it towed off his driveway out of spite, but it wasn't until I admitted that I didn't want to have to ever come back to my dad's house again that he relented.

He still refused to leave until I was ready to go. He said it was so he could make sure I followed him, but we both knew he wanted to be there in case I needed him.

I didn't bother pretending to grumble about him being overprotective or something. Especially because he waited around to make sure Kimberlee was okay, too.

And somehow, she was.

"Why?" I hadn't turned around to see her while I packed up the things I needed from my bedroom, but I could sense her standing in the doorway.

"Why did I stand up for you?" Kimberlee asked.

"No." I shook my head, trying to figure out how to ask what I wanted to ask. "Why... him?"

"Why am I with your father?" she asked.

"How can you *love* him?"

She sighed, walking into my room and sitting on the edge of the bed.

"I love him because hearts are stupid and sometimes convince you to do things that make no sense," she said.

"The only way *that* makes any sense is if you had a heart transplant taken from a death row inmate who happened to be a vengeful masochist," I said.

She laughed softly. "I do not expect you to see the good things about him."

"What good things?" I muttered.

"They are there. But when someone treats you like that, the good is overshadowed by everything else."

I gritted my teeth together and continued packing.

"Witnessing him treat you the way he does overshadows many of those good things for me right now," she said when I didn't say anything.

"Not all of them."

"Enough that I'm questioning a lot right now." Mindlessly, she put a hand on her stomach. "But I've also witnessed him try to be a loving parent and—"

I burst out laughing.

"What?" she asked.

"A loving parent." I snorted. "At what point has my dad done *anything* that would make you think that?"

She sighed again. "He struggles. His first experience with a loving parent was watching your mom after you were born. He didn't have that experience with his own parents."

"Poor baby," I said sarcastically. "How hard for him. I guess that means I should forgive everything without question."

"Of course not," she said. "You don't owe Max grace or sympathy or understanding. That's not a requirement for children to extend to their parents."

I glanced at her, uncertain. She shrugged.

"I don't believe so, anyway. Your parents are responsible for creating a relationship where you would want to do that, should you ever need to, and not out of obligation."

"Wow," I said.

"My perspective of Max is different," she said, looking down at her hands. "Just as he saw many of the things I needed in my life, I saw much of what he needed in his."

I rolled my eyes. "Right. And you told yourself you could fix him. No *really*, you could totally fix him."

She laughed instead of being insulted. "The first thing I told your father when we began to date was that if he wanted to be with me, he needed to fix himself, because it was certainly not my responsibility to fix a man who has every privilege possible in the modern world."

"And has he?"

"He has tried." She pressed her lips together. "He's tried hard enough that it's making walking away difficult, even though what I just saw makes me want to turn and never look back."

I didn't say anything. I wasn't sure that there was anything I could say. She was talking about tolerating and forgiving someone who'd treated me like garbage.

But at its core, I understood it. It would have been so easy if all of this was black and white, but even sitting there in the aftermath of this disaster, after four years of my dad treating me the way he did, even with these unquestionable failures all stacked up and up and *up* in front of me, I didn't want to go.

I didn't want this to be it.

I didn't want to leave knowing I was a disappointment, even though the expectations that made me a disappointment weren't realistic.

I didn't want to leave at all, as stupid as it was. Because while all of it hurt, everything he'd said and done, he was still my dad.

He was the first man in my life.

He was supposed to love me no matter what.

He was the one letting me down.

He was the disappointment.

He was the one who should be sitting here having his entire life fucked up by his actions.

Yet here I was, living through his awfulness, and still practically programmed at a biological level to want to impress him.

After everything, the thought of this being *it* hurt as much as anything else. Because even if I was never good enough for him, something in me would always want to try.

And wasn't that just the—

Ah, shit.

I was going to have to text Ben and tell him he was right about the daddy issues all along.

Because that was the real issue here.

"Nellie?" Kimberlee said softly.

I blinked, my bag coming back into focus and the same clothes I'd been holding a few minutes earlier still clutched in my hands.

"Are you alright?" she asked.

"I'm sorry," I said, barely thinking the words. "I haven't always been the nicest person to you."

"That is the understatement of the century," Kimberlee said, but her voice was warm. "But thank you for saying it, even though I very much understand."

I nodded, putting the rest of my things in my bag. "Do you, like, have somewhere to go? If you leave?"

I wasn't expecting her to laugh, but she did.

"I will be absolutely fine," she said. "Max is the one who would suffer more if we broke up. Financially, at least."

Alarmed and slightly intrigued, I raised my eyebrows. Kimberlee smiled as she stood from the edge of my bed.

"Your father is my hedge fund manager," she said. "He'd hate losing my, and my family's, portfolios."

And I couldn't help it.

I fucking *cackled.*

She laughed with me for a bit, even though I don't know that either of us knew why, then came over and hugged me.

"It will be okay," she promised, which was either arrogant or delusional on her part, because I had no idea how *anything* would ever be okay. But I nodded, then pushed my thumbnail into my forefinger.

"If you leave, like... like permanently," I said, not able to look at her. "Would I... like, can I still... if you keep it or whatever, I guess, but like—"

"If I leave, you can absolutely still meet the baby," she said. "They will still be your brother or sister."

I nodded, a lump forming in my throat.

"And if you are..." she continued, then trailed off.

"I'll let you know," I whispered.

She smiled and patted my shoulder. "For what it's worth, I think it's clear to everyone that you and Jean-Paul are lovely together."

I groaned, my eyes slamming shut. "Not you, too."

"*Oh,*" Kimberlee said knowingly. "It's one of those situations. Well... if it turns out you are, you might as well keep messing around with him. It's not like you could get *more* pregnant."

It felt very, very weird to hear Kimberlee say something like that and even weirder to laugh with her so hard that no sound came out because I couldn't actually breathe, but what was one more weird thing to happen that day?

I didn't know if Kimberlee wasn't living with my dad full-time or if she just didn't bother packing anything, but by the time I finished grabbing what I needed from my room, she and the Porsche were gone from the driveway. JP was waiting for me in the foyer, straightening up from where he was leaning against the wall as I started down the stairs.

"I told Anne-Marie to go home," he said, reaching out to take my bag. "She wanted to stay and check on you, but since people would probably show up soon, I figured the priority was to get out of here."

I nodded, then let him lead me out of my dad's house. The front door shut behind us, the sound of it clicking into place far louder in my mind than it was in reality. I didn't look back until I was in my car, the key turned in the ignition.

The house was quiet. Dark. Formidable in its loneliness.

God, was it lonely.

I spent the drive to JP's trying not to think, my eyes focused on the taillights of his BMW as I followed a little too close so no one could cut me off. He'd given me his address, of course, but if I didn't have to figure out how to get there myself, I wasn't going to. The radio played in the background, just loud enough to numb my thoughts so I didn't start processing any of what my dad had said or the fact that after nearly twenty-two years, I wasn't going to be an only child anymore, and absolutely *refusing* to acknowledge that the little sibling Kimberlee was pregnant with might be an aunt or uncle before they could even sit up.

I knew the second I did, I wouldn't be able to keep my eyes dry, and the last thing I needed was to rear-end JP's BMW because I was crying too hard to notice he'd stopped or something.

When we got to his building, JP rolled his window down and gestured towards the visitor parking. I pulled in and waited by my car like he'd told me to until he'd parked. Once he rounded the corner again, jogging in my direction, I grabbed my purse and backpack and started walking towards him.

"You okay?" he asked when we were close enough.

"Just peachy," I replied flatly. "I have a Schrödinger's baby situation going on here, I'm probably being disowned, I'm going to have a twenty-two-year age gap with a sibling, and worst of all, I'm stuck staying with you."

The bastard laughed and reached for my backpack. "At least your sense of humour wasn't damaged in the hailstorm of drama I got caught up in."

"Yes, because it must be so difficult for you to be witness to my family's drama."

"Finally, someone acknowledges it," he muttered playfully.

I half-laughed but didn't respond. He hesitated, then put an arm around my shoulder as we walked towards his building. And for some reason, I didn't mind it all that much, even though he was still in the t-shirt he'd clearly worn to the gym.

"Are you actually okay?" he asked.

"No," I said.

He hugged me a little tighter, but neither of us said anything else until we reached the door and I realized I was being a jerk.

"Are you okay?" I asked.

He held the door open. "Why wouldn't I be?"

"Anne-Marie told me about your fight with your dad." I bit my lip, not looking at him. "I'm guessing your dad wouldn't be thrilled if he found out that—" I couldn't bring myself to say it, so motioned at my stomach.

He let the door swing closed behind us, his lips curling up slightly. "Or he would be thrilled to know he was right. Either way, on the off-chance Anne-Marie does tell them what happened in excruciating, slightly embellished detail, I expect my mom will call once she's finished hyperventilating to tell me she's too young to be a grandmother."

"Oh."

He grinned, pushing the button for the elevator. "That will be her only concern."

"They wouldn't be hideously ashamed of the fact that you"—I pressed a hand to my mouth and faked a theatrical gasp—"dared to have sex outside of marriage?"

"Now that I've done the unthinkable and refused to do what my dad wants me to, I think they've given up on being ashamed of me and have resigned themselves to hoping whatever embarrassing thing I do is at least funny," he said.

I was surprised when I laughed. JP just smiled, his hand moving to my lower back to guide me onto the elevator once the doors opened. An easy silence fell between us as we rode up and it wasn't until we got into his apartment that either of us spoke again.

"Okay," I said. "Let's get this over with. Give it to me."

"Wow, nothing stops you from being in the mood, huh?" he replied, closing the door behind him.

I rolled my eyes and held out my hand. "The test, JP. Give me the test."

He lifted his eyebrows. "The test?"

"The... the test," I repeated. "The pregnancy test? The whole reason for this mess?"

"Right, of course," he said. "The pregnancy test. The pregnancy test I bought you. The pregnancy test I hid beneath your car. The pregnancy test your dad found and is currently in possession of. That pregnancy test?"

I started lowering my hand before he was halfway done and by the time he finished, I was nodding in reluctant agreement.

"Yeah," I said. "That would be the one."

"Yeah, no," he said. "I don't have it. Want me to go get another one?"

"No," I said.

His neck snapped towards me. "What?"

"No, I want that specific one. Just march right in there and ask my dad for it back."

"I'm guessing that would likely result in my balls being separated from my body."

"Why? It's not like he needs them. He already knows Kimberlee's pregnant."

JP snorted. Which made me smile, even though I didn't want to.

"I'll run and get another one," he said. "And some food since I'm guessing you were planning to eat at the dinner party. Pad thai's good?"

I didn't know if he knew it was one of my favourites or if he was asking to make sure I wanted it, but I was too tired and overwhelmed to care. "Yeah."

"Alright." He set my backpack down. "It's gonna be okay, you know."

"It better be. If you bring back shitty pad thai, I'll never forgive you."

He smiled. "I meant the other thing."

"Thing?"

"Thing...s."

I didn't quite look at him as I nodded. "I know."

Something else was itching to be said, but he decided against it. "I'll be back in a bit. Make yourself at home, okay?"

Chapter Twenty-Five
Merciless

I DOUBTED JP ACTUALLY wanted me to make myself at home.

Not because he didn't want me to feel welcome. But my home was a disaster and JP was suspiciously tidy. His apartment was cleaner than mine had been after I skipped class to clean it that one day and he hadn't even know I'd be coming over.

There were no piles of clothes near the plush armchair in his living room. No remote controls sticking out of the cracks between the cushions on the leather couch, although there was a hideous throw blanket made of not-quite-complementary squares of crocheted yarn slung over the armrest and a few books stacked on the glass coffee table. But the throw blanket was folded neatly and the books clearly had a place they were supposed to go; the well-stocked bookshelf on the wall had gaps that fit the ones he'd pulled out.

So I didn't make myself at home by throwing clothes all over the floor or adding dirty dishes to his empty sink, but I did make myself comfortable. When JP returned not quite half an hour later, I was on his couch curled up in the throw blanket, my feet tucked under me as I scrolled through my phone.

"This is cozy," I said as the smell of pad thai permeated his apartment.

"My apartment?" he asked.

"This blanket." I unwrapped myself and stood. "I see why you have it out, despite it not matching your sleek modern aesthetic."

He chuckled softly. "A friend made it for me."

I tried to fold the blanket as tidily as I'd found it but failed. "They must have really liked you. Or hated you."

"A little of both." He set the boxes of pad thai on the table, then turned and held out a similar white plastic bag to the one my dad had found earlier. "Do you want this now?"

I nodded, my tongue suddenly too big for my mouth, and took the bag from him.

"I'll be right here," he said.

That made things both better and worse, somehow. As I ripped the cardboard box open in the bathroom and pulled out the instructions, I could hear him pulling plates from the cupboard louder than strictly necessary. Shaking, I skimmed the instructions, then took the test out and followed them as fast as possible.

All so I could hurry up and wait for the longest three minutes of my fucking life.

JP's eyes snapped up as soon as I walked into the kitchen. "Well?"

My face turned red, even as I looked away from him. "It'll be a few minutes. I didn't want to wait alone."

I half-expected him to make fun of me, but JP just smiled and started splitting the pad thai between our plates.

"So I went to the same place for this test," he said conversationally. "And wouldn't you know, it's the same guy working. This older guy, probably has a soccer team full of kids at home. Lucky me, he remembers me from earlier. So he goes off about how if the first test was negative, it could be positive, but doing a second test on the same day wouldn't work and I needed to 'tell my woman' to wait until tomorrow. And I get it, he's trying to be helpful, but there's a lineup of four people behind me and plenty of others in the store."

"Let me guess," I said. "You embarrassed the poor guy."

"Of course not," he said. "I just asked if the second girl was less likely to be pregnant if the first girl was."

I rolled my eyes, but there was no stopping the reluctant laugh on my lips. JP smiled, then finished putting the food on the plates before coming to stand next to me.

"Think it's ready?" he asked.

It was. I'd already felt my phone vibrate to say the timer was done. But I stared at the hallway, fear gluing my feet to the floor and my palms to the sides of my thighs.

Which was stupid. It was so stupid. All that was down that hall was a piece of plastic with an answer on it. It wasn't a shark. Or a lion. Or a man with a gun. Or my dad.

It was just an answer.

But I'd never been so scared in my life.

"Babe?" JP asked. "Are you going to check it?"

I nodded, then swallowed hard. "Unless, um. You want to. See if it's ready."

His arm went around my shoulder again and he pressed his lips to the side of my head, then walked to the bathroom with a sense of calm I couldn't understand. I stayed where I was, waiting, until he reappeared a moment later.

"Well?" I asked.

"It's ready," he said.

I stared at him, waiting, my heart in my throat. "And?"

"Oh," he said. "You wanted me to tell you what it said, too?"

"You've got to be fucking kidding me," I said, and stormed forward to push past him to the bathroom.

JP laughed, catching me around the waist. "Babe, wait. I—"

"You're such a f-fucking asshole," I said.

I don't know if it was the stammer or the fact that because he'd grabbed me, he was close enough to see the tears in my eyes, but JP's laugh faded instantly.

"It's negative," he said. "Nell, it's negative."

"I need to s-see it." The words shook, wavering on my voice as I tried to squirm away from him.

"Here." He shoved his other hand towards me. "Look."

I hadn't noticed him holding it. I stopped squirming and yanked the test out of his hand, holding it up to my eyes and staring hard at the little window.

One pink line.

One strong pink line, just like the box had said. Not two. Not even a faint hint of a question of a second line showed.

"Nellie?" JP said. "I wasn't trying to fuck with you. I—"

"Where's your garbage can?"

"What?"

"I want to throw this out and never think about it again."

He showed me where his garbage can was and let me do the honours of tossing the stupid fucking piece of plastic that had changed everything—even though I wasn't fucking pregnant—into it. As soon as I had, I washed my hands again, wiping my fingers along my cheeks to make sure none of the tears had leaked out before taking a breath.

"I'm sorry," he said.

"What happened to never thinking about it again?" I asked. "It's done. It's negative. Now everything can go back to normal."

"Can it?" he asked, raising his eyebrows.

"Of course. Aside from, you know, the whole thing where my dad hates me and all that other stuff. But the rest of it, the... this." I gestured at us. "We can go back to normal."

He looked like he was about to agree. I could see it on his lips, the instinctive response, before it fizzled out. He looked at me, then glanced to the side.

And I knew.

I knew what he was going to say.

I knew what was coming, and my stomach clenched, and I opened my mouth to say something—*anything*—that might stop it, but JP spoke before I could.

"No, we can't," JP said.

"Yes we can," I said.

He shook his head. "Nellie, we have to talk about this."

"No we don't."

"You're not the only one involved." His voice was gentle the same way someone reluctantly pressing a knife into your stomach was gentle. "This isn't fair to me."

"So what, you feel like because you stood up to my dad for me that I owe you an explanation?"

A hint of anger flared in his eyes. "You don't owe me shit and you never will. But just because you don't owe me an explanation doesn't mean I'm not hoping for one."

I stuttered for a moment before glaring at him. "You're lawyering me again."

He half-laughed. "You can't just accuse me of 'lawyering' you when you don't like that I'm right."

"I can do anything."

He smiled sadly. "Well, I can't. I can't do this. I like you—"

"As a friend," I said.

"Nellie—"

"You like me as a *friend*, JP." It came out like I was begging. Pleading. The vocal equivalent of falling to my knees and grovelling with everything in me for him to stop.

But JP was a merciless bastard.

"No," he said. "Not just as a friend."

"JP, please," I whispered. "Not now."

"When, then?" There was regret in his eyes, but he still shook his head. "I've been trying. I thought I could keep dancing around whatever I was feeling—"

"You shouldn't be feeling anything!" The words came out far harsher than I intended them, but he didn't react. "Don't do this to me."

The usual, playful expression on his face was gone, and in its place was one of solemn resignation. "I'm not doing anything *to* you. But after... after everything last time, I told myself I couldn't do it anymore. I need to hold myself to that because I'm not being fair to either of us, and now this... fuck, Nell, I can't pretend to be your friend. It might've started that way, but I can't anymore. I care about you, a lot. More than I want to, trust me. It'd be a hell of a lot easier if I didn't."

"You sure know how to flatter a girl."

"Do you want flattery, honesty, or to pretend there's nothing between us?" he asked bluntly. "You only get one."

I opened my mouth to reply, but the answer caught in my throat. I didn't need him to flatter me. Of course I didn't need that. And I wanted to tell him to pretend there was nothing between us. That was what I had wanted all along.

But I'd be picking a lie.

I could only pick one thing, and I couldn't bring myself to say the word. It stuck in my throat, held back by the throbbing of my pulse through swollen veins, trapped by the dry terror in my mouth.

The bastard knew it, too, and his stupid face softened as he looked at me, practically trembling in front of him.

"None of this is about you," he said. "Or anything you did. Or anything I... I know I'm in your friend zone. I'm not trying to get out of it."

"Then what is the *point*?" My voice shook. "Why are you doing this?"

"Because the last time I had something like this happen—"

"The last time?!" A laugh bubbled out unintentionally. "There was a 'last time' you had a pregnancy scare and then decided to tell the girl you're fuck buddies with that feelings have entered the room?"

It would have been easier if anything I said got to him. Instead, he just took it, not quite looking at me, not quite reacting, not letting my words weaken the resolve he'd mustered up.

"The last time I messed around with a friend and feelings 'entered the room,'" he said. "Because yeah. I've been there before."

"And you let it happen again," I said. "With me. After I asked you not to."

"I didn't *let* it happen." His jaw flexed. "It just did. I thought I could ignore it. I couldn't. And the last few weeks, I've been losing my mind telling myself it wasn't gonna happen again and it is."

"What is?"

He sighed. "Nell, I lost the only other person I have ever in my life wanted to be *more* with. I can't do this again."

I gestured a little too aggressively. "So you think by telling me you're suddenly feeling things I'm just going to give in and give you what you want?"

He shook his head.

"What, then? You're standing here telling me you lost someone because you wanted something more than you agreed on, like I'm going to choose differently than the girl who left you—"

"No one *left*," he said. "That's not what I meant by lost."

"Then what—"

"He died, Nell."

I stopped.

JP wasn't looking at me. His eyes were cast down and to my left, staring at a spot on the floor like avoiding my gaze meant I couldn't see the vulnerability and pain scrawled across his face.

Fuck.

Fuck.

"JP, I—"

"—didn't know." His throat flexed as he swallowed. "I know you didn't. I didn't tell you."

"Why?"

"Why would I?" he asked, flicking his eyes up for a moment. "You're my sister's best friend. I wasn't going to suddenly spill my deepest, darkest secrets to you just because we started fucking."

My throat tightened. He wasn't wrong. I'd spilled more than one of my deepest, darkest secrets to him, on top of his presence during some of the deepest, darkest moments of my life, but I wasn't entitled to his just because he'd put his dick in me.

"It was never supposed to be anything more than fucking around," he said. "That's what Sam and I agreed to. But, like, we were... close. Close enough that when we were both single and busy with school and midterms and internships and all that shit, neither of us thought it was weird to propose we, uh, help each other out." His face turned red. "You take a friendship like that and mix fucking into it and things change."

Pain prickled on my thumb and I realized I'd been picking at it mercilessly, the skin around my nail going from raw to broken, drops of blood blooming along the nail bed. I grabbed the hem of my shirt, rolling the fabric around my thumb as subtly as I could.

"I was the one who didn't want to tell anyone," he continued. "I wanted more, don't get me wrong. The sappy shit. I wanted to fuckin', like, hold his hand in public and stuff. But I was so fucking worried about what people might think. If it would ruin things. What my dad would say."

I both could and couldn't relate. I knew what it was like to not want my dad to know something. But I had the benefit of a second life. Of cities between us. Of being able to safely drop the charade so I could take a break from the fear.

I couldn't imagine what it would be like to hide from *everyone* the way JP felt he had to. But thinking about it hurt.

"We fought about it. It had been at least a year that we'd been messing around exclusively and Sam was sick of it being a secret. He... he told someone." JP shifted in place. "At the party. That night. I left him there. I spent the whole night thinking about it and deciding I didn't want to lose what we had. And then he was gone. I don't know if he even got my text telling him we were okay."

Somehow, the way he talked about it hurt even more. His tone was matter-of-fact; forlorn, but like he barely registered that every single detail made all of it that much worse.

He hadn't just lost someone.

They hadn't just fought about coming out to people.

JP's dad hadn't just told him to hold it together at a friend's funeral.

He'd lost Sam forever. They'd fought the night he died. And that funeral hadn't been for just a *friend*.

"I'm so sorry," I whispered.

JP shook his head. "Don't. I don't want an apology."

"It's sympathy."

"I don't want that either."

"What do you want then?" I wasn't sure if I was annoyed or frustrated or just grasping for something to say. "Or were you telling me this so I'd change my mind and give you a chance?"

He laughed, thankfully, considering it was a pretty harsh accusation. "No. I'm not trying guilt you into being with me, Nell."

"Even though all of this stemmed from you saying you can't lose someone again."

"That's not the part I can't go through." He finally looked up from the spot on the floor, capturing my gaze instantly. "I can go through you not wanting me. Easily. It sucks, but I'll survive. What I *can't* do is be caught in between. No matter what you refuse to admit, there's been something there for a while—"

"There has not," I snapped, my face heating up. "You're wrong."

He shrugged. "Tell yourself what you need to. But I can't keep existing in this fucking purgatory of not being together but not being just friends. I've been there. I've done that. I'm never going to get *out* of it because Sam is gone and I'll never fucking know. I can't keep doing it with you, too."

Silence filled the space between us as I processed what he'd said and the simmering determination beneath his nonchalant attitude.

"How long have you—" I started.

"Months," he said.

"You could've told me when you knew," I said. "It's not my fault you—"

"It is," he said bluntly. "It's my fault, too, but you don't get to walk away blameless. Because I tried, Nellie. But you said no, or don't, or not now. And honestly... Look, I like you. But we were supposed to be friends, and that's not a great way of treating friends. I like myself enough to know I don't have to put up with that."

"So, I've been a bad friend?" I replied, my voice shaking more than I wanted it to.

He studied me for a moment, blue eyes boring into mine. I couldn't look away, but I also couldn't give him what he wanted.

"I'm in love with you," he said.

My stomach dropped.

"And that's not what you want," he continued. "I get that. I'm not asking you to change what you want for me."

"Then why are we having this conversation?" I whispered.

"Because I can't be just your friend."

I nodded slowly, biting my lip for the dual purpose of distracting myself with a brief prick of pain and to keep my lip from quivering.

"If you can't be my friend and I can't be… more than your friend…" I looked up at him, not ready to finish the sentence.

"It's okay, babe." A sad smile made his cheek twitch. "Say it."

Once upon a time, my mom had called JP a heartbreaker.

I'd thought she meant he was a bad person. Because who would want to break hearts? But of course, she'd meant it in the way that moms always knew which little boys would grow up to be the type of men who discarded the hearts of the women who wanted them without care and without mercy.

But she was wrong.

JP wasn't a heartbreaker. He cared too much to be one. He might have been merciless, but not when it came to hearts.

But I guess one of the many things I didn't want to admit JP and I had in common was our ability to be merciless.

Because in hindsight, the pieces were all there. The hints. The realization that he'd been trying to tell me about this for months. Since before the Diamond Gala. Since the night Anne-Marie had nearly caught us in his bedroom, at least.

And I'd ignored it willfully.

I'd ignored him mercilessly.

And now, standing in front of each other, everything spilling out of the slashes he'd put in the surprisingly delicate wall of ignorance, I was going to have to keep being merciless.

I was going to have to be the heartbreaker.

And I wasn't quite sure whose heart it was.

"This is it, then," I said. "We're not friends anymore."

"Okay," he agreed quietly. "We're not friends anymore."

I pressed my lips together. "Alright. I'm gonna go."

"You don't have to," he said. "You can stay in the guest room or—"

"You wouldn't do that for someone you're not friends with."

He stopped speaking, then nodded once. "Right."

I mirrored his nod, not looking at him. "Okay. Bye, JP."

He watched silently as I turned to leave his apartment. Just as I opened the door, he spoke one last time.

"I'll miss you, Nell."

Chapter Twenty-Six
I Drove All Night

I listened to Celine Dion on the way home.

Not because I wanted to. I just didn't bother plugging my phone into the car and whatever Montreal radio station I picked up had some kind of tribute to Celine night going on.

It wasn't that I didn't want to, either. I had no objection to Celine. She was a national treasure, not that I'd even risk hinting otherwise while in Montreal.

I just didn't want anything.

Everything was numb. My hands. My feet. My heart. My mind. It was like I'd overloaded and instead of shutting down, I froze, a shell of whatever was supposed to be sitting in the driver's seat of a Honda Civic trying not to get sideswiped by an Uber doing one-thirty in the seventy zone on Autoroute 20.

It was a mercy in the mercilessness that had been that day. I didn't *want* to think. I didn't *want* to hurt. I didn't *want* to feel.

I just drove.

For a while, anyway.

Celine was singing about how things were all coming back to her when I started feeling again. Hunger, mainly, since all I'd eaten since lunch was a single donut.

Unfortunately, that reminded me I'd bought a bunch of donuts, and I brightened up for all of a second before realizing I'd left those donuts at my dad's house.

I was almost more upset about leaving the donuts behind than leaving JP.

That was a lie. I couldn't even pretend to convince myself it was true.

But I didn't want to think about JP.

Food, on the other hand, was a necessity. I wasn't going to make it back home if I didn't eat *something*, especially since I'd also left the pad thai JP had bought me at his house because—

Fuck.

I was thinking about JP again.

I turned the radio up and let Celine's voice bounce around my skull, then switched lanes so I could take the next exit, since I also needed gas.

The gas station I pulled into had a Tim Hortons attached to it. It wasn't my first choice of food, but I was pretty sure anything would taste like ashes in my mouth right then, so it didn't matter. After filling up my car, I went inside and ordered, then wandered to the bathroom while I was waiting for it to be made.

Then, because something in the universe thought it was just *hilarious* to fuck with me, I left the bathroom, brought an overpriced pack of tampons up to the cashier, and went back to put one in before picking up my bagel and Iced Capp.

The radio station cut out just after I left the gas station, but I apparently decided I needed my own Celine tribute night and pulled up her discography on my phone. Plugging it in, I turned the volume up, turned my thoughts down, and drove.

And drove.

And drove.

When I got to Ottawa, I looked at the exit.

And I kept driving.

And driving.

And driving.

It was after midnight when I pulled up to the place I hadn't thought of going. Instinct more than anything had brought me there. That was the only justification I had, especially as I turned my car off and hesitated.

It was late, but the lights were still on. Of course they were; I had to get my night owl tendencies from somewhere.

But still. Maybe I should go home.

Which would've been as stupid as driving here in the first place, of course. I wouldn't make it home without falling asleep.

So I got out of the car. I walked up to the door. I rang the bell because even though I knew I could just walk in, it was the middle of the night and I hadn't called. I heard the TV blaring and a confused voice and a few moments later, the front door opened tentatively, revealing a chubby man who looked about my age with thick brown hair, pale olive skin, and furrowed eyebrows.

"Who are you?" I asked, frowning.

"Uh... Jack," he said.

"What are you doing here?"

"I live here," he said.

"Since when?"

"Since—you know, I don't have to answer that," he said. "Can I help you with something?"

"Depends. Am I delirious or did my mom secretly move without telling me her new address?"

Jack's confusion lingered a moment longer before his eyes widened. "Oh, shi—"

"Nellie?" came a panicked yelp, and a second later Jack was shoved out of the way.

"Hi Mom," I said. "How was Vegas?"

My mom stared at me. Her hair was pulled up in a messy ponytail and part of the hem of her baggy pyjama top was tucked into the waistband of her shorts.

"It was good," she said, her voice strangely high. "We had—um." She cleared her throat. "*I* had a lot of fun."

"With the friend I'm not supposed to know about?" I asked.

My mom's eyebrows pinched together. "Well... yes."

"Don't worry. I'll pretend I didn't see him."

A single bubble of laughter popped out of her mouth. "No, it's fine. It's... um..." She waved behind her and Jack reappeared, a wary look on his face. "This is, um, Jack."

"Hi," I said. "Are you older than me?"

My mom's face turned red, but Jack just nodded. "I'm twenty-seven."

"Cool."

"Is that a problem?" my mom asked.

I shrugged. "I don't think it matters as long as it's someone older than I am. Though I guess it's a lot less weird when it's not a girl."

"What?" Jack whispered.

"She means her dad," my mom said quickly. "He... well. Anyway. So you're not mad, hon?"

"Why would I be mad?" I asked.

She bit her lip nervously. "Well, I know I haven't dated much or anything. And Jack is, um, staying here. And he is a little younger than me, so..."

"I'm not mad, Mom."

Her lips pressed together and she looked like she was holding back tears. "Well, come in. No point in standing at the door."

I was pretty sure I cockblocked Jack, based on the state of the blankets on the couch in the living room, but he still graciously excused himself upstairs while my mom and I went to the kitchen.

"You know I'm thrilled to see you, hon," my mom said as she grabbed a couple of water glasses from the cupboard, then changed her mind and grabbed the wine glasses. "But what's going on?"

"I just needed to see you," I said, not looking at her. "And I felt like driving."

"You drove?"

I nodded.

She let out a bright caw of laughter, shaking her head so her ponytail swung from side to side before pouring wine for each of us. "Oh, Daughter of Mine. I adore how impulsive you are."

And I know she didn't mean to.

She couldn't have known.

But she said that and my lip trembled, and even though I immediately curled it into my mouth, she saw it.

"What's wrong, Nell?" she asked, her voice soft. "I know you didn't just drive four and a half hours to surprise me."

"Closer to seven, actually," I mumbled.

"What?" she asked.

I dragged my fingernail along my thumb, holding in a wince as it hit the spot I'd picked raw earlier. "So if I wasn't mad about your thing, you can't be mad about my thing, okay?"

"It would be so nice if that was how it worked," she said. "But it's not."

"Oh," I said. "Never mind, then."

She laughed again. "Tell me. I promise I'll *try* not to be mad."

And what was I supposed to say to that? "Well, before I can tell you everything, I need to tell you I've spent the last four years attending a bunch of fancy events to make my dad look good in exchange for the four years of tuition and living expenses you specifically told me not to ask for because you didn't want me to get hurt by the sociopath you had the misfortune of conceiving me with?"

I sure hope so, since that was basically what I said.

I wasn't sure how she'd react. I'd always assumed she would be angry, but that was because I was terrified of the far more likely option.

You know. The one where she was as disappointed in me as she was hurt by my actions.

As I spilled all my admissions, I almost expected her shoulders to sag. For her to look down, hoping I didn't see her eyes water. For her to sigh, trying to hide the fact that I'd found a condition that lessened the unconditional love she was supposed to have for me.

She wasn't looking at me when I finished speaking. Her eyes were set on the table, her head tilted just enough that I couldn't make out what was on her face even if it hadn't been unreadable. For a long moment, neither of us spoke.

"Mom?" I finally said. "Please don't hate me."

She chuckled. "I could never, *ever* hate you."

"But you're mad that I asked Dad for help?" I said.

She took a deep breath, then let it out in a sigh before looking up.

"No," she said. "I already knew that, Daughter of Mine."

Chapter Twenty-Seven
Fucking Excuse Me?!

When all was said and done, it was the government that sold me out.

"Don't mess with the tax man," my mom said, laughing as I stared at her incredulously.

"But I never even filed any taxes," I said.

"Well first of all, you should have," she said. "And second of all, yes you did."

"I think I would know if I filed taxes, Mom," I said.

"I think I would know if I prepared your tax return every year and you signed it without looking even though I've always told you not to sign anything without reading it," she shot back.

I opened my mouth with the assumption that I'd think of a response, but I didn't.

"The first red flag was that you never got a T4 for the job you apparently had," she said. "But your father also called to discuss the tuition credit, so—"

"Dad *called* you?!" I asked.

"Well, Pierre called," she said. "I haven't spoken to your father for years because he knows I'll hang up on him. So he gets Pierre to do it, since

Pierre is slightly more tolerable. Though I wouldn't necessarily piss on him if he was on fire, either."

"So you knew," I said. "The whole time."

She nodded.

"You never said anything."

My mom nodded again. "I thought about it. Trust me. After Pierre called, there were a few times I almost rented a car and drove myself to Ottawa to scream at you. And you know how I feel about driving. But once I'd calmed down, I thought about how you're my daughter."

I must have looked confused, because she snickered and put her hand over mine.

"You know what I did after I got pregnant and my parents said they'd never approve of me marrying Max because he was bad fucking news?"

"Married him?" I guessed.

"Married him," she repeated, nodding. "And what did you do when I made it clear you should never ask your dad for money?"

"Asked Dad for money," I whispered.

She smiled wryly. "I spent over a decade fighting to prove I'd done the right thing like I hadn't been second-guessing myself from the moment I let your dad put a ring on my finger."

"You never loved him at all?" I asked.

"It makes me nauseous to admit, but I... *did*." She made a disgruntled noise that sounded a bit like a retch. "I loved him in a way. But when I finally gave in and admitted I should've never married him, I told your grandma I was leaving and you know what she said?"

"She told you so?"

"Yep."

I wrinkled my nose. "Ugh."

"There's a reason I haven't seen your grandparents since." My mom looked down at her hands, tapping her fingertips on the table. "I love you more than I despise your father. I wasn't about to do something that made *him* the reason you walked away from me."

I stared into my glass of wine, not sure what to say.

"I know I messed up when I refused to let you ask him for help," she said. "Am I thrilled you lied to me for four years? Of course not. But seeing as I would've done the same thing, I can't say shit, Daughter of Mine. I just wanted what was best for you and part of me didn't want to remember that while he might've been my husband, he was your *father*. There's a big difference."

"I would fucking hope so," I muttered.

My mom cackled, sipping her wine before grabbing the bottle and topping both of our glasses up. "Look, I'm never going to like the man. What happened with us was too deep. But being ten years removed from it all makes it easier to look back and see that he tried, in his own way. He just... he didn't know how." She paused to sip her wine, so I took a sip too. "You know, I always thought his dad murdered his mother."

Wine spurted out of my mouth. My mom handed me a napkin, continuing even as I coughed.

"I don't know for sure, and obviously your father would've never known. He was young. But it was one of those suspicious 'accidents' that never got looked into, and then his dad remarried within months." She shrugged. "I met his stepmom once, at his father's funeral. I swear to God, they based Cruella de Vil on the woman. And his dad was no better. Your father never forgave him for—" She stopped, frowning. "This probably isn't something we should be talking about."

"I mean, maybe it is," I said.

She twisted her mouth to the side, then sighed. "Look, it's one of those things that even sitting here, knowing how much I despise him, I can't help but hurt for him. But at least when I knew him, he always—*always*—used it to justify not being better than he was. And

I don't want to tell you this if it's going to guilt you into accepting anything less than full respect from him."

My stomach clenched as I thought about earlier that night, when I'd thought JP was doing the same thing to me. "It won't."

There was another moment of hesitation, but after taking a long sip of wine, my mom told me the story.

And no, it didn't excuse how my dad treated me.

But if it wasn't for the fact that *he* was my dad, I might have felt empathy for what he'd gone through.

Because he'd learned when he was younger than me that everyone had a price. And he'd learned it after his high school girlfriend had gotten pregnant—since apparently all the problems in my dad's life revolved around him not being able to keep it in his pants, which was kind of horrifying to think about considering where all my problems were currently stemming from—and his father found the amount of money it would take for that girl to end the pregnancy and leave my dad.

Even though he'd loved her.

He'd wanted to be with her.

So much that he was going to give up everything to run away with her.

So yeah, I got it. And yeah, it explained a bit of his reaction earlier that day.

But it didn't take away how much it hurt.

"When I finally said I couldn't do it anymore, he was desperate for me not to take you," my mom said as I polished off my wine. "But I told him he had eleven *years* to prove he could be better than his father and I couldn't watch him use you to try to fix himself. And maybe that wasn't what he was doing. He's misguided, but he tried to do what he could with what he had. And really"—she paused to take a sip of wine—"that's what I tried to do, too."

"Yeah, except I'm pretty sure you wouldn't call me a stupid slut in front of a bunch of people because you found out I might be pregnant,"

I said because I was tired and emotional and a little too drunk to think properly.

"No, probably not," my mom said, surprisingly nonchalant. "But to be fair, I told you this whole story before just now remembering that he's about as appealing as a turtle shit dildo and also, fucking *excuse me*?!"

My eyes shot up as her voice rose in both volume and rage. "Wait, I—"

"He called you—wait, are you—" She didn't even finish speaking, just lurched forward and yanked my wine glass towards her, some of it sloshing out from the force of her movement. "You can't drink when—"

"I'm *not*," I said. "I just thought I might be and Dad... Dad found out."

My mom looked at me, patches of red on her cheeks and a doubtful look on her face before she slowly slid the wine glass back to me.

"Nellie," she said calmly. "I need you to please explain right now what. The. Actual. *Fuck*."

And so I explained what the actual fuck, that my period had been late and I'd freaked out and I'd called someone to bring me a pregnancy test, only my dad had seen them leaving it for me and found it before I could, and he'd lost his shit on me in front of everyone.

Which didn't give much more context than what I'd first blurted out, so unfortunately, my mom had follow-up questions.

"Who... I mean..." She tapped her hands on the table. "Do you have a boyfriend?"

"No," I said.

She lifted an eyebrow. "So who—"

"This guy. That I had an arrangement with." My face was burning. "It's over now."

She folded her arms. "Some guy? How did you know him? Because if you were only going to Montreal for stuff with your dad, there are only so many types of men you'd be seeing, and—"

"It's not like that," I said.

"He's not some rich little fucker who wouldn't treat you the way you deserve to be treated?"

I couldn't bring myself to look at her. "He… I mean, he's a good guy."

"Nellie—"

"It was JP. JP Marchand." I rubbed my thumb against my forefinger. "From next door."

That didn't seem to be better than whatever she was picturing. "The little mini brown-noser version of Jean-Luc?"

I snorted. "He's not like his dad."

"No? He didn't become some big-shot lawyer working at his dad's firm like they'd always planned?"

"Well, yes, but—"

"Nellie!"

"He just quit because he didn't agree with his dad on a pretty nasty client." I folded my arms. "Also he stood up for me to Dad."

She nodded slowly. "Alright. And you and JP are…?"

"Just fri—" I stopped myself. "Nothing."

"Nellie."

"It was just supposed to be for fun," I said. "He caught feelings, so it's over."

She frowned. "Why is it—"

"I don't want to talk about JP," I said.

She lifted a hand in concession. "That's fine. I have other things to focus on. Like waking Jack up so he can drive me to Montreal to kill your father."

I tried not to laugh. "You can't kill him."

"I can do anything," she said.

"You'd leave a baby fatherless?"

"Hon, I know it's hard to hear, but you're a couple weeks away from twenty-two. You're not a baby anymore."

"Not me," I said. "The other baby."

My mom paused, then lifted her glass to her lips and drained it. She stood up, but instead of going to wake Jack so she could go to Montreal and kill my dad, she went to the fridge and got another bottle of wine. Returning to the table, she twisted the cap off and the sound of liquid glugging from the bottle filled the kitchen. Once her glass was full nearly to the brim, she set the bottle down, put the cap back on, and lifted her glass again to take a long swig.

"The what now?" she asked after setting it down again.

"Dad's fiancée is pregnant. Except she might be leaving him over this whole thing. Actually, I think you'd almost like Kimberlee."

When all was said and done, we went through two bottles of wine and even though she stopped threatening to kill him, I had to stop my mom from trying to call my dad three times. I don't know if she actually would have, but it didn't matter; the fact that she was willing to do it at all healed something I wasn't fully aware had been scarred. And between that and the wine, I finally broke down and sobbed about everything while my mom hugged me.

And wasn't that really the whole reason I'd been drawn there?

We ended up sleeping in my room, I think partly because my mom didn't want to wake up Jack—who was obviously sleeping in her room—and mostly because she wanted to tell me about Jack, now that I knew about him.

"Persistent little fucker," she slurred as we curled up in bed. "Told him eighty bazillion times he was just a baby and now look at me. Smitten like a fucking school girl."

He was indeed the owner of Jack's Cafe in the same shopping complex that my mom's liquor store was in, despite being only twenty-seven. It had always been his dream, he'd said, and when he came into some unexpected money, it was the first thing he thought of.

"He makes me feel pretty," she mumbled.

"He better, or I'll kick his butt," I replied.

"*Shh*," my mom hissed, giggling. "These walls haven't gotten any thicker since you moved out. He might hear you and he has to work early tomorrow. Or, well... today."

"I can hear you," came a muffled but sleepy response from the other room. "And don't worry. I'd kick my butt, too."

We giggled ourselves to sleep and it wasn't until the next morning, when I woke up feeling better about life in general and worse than I would have if I hadn't gone through two bottles of wine with my mom over the course of a huge, life-altering conversation, that I thought of something else I wanted to talk to her about.

"Hey, did you ever think I might have ADHD?" I asked my mom after Jack had dropped by with breakfast and coffee for us, earning my absolute but still somewhat conditional approval to keep dating my mom.

My mom snorted into her poppyseed muffin. "Oh, God. This again?"

I raised my eyebrows. "Again?"

"Oh, some teacher thought you had it when we were still in Montreal." She took a bite of the muffin. "She had it out for you. You were just being a kid who was going through some stuff at the time and she didn't like that you wouldn't sit down and listen."

I picked at the croissant I'd been dipping in my coffee, not looking at her. "I'm getting assessed in a couple of weeks."

She sighed, tearing off another piece of muffin but not putting it in her mouth. "Nell, you know I'm always gonna think you're extraordinary, but medically, you're perfectly normal. You were a normal kid who had normal behaviour problems and found normal solutions. Just because you have some quirks here or there doesn't mean you're sick in the head."

"It's not a sickness," I said.

She waved it off. "Whatever. I mean—"

"No. Not 'whatever.'" I frowned down at my croissant. "You're making it sound like there's something wrong with me when it's just how my brain works."

"You don't even know if that's true."

"Mom." I looked up at her. "Even if I don't have it, it's not how you should refer to it."

She lifted her hands in surrender. "Fine. But regardless, I mean that I don't want you to be disappointed if you don't get the answer you want."

"I don't want any particular answer," I said. "I just want an *answer*."

"Well, I'm no doctor, but my answer is you don't have it. You know why?"

"Because you don't believe in it?" I asked, trying not to sound dejected.

She shook her head. "Whether I do or not doesn't matter. What does is that you and I are like two peas in a pod." She popped the rest of her muffin in her mouth. "And if I don't have ADHD, Daughter of Mine, you don't have ADHD either."

Chapter Twenty-Eight
Go *clap emoji* To *clap emoji* Therapy *clap emoji*

"OH, YOU ABSOLUTELY HAVE ADHD," Dr. Klum said, shuffling some papers from the folder in his hands. "Definitely. I knew that about three minutes into the appointment."

"Oh," I said. "But I've been here for an hour."

"Yes, well, the rest of this has been trying to figure out how severe it is, but you've got a lot of trauma mixed up that's gonna make it hard to figure out what's your brain wiring and what's a 'daddy issue'—and remember, those were *your* words, not mine." He found what he was looking for and bit the lid off his pen. "But I don't do talk therapy. You'll need a psychologist for that."

"If it was that obvious, how did no one know before now?" I asked.

Dr. Klum blew out a loud breath of air. He was a heavy-set, high-energy man with wide brown eyes, medium brown skin, and a lack of fucks to give. I'd liked him immediately when I walked into his office; everything he'd said was straightforward and to the point, like he had no patience for games.

"Honestly, Nellie, you're damn good at masking," he said.

"Thanks," I replied.

"Not a compliment in this context."

"Oh."

"What it means is that you're very, very good at hiding things that are giving you trouble," he said.

"But I wasn't trying to hide anything."

"And therein lies some of the difficulty in diagnosing ADHD for anyone who isn't a standard Caucasian male." He sat back, crossing an ankle over his knee with a self-satisfied smirk on his face. "You've been so conditioned to hide the symptoms that you don't realize how convoluted a system you've had to create to manage your time so no one realizes you're falling behind. Then something happens that worsens your ADHD symptoms and your systems no longer work. That means the fake persona you've created to cater to everyone else is too tired to keep covering your own ass. And lucky you, this can be caused by anything. Stress. Lack of sleep. Hormones. Diet. Trauma." He pointed his pen at me. "I'm guessing something happened around the time you started noticing the issues with being late and not being able to focus and all that getting worse."

It could've been a few different things, actually. Which was kind of the point, I guess, but also, he had to be wrong.

"What fake persona?" I asked. "I don't *fake* who I am—"

"Have you ever felt the need to hide who you are to impress people?" he asked.

"No, of course—"

And then I stopped and frowned. The smug look on Dr. Klum's face widened.

"See?" he said.

"No." I folded my arms. "I was doing that because my *dad* wanted me to impress people."

"And now you see my conundrum from the last hour," he said. "Is that ADHD or is that trauma?"

"I guess we'll never know," I muttered.

"Wrong. We're finding out." He started writing on one of the papers in his lap. "You need therapy."

"That's it?" I asked. "Just therapy?"

"And meds. You're okay with taking pills?"

"Uh... mostly," I said. "Like, I was on the pill but after this, um, thing that happened a few weeks ago, I went to get an IUD. Because I forgot to take a few of them."

"Smart," Dr. Klum said. "Well, they don't have an IUD for ADHD meds, so we'll have to stick with Vyvanse. Set an alarm on your phone or whatever to remember to take it. We're gonna get you on a starting dose, but we'll move up fairly quickly because—and now, don't take this as enabling or excusing you buying Adderall or whatever your dumbass TA sold you, because I am *very* firmly telling you to never do that ever again—but since you *did* do that and seemed to have a good reaction to whatever you took, I'm confident we can nail your dosage without too much trouble. If not, we try a different med until we find the right one."

"So this whole mental health thing is really just throw it at the wall and see what sticks, hey?" I asked.

"Professionally speaking, no, it's much more complex than that," he said. "Personally speaking, absolutely. Brains are complicated and what works for you won't work for someone else. But for now—ADHD. Meds. Therapy. Seriously. You have a lot to work through."

That was the understatement of the fucking century.

It was a bit of a surprise that Dr. Klum said he'd known three minutes into the appointment seeing as I was ten minutes late. And as I'd explained to him, I was ten minutes late because my dad had called.

"You couldn't hang up on him?" Dr. Klum had joked.

"Oh, he would've lost it if I did," I'd said. "But I would've had to answer for that to happen."

"Why didn't you answer?" he'd asked.

And then I spent the next twenty minutes blabbing about the entire shitshow that was my life.

For a few days after what I referred to in my head as the Pregnancy Fiasco, I hadn't heard a word. Not from my dad. Not from Kimberlee. Obviously not from JP. Not even Anne-Marie knew what was going on.

"Kimberlee's Porsche is on the driveway again," she'd informed me on the following Tuesday. "But I did not see her go into the house or either of them leave. And she missed an event on Wednesday night that I know she was supposed to attend."

But a couple of days after that, my dad called.

It might have been the first time in my life I looked at my phone screen and didn't feel the inherent need to answer. I'd watched it ring, his name flashing on the screen like a warning sign, until it went to voicemail.

Then, when my phone vibrated to tell me I had a new voicemail, I deleted it without listening to it.

I'd repeated the same thing the next day, and the next, and even when he'd called during Dr. Spitzki's class, I'd watched it ring. Which I could only do because I'd turned the ringer off for once because I was so tired of my dad trying to call.

By the time my ADHD assessment rolled around, my dad had taken to not only calling daily, but texting.

Texting.

My dad did not *text*.

But I'd muted that conversation so the notifications didn't show on my phone at all.

"I guess I could block him," I'd said to Dr. Klum. "But it seems so final. Or what if I want to read the messages one day?"

"Very valid," Dr. Klum had said. "But, ah, how did this make you late for your appointment?"

"Oh," I'd said. "Because I missed my 'You have to leave the house in eight minutes' alarm when I silenced my phone."

"Why eight minutes?" he'd asked.

"Because ten minutes makes it feel like it's not that much of a rush and five minutes is too late," I'd said, like it was perfectly normal.

I hadn't known what to expect from my assessment, but it had gone by smoothly. Once he'd reiterated for the eighty millionth time that I needed a therapist—"I'm gonna need therapy to process the trauma of you telling me how much therapy I need," I said at one point, and Dr. Klum shrugged and said if that was what it took, then he was fine with it—he handed me the prescription and gave me strict instructions to book another appointment in a month to follow up with him.

And that was it. I walked out of his office with a prescription in one hand and a diagnosis in... well, not the other hand. But in my mind and medical file, I guess.

"So what are you going to do now?" Sydney asked over beers at Lou's Pub that night once I'd finished telling her that Glitch, Ms. Travers, and Ben had all been unbearably right.

"Go to therapy, I guess," I said. "And fill my prescription. And then just, like, function as a human being?"

She laughed. "I meant about classes. This all started because you wanted an extension from Glitch. Are you gonna ask them for one? You have a case study due next week."

"Yeah, but it's done."

"Seriously?"

I nodded, not looking at her. "And the one after that. And everything else for the rest of the semester."

"After all that," she said. "Well, I guess you had to be doing something while we weren't hanging out."

I shifted uncomfortably. She wasn't wrong. It wasn't that I was actively avoiding Sydney. I wasn't actively avoiding anyone.

Except my dad.

And Kimberlee, I guess, by association.

And Anne-Marie a little, though not completely. Just when I couldn't handle her particular brand of chaotic energy, which had been a lot the past few days.

But no one else. It wasn't like I was avoiding JP. You can't avoid someone who isn't trying to reach you.

But I was inactively avoiding people. Inadvertent avoidance, as it were. Because as it turned out, a great way to distract myself from everything going on was to simply do my homework.

And then every single time my phone went off and I couldn't stop reliving the things my dad said to me, to do more of it.

And whenever I started thinking thoughts I didn't want to think, when I started remembering blue eyes and a smirk that turned to a smile showing off a crooked tooth on the left side of his mouth and how fucking angry I was that he'd gone and done the one thing I'd asked him not to—

Well, you get the picture.

Homework was the answer. Homework, and rewatching documentaries when I was done with my homework, and sleep. I hadn't even been listening to the *Why Am I Like This* podcast. And this beer with Sydney was the first time I'd gone out in nearly two weeks.

The server saved the awkwardness of the conversation by walking up to our table at that moment to ask if we wanted a refill.

"Yeah, absolutely," I said.

"Not for me," Sydney said.

"Oh," I said. "Well, never mind then."

Sydney shrugged apologetically as the server walked away to get our bills. "I have to get home soon."

I looked at her, feigning offense that wasn't entirely fake. "But it's Friday night!"

"I have to be up early tomorrow," she said.

"For *what*?" I asked.

Her eyes didn't quite meet mine and her face was turning pink at a steady pace. "I, uh... I'm going away for the weekend. With Reid."

I almost spilled my beer. I didn't, because the glass was empty and I didn't actually knock it over, but if I'd had some left, I might've purposely tried to spill it to express how absolutely shaken I was by that statement.

"What?!" I said instead. "Where? And like... together?"

"Oh God, of course not," she said, though the way her eyebrows pinched together betrayed something painful. "Not together-together. We, um..." She swallowed, then twisted her glass on the coaster. "We're *goingtomontrealtotellolivierswife.*"

The words spilled out the way my imaginary beer had, pooling between us as I processed what she'd said.

She still hadn't told either Olivier or his wife what she knew. I didn't fully understand why she couldn't bring herself to do it. Like yeah, it was scary, and yeah, it shouldn't have been her problem to deal with, but it was painful watching her stuck in a place between decisions, not willing to end things without saying why but not willing to reveal what she knew.

But I was the absolute last person who should judge her for something like that. And I'd told her I would support whatever she did, but...

"Without me?" I asked, trying not to sound hurt even though I was definitely fucking hurt.

Her face twisted regretfully. "I didn't think you'd want to go to Montreal. And you've got so much other stuff going on that I—"

"I still want to be there for you, Syd," I said. "You're my best friend."

"I know. But I didn't want to add more to your plate. You've got a lot to handle right now."

She didn't say it condescendingly, but that didn't change the fact that it felt that way.

"You could've let me make that decision for myself," I said. "Or at least told me you were going instead of hiding it from me."

She looked down at the table as she fidgeted with her glass again. "I've been worried about you."

"Worried about what?" I asked, rolling my eyes. "I'm fine. I'm completely fine."

"Are you?" she asked. "Because—"

"I am *fine*, Syd," I said.

She twisted her mouth to the side but thankfully dropped it. "Does it help if I say I didn't decide to go until yesterday and I wasn't sure if you wanted that on your mind during your assessment?"

"A little," I muttered.

"Well, that's what happened." She sighed and leaned against the back of the booth. "Olivier's been suspicious for a while. It's been two months since I've seen him and, like, over a month since we've really talked. I keep telling him I'm busy with school but he got annoyed when he said he'd come out to visit for a weekend and I turned it down. But I hadn't figured out how to tell Clara yet. Or what I was going to do. I didn't want him to *be* here."

"Okay," I said.

"Well, Reid pointed out the fact that Olivier doesn't know that I know he's married," she continued. "So if I happened to run into him and Clara unexpectedly..."

I saw where she was going with it. "How would you do that?"

She pressed her lips together, not quite smiling. "Well, see, here's the thing. He's getting an award."

"For Montreal's Biggest Scumbag?"

"Close. For being a good cop or something like that. As a result of—get this—Clinton's arrest."

A laugh burst out of me. "Clinton's arrest? The one where his *wife* did all the work?"

"Mm-hmm, yep." The not-quite-a-smile widened into an actual one. "Of course he didn't tell me about it, but I checked Clara's socials and she made a post about it. So I bought a ticket to go down and 'surprise him' at the event."

I couldn't help but grin. "That's devious."

"Reid suggested I ask you to come with me, actually. He was going to come either way because he said he wants to make sure someone's looking out for us, which I told him was kind of sexist but also, he's bigger than Olivier and could probably kick his ass if things went badly. So I wasn't going to say no."

We got our bills and paid them, then walked home. It wasn't until we were at our building that Sydney mentioned it again.

"If you do want to come, Nell, you know I'd love to have you there," she said.

"It's okay," I said. "I have… you know. Homework and stuff."

She nodded, though there was something remorseful on her face. "If you change your mind, you know where to find me. I can kick Olivier's ass to the curb and then we can go out clubbing. With Anne-Marie, maybe."

I appreciated the offer, but turned it down. Partly because she made a point of telling me Reid had gotten his own hotel room because roommates or not, sharing a room felt weird. Which meant the hotel would probably end up with only one room, so maybe she and Reid would finally get their heads out of their asses and hook up.

But I said no mainly because Syd was right.

I didn't have any desire to go to Montreal.

Chapter Twenty-Nine
Poof, Everything Is Fixed

CURIOSITY FINALLY GOT THE best of me later that night.

I only answered because I was at least sixty-three percent sure it wasn't my dad. It was after eight and he rarely had his phone on him after seven; anything urgent was routed through Pierre. And sure, he could've been trying to trick me into answering by doing things I didn't expect, like texting me.

But I was also convinced he was far too proud to hide his name when he called.

"If you're calling at a weird time and using Kimberlee's phone under the assumption that I'd pick up, you're right, but I'm going to hang up if this isn't her," I said when I answered.

"So you are ignoring Max, then?" Kimberlee asked, laughing softly.

"Of course I am," I said. "Why would I want to talk to him?"

"I wanted to be sure. He said he has been trying to reach you but that you wouldn't respond. I didn't know if I should believe him or not."

There was a lot more to her words than what she said. I picked at my thumbnail, not sure what to feel. "So you're taking him back, then?"

"There are conditions," she said, which obviously meant yes. "One of the biggest is that he needs to apologize to you."

I laughed so hard I dropped my phone.

"Damn, Kimberlee," I said when I finally managed to control myself and picked it back up. "I never pegged you to be a comedian."

"I like to tell a joke as much as anyone," she said. "Though I'd love to know what I said that was so funny."

"My dad doesn't apologize."

"He apologized to me."

"And you believed him?"

"I did. I do." She sighed. "He is destroyed right now, Nellie."

Good, I wanted to say. Good, and good riddance, and good fucking bye.

Instead, I sank onto my couch and closed my eyes. "You heard what he said to me."

"I did. It was unacceptable. And he knows if I ever hear anything like that again, I will be out of his life faster than he can blink," she said.

"And you think he's telling the truth. That he's not faking all of this remorse because you're pregnant and he doesn't want you to take his kid away?"

"I truly do not think Max is faking anything right now."

"How can you be so sure?"

"People cannot fake tears like the ones I saw from him."

I snorted. "My dad would never let anyone see him cry. If he's even capable of it. I wouldn't be surprised if he'd had his tear ducts removed during one of those Botox appointments he pretends he doesn't get."

"I know what I saw, Nellie. You do not have to believe him, or accept his apology, or do anything you do not want to," she said, then paused for a moment. "I do not know how much you know about Max's past—"

"More than I did before," I said. "My mom told me some of it."

"It is very hard for someone to realize the things they thought were normal are anything but," she said. "That doesn't excuse any of what he did. Ever. But he is trying to change. He truly is."

I wanted to believe her. But even after everything, I didn't know if I could trust her. Especially over something as fantastical as claiming my dad had *cried*.

My dad was the kind of man whose smile never reached his eyes. If a smile couldn't reach them, how could anything else?

"What are you going to do if I don't let him apologize to me?" I asked. "If that's one of your conditions?"

"I would never make you speak with him. I only needed to know he tried."

I swallowed hard. "Well, he did. If he wants to go ahead and stop trying, that would be great. I'm not gonna answer."

Because he didn't deserve to apologize.

He didn't deserve my forgiveness.

He didn't deserve to have me in his life.

I was so tired of trying to be the daughter he wanted. I wasn't very good at it, but he'd also never wanted a daughter in the first place. Neither of my parents had expected me.

But at least I'd never felt like my mom didn't want me.

There was no reason for me to talk to my dad. Harsh as it was, he'd given me what I needed from him. My tuition was paid for. I thought he'd paid for my rent on a yearly basis, but even if he didn't, I still had the money my mom had saved for me for university. She'd transferred it to my account in my first year, but I hadn't touched a dime of it; my dad had covered everything.

So I had a cushion. And I had friends in Ottawa who would help me out if I needed it. And even though Jack was living with my mom, my room was still there if I really had no other option.

I'd asked my dad for money. Nothing more.

He'd asked me to attend social events for him. Nothing more.

Everything else he'd given me and that I'd given him was extra. The things that we did because we were connected by blood and a piece of paper someone had put his name on twenty-two years earlier saying he'd contributed to my existence.

I had no reason to forgive him.

No reason except that I wanted my dad to accept me.

I'd asked for his money, but I'd wanted his support. I'd wanted his pride. I'd wanted to feel *wanted*. But I didn't know if he was capable of wanting me as the daughter I was, rather than the one he tried to curate.

I doubted *he* knew if he was.

I didn't say any of that to Kimberlee. She didn't make me justify anything. She just accepted my "no" and told me about her latest prenatal appointment, then wished me a good night and hung up.

So I guess I was justifying it all to myself.

For a long time, I sat in silence, staring blankly at the TV in front of me, thinking in circles until I was dizzy. Then, hands shaking, I unlocked my phone.

I'd deleted all the voicemails, but the messages were there. I hesitated before tapping on his name, not sure if I wanted to know what they'd say. My mind had already filled in a number of options, each both more and less likely than the last:

Eleanor, answer my calls or I'll have your landlord evict you.

Dear God, grow up and show some class. Call me by the end of the day or I will ensure you cannot graduate this year.

Enough is enough, Eleanor. There is an event you must attend otherwise I will take you to court. Oh, you do not believe a father can sue his daughter? Perhaps you should have gone to law school after all so you'd know better. As it stands, I'm sure Jean-Paul will provide legal advice if you are able to take his penis out of your mouth long enough for him to string a coherent argument together.

But when I finally summoned the courage to click on the chat, the messages there were ones I'd never expected.

They escalated in a similar way. Short, to-the-point ones that grew longer and longer with each one sent. All of them similar, none of them threatening, most inappropriately businesslike, and only one of them that mattered.

Dad

> Please answer your phone.
> From Dad.

> Please listen to my message. I would like to say something to you.
> From Dad.

> I know you are ignoring me. I understand. I would still like to speak to you when you have some time.
> From Dad.

Nellie, I need to speak with you about what happened the last time you were here. I would appreciate the opportunity to discuss the situation and attempt to come to a resolution. From Dad.

I have not told Kimberlee yet that this will be the last message I send you. I expect she will tell you she has requested I apologize to you as a condition of her accepting my apology to her. I have not told her yet I have been trying to reach you since before she spoke with me and I cannot bring myself to keep pressing when I am very aware that you are not interested in hearing from me. Nor have I told her that I cannot apologize to you. Because there is no apology on Earth I would accept from someone who hurt my daughter the way I have, and I cannot advise you to accept mine. Regardless of that, please know I am sorry for how I have treated you, both this most recent visit and all the times prior that I must apologize for. I love you very much, ma fille ange.
Love Dad.

And I cried.

Because of course I did.

And when I was done crying, I cried some more, because apparently I wasn't actually done.

And then I picked up my phone again.

"'Lo?" Sydney mumbled.

"Syd?"

"Nell? It's... dude, it's two a.m."

I blinked at the clock. "Shit. Sorry. I didn't realize."

"What—" She stopped to cough, then stifled a yawn. "What's wrong?"

"Can I come with you tomorrow?"

"Today."

"Huh?"

"It's two a.m. We leave at eight. We're splitting gas for Reid's truck three ways, you're on the hook for coffee, and I call shotgun."

The line clicked dead. After I got up and threw a bunch of clothes in a bag for the next day—today, as Syd had said, but in my mind days started after I'd slept regardless of the actual time—I typed a quick message.

Me

I will be in Montreal tomorrow. We can meet for lunch. John Jean's Pub.

Just before I went to sleep, my phone buzzed with a response.

Dad

Thank you, Nellie.
Love Dad

When my dad arrived at the restaurant the next day, the first thing I thought was that he looked old.

It wasn't a bad thing. He looked old in a natural way, like the uncertainty and remorse on his face were dynamite that had blasted away cliffs and crevices to reveal the man beneath, an actual human who had taken stone after stone that was thrown at him and stacked it until he became the unfeeling mountain he was.

He looked like a man who could cry.

"I thought Kimberlee would come with you," I said when he walked up to the table.

"I asked her not to," my dad replied. "But if you would like her to attend, I can call and—"

"No," I said. "It's fine."

He nodded once, stiffly, and sat down.

"I ordered some of Dee's Nuts," I said. "The ones we had last time."

"Thank you," he said.

There was a long, awkward silence.

And then, without prompting, my dad began to talk.

He told me things he'd never said before. Things he'd never shared before, because why would anyone share things like that with a child? Things that hurt to hear as much as it hurt to know that I couldn't excuse the things he'd done because of them, not that he was asking me to. Things he never wanted me to know about because he thought if I knew how broken he was, it would make me think he didn't want me.

Of course, he didn't say any of it like that. Everything came out in a business-like tone, like he'd constructed the words a certain way and fit them all together neatly. But it didn't seem *fake*. I could fill the rest of the emotion in myself and realize that it was the best he could do right now, that what I saw in front of me was the result of all the work he'd done with Kimberlee's help.

And yet, after all that, the thing that made me realize his apology was genuine was that he didn't invite me to his dinner party that night.

I mean, he did.

But he didn't insist I attend.

"It was planned before I knew you would be here today," he said. "But you do not need to come. Or if you would like to come stay in your room, we will cancel it. I will call—"

"It's okay," I said. "I have a hotel. With Syd. And we have, um, plans tonight."

He nodded. "I understand."

I don't know if he actually did. It didn't matter, not when there was so far to go before anything was truly solved. I didn't magically walk away from lunch with my dad feeling like twenty-two years of the mess that was our relationship had been wiped away.

But he asked about my life while we had lunch. I told him about my ADHD assessment and he listened thoughtfully. Instead of deciding it was a flaw to hide so I could be his perfect daughter, he asked what I needed from him for support, then told me to have whatever therapist I ended up working with call Pierre to put a payment method on file.

And he smiled when I told him about the grade I got on my midterm paper, and said that he was glad I'd done well even though I hated the class, and didn't twist it to suggest I go to law school again.

So no, nothing was completely fixed. But I walked away with maybe one or two less of those issues I had with my daddy, as it were, so it wasn't all for nothing.

And maybe, with time, it would be something.

"So it was good," I said to Sydney as we did our makeup to go out to the club that night. "I think things are really looking up, actually."

"About time," she said in a dejected tone. "You deserve it."

I grimaced. "I'm sure things will work out for you, too. Something must have happened for Olivier to not be at the luncheon."

"Yeah," she said vaguely, dabbing more blush on her cheeks.

"Did you call him or anything?"

She shook her head.

"It just doesn't make sense. How did he—"

"If I knew, I'd tell you." She took a breath in and let it out. "Let's not let it get in the way of celebrating for at least one of us. I *am* super happy for you."

"Thanks." I smiled. "It's great, actually. I'm getting treated for ADHD, I'm talking to my friends again, I'm not gonna fail that one class, everything's good with my parents. It's like, *poof*, just like that, everything's resolved and there are definitely no loose ends for me to finish tying up."

Chapter Thirty
No It Isn't, You Fucking Liar

"YOU'RE SO FULL OF shit," Reid said.

I scoffed loudly, partly because I was offended and mostly because I forgot he was in the hotel room with us. "Excuse me?"

"No, he's right," Sydney said. "It's not resolved at all, you fucking liar. What about JP?"

"What *about* JP?" I asked.

She gave me an unimpressed look that smeared mascara along her brow bone. "Nell."

"Don't 'Nell' me," I said, passing her a Q-tip. "There's nothing to resolve there. I don't want a relationship. JP does. We're not together. Poof. Fucking resolved. Now we can go out and I can be my slutty, fun self and find some French guy to celebrate with."

"I don't believe that for one second," she said.

"I don't really care what you believe," I said, annoyed. "I don't want JP."

"Not at all."

"Not even a little bit."

Reid coughed in the background. *"Sureyoudon't."*

"No one asked you," I said.

"Okay, but he's still not wrong," Sydney said. "Ignoring what happened with JP isn't going to make it go away."

"Nothing *happened*," I said. "He had feelings he shouldn't have had and we ended things."

"And you're sad about it."

"I am *not*."

"You've been moping for weeks. You—"

"I haven't!" My voice pitched up and I tried to calm the flare of anger that was warming my cheeks. "I had a huge falling out with my dad. That was the main issue."

"You had a pregnancy scare and a breakup at the same time," she said. "And no matter how much you insist you don't like JP, I've been listening to you talk about him for months now and—"

"Syd, I don't want to hear it," I said.

"Even things with Anne-Marie aren't the same. Sure, you're talking again, but—"

"Anne-Marie has finally accepted that me and JP are never getting together," I said. "If *she's* stopped bothering me, you have no excuse."

Unfortunately, that turned out to be both bullshit and a total setup, which I found out approximately three minutes later when someone knocked at the hotel door.

"What are you doing here?" I asked as Anne-Marie breezed past Reid into the room, Remy trailing behind her.

"*Bonjour, chérie*," she said, her tone bright and almost business-like. "We cannot stay long. We're going to the dinner party at your father's because my dad is trying to make a good impression on the Martelles. They threatened to stop working with him because he won't drop the Thibaults but—"

"Wait," I said. "The Martelles are going to the dinner party?"

"Yes," she said. "Why?"

Oh, just the little thing where my dad had offered to cancel the whole party for me and as much as I'd realized that was a big deal, I hadn't realized *how* big it was. "Nothing."

Anne-Marie shrugged. "Anyway, I have some things to say to you, *chérie*."

"To me?" I asked.

She nodded. "You and Jean-Paul."

"You've got to be fucking kidding me." I put my makeup brush down on the dresser a little harder than necessary.

Well, a lot harder than necessary. The powder on the end puffed into the air and my lipstick nearly flew off the edge of the dresser, but Sydney caught it in time.

"Kidding you about what?" Anne-Marie asked. "You have not been yourself and—"

"Says who?" I demanded.

She gestured at Sydney. "Your friends who see you every day. And I am worried about you, too. Even Jean-Paul is worried, and he—"

"Why the fuck would JP be worried?" I asked. "And why are you all talking about me?"

She ignored my second question. "Because he knows you. He may not outright say it, but I know he is worried."

"He doesn't know anything about me," I said.

"He knows enough to be in love with you."

Anger lurched up my chest and into my throat. "I wouldn't trust him to know the difference between a hat and his own ass if he thinks he's in love with me."

Anne-Marie looked amused, despite the way I was glaring at her. "I seem to have hit a nerve."

"Yeah, you have. The nerve where you *said* you weren't going to bring this shit up with me again. I know it's weird that I fucked your brother, Anne-Marie, but it's not up for discussion."

She tapped her fingers against the dresser, then leaned on it. "You know, you are right."

"Thank—"

"It *is* weird that you fucked my brother and lied to me about it," she said. "So perhaps I am entitled to say a few words before we drop it completely."

"I—" I started, but nothing followed it.

Because she wasn't wrong. She was playing off the guilt she knew I had about the situation, but she wasn't *wrong*.

Anne-Marie smiled, the corners of her large brown eyes crinkling. "As I thought. Now, Nellie, *chérie*, listen to me. You and Jean-Paul are perfect for each other. You have been in love—"

"Stop right there," I said. "No, I haven't. And I am not."

She waved a hand at me. "Call it what you want. Anyone with even fifty percent of their vision remaining in a single eyeball could see that."

"It is pretty obvious," Remy said.

"It is not!" I said.

"No, it is," he said. "Even before everyone knew you were sleeping together, it was obvious."

"If you are too stubborn to admit it, that is to your detriment," Anne-Marie said before I could snap back at Remy again. "You spent a summer loving him, you loved him enough to let him take the virginity you oh-so-virtuously prized when we were eighteen—"

Blood drained from my face. I had never admitted that to Anne-Marie. "He *told* you?"

"In excruciating detail." Perfectly white teeth gleamed at me through Anne-Marie's grin, though there was a hint of regret in it. "It was partially my fault. I think perhaps Jean-Paul thought it would disturb me enough to make me go away. But I am very persistent."

"No shit," I muttered, not looking at anyone in the room.

"Nellie, he cares for you deeply," Anne-Marie said.

"He didn't tell you that."

"He told me he popped your cherry," she said smoothly. "What else do you think he's told me?"

It was a good point. I didn't say anything else.

"*Chérie*, even if you do not want to be with him, get closure." She opened her purse, taking out a Post-It note like the ones JP used to leave on my car, and held it out to me. "He feels awful about things happening the way they did. Deny it all you want, but you do too. You would both feel better if you talked things out."

"What's that?" I asked.

"My brother's new address," she said. "He moved to start his new job. You can go see him."

I stared at the Post-It for a moment, then flicked my eyes up to Anne-Marie. Slowly, I reached out to take it.

Then, holding her gaze, I crumpled it up and put it in my mouth.

"How does that taste?" she asked patiently as I chewed.

I spit it into my hand, then threw the saliva-soaked clump of paper into the garbage can. "Like winning."

Anne-Marie and Sydney shared a look, then Anne-Marie shrugged.

"Alright, *chérie*," she said. "I have said my piece. I will not bring it up again."

"None of you better," I said, glancing at Sydney from the corner of my eye.

"I make no promises," Reid said from the bed.

I was still grumbling angrily as Anne-Marie said goodbye and left. Sydney didn't say anything once the door was shut and I leaned into the mirror, aggressively putting on way too much blush.

"Is your plan to sit around here the rest of the night, Reid?" I asked. "Or are you coming out with us? Because you can if you want but make it clear you're with Syd so it doesn't mess up my chances of getting laid."

"Yeah, I'd rather not do that," Reid said, flipping through the channels on the TV.

Sydney didn't say anything and Reid wasn't looking at her, which made it even more impressive that he knew hurt had flashed across her face.

"Because clubs aren't my scene," he added quickly. "Not because—"

"Shut up," Sydney muttered. "Are you almost done so we can go, Nell?"

"It's like, seven o'clock," Reid said. "What clubs are open this early?"

"We'll stop for food first," I said.

"I'll come with you guys for dinner," he said.

"Maybe you should order a pizza or something," Sydney said, then closed her eyes so she could put on her setting spray.

I ignored the two of them, instead going to my bag and digging out the dress I'd wanted to wear.

And then, when I couldn't find it, I pulled out the dress I'd actually brought.

Which was the same fucking dress I'd brought to Mont Tremblant for JP's work thing.

Which was fine. It was a cute dress. I could get away with it at a club. It was short and fit me nicely and was revealing in a classy sort of way.

But I wasn't going for classy.

"Wow," Reid said when I walked out of the bathroom a while later. "That's..."

"Did you cut up your dress?" Sydney asked, frowning.

"I had a vision," I said, tugging the edge of the now-incredibly-mini skirt down a bit.

"A vision of your tits falling out?" she asked.

"It's not that low cut," I said.

She raised her eyebrows, then walked over and hooked a finger in the bottom of the even deeper V I'd cut into the neckline of the dress. "I can literally see your tattoo when I do this."

"Also my nipples. So win-win." I pressed the fabric down again. "Come on. I want to go out and I'm not ending the night until I get fucked or fucked up, whichever comes first."

And if I had to put money on it, I was going to say it would be the former, based on the fact that we were in the club for about twelve seconds when we were sent our first drink.

"Told you the dress was a good idea," I said to Sydney as the bartender pointed out the gentlemen our drinks were courtesy of.

"I never said it wasn't," she said. "I just said your tits would fall out."

I smiled prettily at the two men the bartender had motioned to, then took a sip as I looked around the room.

We'd left the hotel closer to eight and grabbed dinner, but it was still early enough that the club wasn't in full party mode yet. That was fine by me; I didn't need a club full of people to find someone to sleep with, and the faster I found someone, the faster I'd be able to go get laid.

And there were enough people there for me to be a little choosy. A bachelorette party was getting table service at one of the large booths in the corner and a couple of guys hovered around the DJ booth, trying to get him to play their requests. A couple who seemed to be really into exhibitionism ignored everyone's glances as they made out on the mostly empty dance floor and a few groups of friends sat at various tables and booths throughout the bar. Most of them looked to be tourists who didn't realize Montreal's night life started later than they thought it should, but there were clearly some locals there.

I say clearly, because I knew them.

"Syd," I said. "Fuck me if I'm wrong, but is that—"

"Mother *fucker*!" Sydney gasped, her eyes going wide.

"And that's her?" I asked.

She stared, nodding slowly as Olivier slung his arm around his curvy redheaded wife, Clara, who was sitting next to him at one of the high-top cocktail tables with another couple. I didn't recognize the woman, but the guy, on the other hand...

"That's Cody," I said. "The groom from the bachelor party the night we met them."

Sydney nodded, her lips pressed tightly together. I elbowed her excitedly.

"Now's your chance, Syd!"

"Let's just go to a different bar."

My head snapped towards her. "What?"

"I—"

"You came to Montreal to deal with this," I said. "Just because he wasn't at the awards thing—"

She shook her head slowly, her face twisting. "Nell, I can't. I... I just want to go."

"I'll do it," I said.

"You don't have to—"

"I know I don't have to," I said. "But remember when I said I wanted to get fucked or fucked up?"

"Yeah, but—"

"I think getting into a fight should be added to the list."

"He was at the luncheon," she said.

I gaped at her. "*What*?"

"I chickened out." Her voice shook. "I saw him there with her and I just... I don't want to hurt her."

"She needs to know he's cheating, Syd," I said.

"Yeah, but in public?" She chewed her bottom lip. "I don't want to embarrass her. And I... what if he..."

She didn't have to finish for me to know how scared she was. She didn't have to justify it, either. Not when there was a non-zero chance of Olivier doing something that could hurt her. Both of us watched the table and a few moments later, Olivier stood, gesturing towards the bar.

Perfect.

"Let me do it," I said. "Then you don't have to worry."

She hesitated, then her shoulders sagged in defeat. "Fine. Just be nice about it, okay?"

"I'll see what I can do," I said.

"Nell—"

But I'd already started across the bar towards the table.

"Excuse me!" I shouted over the music when I was close enough. Three sets of curious eyes turned to me. "Hi! Cody?"

Cody blinked, confused. "Uh... yeah?"

I grinned. "I know you don't remember me. We met at your bachelor party."

He glanced nervously at the woman sitting next to him, who'd stiffened. "Did we?"

"Don't worry, it was nothing bad," I said to his wife. "My name's Nellie. I helped the guys out with a scavenger hunt and just wanted to come over and say congratulations."

"The scavenger hunt," Cody repeated, his forehead creasing before realization dawned on him and he burst out laughing. "Oh, shit! Baby, this is the girl who gave me her panties and made out with Christian and Jesse."

"I did way more than make out with them," I said.

His wife squealed with laughter and pressed her hands together. "Oh my *God*! He told me all about that. And"—she clapped excitedly—"you know Christian and Jesse have been together basically ever since?"

An excited grin spread on my face. Not because I finally knew I'd been right about Christian and Jesse, but because she'd given me the *perfect* opening. "Oh, *good*! I'm so glad to hear that. They were adorable together. And, like, what a nice thing that multiple relationships got started at that party, you know? That's such good karma for your marriage."

"Multiple relationships?" Cody's wife repeated. "Who else—"

"No one," Cody said. "It was only Christian and Jesse."

"No, there was one more!" I said brightly. "My friend Sydney and your best man."

And the thing was, even if I *hadn't* been faking the whole thing, I would've instantly known something was wrong. The attitude at the table shifted; Cody wasn't looking at me, but his wife's smile disappeared and from the corner of my eye, I saw Clara sit back.

But I was faking it, and I figured I'd go for the nuclear option.

"It wouldn't have been my best man," Cody said. "Maybe someone else?"

"I could've sworn she said Olivier was your best man," I said. "She's been here to visit him a few times since. The cop with the curly brown hair? They made out in front of *everyone* and she went back to his hotel. He's been spoiling her rotten, honestly, getting nice hotels for her every time she visits. It's so hard to find good guys like that these days, you know?" I smiled stupidly before turning to Clara. "Do you know him, too?"

Clara stared at me, silent. After a moment, her eyes trailed to something behind my right shoulder and stayed there.

And I knew he had to be behind me.

"Yes," she said. "Olivier is my husband."

"I sure am," said the voice behind me. "Who—"

And then he looked at me and stopped.

"Did you know about this?" Cody's wife asked.

"I... what..." Cody said.

"Did you know?" his wife asked. "Did you know your best friend is cheating on my sister?"

Oh.

Oh *shit*.

"Wait," Olivier said. "Wait, I can explain—"

"Did you know, Cody?" his wife demanded. "Did you see him make out with this girl 'in front of everyone'?"

"What girl?" Olivier said. "I've never seen this girl before in my life."

"Surprising, since it's apparently her friend you've been fucking," Cody's wife said.

Through it all, Clara just stared at the table. I looked at her, then at Olivier, who was glaring daggers at me.

"Oops," I said. "My bad. Good luck with that."

And then I walked away.

Chapter Thirty-One
Problem Solver

I DIDN'T WALK DIRECTLY to Sydney in case Olivier came after me, but when it was clear he was preoccupied with whatever was going on, I doubled back and met Syd where I'd left her. She was staring at the table, her lips parted and her drink empty.

"Well, that went both better and worse than expected," I said. "So it turns out Clara is Cody's wife's *sister*."

"Nellie," Sydney said, her voice hollow. "What happened to being nice?"

"How nice can you be when you're telling someone their husband is cheating?" I asked.

"Yeah, but I didn't want to embarrass her!"

"I didn't say anything embarrassing—"

"Look at her!" Sydney's voice wavered. I glanced back at the table, where Clara was clearly fighting back tears. Olivier grabbed her arm and she batted it away. A second later, Cody's wife doused Olivier with the rest of her frozen daiquiri and then took Cody's beer and dumped it on his head.

"It's not even just Olivier and Clara now," Sydney said. "Now it's two couples I broke up."

"You didn't do shit," I said. "You'd rather let those women be with dirtbags who lied to them instead of letting them know the truth?"

"Put yourself in their shoes," she said. "Would you want to be embarrassed like that in public?"

I rolled my eyes. "I'd never be in those shoes in the first place. I'm never doing relationships and that means I'm never getting married."

"Yeah, but have some fucking empathy," she snapped.

I gaped at her. "Are you seriously arguing for not telling them?"

"I'm saying you need to think about how your actions affect other people." She blinked rapidly. "Neither of those women deserved that."

I didn't know if embarrassment or anger was heating my cheeks. Maybe it was both. Sydney had a point, in a way. Yes, both of them had deserved better than that, but they'd thank me one day.

Maybe.

Or maybe it was just another way that I'd fucked up.

"Maybe we should go back to the hotel," Sydney said

"Why?" I asked.

"You're spiralling."

"How am *I* spiralling?"

"You're not being yourself," she said. "You're doubling down on this relationships-are-bullshit thing because you're obviously hurt about things ending with JP and—"

"Watch it, Syd," I said.

"I am saying this as your friend," Sydney said. "You are lying so obviously that it's painful. You are so stubborn you're refusing to admit how miserable you are. You're so unwilling to admit you have feelings for him that you're trying to solve it by finding a random person to hook up with, but you can't solve every problem by spreading your legs, Nell."

I didn't say anything.

I didn't say a single fucking thing.

"Wait," Sydney said a moment later. "That came out—"

"Ladies," said an unfamiliar voice. "I hope the drinks we sent over didn't cause this tension."

I turned to see the two guys the bartender had pointed out standing nearby. One was taller, with light brown hair and pale white skin, wearing a buttoned shirt and chinos. The other was shorter and looked like he lived in a gym, with thick biceps that strained the fabric of his polo and big, puppy dog eyes.

I liked the tall one.

"Yeah," I said. "You'll do."

He raised his eyebrows. "What was that?"

"I said you'll do." I downed the rest of the drink one of them had bought me and put the glass on the bar. "Let's go dance."

"Nellie, wait," Sydney started.

"You can leave if you want," I said. "But I have to go solve some problems."

And I grabbed the man's hand and dragged him towards the dance floor.

"Well, you know how to go after what you want," he said.

Or at least, I think he did. The music was so loud I could barely think.

"Yeah," I shouted. "What's your name?"

He said something. I wasn't exactly sure what. He had a strong French accent to begin with, but paired with the volume of the music, all I could guess was that it started with an *F* sound. Felix, maybe?

It didn't matter.

I didn't need to know his name.

Our dancing started innocently enough. My body didn't touch his as I swayed to the music, my hands grazing his arm the only form of contact. For one or two songs, we stayed that way, just teasing each other as we moved to the music.

I let him be the one to make the next move; as my fingers trailed down his arm, he turned his palm up to catch my wrist and tugged me closer to him. He leaned in, his lips moving, but I shrugged helplessly.

"The music is too loud!" I shouted, and he smiled and returned the gesture before putting a hand on my lower back and pulling me hard against his body.

I took a sharp breath as we pressed together, inhaling the scent of overpriced cologne and subtle sweat. Closing my eyes, I focused on the feel of his fingers as they trailed down my sides, strong hands pulling my body closer to his. There was a comfort to his body, a gentle familiarity that made me relax against him. I took another deep breath, then frowned.

Familiar, but not quite right.

There were a few things wrong with that, namely that I'd never met Felix before and there was no reason for him to seem familiar. Something tugged at the back of my mind, but I ignored it, instead reaching up and running my hands along Felix's chest. His hands moved up and down my sides in a way far too intimate for a man I'd spoken a handful of sentences to. Still, I kept dancing, and I kept letting him touch me, and I kept thinking the woodsy citrusy scent of his cologne was too spicy.

Too spicy compared to what, I didn't know.

He moved one hand to the small of my back, holding me even closer. I rested my hands on his shoulders, trying to ignore that déjà vu-like sense creeping through my nerves. My tension must have been palpable: moments later, Felix's lips brushed my ear.

"What is wrong?" he shout-asked.

I shook my head as if doing so would shake off the strange feeling and grinned, looking up at him. "Nothing!"

Without warning, he tightened his grip on me, making me gasp as his body crushed against mine. I looked up at him with wide eyes, and he raised an eyebrow at me questioningly. Before he could speak or I could think, I pulled his face to mine and kissed him as hard as I could.

It surprised him; that much was evident by the way he jumped. It was just as apparent that he wanted it, though; as soon as he recovered, he kissed me back, his hips grinding into mine. I smirked against his mouth, responding by pushing my chest into his, and I felt him exhale against my lips.

He pulled back and said something, but again, I couldn't hear it.

"I don't read lips!" I shouted.

He leaned in and brought his mouth next to my ear. "I said, keep dancing like that on me and I might start wondering if there's something else you are looking for."

Turning my head slightly, I spoke into his ear. "Are you wondering how long you have to put up with the dancing charade before you ask me to go home with you?"

"Forward, are you?"

I pressed my body tighter to his, already feeling his body reacting through his chinos. "You seem to like it."

"Well, maybe," he said.

I raised my eyebrows and swayed my hips. "Maybe? So that's just your phone vibrating in your pocket?"

The shifting of my hips had the desired effect. Felix's cock twitched again and he smirked.

"Maybe I'm just very happy to see you," he said.

I kissed him again, and again, breathing softly as his lips worked mine, and his fingers dug into my skin as he pushed his bulge against me. Usually, that would get a reaction of my own underway. I waited patiently for those tingles of desire to start, for my panties to dampen and my nipples to harden, but they didn't.

Frowning, I kissed Felix harder, slipping my tongue into his mouth. He exhaled a soft sigh, his hands moving to my ass and squeezing. His tongue flicked against mine, and again, I waited for that shot of arousal to course through me.

Nothing happened.

Frustrated, I moved my mouth to his neck. Felix groaned, the sound making his neck vibrate beneath my lips, and he kissed the side of my head. His hips rolled, pushing his erection against me again as his lips found my ear.

"Why are you teasing me like this?" he asked.

"I'm not teasing," I said. "That would imply I have no intention of going through with this."

He swore softly enough that I wasn't sure exactly what he said. "What if I took you to my car? I'm parked out back."

I had no problem fucking anyone in a car. "You have a condom?"

He nodded. "Let me settle the tab so they do not stop us on the way out."

He subtly adjusted the front of his pants before leading me to the bar, his hand on the small of my back. I waited, leaning against the bar as he asked for his credit card, my heart racing as I tried to ignore the fact that Felix was barely turning me on. It was because it had been a while, I told myself. I hadn't fucked anyone new since Ben, technically, and that had been at the start of the summer.

I'd almost convinced myself when the bartender brought Felix's credit card over and Felix took out his wallet to put it away.

"What's that?" I asked, staring at the leather.

He frowned. "What?"

"That!"

"My wallet?"

"No." I pointed at the monograph in the corner. "What are those initials?"

He frowned, a mix of confusion and amusement. "My initials."

"I thought your name was Felix."

He laughed and shook his head. "No. *Phillipe*." He tapped each of the letters on the wallet. "Jean-Phillipe MacKay."

JPM.

Nausea hit me at the same time as the realization that I'd picked the fucking knock-off version of JP to dance with. I'd had the opportunity to dance with a guy who was completely different, but here I was with Phillipe.

Brown hair instead of blonde, but in this light, almost the same.

Confident hands, but they didn't know how to touch me.

His voice smooth, but too French.

His outfit stylish and put together, but it didn't fit him quite right.

Woodsy, citrusy cologne, but it didn't have the subtleness of JP's.

And no sparks when he kissed me.

"Oh no," I whispered.

Phillipe frowned. "What is wrong?"

"I... I have to go," I said.

The frown deepened. "Wait. Go where?"

"I have to—"

"You said you were not a tease, baby."

He wasn't even calling me the right nickname. "I'm not. I just realized—"

He took a step forward, effectively trapping me between him and the bar. "Then why are you teasing me?"

One time, a man with horrible breath and even worse sweatpants cornered me alone at Les Bleus.

One time, Clinton Thibault was his usual horrible self while we were alone at a luncheon in the Marchands' backyard.

One time, my dad was about to scream at me for asking what a blowjob was at a wedding. One time, he *had* screamed at me, calling me a slut for daring to try to find out if I was pregnant.

Each of those times, JP had inconveniently shown up right when I needed him.

Each of those times, he'd stepped in, not to protect me but to back me up.

Each of those times, I'd taken it for granted.

For a moment as Phillipe pressed me against the bar, I hoped JP would magically appear. But he wouldn't. He only ever did that when we were friends, and we weren't friends anymore.

We weren't anything anymore.

And I hated it.

"You need to leave me alone," I said to Phillipe.

"You need to tell me why you're such a fucking—"

"Finish that sentence and I'll rip your balls off before you even get a chance to take your hands off my friend."

Sydney worked her way between me and Phillipe, giving exactly zero fucks about shoving him out of the way so she could get in front of me. Phillipe stepped back, a look of offense on his face.

"I just want to know what happened," he said. "One second she wants to fuck me and—"

He said more, but I didn't hear it. Sydney pulled me away from the bar, then threaded her arm through mine.

"Leave?" she asked.

"Leave," I agreed, and we hurried for the exit.

Chapter Thirty-Two
You're Just A Bad Person

IT WAS COLD.

Refreshingly cold.

Soberingly cold.

It probably wouldn't have felt so cold if I hadn't sliced my dress down to my sternum and trimmed it into a mini skirt that barely covered my ass cheeks. But even if I'd been clad in a parka and snowpants, I think I would have still been shivering uncontrollably.

The moment my heels hit the sidewalk outside the club, I started power walking down the block. Sydney followed, her longer legs keeping pace with me easily, though she hung back a few steps anyway. We wove through a few groups of people dressed in slightly less revealing clothing than I was, each body between me and that club cutting through the uneasy sensation Phillipe's hands had left on my body.

Neither of us spoke for about three blocks, once we were away from the businesses and in front of a low-rise apartment building.

"Nellie—" Syd started.

"Leave it to me, right?" I interrupted, the words coming out in a shaky laugh. "I don't want to talk about JP, think about JP, admit anything about how I feel or don't feel about JP, and then I pick the one guy in the bar who looks like a knockoff version of him."

"Well, that—"

"—could mean nothing, I know," I said. "Maybe I just have a type. Maybe that's my thing now. A world full of sexy fucking people and I'm into tall snarky bastards who wear chinos and own monogrammed leather accessories."

"Does JP—"

"—own a monogrammed wallet? Probably. The bastard wears bespoke fucking shoes. But you know, I was sitting there trying to figure out why I wasn't attracted to him. I'm attracted to, like, *everyone*. So maybe it has nothing to do with JP."

"That seems—"

"—like a stretch? Yeah." I stopped walking, raising my hands to my head as I turned to her, doing everything I could not to beg for an answer. "What am I supposed to *do*, Syd?"

"Well, you—" She stopped, like she was waiting for me to say something, but continued when I didn't. "You could try telling JP you're in love with him."

The words were so blunt, it was like being hit in the stomach by a… I don't know. By a large blunt object. So blunt and so hard it bruised as it winded me. "I'm not."

"You most def—"

"I am *not*!" I repeated, the words ringing off the side of the building beside us. "I don't love him. I *don't*."

Sydney let out a heavy breath. "You know, I'm putting up with a lot of shit from you right now. Maybe you could stop and listen to me for five seconds?"

I opened my mouth, but the angry retort that I'd instinctively leaned towards faded as I looked at my best friend. Despite not doing what she'd wanted me to earlier that night, despite not letting her finish a fucking sentence because apparently I couldn't control my mouth for longer than a heartbeat at a time, she was looking at me patiently, her mouth set in a straight line but her eyes round and full of... pity?

No, not pity. Not sympathy, either.

She was looking at me with leniency. Like she was giving me far, far more grace than I deserved.

"You're right." My voice caught on the lump in my throat. "I'm sorry."

Sydney laughed, the sound shocking both of us. "I don't think you've ever apologized to me before."

I snorted, then laughed, then brushed my hand across my face to catch the tears that leaked onto my cheeks. She wasn't the first person to tell me I didn't apologize very often. She probably wouldn't be the last.

But fuck if it didn't make me feel like garbage to know that's what people thought about me.

Without a word, she hugged me, and kindly didn't comment on the fact that I started crying on her.

"I'm sorry I'm a shitty friend," I said into her chest.

"You aren't a shitty friend, Nell," she said. "You're just a bad person overall."

I choked.

Like, legitimately choked on the air I sucked in as I laughed, coughing as it caught in my throat and forced the rest of the tears out of my eyes because I couldn't breathe. Leave it to Syd to know me well enough that she could tell that was what I needed.

"I'm sorry too," Sydney said through her own giggles.

I drew in a deep breath, trying to calm myself. "Don't. It's fine. Let's just... let's not let this get between us? If that's okay?"

"Never." She dug into her pocket and handed me a Kleenex, then pressed a loud, smacking kiss against the side of my head. "So let's get into it. Why don't you want to be with JP?"

I sighed. "I don't want a rela—"

"Nope," she said. "Try again."

"But I don't—"

"The truth, Nell." Sydney crossed her arms. "The actual, real truth."

"Relationships aren't for me," I said. "I don't know what else to—"

"The truth," she repeated. "Because I've heard that bullshit a thousand times and I don't believe it."

"What's so hard to believe?" I gestured in the general direction we'd just walked from. "Look at Olivier and Cody and their wives. Why the fuck would I want that? Why would I want to tie myself to one person and then sit in a bar having my whole life turned upside down because that one person fucked me over? Why would I want to give up going out and doing whatever I want whenever I want with *whoever* I want for the chance to waste twelve years with someone I despise to prove a point I don't even want to prove?"

Sydney frowned. "That was oddly specific."

"I... no it wasn't," I said, but I knew my face was turning red even as I looked away from her. "It was just an example."

"An example of what happened to your parents," she said.

I didn't confirm or deny it. "It's not unreasonable. Relationships ruin lives."

"You can't believe that about every relationship." She gestured vaguely. "Look at my parents. They're still together. JP's parents are married. And look at Ben."

"Ben," I repeated. "My *divorced* psychology professor?"

"Ben's the best example," she said. "Did he or did he not just come back to Ottawa to help his ex-wife through surgery? They still have a great relationship, Nell. It didn't ruin his life at all. Things aren't *ruined* just because they end."

She waited, but I didn't know what to say.

"So one last time," she said, her voice soft. "Why don't you want to be with JP?"

"What if he turns out like my dad?"

She tilted her head to the side. "How do you figure?"

"My mom loved my dad at one point and now look at him." I licked my lips, trying not to cry again. "JP is part of a life I don't want. He grew up with those same dinner parties and galas and shit. The backroom deals and who-knows-who and... I don't *want* that."

"I thought JP didn't want that either."

"He could change his mind."

"So could you."

"I would never."

Sydney tilted her head back, looking up at the dark sky like answers would fall from it. "Nell, JP gave up a fully funded *life*. He quit a cushy job with a massive firm that was going to be handed to him one day, all because he wanted something *morally* better than what he had. You're sitting here thinking him turning into someone like your dad is a forgone conclusion when there's no basis for it, Nell. He's told you he doesn't like your dad. He's *stood up* to your dad."

I brought my hand to my mouth, sticking my thumbnail between my teeth. "Even if that's all true, why should I have to give up the life I love to be with him? Like, I want to go out. I want to hit on people. I *like* embracing that part of me, Syd. I like being a—"

I was going to say "slut," but apparently, some of the embracing I'd done of the word had been shattered by my dad using it. Swallowing hard, I continued without looking at Sydney.

"I like the person I am. I don't want to give that up."

"Why would you?" she asked. "How many times did JP say he loves the idea of you getting fucked by someone else?"

I rolled my eyes. "He wouldn't let me—"

"Ah, ah, ah. First of all, he doesn't get to tell you what to do," she said. "Second of all, the Martelles."

"What about them?"

She looked at me incredulously. "Claire? Claire's fiancée? Claire's girlfriend? Claire's girlfriend's husband-boyfriend-partners-whatever? Don't pretend like you don't think something untraditional wouldn't be an option. If you and JP talked about it and couldn't find something that worked, then fine, but I don't believe he wouldn't be *just* as into other people as you would be."

That was also a very good point, which was a bit worrisome. "You don't know that, though."

"Neither do you. It's not like you and JP ever really talked about the whole marriage-babies-monogamy thing."

"Yeah, because why would we? We were just fri—"

She let out a loud, unattractive fake buzzer noise that made me jump. "*Eeehhh.* Nope."

"Yes, we were," I said.

"Right. The whole thing where you went on dates with each other, helped each other out, told each other your deepest darkest secrets... you know damn well you haven't been 'just friends' for a while, Nell."

"Shut up," I mumbled, sort of jokingly and sort of not. Sydney snickered. "None of this even matters."

"Why not?"

I stared at the sidewalk, my shoulders slowly sagging as part of me seemed to deflate. "I blew it."

"His dick? Yes, multiple times. I know. You've told me."

"My chance."

The words came out so small I almost wondered if I'd actually said them. I had, obviously, because Sydney shook her head.

"You honestly think he wouldn't give you another one?" she asked. "He told you he was in love with you two weeks ago."

"What am I supposed to say?" I said. "I've been saying I don't want a relationship for... well, forever. And now I'm supposed to admit to him I was wrong?"

"You don't have to be wrong to change your mind," she replied. "You could just... you know... experience personal growth."

"Ugh. That sounds terrible."

"I know, but it's what adults do. I think."

I laughed thickly, trying not to cry. "This is stupid. I don't like feelings."

"But you do like JP," she said.

"I... might."

"Might?"

I sighed. "Might... definitely."

"So go talk to him."

"I don't know if texting him out of the blue is the best—"

"No, Nellie. Go *talk* to him." She looked at me pointedly. "Face to face."

"He moved. I don't—"

"Anne-Marie gave you his new address."

"And I *ate it*," I said. "You were there."

"Technically, you threw it out after chewing it, but you could just ask Anne-Marie for another—"

"Syd, I would give my dad a detailed breakdown of all the people I've hooked up with before I would bring Anne-Marie into this," I said.

She burst out laughing. "She said you'd say that."

"What?"

"Well, not exactly that, but pretty close." Sydney put her hand in her pocket and pulled out a folded and slightly crumpled piece of paper. "She ran out of Post-Its after you ate his address."

"She did *not*," I said, reaching forward to take the paper from her hand.

Sydney yanked it away before I could snatch it from her. "We agreed I would only give it to you if you promised me one thing."

I stared at her as a shit-eating grin spread across her face.

"Never mind, then," I muttered, then turned on a heel.

"Wha—*wait!*" she exclaimed. "Nell, wait!"

"I'm not playing this fucking game," I said. "You two think you're so goddamn smart and you know everything but—"

"It's that you have to go see him *now*," she said. "You take this address, you plug it into Uber, and you go to talk to him *now*. No chickening out. No sleeping on it. No procrastinating until you can justify not following through. You go see him tonight."

I still should have said no. I didn't even know where JP was. Then again, if Anne-Marie was making me promise to see him, he was obviously still in Montreal. But still. I hadn't been drinking heavily—chugging one drink at the bar didn't count, and I'd only had one at dinner—but I was emotional. I'd already had one big, heavy, life-changing conversation that day.

So really... what was one more?

"Fine," I said. "I promise. I'll go see him now."

Sydney did a strange sort of jig, her face lighting up with a smile as she unfolded the crumpled paper. "Oh thank God. I can't believe I actually did it. This is one of the top accomplishments of my life, Nell. I'm gonna put this on my resume and—" She looked down at the paper and the smile disappeared from her face. "Uh... oh."

"What?" I asked.

"Um... well... on the off-chance you actually do end up getting married one day, I'd like you to please remember when picking your maid of honour that *I* believed in you far more than Anne-Marie did," she said.

"What are you talking about?" I asked.

Sydney bit her lip. "I think she thought it would take longer for you to figure this all out."

Frowning, I reached for the paper again. This time, Sydney let me take it, and I looked down at the address.

Then I looked back up at her. "You've got to be fucking kidding me."

Chapter Thirty-Three
Hull

THREE CANCELLED UBERS AND two hours later, I looked longingly at my apartment building.

One minute after that, the Uber passed it and continued towards the Ottawa River.

Ten minutes after *that*, I was back in Quebec, getting out of the Uber in front of a twenty-floor condo building overlooking the other side of the Ottawa River.

Because of all the places in all the world—or at least in Quebec—JP had moved to Hull.

Fucking *Hull*.

I couldn't see Hull from my house, but only because there were other buildings and a slight exaggeration in the way. But the address scrawled in Anne-Marie's loopy handwriting on the crumpled piece of paper Syd showed me was barely ten minutes from our building. Hull was technically in Gatineau, which was in Quebec, even though I'd had to drive from Quebec through Ontario and back into Quebec to get there, but it was all part of the same metropolitan region as Ottawa.

Basically, JP had moved to the same city as me and hadn't said a fucking word about it.

Part of me was angry. Part of me raged at JP's audacity. More than usual, anyway. Because it had to be audacity, right? It was obnoxiously audacious of him to have assumed I wanted to be with him so confidently that he got a job at a law firm in Hull and moved there. Luckily there were two hours between me promising I'd talk to him immediately and actually being able to talk to him so I could think on it a bit more and calm down.

Because there were only so many places he could go that would hire him without it getting back to his dad. Montreal had been out of the picture completely. Quebec City would've been almost as risky, considering he'd articled there. So aside from coincidence, it likely had nothing to do with me.

Maybe.

The Uber left before I could chicken out and jump back in, so I had no choice but to go into the building. Other than calling another Uber or something, but I promised.

I promised, and in my heart, I wanted to, even though the rest of me wanted to cower.

The building was on the newer side and while there was still a foyer to trap people before they got buzzed in, it also had a lobby with gleaming floors and a large reception desk. I didn't pay much attention to it until I reached the intercom system and pressed a few buttons, only for the screen to go blank and a speaker to buzz loudly before I could finish typing the number.

"This is private property," said a gruff voice through the speaker.

"I'm aware," I said, glancing around until I realized a security guard sat at the reception desk, glaring at me through the glass wall between us. "I'm here to see someone."

"You ladies always are," he said snidely. "You can't just look up your client's name on the list. You need their private number. Otherwise, they have to come down and collect you themselves."

"Client?" I repeated.

He gave me an unimpressed look, his eyes flicking down, but it took me another moment before I realized what he was saying.

"Okay, well, not that it's any of your judgy ass's business," I said. "But I was out at a club and now I'm here to see a friend."

"Still can't get in without the number," he said.

"I *know* the number," I said. "If you'd let me type the damn thing in."

The speaker clicked off. He gestured at the wall snidely, as if to say "Go ahead." After mouthing "Thank you" at him as sarcastically as I could, I dialled JP's number. I could feel the security guard's eyes on me as the call connected and tapped my foot, waiting for it to ring.

And it did.

It rang once, and there was no answer.

It rang again, and still nothing.

A third time, and my breath hitched as if in preparation for the embarrassment I'd have to face when JP didn't let me in.

A fourth ring, and I almost winced.

And then the line clicked.

"Hello?" JP asked breathlessly.

"Hi," I said. "I'm here to sell a two-dicked dragon dildo to Giovanni Cockeverlasting from the Monster Fucker Ottawa group."

There was a long, confused silence.

"Nellie?" he finally said.

"Yeah."

He paused again. "What are you—"

"I need to talk to you."

"It's—" There was a rustling sound. "It's midnight."

"Were you asleep?"

"No, I just... how did you—"

"Anne-Marie."

He laughed. "Fucking Anne-Marie."

"I know. But look, the security guard down here is trying to set me on fire with his mind because he thinks you're paying me to be here, so can I come in?"

"Oh, shit. Uh—" There was another rustling sound. "Uh, yeah. Come on up."

The speaker clicked off, replaced by the buzz of the door unlocking. I pulled the door open and looked at the security desk, where the guard had suddenly become very interested in something on the other side of the room, and remained that way as I waited for the elevator.

The building might have been twenty stories, but JP only lived on the eighth floor, so it didn't take me long to get to his apartment. Still, I walked slower than I usually would, telling myself it was to give JP more time to get ready and definitely not because I was terrified to talk to him.

Even still, when I finally knocked on the door to his apartment, it took longer than expected for the door to swing open. Once it did, it revealed JP standing there, looking flustered in a way I'd literally never seen him look before. His shirt, usually so carefully pressed, was rumpled, the buttons done up through the wrong holes so the untucked hem sat unevenly on his waistband. His face was pink and his hair was tousled and sticking up on one side.

I was pretty sure I'd never been more attracted to anyone in my life.

"Hi, I'm from the Banjo Brotherhood, here to talk to you about our lord and saviour Mullet Bubba," I said.

"If those are standard issue uniforms, I'm in," he said, eyes flicking down at my dress.

"I'm not sure we have them in your size, but I can check with Betsy-Mae," I said.

His mouth twitched. "I'm glad to hear this is a religion thing. I was a little worried that not talking to you for a couple of weeks had made you decide on a new career path."

"You know what they say. Do what you love and you'll never work a day in your life."

That earned a laugh. "So did you actually get in a fight with a guy with knives for hands or—"

"I was at a club," I said.

"And Sliced and Diced Chic went against their dress code? What's it called so I know never to go there?"

"You don't have to worry about that."

"Help a guy out. I'm kinda new to town."

I shifted in place, not quite looking at him. "I'd love to, but I, uh... I have something else to talk to you about."

The half-smile faded off his lips. "That's fair."

There was a heavy pause.

"So... can I come in?" I asked.

"Right, yeah," JP said. "Of course."

He stepped back, holding the door for me, and something almost like shyness washed over me as I walked into the apartment.

The place looked settled in, even though he'd only moved sometime within the past couple of weeks. There were no moving boxes waiting to be unpacked and his fastidious tidiness meant that aside from a few plates sitting on the drying rack and the hideous handmade throw blanket tossed carelessly across the back of the couch, it could have been a model apartment. Most of it was dark, but a warm yellow light glowed over the sink and another light from down the hallway came from what was probably his bedroom.

"Nice apartment," I said awkwardly.

"Thanks," he said. "It's not quite as, uh, new as my old place was, but I like the layout better."

I couldn't bring myself to look at him, instead glancing around like I was taking everything in. "It's very, um, modern."

"Thanks," he said again. "So, there was something you wanted to—"

"Is this granite?" I asked desperately, moving into his kitchen.

JP laughed. "Nell, I'm more than happy to show you around, but I feel like you didn't pick midnight on a Saturday to pop by for a tour of my new place. What's going on?"

I jabbed my forefinger into my thumb. "I'm stalling, okay?"

"I got that. Wanna maybe tell me why?"

I turned to him slowly, afraid if I moved any faster, I'd faint. My heart pounded so hard I could feel it in my skin.

"Yeah," I said. "I... should do that."

He waited patiently, his eyebrows raised as he bit back a smile. I looked at the wall behind him, unable to meet his eyes.

"I wanted to talk about... what you said." I swallowed hard. "The last time we saw each other."

"Okay," he said.

"I thought maybe, um..." I trailed off, thinking, then sighed in frustration. "Fuck, how do people do this?"

"Do what?"

I bit my lip, my face burning. "Tell people they want... things."

"What kind of things?"

"You know what kind of things," I mumbled.

"Nell, are you here to tell me you like me?"

"Ew." I cringed, almost shuddering. "Ugh. Gross. Don't say it like that."

His mouth twitched into a smirk. "So that's a yes?"

"It's a... a..." I sighed. "Yes. I might've done some thinking and... and when I was thinking, I thought, like... like maybe if I... I sort of realized that—"

"—that if you came crawling back, I might give you another chance?" he finished.

It was meant to be a joke. I knew JP's voice well enough to know that he was trying to tease me. But the words still made heat rise up my neck and through my cheeks as my stomach curled in painful embarrassment. I paused, then shook my head.

"Nope," I said.

He looked surprised. "What?"

"Never mind." I turned on my heel. "This was a bad idea."

He didn't have time to react before I strode back to his door, yanking it open and marching back into the hallway. I was only a few steps away when the door flew open again.

"Babe, I was joking!" he said.

"Whatever," I grumbled.

"Nellie, wait," he said, touching my arm to stop me. "Please."

"If you're already making fun of me, I can't do the rest of it," I said. "I thought I could, but I can't."

"Can't what?" he asked.

"This is hard enough. I might be... be... like, have changed my mind or whatever. But if you want me to grovel, it's not happening. Especially if you're just going to laugh about it."

"I won't, babe," he said, and his voice was as solemn as I'd ever heard it. "I promise. I will be as serious about this as you are. And for the love of God, don't fucking grovel. Of *course* I don't want that. Tell me what you thought you could do."

I took a shallow breath, steadying myself, and tried to think of everything I'd spent the last two hours meticulously planning out in the back of an Uber.

So of course, I couldn't remember any of it.

"I don't know how to do this," I said. "This... feeling. The feelings thing." I folded my arms and turned back to him. "I don't like it."

"I know you don't."

"What I know about relationships is that I hate them. I hate feeling like someone owns me. I hate feeling like I have to answer to someone."

"That's not what relationships are," he said. "Or if it is, it's not what I want, either."

"And you... you're like... you know what my dad is like," I said. "I don't want that life. I don't want to be controlled by money."

"I don't either," he said. "I don't want the kind of life my parents have or that your dad has. If I never have to attend another charity gala, I'd die happy. Unless you promised me anal again, in which case, I'd strongly consider attending another charity gala."

It was funny, but my chest still felt hollow with fear. "Okay, but what about, like, life? Like, I'm in school. I'm gonna probably have to move one day because I want a career. I don't want to give that up and pump out a bunch of babies or something."

"Not that I'm saying that's what I want, but you know we could date or whatever for a while before having big, serious, rest-of-our-lives conversations, right?" he asked.

"Maybe you can. I can't get into this if I think that's where it's going to go."

"Well, it's not," he said. "Or maybe it is, if you end up wanting that. I'm just saying we can talk about anything. If you wanted to."

"Anything?"

"Of course."

"What about sex with other people?"

My heart skipped a beat or five before returning to its normal pace. If anything was going to trip him up, I thought it would be that, but JP didn't even blink.

"I would listen to you talk about or, God willing, watch you fuck literally anyone you wanted, whenever you wanted, as often as you wanted," he said. "Look, you talk about relationships like they have all these set-in-stone rules, but that's never appealed to me. We can make something that works for us. We can decide what we want it to be, okay? All I want, all I really, truly, actually want, is—"

"You're going to say something super cheesy, aren't you?" I said.

"Yes, I am," he said. "Because I fucking need to. All I want is to be with you. However that happens, I don't care."

"Even after..." I swallowed hard. "Like, what I said a couple of weeks ago?"

"Yes."

I couldn't quite look at him. "I kind of want that, too."

"So what's stopping us?" he asked.

"I'm scared."

The words were out of my mouth before they even registered in my mind. I heard them for the first time at the same time JP did.

"Scared of what?" he asked.

"Just... scared," I said.

His mouth twitched. "Scared of how much you love me?"

"*Like* you," I said. "Don't push your luck."

"I'm not," he said. "It's not a joke, Nell. I'm in love with you. And yeah, that scares the shit out of me too."

I looked up at him, half-expecting to see a smirk on his face, but his expression was almost pained its seriousness. "It does?"

"Of course it does," he said. "I haven't felt like this about anyone, ever."

I frowned. "You don't have to lie to me."

"How is that—"

"You loved Sam." He stared at me, lips parted, and I shifted awkwardly. "I don't mean that in a bad way. Just that... that you loved him. And that matters. Don't pretend you didn't just to make me feel special."

His throat flexed and he blinked rapidly a few times before he spoke.

"I loved him differently," he finally said. "Maybe one day it would've been like this, yeah. But it wasn't the same as how I feel now. That doesn't make it mean anything less for him, and it doesn't mean anything less for you. So yeah, it's new to me. Yeah, it's scary. But it's also… I dunno. Exciting."

"What if it changes things?" I asked.

"It will," he said. "Absolutely, it will. I mean, it damn well better. Hopefully, we can stop sneaking around to fuck and, you know, fuck whenever."

I tried not to laugh, but it was futile. JP smiled.

"I think they'll be good changes," he said. "I really do."

I looked at him for a long moment, then nodded. "Okay."

"Okay?"

"Yeah," I said. "So is there some kind of ceremonial words I have to say or are you just, like, my boyfriend now?"

"Only if you're my girlfriend now," he said.

"I mean, I guess. Still kind of gross, though."

When he took me into his arms, we were both laughing, and when he brought an arm to my neck and tilted my face up to kiss me, I couldn't stop smiling. I rested my hand against his side, relaxing into the acceptance and relief and fear and familiarity. Into the scent of his cologne and the warmth of his body.

Into him.

And then, just as I thought to myself that I never guessed how fucking *good* this would feel, JP's apartment door opened.

"Seriously?" said a woman's voice. "What the actual *fuck*, JP?!"

Chapter Thirty-Four
Might Definitely

THE WOMAN STANDING IN the doorway to JP's apartment was, for lack of a better term, wet dream material.

She was nearly as tall as he was and had the kind of bouncy curls in her shiny blonde hair that made me think of a shampoo commercial. Between the high cut of her cheekbones, the upturned corners of her green eyes, the tanned beige of her white skin, and the body that was toned as close to perfection as one could get without developing actual visible muscles, I would've bet my sliced-up designer dress she was an actual model.

In short, she was gorgeous. Mindbogglingly gorgeous. And she was wearing a shiny silver halter top that showed off an overly generous amount of cleavage. Given that her breasts were literal chef's-kiss-perfection, that wasn't a complaint, except for the fact that they distracted me to the point that I forgot where I was for a second.

"Who's this skank?" she demanded, glaring at me.

Scratch all of what I said before.

The woman standing in the doorway to JP's apartment was, for lack of a better term, wastefully hot. As in, it was an actual tragedy that perfect breasts like hers were wasted on someone who defaulted to calling *me,* the person who had no idea she was there, a skank when JP was the one who had an entire other woman waiting in his apartment while he kissed me.

"I'm Nellie," I said. "Who the hell are you?"

"I'm Paige," she said.

"Cool," I said. "What are you doing here?"

She looked at JP, stunned offense on her face.

"Right," he said awkwardly.

And that was it. An uncomfortable silence stretched between us as I stared at Paige, who looked from JP to me and back to JP again. No one spoke until she finally and unfortunately folded her arms across her chest.

"So, what, some random chick in an awful dress shows up in the middle of the night and you decide you want to fuck her?" Paige asked. "Instead of *me*?"

"Well, that's not quite—" JP started.

"You had another woman in your apartment this entire time?" I asked, raising my eyebrows.

JP's eyes sparkled as he fought back a laugh. "Well, we were... you know. Not *together*, Nell."

Paige let out a loud scoff. "Oh, fucking *classic*."

"Classic?" JP repeated.

"You have, what, one fight with your girlfriend and go out prowling for someone else?" she said.

"No," he said. "She wasn't my girlfriend when—"

"Oh, so you were on a break?" she scoffed, looking at me like I would suddenly have solidarity with her. "What a fucking pig."

"Hey!" I glared at her. "Don't call my—" I grimaced suddenly, nearly gagging. "Oh, God. I can't believe I'm about to say this."

JP's fight not to laugh turned into a battle he was destined to lose, though he attempted to hold on by turning his head so he didn't have to look at me as my face burned red.

"What?" Paige said.

"Don't call my *boyfriend*"—I suppressed another gag—"a pig."

"Your 'boyfriend' was just in here with *me* and made no mention of the fact he was in a relationship," she said.

"That would be because he wasn't in a relationship," I said, mirroring her stance and folding my arms over my chest. "We *just* agreed we were going to do this stupid boyfriend-girlfriend thing."

She frowned in bewilderment. "So mid-hookup with *me*, he came out here and picked *you* instead?"

"Yeah, that's exactly what happened." I didn't know if that was entirely true, but it seemed accurate and Paige was pissing me off. "And maybe I would've asked if you wanted to stick around and fuck us, but—"

"What?" Her mouth dropped open even further. "*What*?!"

"Well, it's been a while." I motioned towards at JP. "We haven't talked for, like, two weeks. And I wasn't opposed to you joining in because usually he has good taste, but only aesthetically apparently, since you're kind of an asshole."

JP lost the battle gracelessly. His eyes squeezed shut and he put a hand over his mouth, but his attempt to muffle his laughter resulting in a sound similar to the one people make when they're about to hawk a wad of phlegm into a napkin.

"Did you j-just—" He stuttered, then coughed in an attempt to compose himself. "Did you just propose a threesome? For our... our... I don't know, our first fuck as an actual couple?"

"No," I said. "I *would've*, but she called me a skank and I don't fuck mean girls."

He started laughing so hard he couldn't speak. Paige looked from him to me, then let out a disgusted scoff.

"You two are the worst," she said, turning and snatching her purse off the table near the door before storming past us. "You freaks deserve each other."

Which was fair, especially considering she wasn't even halfway down the hall before JP pulled me into his apartment.

"You are *such*"—I paused as he pressed his lips to mine so I could kiss him back—"an asshole."

"I know," he groaned, moving his lips to my jaw and then to my neck. "I feel bad."

"I can tell."

His chuckle felt warm against my skin. "I swear to God, I just met her earlier tonight. When I realized you were here, I told her something came up, but she wasn't taking the hint and then you knocked and—"

"Did you fuck her?"

"I got home ten minutes before you got here."

"...so yes?"

"You think I finished that fast?"

"I've definitely finished you off faster than that."

"You're the only one who makes me come like that." He nipped at my neck. "Only you, babe. She and I were just making out."

I shivered, maybe because all the heat in my body was starting to pool in my core. "So you had a woman that hot in your apartment for ten minutes and you didn't even get into her panties? Loser."

"I know." His hands slipped down my sides and around to my ass. "I didn't even get the chance for a final hurrah before you got your claws in me."

"'A final hurrah?' Okay, Grandpa."

He let out a soft noise, using his hips to guide me backwards towards the hallway. "You should be nicer to me. I gave up a sure thing for you."

"I'm *so* sorry I ruined your one-night stand."

"You better be." He kissed me as we reached the room down his hall that had the light on, which was his bedroom, like I'd guessed. "The things I do for love."

Goosebumps raised on my arms. "Ew. Stop saying you love me."

"No." He kissed me again. "I won't lie to you. I fucking love you, Nell."

And I didn't know what to say.

I knew what I *should* have said.

But I didn't know if I could.

It didn't matter. JP didn't seem to care about hearing it, not right then. He slipped his tongue into my mouth, sighing as he tasted me, then let go of my ass so he could reach up and brush my hair away from my cheek.

"Besides," he continued casually. "Right now, it's very, very important that you know I love you."

"Why?" I asked.

He didn't need to answer. I figured it out by the second syllable of the word. And yes, "why" was only a one-syllable word, but I figured the "aye" I let out as my back hit the mattress and the air puffed out of my lungs counted a second syllable.

So no, he didn't need to answer, but after putting a hand on each of my thighs, he did anyway.

"Because, babe," he said, wrenching my thighs open. "I want you to remember I'm fucking you like this because you're *mine*."

And then he moved over top of me and pinned my arms to the bed.

"J-JP," I tried to say, but he absorbed my cry with his lips.

"Red, right?" he murmured.

"Huh?" I gasped.

"If you want me to stop." He nipped at my lower lip. "You'll say red?"

Oh, fuck.

Fuck.

"Yes," I whispered.

"Or I can stop right now."

"Don't you fucking dare," I said, and the wicked grin JP flashed at me was almost enough to make me beg for him to fuck me right then.

And maybe it should have bothered me that the sheets he'd tossed me onto were messed up. That a hint of warm vanilla lingered on his pillow as he kissed me, perfume or shampoo or hairspray that was left behind by someone else. That his cock pressed against the thin fabric of my lacy pink thong, already wet because my pussy was fucking *soaked* for him, and it was hard beneath the fabric of his pants, and I didn't know if I'd made it that way or if it was the other woman he'd had in here moments earlier.

But it didn't bother me.

I didn't care.

If anything, it calmed me, a reminder that I hadn't just signed my happiness away for him. I couldn't fault JP for sleeping around; I was a lot of things, but I would not be a hypocrite. But more than that, it made me feel like whatever happened between me and JP would be okay.

That he'd laughed, but hadn't said no when I suggested bringing someone else to the bedroom with us.

That he didn't want my skewed idea of a relationship.

That the only relationship he wanted was the one we defined for ourselves. I didn't know what that meant. I didn't know if it was the forever type of relationship or if we'd even last until Christmas.

But God, did I want to find out.

He started by marking my neck. I couldn't remember the last time someone left a hickey like that on me, nor could I remember a time that I liked it so much. His mouth claimed me, sucking and nipping at the tender skin until I couldn't stop myself from writhing beneath him, trying to get his bulge to line up with my clit so I could give into the friction I was craving.

Of course, he didn't let me. He finished leaving proof of his kiss on my neck, then finally let go of my arms so he could tug my dress up.

"There's a z-zipper," I said when the skirt was around my waist and he couldn't get it any higher.

But he just grabbed the front of my dress and pulled until the cut I'd made to deepen the neckline tore the rest of the way down the dress, and since I'd cut the hem off when I shortened it, the entire thing split in two.

"Or you could just ruin my dress," I continued.

"It was ruined before I got my hands on it," he said. "There's no way my girlfriend was going to wear that out in public again."

I tensed, the internal red flags rising.

"Because if she's gonna show off her phenomenal fucking body, it's going to be in something made to do just that," he continued, casually pulling the destroyed fabric off me. "Not a hacked-up gown she only bought because her dad approved of it."

The red flags lowered, as did JP's head. He brought his lips to my bared breasts, pressing his face into my cleavage before taking my left nipple into his mouth and sucking for a moment before carefully sinking his teeth into the tender nub. I cried out, not able to stop myself from squirming beneath him, though I could only do so much from the way he was holding me down.

"JP," I whispered. "Please."

"Please what?" he mumbled, my tits muffling his voice.

"I... I need..." I slammed my eyes closed. "Don't make me wait."

He chuckled and bit my nipple the slightest bit harder before moving his lips to the underside of my breast. He kissed one, then the other, before teasing his tongue down to my ribcage. Large hands gripped my waist, his fingertips digging in possessively as he left more little purple marks on my stomach.

And then just as my belly button piercing brushed his chin, I tensed.

"Wait," I said.

"Thought you didn't want to," he said.

I bit my lip. "Yeah, but for you to fuck me. Not to go down on me."

He lifted his head, eyebrows raised so high that they had an almost cartoonish arch. "What's wrong?"

"Nothing. I—"

"You are *not* the girl who turns down getting eaten out," he said.

My stomach flipped and heat crawled up my neck. "Let me go clean up a bit first."

He frowned. "Since when have you worried about that? More importantly, since when have you thought I *care* about that?"

My face had to be fully red. "I don't usually. But I also don't usually go to fuck someone after sitting in an Uber for two hours."

The frown deepened. "What were you doing in an Uber for two hours?"

"Well, when you drive the speed limit from Montreal, that's how long it takes."

His mouth stayed half-open as he stared at me. "What were you doing in Montreal?"

"I went to talk to my dad, but Syd and I went out and—"

"And you Ubered back *here*?" he asked incredulously.

I suddenly felt even more exposed than when I was just mostly naked in front of him. "I had a... a realization. And Syd said she'd promised Anne-Marie she would only give me your address if I went to see you right away. Neither of us knew you were *here*."

"So you..." He trailed off, something deep filling his eyes. "You didn't have to do that, babe."

"I know, you wanted to get laid by your hot model one-night stand, but—"

He leaned in and kissed me, cutting me off.

"I love you," he murmured against my lips. "I love you so fucking much. And I would've still loved you tomorrow."

"I—" I started, but he kissed me again.

"And as a reminder, I told you to remember that while I fuck you," he said, his voice lowering. "Because you're mine, and that means if I want to eat you out, I'm going to. *Especially* since your poor, sweet pussy has been waiting even *longer* than I thought to find its way back to me."

I think I started to say something again, but if I did, I couldn't remember what it was. JP moved faster than I thought possible, grabbing my legs and lifting them so he could peel my thong off and toss it unceremoniously to the side before letting my legs drop back to the bed. He parted my thighs again a second later and buried his face between my legs hard enough that I was a little worried he broke his nose.

Not for long, though.

"Oh, *fuck*," I moaned as JP eagerly licked along my slit, splitting my folds with his tongue and teasing my needy entrance. I writhed beneath him until he brought his hands to my hips and held me down while he ate my pussy like he was starving and for some reason couldn't have an actual meal until he'd made me come on his face.

Which didn't take him long.

It only took him sawing one thick finger into my pussy and curling it to hit my G-spot to bring me to the edge. A second finger joined it and my eyes rolled back in my head. His mouth closed over my clit, sucking and swirling all at once, and I reached down. His hair was soft between my fingers and I could feel his sparkling blue eyes on me even as I slammed my own shut because oh, *fuck*.

Oh, I was going to fucking come.

He heard me gasp it. I knew he watched me do it, even though I wasn't watching him watch me. I didn't mean to pull his hair, but the pleasure flooding my body was too intense to not have something to hold onto. My back arched and I cried out, riding JP's face as much as he was devouring me.

It lasted a while. Too long, somehow, and of course, never long enough. JP kept licking and as the intensity passed and my clit got sensitive, I tried to pull his head away.

He took his fingers out of my pussy, batted my hand away, and kept licking.

"I-It's too much," I gasped, trying to squirm away. "J-JP—"

"Not done with what's *mine*," he growled, then sucked on my clit.

"S-Sensitive," I stammered. "Please, it's—"

"You can handle it, babe." He pressed a kiss to the top of my mound, giving me a moment's break. "All you have to do is lie there and let me spoil you."

And fuck.

Fuck.

He kept going, and I kept squirming and writhing and shuddering until the sensitivity gave way to pleasure again. Then I stilled, panting as JP started all over again, sucking and licking and fingering me until I had my thighs clamped around his head and was bucking up into him as I cried out my pleasure.

When my second orgasm was over and my legs fell away from JP's ears, he finally pulled away and sat back on his knees.

"S-Sorry," I whispered shakily.

JP wiped the back of his hand across his mouth and grinned before leaning in to kiss me.

"If I ever complain about making you come like that, feel free to sit on my face and suffocate me," he said.

"Deal," I whispered.

He kissed me again, and again, and his body got closer and closer to mine. He was still dressed, still wearing that stupidly buttoned shirt, but I hadn't noticed he'd unbuttoned his pants at some point, likely to relieve the pressure on his throbbing cock. I could feel the heat radiating off his swollen shaft even through the fabric of his boxers, his tip pressing needily into my inner thigh as he let me taste myself on his lips and tongue. He was holding it together, pretending to be patient and in control, until I shifted my hips so he pressed against my pussy instead of my thigh.

That was when his knees buckled and he groaned.

"Fuck," he said. "I need you, babe."

"Don't call me babe," I murmured.

He laughed. "Should've said something before you agreed to be my girlfriend, babe. Because now I'm gonna call you what I fucking want to."

"Asshole," I said, but I didn't bother trying to hide that I was laughing.

"See? I let you call me a pet name." He rubbed his cock against me and sighed. "Though I think the one I gave you is a little sweeter."

"I can stick with 'bastard,' if you like," I said, reaching up to unbutton his shirt and push it off his shoulders.

"Mmm, babe, please," he moaned. "I'm already hard enough to cut glass. Keep this up, and I'm just gonna jizz in my boxers."

I reached down, pushing his pants as low as I could before taking his cock out. "Why do that when I have a perfectly good pussy right here?"

JP's breath hitched as I notched the head of his cock against my pussy. "Nell, are you—" He stopped to draw in a breath as if to steady himself. "You're on the pill, but—"

"Not anymore," I said.

He jerked back, apparently forgetting I was holding his cock, so it accomplished nothing. It would have almost been funny, except for the sheer panic that paled his face and made me let go of him.

"I got an IUD," I added quickly. "After what... happened. So I don't have to remember to take pills anymore."

He swallowed hard, glancing down. "It's a damn good thing you're as hot as you are. If anyone else had scared me like that, I probably would've gone soft."

"We can use a condom if you want," I said. "I'm okay with whatever but I understand if you don't trust me anymore or—"

"Of course I trust you." He leaned in and kissed me. "You sure you're okay with not using one?"

"Mm-hmm," I breathed.

"I'm not pulling out." He shifted slightly, his bare cock rubbing against my slit. "I don't care if it's in a condom or not, you're mine and that means I'm coming inside you."

"You better," I said. "I might be yours now, but we both know you've *always* been mine."

His eyes locked on mine, both of us silent.

Then, slowly, without so much as a blink to break our gazes, he pushed inside of me.

He told me he loved me as he fucked me. More times than I could count and nowhere near as many times as I wanted to hear it. I'd never, ever admit how his words made me shiver, how my heart perked up and my stomach flipped and parts of me melted as he said it again and again. He said it just before I came, and while I was coming, and in the heated moments afterwards as he thrust inside me faster and faster, chasing his own orgasm.

"You're going to get sick of hearing this," he said, still inside me as he caught his breath after coming, "but I love you."

"I'm sick of it already," I said, holding him in place with my legs.

"Mmm," he said, resting against me. "Not gonna stop doing it, though."

"I know," I said. "Good thing you're good in bed."

It wasn't all that funny, but for some reason, JP laughed hard enough that he had to roll off of me. Maybe it was because everything was heightened and emotional and exhausting, but it didn't matter. What mattered was that he pulled me in close and wrapped his arms around me.

"Careful now," he said, still chuckling. "Say stuff like that too often, and I might start to think you actually like me, Nell."

"I dunno if I like you," I said. "I might love you, though."

His breath caught almost imperceptibly, but there was no hiding it when I had my ear pressed to his heart. "Might?"

I bit my lip, then pressed a tiny kiss to his chest. "Might... definitely."

And I couldn't see his face, but from the way his arms tightened around me and the kiss he pressed to the top of my head, I was pretty sure he was smiling.

Epilogue

"Hmm. Well, I cannot say I am surprised, Eleanor—"

"Nellie," I said immediately.

"It's Nellie, Max, not Eleanor," I heard Kimberlee say in the background.

I bit back a grin; my dad didn't have me on speaker phone, so Kimberlee couldn't have known I corrected him. It was kind of nice having her on my side.

My dad sighed. "My... apologies. I am not surprised, Nellie. I just want to ensure he is the sort of person you see yourself being with long-term."

"I don't know," I said. "I haven't thought that far ahead."

"Clearly."

I bristled at his cynical tone. If my dad was the horse, Kimberlee was leading him to the kind of water that would make him a better person, but he hadn't quite gotten the hang of drinking it yet.

"You told me once I could do worse than JP. At the Diamond Gala," I said.

"That was when he had a promising job at a prestigious law firm."

"Money isn't everything," I said.

"Certainly not, but critical thinking and decision-making skills should be key attributes in a partner."

I rolled my eyes. "I wasn't aware I was supposed to treat relationships like a job interview. Here I thought if he treated me nice and was good in bed, it was a win."

That was probably a button too many to push, which I realized after I'd said it, but maybe my dad had taken a sip of the water after all. Instead of blowing up, he took a deep breath and let it out.

"I do not need to hear that about my daughter." The words were stiff, as though they were being spoken through a clenched jaw. "I understand you're an adult, but—"

"Right," I said. "I'm sorry."

He cleared his throat. "In any case, I urge you to think about this decision a bit before committing to anything in particular with Jean-Paul. I can't imagine his parents will be particularly pleased with the situation, given what happened last month."

"Probably not," I said. "But we're about to find out."

"What?"

"Oh, that's why I called. We're on our way to the Marchands' and I thought you might want to have coffee or something while we're in Montreal," I said. "JP's driving. Also, I guess I should've mentioned you're on speaker."

"Hi, Mr. Belanger," JP said cheerfully.

His anger practically dripped through the phone. "Eleanor, take me off speaker phone—"

"Max!" I heard Kimberlee say in the background.

He took another deep breath, then told her in rapid, clipped French what was going on. After a moment, she sighed.

"Let me talk to her," she said, and the phone rustled. "Nellie?"

"Wow, you're going to have to teach me how you whip guys into shape like that," I said.

"Unless it involves actual whips, we're not interested," JP said loudly.

I waved a hand to shush him, though Kimberlee laughed. "I do not believe you're purposely antagonizing Max—"

"I'm not," I said. "I only blurted out one thing without thinking about it first, which is a huge improvement. And I didn't have a chance to tell him we were on speaker before he started asking me questions."

"I buy approximately half of that," she said.

"If he would stop being so judgmental in the first place, it wouldn't be a problem. It's not my fault he said JP is terrible."

"I did not hear him say anyone was *terrible*, but he is being protective. I wouldn't say that is his fault, either."

"Right. It's actually JP's fault, mostly because he's terrible."

"That's true," JP said.

Kimberlee chuckled. "You can certainly feel the love between the two of you."

"Ugh. Don't say that. I barely tolerate him," I replied.

"And she's a complete annoyance," JP said.

There was a pause, then Kimberlee sighed. "I am going to assume I did not hear that since I am certain you took us off speaker phone when your father asked you to."

"He never actually asked me to," I said.

She stifled a laugh, then took a steadying breath before promising to help my dad see JP didn't suck as much as he thought JP did. I promised to actually take them off speaker phone next time, then hung up.

"Well, that's your parents taken care of," JP said.

"I don't know which was worse," I said.

He raised his eyebrows. "You can't decide if your dad who tried to convince you I'm not good enough for you because I have no critical thinking skills is worse than your mom telling me she's been saving the engagement ring your dad gave her so your future husband could give it to you one day?"

"You're right. Anyone assuming I'm going to marry you one day is the far worse option."

He chuckled. "And here I thought the concept of it being your *divorced* parents' ring was the problem."

"I guess that's a little weird, yeah." I looked out the window, shaking my head. "I can't believe you talked me into this."

"Into what?"

"Telling people." I folded my arms. "We could've not said anything and let people figure it out themselves."

"I think when you're officially boyfriend-and-girlfriend, you're supposed to tell people about it," he said.

"It's been a week."

"And what a week," he murmured.

I bit back a smirk. It *had* been a pretty good week. I hadn't left JP's apartment until Monday morning. He'd driven me to campus so I could meet Sydney and get my laptop and books, then rushed to my first class wearing a pair of JP's sweats and one of his hoodies.

That night, he came over under the guise of getting his clothes back. Unfortunately, that was after he'd gone home from work and changed, so I sent him home short a second hoodie the next morning.

I spent Tuesday night at his place. On Wednesday, he was late for work because I realized I'd forgotten my new ADHD medication at my apartment, so he sped over to grab it for me. We spent Wednesday at my place, but on Thursday, both of us must have thought the other was tired of all the great sex we were having or something, because he went back to his place after work.

So of course, that was the night Anne-Marie called.

"Why have you been avoiding me, *chérie*?" she'd asked.

"I don't know what you're talking about," I'd replied, despite knowing exactly what she was talking about. I'd actively been avoiding her since JP and I decided we were a *thing* because I didn't want to hear her "I told you sos."

Except apparently, Anne-Marie didn't *know* that JP and I were a thing.

"Of course I didn't say anything," Sydney had said when I asked if she'd told Anne-Marie about giving me JP's address. "You think I'm risking my eardrums listening to her scream when she finds out she was right?"

"She didn't demand you tell her the moment you gave up the note with the address?" I'd asked.

"She asked me to tell her if I gave it to you," she'd said. "It's not my fault she didn't specify *when* I had to tell her."

"Of course I didn't tell her," JP had said when I called him after hanging up with Sydney. "It'll be way funnier to see her face in person."

"Great," I'd said. "So now I'm stuck going to Montreal and having to tell her."

"Why would you have to go to Montreal?" he'd asked.

"Because she made me feel guilty for not talking to her all week and I agreed to go out with her to the clubs for my birthday," I'd said.

"When's your birthday?"

"Saturday. Thanks for the great gift, bastard."

He'd laughed. "Well, I didn't know that."

"You could make it up to me by figuring out how we tell Anne-Marie about this," I'd said.

"Tell you what," he'd said. "Take off your panties and touch yourself for me a little, and we'll call it a deal."

"You could come over here and touch me yourself."

"I plan to. But I want to listen to you do it first. For old time's sake."

We'd never actually had phone sex before, but it was pretty hot, so I didn't bother correcting him.

After he listened to me come, he came over and made it happen again. Then he'd suggested his birthday gift to me include getting a hotel in

Montreal for the weekend so I could go out with Anne-Marie, plus do the two-birds-one-stone thing and have dinner with his family so they could *all* find out about our relationship at once.

"We might as well get this shit out of the way now," he'd said. "We can tell your parents. And selfishly, it'd probably be easiest if my parents talk to us, rather than get half the story from some gossip."

"Like Anne-Marie?" I'd mumbled.

"Exactly."

"You figured out how to tell her?"

"I have absolutely planned how she's gonna find out," he said, nodding. "And it's not like I'm going to surprise my parents with an unexpected dinner guest."

So that was how I ended up spending my Friday night in JP's car on the way to Montreal for the second time in as many weeks. I'd procrastinated calling my parents until we were on the road and once we had, all that was left was to stress about telling JP's family.

"It's going to be okay," JP said, and I realized I'd been lost in thought for long enough that we were nearly in Montreal. "I mean, I'd say something like 'My parents love you' or 'You'll impress them,' but we both know I'm full of shit."

"Thanks," I said. "You sure know how to make a girl feel better."

"The day my girl worries about impressing my parents instead of being herself is the day I question if you've been replaced by a pod person," he said.

I pretended hearing him call me his girl didn't make my stomach feel all fluttery. "Shut up."

He chuckled. "Look, your dad took it better than you'd thought."

"Hardly," I scoffed. "That was Kimberlee's doing, and he's probably starting to wonder if giving into her every whim is worth it. Chances are he's going to realize his balls are firmly stored in her purse and lose his mind."

"Well, maybe. Or, maybe he loves her and he's just learning."

"Yeah, and maybe I'm going to join a convent."

He snorted. "Well, your mom was fine with it."

"She's as much of a hopeless romantic as she is a hypocrite." I raised the pitch of my voice in an imitation of my mom's. "'Oh, how *sweet*. The boy next *door*. As if I didn't just refer to him as a brown-noser version of his dad. Because now it's *impressive* that he's a *lawyer*.'"

JP smirked. "They all say that until they find out how much of my work is pro bono right now."

"No one outside of lawyers has any concept of what that means."

"You do," he said.

"Yeah, well, sometimes I've got a lawyer inside me."

He burst out laughing, shaking his head. "You would've made a good lawyer. Seriously."

"Stop saying that. I have some self-respect, you know."

"Big words from someone who's fucking me."

The jibes continued until he turned down his parents' street, and I fell quiet, staring out the window. He reached over to cover my hand with his.

"Honestly, babe, they'll be happy that I'm happy," he said. "My dad's starting to get over me leaving the firm, and I think they'll mostly be impressed that I'm serious enough about someone to bring them home. I haven't done that since I was in high school."

"Way back in the day?"

I smirked as he flicked my palm before returning his hand to the steering wheel. We drove past my dad's house and JP turned into the driveway next door. He turned the car off as I hesitantly regarded the large house in front of me.

"Are you okay?" he asked softly.

"I'm fine," I muttered, then opened my car door. "Let's get this over with."

He took my arm as we walked up to the front door. Whether it was a sign of support or to keep me from running was anyone's guess, though I'd have put money on keeping me from running.

JP knocked on the door but didn't wait for an answer before swinging it open. The Marchands' house was so large that no one would likely have heard it, anyway. Still, as the door swung closed behind him, he called out.

"Anyone home? I'm here!"

"They're in the living room," said a voice from the stairs.

I jumped at the unfamiliar voice and looked up to see Marc-Andre, JP's younger brother, bounding down the steps. He froze when he saw me.

"Oh. It's Nellie," he said.

"Hi," I replied awkwardly.

Marc-Andre glanced at JP, then shrugged and made his way down the hallway.

"What was that about?" I asked as we followed him.

"That?" He held my arm tighter, lowering his voice as we rounded the corner to the living room. "Well, you know how I said I was going to tell my parents I was bringing a guest for dinner?"

I instinctively tried to dig my feet into the tile floor, which went about as well as one would expect. "Wait, you didn't—"

"I told them! I just might not have mentioned you were the person I was bringing," he said.

I looked up at him. "But you said you figured out how you were telling Anne-Marie."

JP smirked, his eyes sparkling. "I said I'd planned how she was finding out."

Oh, fuck. "You fucking bastard. I swear to God I—"

"Hey, Mom!" he said loudly as he tugged me into the kitchen and living room area. "Hey Dad. You remember my girlfriend Nellie, right?"

Mr. Marchand's eyebrows raised as he looked at us. Della Kinsley's lips were in a comical O-shape.

"What—" Mr. Marchand began to say.

From the couch, Anne-Marie shrieked so loudly that Remy, who was sitting beside her, winced in pain and I was pretty sure the wine glasses on the table cracked.

"I *knew* it!" she shouted, leaping up and bounding across the room towards us.

"I'll make it up to you later," JP muttered in my ear just before letting go of my hand so when Anne-Marie threw her arms around me, it was only her and me who went crashing to the floor.

"It's about time!" she screeched in my ear. "I am going to *kill* Sydney, she *promised* she would tell me when she gave you the address! I thought it would take longer, honestly; what day did it happen? Why did you not call me? When did—"

And somehow, even though he'd completely betrayed me, I laughed.

It was a smart plan, as much as I'd hated to admit it. He'd make it up to me, sure, but I'd definitely find a way to get back at him.

Because of course he hadn't wanted to tell her on his own.

Of course he'd made sure I was around to take the brunt of Anne-Marie's excitement.

Of course he'd been careful how he phrased things so I wouldn't remember, right up until we were walking into his parents' house, that I always had to be on my game around JP Marchand.

Because if I wasn't, he might convince me to do something stupid, like fall in love with him.

And God, did I love that bastard.

The End... for now!
Nellie and JP return in the special Christmas novella Sleigh Me If You
Can, coming October 2024!

Acknowledgments

Nellie's journey started as a writing exercise.

Three-ish years prior to the publishing of this series, I was publishing my writing online for free and I wanted to challenge myself to write an ongoing series of short stories that hit multiple categories. From a practical standpoint, a college student was the perfect character: there were plenty of opportunities for her to get up to all sorts of shenanigans.

The rest of her character development surrounded creating a woman who was empowered by the things I, and many others, have always been told are flaws.

Nellie is stubborn. She's unapologetic. She's brash, competitive, short-sighted, petty, and non-committal. She's lazy, disorganized, careless, and flighty. She has a hot temper, intense mood swings, and gets bored easily. She's overtly and shamelessly sexual.

And she's loved for it, not just by her friends and lovers in the books, but by so many readers that she won the reader's choice award for Literotica's Sexiest Female Character in 2020. And most importantly, by herself. Nellie likes herself. She is charismatic and adventurous and confident.

Many authors will tell you they put a piece of themselves into each character, intentionally or not. That is very true of Nellie. She represents someone I both relate to and wished I could have been. But it wasn't until

I sat down to "reboot" the series into the iteration you've just read that I realized there was something massive about Nellie that I'd never known.

Because I had to start my own ADHD journey to realize that as a woman with undiagnosed ADHD, I'd written a woman with undiagnosed ADHD.

When I had that moment of realization, I cried. I still cry about a bit, honestly. I'd given her a laundry list of symptoms that I'd never realized were symptoms and insisted that she be loved for the struggles I'd always been ashamed of. The ADHD plotline doesn't appear in the original short stories at all, but Nellie's character hasn't changed between the two versions. She was always just a girl who wanted to be appreciated for who she was, who felt like she had to put on a mask to impress people, who didn't always understand why she is the way she is.

Much in the way that Nellie is often the person I wish/wished I could be, parts of her ADHD journey are things I wish I could have had happen during mine. I wish I'd found out earlier. I wish someone would have noticed the symptoms I didn't know about. I wish my assessment hadn't taken months of waiting only to be failed by the medical system. I wish my psychiatrist was Dr. Klum. Nellie's journey represents an idealized version of ADHD assessment and diagnosis that most people would not ever experience. It might not be realistic, but it was necessary, because for me, Nellie needed to represent hope.

All that is to say, I want to acknowledge and thank all the people who have connected with Nellie, whether it be through the original short stories or through the If You Can series. I would especially like to thank those of you who shared your knowledge or experiences with me so I could better represent this neurotype.

I also need to thank my beta readers, proof readers, and feedback givers: Charlie, Kristi, Lisa, Sam, Jenine, and Becca. Thank you for helping this book become what it is!

Nazarea Andrews from Inkslinger PR is amazing and keeps me sane.

Thanks to Paul M, Kevin Matheny, PM, KJ, MidNyt, RP, Alex, and GW, and all my incredible supporters on Patreon.

My friends and family deserve so much gratitude for their support, their willingness to listen to me talk about my characters like they're real people, and their patience when I compare everything in my life to that thing I'm writing about. A special shout out to the members of the STFUARSBLAGG club, to Becca and Rachel for being the world's best cheerleaders, and to Nora for being there for me whenever I need her. Also, thank you to Karissa, the inventor of the Sniff, Sip, Shoot. No one pukes on the side of the road in Niagara On The Lake more gracefully than you do <3 I also need to thank you to the Basement Yard Podcast for inspiring the Spit or Swallow game, and to Joe and Frankie living in my head as inspiration for the Why Am I Like This podcast.

To my sweet doggos Cheddar and Pumpkin, thank you for not pooping on the carpet today.

And as always, to my husband, who puts up with my shenanigans, lifts me up when I begin to doubt myself, celebrates the little and big wins with me, and showers me with patience and understanding when I need it: I love you. I love you more. I love you most.

Xoxo, Cheryl

A Note About Neurodiversity

Neurodiversity representation in media is an important but complex topic.

In addition to my own diagnosis, this book has been reviewed by multiple other neurodiverse readers and a large amount of due diligence has been done in ensuring neurodiverse characters are depicted in a respectful and accurate way.

That being said, "diversity" is a key component of neurodiversity. My experience is different from my beta readers and their experiences are different from the countless others with neurodiverse brains. There is no way to represent the vast array of symptoms, neurotypes, etc. that people may have in a single book series. I have done my best to represent multiple experiences in an accessible way, which means that not every aspect of the characters may match the experiences other members of the neurodiverse community have, and there is a greater focus on the more "common" types of symptoms and behaviours neurodiverse people may have.

In addition, health care varies from country to country, including accessibility to mental health professionals and medication. Please note that while based in reality and certainly possible, Nellie's diagnostic journey, quick diagnosis, and the character of Dr. Klum are written as idealized versions of the psychiatric care I, and many others, wish we had received.

Nothing in this book is intended to be medical advice. While I know readers may relate to the neurodiverse characters—Nellie, Remy, Glitch, Reid, Vicki (undiagnosed), or any other characters presented as neurodiverse—that is not an indicator of ADHD, Autism, etc. and does not replace a diagnosis or professional medical opinion.

My intent is not to ever invalidate anyone's experience and I want to assure you that your experience is valid, even if it differs from or opposes the small slice of neurodiversity represented here. In addition, language, knowledge, and research is constantly changing. I have done my best to keep facts accurate and use accepted/supportive language, but if something is standing out as glaringly wrong, *please* do not hesitate to reach out to me directly at info@cherylterra.com.

En Francais, S'il Vous Plait

Or, a List of Quebecois Words and Phrases In This Book

As the If You Can series is set partially in Montreal, there are several Francophone and bilingual characters. For practicality's sake, the book is mainly written in one language and it may be noted in the text whether a character was speaking French or English. However, there are points where specific words or phrases are kept in French. For those who would like a translation, they are listed on the following page.

ma chouette: "my owl," term of endearment like sweetie/darling

ma puce: "my flea," term of endearment like sweetie/darling

cherie: "dear"

ma fille ange: my angel girl/my angel daughter

Mon beau loup: my handsome/beautiful wolf, term of endearment for a boyfriend

S'il vous plaît?: "if you please" or "please"

Saisons de Changement: Seasons of Change

Crisse de tabarnak: Quebec sacre/profanity, "what the fuck" or "holy fuck"

ma nounoune: affectionate/teasingly saying "my silly girl"

mon chenille: my caterpillar, not a common term of endearment

son papillion: her butterfly

ma cherie!: my dear

Est-ce que tu apprécies la fête?: Are you enjoying the party?

Je suis désolé: I am sorry

Crisse d'ostie de tabarnak: more sacres

D'où vient ce vin?: Where did this wine come from?

C'est pas le vin que j'ai demandé pour les tables: This is not the wine I requested for the tables

Ce vin est sur les tables des dirigeants. Monsieur Richard a insisté pour que nous changions le vin sur les tables d'hôtes: That wine is on the head tables. Mr. Richard insisted we change the wine on the guest tables.

Ostie de fucking crisse, qu'est que-fucking-tabarnak: Big expression of shock as implied by the mix of sacres and English

Tu es un gros plein de merde: You are a huge pile of shit/you are a fat, shitty man/you are full of shit

dep: depanneur, a corner store in Quebec (similar to a bodega)

Character List

This page is meant to be a reminder of basic character information and appearances in the context of what you've read so far. This means that while no spoilers for this book will appear here, additional revelations or information may be different in later books of the series.

Nellie Belanger: Justified main character syndrome on account of being the main character. Rosy white skin, slightly chubby, blonde hair, brown eyes, 21 years old. Forensic science student attending Ottawa Tech, currently living in Ottawa but spending much of her summer in Montreal. Known for being joyfully promiscuous and unapologetically against commitment.

Jean-Paul "JP" Marchand: Disgustingly good-looking and aggravatingly smart lawyer who is the older brother of Anne-Marie Marchand. 26, tall, tanned light beige skin, thick wavy blonde hair, blue eyes, wide smile with one crooked tooth. Works as a junior associate at his dad's law firm, lives with his parents temporarily while waiting for his condo to finish being built. Has been secretly hooking up with Nellie since the start of the summer.

Anne-Marie Marchand: Nellie's childhood best friend and next door neighbour. Tanned medium white skin, dyed blonde hair, brown eyes, tall and thin. Flighty and slightly out of touch at times but loyal AF. Lives in Montreal and speaks with a distinct Quebecois accent, peppering her dialogue with both French and English phrases. Thinks Nellie and her brother, JP, are perfect for each other, is unaware that Nellie and JP have been secretly hooking up for months.

Sydney Amhurst: Nellie's best friend. Tall-ish, pale skin, reddish-blonde hair, hazel eyes, athletic build. Currently lives in Ottawa and also attends Ottawa Tech. Regularly goes to Montreal to visit Olivier, who's not really her boyfriend but sort of. Definitely not in love with her roommate.

Ben Cameron: Forensic psychologist and professor at Ottawa Tech. Late 30s, medium gold-beige skin, thick brown hair with a grey streak above the left temple, hazel eyes, average height. Sydney calls him Professor Sexy. Nellie and Ben had a summer fling before he moved to California for a year of sabbatical at the end of the summer.

Maximillian Belanger: Nellie's father. Mid-50s hedge fund manager who places a high level of importance on appearances. Greyish blue eyes, straight nose, light olive-toned skin, thick black hair, shorter than average. Lives in Montreal.

Kimberlee Dunn: Max's current girlfriend. Appears to be in her mid-thirties, light brown skin, dark brown hair, large eyes, and about the same height as Max. Involved with a number of charities and associations. Lives in Montreal.

Vicki McCauley: Nellie's mother. Mid-40s, manages an LCBO liquor store. Left Max 10 years ago. Brown eyes, long, frizzy blonde hair, rosy white skin, taller than Max. Flighty and impulsive, doesn't drive. Lives in Toronto.

Remy Tremblay: Anne-Marie's boyfriend. Tall, dark brown skin, coiled hair usually kept in twists or braids, brown eyes. Stoic and serious. Autistic.

Marc-Andre Marchand: The youngest Marchand child. He exists and has brown hair.

Jean-Luc Marchand: JP and Anne-Marie's father. Looks similar to JP, overly serious. Highly successful lawyer who has his own practice. His family comes from money.

Della Kinsley: JP and Anne-Marie's mother. Very involved in the charities, associations, and events. More down to earth than her husband.

Clinton Thibault: Son of one of Max's major investors. Lives in Montreal. Wavy blonde hair, pale blue eyes, and a distinct lack of understanding of the word "No." Despite Nellie's disdain for him, is interested in her, which her dad approves of. JP agreed to take Nellie to the Diamond Gala so she didn't have to go with Clinton.

Olivier: a police officer Sydney went home with after they met during a bachelor party Olivier was attending. Light brown hair, an inch or two shorter than Sydney. Lives in Montreal.

Reid: Sydney's roommate and childhood friend. Lives in Ottawa. Has ADHD.

Hope: Reid's newest girlfriend after he and Alison broke up because Alison was into sexual things he wasn't willing to do, including humiliation and cuckolding. Does not like Sydney or Nellie.

Sam: JP's friend who was killed in a car accident with an impaired driver 6-7 years earlier. Reddish-brown skin, brown hair, had ADHD and was in law school in Montreal. JP was devastated but his father told him to hold it together during the funeral because he didn't want JP to embarrass him, so has never truly had a chance to mourn his friend.

Bruno: Friend of Remy's who agrees to be Nellie's date for social obligations over the summer but ditched her after his crush, Niko, expressed interest in being his date. Lives in Montreal. White skin, dark brown hair and eyes. In Nellie's words, looks like he's one hair straightener accident away from a 2006 Myspace photo.

Niko: Bruno's boyfriend. Brown hair, mustache, swollen biceps, tanned beige skin.

Claire Martelle: billionaire heiress to a cosmetics empire in a polyamorous relationship, befriended Nellie at a few of the galas she attended over the summer. Late 30's, long brown hair, white skin, impish face, often wears a tux to fancy events. Has a horrendously grating laugh.

Julie: One of Claire's partners (current fiancee) Curvy with blondish-brown hair, white skin, and a pretty smile.

Pia Martelle: Multi-billionaire founder of a large cosmetics company called The Martelle Makeup Group.

Jack: a guy who owns a cafe. Chubby, thick brown hair, olive skin, 27.

Glitch: Mid-20s law student, Nellie's TA for her Forensic Science and Law class. Non-binary, waist-length brown hair, beige-white skin, thin, "stoner chic" style.

Louie: An unlawyerly lawyer who runs a personal development conference and believes in genuine connection between lawyers and clients. 50s, short cropped brown hair, olive skin

Brandon: Nellie's friend. Chubby, wild brown hair, ruddy white skin. Just friends despite people thinking they would be a good couple because Brandon wants a serious relationship and Nellie doesn't. Plays DnD.

Calvin: Nellie's friend. Filipino, wide nose, brown skin. Excellent cook. DnD Dungeon Master.

Join The Chaos

Every hot mess deserves a happy ending.

Get exclusive bonus scenes, short stories, novellas, and more by joining my newsletter: **cherylterra.com/newsletter**

Find even more bonus content, early access to new work, and weekly updates that I sometimes actually do post every week on my Patreon (free tier available!): **patreon.com/cherylterra**

Also By Cheryl Terra

Also By Cheryl Terra

Find all of Cheryl's books at cherylterra.com/stories

Aurora Flats Series

Fate and Fried Chicken

If You Can Series

The Boy Next Door
Kiss Me If You Can
Hold Me If You Can
Keep Me If You Can
Sleigh Me If You Can

Unicorn Confessions Series

The Unicorn Confessions
Unicorn For Sale
Death of a Unicorn

Love Across Canada Series

Get Over It
The Devil Made Me
Runaway
Finding Home

Standalones

When It Rains
Hearts at Play: Special Edition
One Little Question
What Happens In Vegas
Selfish Love
Another Last Call